"You're a wicked influence, Aaron,"

she said mischievously, for the first time sounding as if she had let down her guard with him.

"Wicked is more fun, and you know you agree," Aaron said softly, standing close in front of her. "I'll show you tonight when we're together."

"Oh, no, you won't. I don't need you to show me one thing. We'll have dinner, talk a little and say good night. That's the agenda. Got it?"

"Oh, I have an agenda. I had it the moment I walked through the door and saw you sitting there with Cole. My agenda is to get you to take down your hair."

"Amazing. One of my goals is to keep my hair pinned up, so one of us is going to fail completely," she said, her blue eyes twinkling.

Eager to be with her for the whole evening, to flirt and dance and hopefully kiss, he leaned a bit closer. "If I placed my fingers on your throat, I'll bet I'd feel your pulse racing. You want the same thing I do."

* * *

Pregnant by the Texan
is a Texas Cattleman's Club: After the Storm
novel—As a Texas town rebuilds, love
heals all wounds…

PREGNANT
BY THE TEXAN

BY
SARA ORWIG

MILLS & BOON

Published in Great Britain 2014
by Mills & Boon, an imprint of Harlequin (UK) Limited,
Eton House, 18-24 Paradise Road, Richmond, Surrey, TW9 1SR

© 2014 Harlequin Books S.A.

Special thanks and acknowledgement are given to Sara Orwig for her contribution to the TEXAS CATTLEMAN'S CLUB: AFTER THE STORM series.

ISBN: 978-0-263-91486-3

51-1214

Harlequin (UK) Limited's policy is to use papers that are natural, renewable and recyclable products and made from wood grown in sustainable forests. The logging and manufacturing processes conform to the legal environmental regulations of the country of origin.

Printed and bound in Spain
by CPI, Barcelona

Sara Orwig lives in Oklahoma. She has a patient husband who will take her on research trips anywhere, from big cities to old forts. She is an avid collector of Western history books. With a master's degree in English, Sara has written historical romance, mainstream fiction and contemporary romance. Books are beloved treasures that take Sara to magical worlds, and she loves both reading and writing them.

With a big thank-you to Stacy Boyd, Harlequin Desire Senior Editor, and Charles Griemsman, Harlequin Desire Series Editorial.

Also, with love to my family.

One

Early in December as the private jet came in for a landing, Aaron Nichols looked below. Even though the tornado had hit two months earlier, the west side of Royal, Texas, still looked unrecognizable.

No matter how many times he had gone back and forth between Dallas and Royal, he was shocked by the destruction when he returned to Royal. The cleanup had commenced shortly after the storm, but the devastation had been too massive to get the land cleared yet. Hopefully, he and his partner, Cole Richardson, could find additional ways for R&N Builders to help in the restoration. As he looked at the debris—the broken lumber, bits and pieces of wood and metal, a crumpled car with the front half torn away—he thought of the lives wrecked and changed forever. It was a reminder of his own loss over seven years ago that had hit as suddenly as a storm: a car accident, and then Paula and seventeen-month-old Blake were gone. With time the pain had dulled, but it never went away and in moments like this when he had a sharp reminder, the hurt and memories hit him with a force that sometimes made him afraid his knees would buckle.

Realizing his fists were doubled, his knuckles white, he tried to relax, to shift his thoughts elsewhere. He remembered the day in October when he had met Stella Daniels during the cleanup effort. He thought of their one night together and his desire became a steady flame.

He hoped he would see her on this trip, although since their encounter, he had followed her wishes and refrained from calling her to go out again. The agreement to avoid further contact hadn't stopped him from thinking about her.

At the time he and Stella parted ways, he expected it to be easy. In the seven years since he lost his wife and baby son, women had come and gone in his life, but he had never been close to any of them. Stella had been different because he hadn't been able to walk away and forget her.

He settled in the seat as the plane approached the small Royal airport. Royal was a West Texas town of very wealthy people—yet their wealth hadn't been enough to help them escape the whirlwind.

Almost an hour later he walked into the dining room at the Cozy Inn, his gaze going over the quiet room that was almost empty because of the afternoon hour. He saw the familiar face of Cole Richardson, whose twin, Craig, was one of the storm's fatalities. A woman was seated near Cole. Aaron's heart missed a beat when he saw the brown hair pulled back severely into a bun. He could remember taking down that knot of hair and watching it fall across her bare shoulders, transforming her looks. Stella Daniels was with Cole. Aaron almost whispered "My lucky day" to himself.

Eagerness to see her again quickened his step even though it would get him nowhere with her. He suspected when she decided something, she stuck by her decision and no one could sway her until she was ready to change. Her outfit—white cotton blouse buttoned to her throat and khaki slacks with practical loafers—was as severe and plain as her hairdo. She wore almost no makeup. Few men would look twice at her and he wondered whether she really cared. Watching her, a woman who appeared straitlaced and plain, Aaron couldn't help thinking that the passionate night they'd had almost seemed a figment of his imagination.

As Aaron approached them, Cole stood and Stella glanced over her shoulder. Her gaze met Aaron's and her big blue eyes widened slightly, a look of surprise forming on her face, followed by a slight frown that was gone in a flash.

He reached Cole and held out his hand. "Hi, Cole. Have a seat."

"Aaron, good to see you," Cole said. Looking ready for construction work, he wore one of his T-shirts with the red, white and blue R&N Builders logo printed across the front. "You know Stella Daniels."

Bright, luminous eyes gazed at him as he took her hand in his. Her hand was slender, warm, soft, instantly stirring memories of holding her in his arms.

"Oh, yes," he answered. "Hi, Stella," he said, his voice changing slightly. "We've met, but if we hadn't, anyone who watches television news would recognize you. You're still doing a great job for Royal," he said, and she smiled.

One of the administrative assistants at town hall, Stella had stepped in, taking charge after the storm and trying to help wherever she could. It hadn't taken long for reporters to notice her and start getting her on camera.

Aaron shed his leather jacket and sat across from Cole, aware of Stella to his left. He caught a whiff of the rose-scented perfume she wore, something old-fashioned, but it was uniquely Stella and made him remember holding her close, catching that same scent then.

"I'm glad to have you back in Royal," Cole said. He looked thinner, more solemn, and Aaron was saddened by Cole's loss as well as the losses of so many others in town. He knew from experience how badly it could hurt.

"I know help is needed here, so I'm glad to be back."

"Thanks," Cole said. "I mean it when I say I appreciate

that. When you can, drop by the Texas Cattleman's Club. They're rebuilding now and moving along. They'll be glad to have you here, too."

"Our club friends in Dallas said to tell you and the others hello."

Cole nodded as he glanced at Stella. "Getting to the business at hand, Stella and I were talking about areas where more lumber is needed—all over the west side of town, it seems."

"Each time I see Royal, I can't believe the destruction. It still looks incredible. I've made arrangements to get another couple of our work crews here."

"R&N Builders have helped tremendously," Stella said.

"I'm sure everyone in town thanks you for doing such a great job right from the start, Stella—acquiring generators, getting help to people and directing some of the rescue efforts. When disaster happens unexpectedly like that, usually all hell breaks loose and it takes a calm head to help the recovery," Aaron stated.

"Thanks. I just did what I could. So many people pitched in and we appreciate what R&N Builders, plus you and Cole individually, have donated and done to aid Royal."

"We're glad to. Everyone in the company wanted to help," Cole replied. "So we're adding two more work crews. Stella, you can help coordinate where they should go. I asked men to volunteer for the assignment. They'll be paid by us the same as if they were working on a job at home, but R&N is donating their services to help Royal rebuild."

"That would be a tremendous help," Stella said. "Local companies are booked solid for the next few months. There's so much to be done that it's overwhelming."

"Also, we might be able to get one of the wrecking companies we work with to come in here and pick up debris. I doubt you have enough help now when there's so much to clean up," Aaron said.

"We need that desperately. We have some companies from nearby towns, but we can use more help. There is an incredible amount of debris and it keeps growing as they get the downed trees cut up."

Cole made a note on a legal pad in front of him.

"Right now I wonder if we'll ever get all the debris cleared. It would be great to have more trucks here to help haul things away."

Stella made notes as they discussed possibilities for the next hour. Even as he concentrated on the conversation, Aaron could not keep from having a sharp awareness of Stella so nearby. He wished she had not asked him to back off and forget their night of passion.

He'd done so, but now that he was back in her presence, he found it difficult to keep memories from surfacing and wished he could take her out again, dance with her and kiss her, because it had been an exciting, fun night.

Her long slender fingers thumbed through the notebook she held as she turned to a page of figures. He recalled her soft hands trailing across his bare chest, and looked up to meet her blue-eyed gaze.

She drew a deep breath and her cheeks flushed as she looked down and bent over her open binder. Startled, he realized she had memories, too. The idea that she had been recalling that night stirred him and ignited desire. He wondered how many men paid no attention to her because of her buttoned-up blouses and austere appearance. Her actions that night hadn't been austere. Aware he should get his thinking elsewhere, he tried to focus on what Cole was saying.

At half past three Cole leaned back in his chair. "Sorry to have to break this up. You two can continue and, Aaron, you can fill me in later. I'm going out to a long-time friend Henry Markham's ranch to stay five or six days. He invited me out. He also lost his brother in the storm and he's had a lot of damage, so I'm going to help him. I'll see you both next week and we can continue this."

"Don't forget," Stella said, "I have to leave town for part of the day tomorrow. I'll be back in the afternoon." As Cole nodded, she looked at Aaron. "I'm flying to Austin where my sister lives."

"If you need to stay longer, you should," Cole said.

"I don't think I'll need to stay. Just a short time with her and then I'll be back."

Cole glanced at Aaron. "I'm glad you're here, Aaron. We've got good people running the place in Dallas while we're gone, so everything should be all right."

"It'll be fine. George Wandle is in charge. And if anything comes up he promised he would call one of us."

"Good deal." Cole stood, pulled on a black Western-cut jacket and picked up his broad-brimmed Resistol hat. "Thanks, Stella, for meeting with me."

"All the thanks go to you and Aaron for the help you and your company are giving to Royal. You've been terrific."

"We're glad to help where we can. Aaron, if you need me for anything, I have my phone with me."

"Sure, Cole."

Aaron watched his partner walk through the restaurant and then he turned back to Stella. "It's nice to see you again."

"Thank you. It's nice to see you, too. I really mean it. Your company has done so much to help."

"There's still so much more to do. How's the mayor?"

A slight frown creased her brow as she shook her head at him. "Since the mayor was in the town hall when it sustained a direct hit, he was hurt badly. He was on the critical list a very long time. He's hurt badly with broken bones, internal ruptures and complications after several surgeries. He was in the ICU for so long. With all the problems he's had, he's still a long way from healed."

"That's tough. Tough for him, for you, for all who work for him and for the town. The deputy mayor's death complicated things even more. No one's really in charge. You've sort of stepped into that void, Stella."

"I'm just doing what I can. There are so many things—from destroyed buildings to lost records and displaced pets. Megan Maguire, the animal shelter director, has worked around the clock a lot of the time. It just takes everybody pulling together and it's nice you're back to help."

He smiled at her. "Maybe, sometime, you need a night out to forget about Royal for a few minutes."

"Frankly, that sounds like paradise, but I don't have time right now. Someone texts or calls every other minute. This has been one of the quietest afternoons, but this morning was a stream of calls."

"Royal could manage without you for a couple of hours."

"Don't tempt me, Aaron," she said, smiling at him. "And I won't be here tomorrow."

"I have the feeling that you're working late into the night, too."

"You're right, but every once in a while now, there'll be a lull in the calls or appointments or hospital visits. Lately, I've had some nights to myself. While you're here, let me show you which projects Cole has finished and where we need the work crews next."

She spread a map on the table and he pulled his chair closer to her. Aware of her only inches away now, he once again inhaled a faint scent of her rose perfume. He helped her smooth the map out and leaned close, trying to focus on what she told him but finding it difficult to keep his attention from wandering to her so close beside him.

She showed him where they had repaired houses and finished building a new house. Stella told him about different areas on the west side of town, which had taken the brunt of the storm, the problems, the shortages of supplies, the people in the hospital. The problems seemed staggering, yet she was quietly helping, as were so many others she told him about.

He wondered if she had suffered some deep loss herself and understood their pain. He wouldn't ask, because she probably wouldn't want to talk about it. He didn't want anyone to ask him about his loss and he hadn't reached a point where he could talk about it with others. He didn't think he ever would. The hurt was deep and personal.

"Aaron?"

Startled, he looked at her. "Sorry, I was thinking about some of these people and their terrible losses. Some things you can't ever get back."

"No," she answered, studying him with a solemn expression. "Houses can be rebuilt, but lives lost are gone. Even some material possessions that hold sentimental value or are antiques—there's no replacing them. You can't replace sixty-year-old or older trees—not until you've planted new ones and let them grow sixty or seventy years. It tears you up sometimes." She smiled at him. "Anyway, I'm glad you're here."

"We'll just help where we can. To have a bed and a roof over your head is good and we need to work toward that for everyone."

"Very good. You and Cole are a godsend," she said, smiling at him and patting his hand.

He placed his hand on hers. Her hand was soft, warm,

smooth. He longed to draw her into his arms and his gaze lowered to her mouth as he remembered kissing her before.

She slipped her hand out from under his. "I think they're beginning to set up the dining room for tonight. I wonder if they want us to leave," she said. Her words were slightly breathless and her reaction to him reinforced his determination to spend time with her again.

"We're not in anyone's way and I doubt they want us to leave."

"I didn't realize how long we've talked," she said.

"Have dinner with me. Then I'll give you a ride home tonight."

"I'm still staying here at the inn until the repairs are done on my town house," she said.

"I'm staying here, too, so I'll see you often," he said. She had a faint smile, but he had the feeling that she had put up a barrier. Was she trying to avoid the attraction that had boiled between them the last time they were together? Whatever it was, he wanted to be with her tonight for a time. "Unless you have other plans, since we're both staying here, then, by all means, have dinner with me."

There was a slight hesitation before she nodded. "Thank you," she replied. Even though she accepted his invitation, she had a touch of reluctance in her reply and he had the feeling she was not eager to eat with him.

"Is this headquarters for you?" he asked, his thoughts more on her actions than her words.

"Not at all. I'm not in charge—just another administrative assistant from town hall helping like the others."

"Not quite just another administrative assistant," he said, looking at her big blue eyes and remembering her passionate responses. For one night she had made him forget loss and loneliness. "Should your town house be on our list of places to help with reconstruction?" he asked her.

"Thank you, no. The damage wasn't that extensive, but I was pretty far down on the priorities list. I finally have the work scheduled and some of it has already started. I'm supposed to be back in my place in about a week. Thank goodness. I want to be there before Christmas."

"Good, although I'm glad you're staying here in the hotel because that means we can see each other easily," he said, deciding he would get his suite moved to whatever floor she was on. "They're setting up for tonight and I need to wash up before dinner. Want to meet again in an hour?" he asked her.

"That's a good idea. I've been busy since seven this morning and I'd welcome a chance to freshen up."

As they walked out of the restaurant, he turned to her. "What floor are you on?"

"The sixth floor. I have a suite."

"The same floor I'm on," he said, smiling at her.

"That's quite a coincidence," she said in a skeptical voice.

"It will be when I get my suite moved to the sixth floor, after seeing you to your suite."

She laughed. "I can find my own way to my suite. You go try to finagle a suite on the sixth floor. I don't think you can. It's hopeless. Every available space has been taken because of so many homeless folks having their houses repaired after the storm. People reserved every nook and cranny available in Royal and all the surrounding little towns. Some had to go to Midland, Amarillo and Lubbock. We're packed, so I don't think I'll see you on my floor."

"So you approve if I can get a suite," he said.

"I figure it won't happen," she answered, looking at him intently.

"Not if you don't approve," he said.

"I don't want more complications in my life and you're

a wicked influence, Aaron," she said mischievously, for the first time sounding as if she had let down her guard with him.

"Wicked is more fun and you know you agree," he said softly, standing close in front of her. "I'll show you tonight when we're together."

"Oh, no, you won't. I don't need you to show me one thing. We'll have dinner, talk a little and say good-night. That's the agenda. Got it?"

"Oh, I have an agenda. I had it the moment I walked through the door and saw you sitting there with Cole. One of the goals on my agenda is to get you to take down your hair."

"Amazing. One of my goals is to keep my hair pinned up, so one of us is going to fail completely," she said, her blue eyes twinkling.

Eager to be with her for the whole evening, to flirt and dance and hopefully kiss, he leaned a bit closer. "If I placed my hand on your throat, I'll bet I'd feel your pulse is racing. You want the same thing I do. I'm looking forward to dinner and spending the evening together."

"I'm looking forward to the evening, too, so I can talk to you more about how you and your company can continue to help with the restoration of Royal. You're doing a wonderful job so far, and it's heartwarming to know you're willing to continue to help."

"We'll help, but tonight is a time for you to relax and catch your breath. It's a time for fun and friendship and maybe a kiss or two to take your mind off all the problems, so don't bring them with you. C'mon, I'll walk you to your door," he said, taking her arm and heading to the elevators.

She laughed. "Well now, don't *you* have a take-charge personality."

"It gets things done," he answered lightly as they entered

the elevator and rode to the sixth floor. When they got off, she walked down the hall and put her key card in a slot. As she opened the door, she held the handle and turned to him.

"Thanks, Aaron. I'll meet you in the lobby."

"How's seven?" he asked, placing one hand on the door frame over her head and leaning close. "It's good to see you again. I'm looking forward to the evening."

Her eyes flickered and he saw the change as if she had mentally closed a door between them. "Since I'm leaving town tomorrow, let's make it an early evening, because I have to get up at the crack of dawn. My life has changed since you first met me. I have responsibilities now that I didn't have then."

"Sure, whatever you want," he said, wondering what bothered her. For a few minutes downstairs she had let down that guard. He intended to find out why she was now being distant with him. "See you at seven."

"Bye, Aaron," she said, and stepped inside her suite, closing the door.

As he rode down in the elevator, his thoughts were on her. He knew she had regretted their night of lovemaking. It was uncustomary for her and in the cool light of day, it upset her that she had allowed herself to succumb to passion. Was she still suffering guilt about that night?

He didn't think that was what had brought on the cool demeanor at the door of her suite. Maybe partially, but it had to be more than that. But what else could it be? He intended to find out.

He took the elevator back down and crossed the lobby, determined to get a suite on the sixth floor even if he had to pay far more to do so.

It turned out to be easier than he had thought because someone had just moved out.

My lucky day.

Two

Stella Daniels walked through the living room of the suite in the Cozy Inn without seeing her surroundings. Visions came of Aaron when he had strolled to the table where she sat with Cole. Looking even better than she had remembered, Aaron exuded energy. His short dark blond hair in a neat cut added to his authoritative impression. The warmth in his light brown eyes had caused her heart to miss a beat.

She had a mixture of reactions to seeing him—excitement, desire, dread, regret. She hoped she'd managed to hide her tangled opposing emotions as she smiled and greeted him. Her first thought was how handsome he was. Her second was happiness to see him again, immediately followed by wishing he had stayed in Dallas where the company he shared with Cole was headquartered. His presence complicated her busy life more than he knew.

She'd offered her hand in a business handshake, but the moment his fingers had closed over hers, her heartbeat had jumped and awareness of the physical contact had set every nerve quivering. Memories taunted and tempted, memories that she had tried to forget since the one night she had spent with Aaron in October.

It had been a night she yielded to passion—which was so unlike her. Never before had she done such a thing or even been tempted to, but Aaron had swept her away. He had made her forget worries, principles, consequences, all her usual levelheaded caution, and she had rushed into a blissful night of love with him.

Now she was going to pay a price. As time passed after their encounter, she suspected she might have gotten pregnant. Finally she had purchased a pregnancy kit and the results confirmed her suspicions. The next step would be a doctor. Tomorrow she had an appointment in Austin. Her friends thought she was going there to visit her sister; Stella hadn't actually said as much, but people had jumped to that conclusion and she had not corrected anyone. She did not want to see a doctor in Royal who would know her. She didn't want to see one anywhere in the vicinity who would recognize her from her appearances on television since the storm. If a doctor confirmed her pregnancy, she wanted some time to make decisions and deal with the situation herself before everyone in Royal had the news, particularly Aaron.

Tomorrow she would have an expert opinion. Most of the time she still felt she wasn't pregnant, that something else was going on. It had only been one night, and they'd used protection—pregnancy shouldn't have resulted, regardless of test results or a missed period.

She studied herself in the mirror—her figure hadn't changed. She hoped the pregnancy test was wrong, even though common sense said the test was accurate.

Given all that was going on, she should have turned Aaron down tonight, but she just couldn't do it.

She looked at her hair and thought about what he had said. She would keep it up in a bun as a reminder to stop herself from another night of making love with him. In the meantime, she was going to have dinner with him, work with him and even have fun with him. Harmless fun that would allow them each to say goodbye without emotional ties—just two people who had a good time working together. What harm could there be in that?

Unless it turned out that she was pregnant. Then she couldn't say goodbye.

She showered, took down her hair to redo it and selected a plain pale beige long-sleeved cotton blouse and a dark brown straight wool skirt with practical low-heeled shoes. She brushed, twisted and secured her hair into a bun at the back of her head. She didn't wear makeup. Men usually didn't notice her and she didn't think makeup would make much difference. The times she had worn makeup in high school, boys still hadn't noticed her or wanted to ask her out except when they were looking for help in some course they were taking.

An evening with Aaron. In spite of her promises to herself and her good intentions, the excitement tingled and added to her eagerness.

When it was time to go meet Aaron, she picked up a small purse that only held necessities, including her card key, wallet and a list of temporary numbers that people were using because of the storm. She wouldn't need a coat because they wouldn't be leaving the Cozy Inn.

When she stepped off the elevator, she saw him. She tried to ignore the faster thump of her heart. In an open-neck pale blue shirt and navy slacks, he looked handsome, neat and important. She thought he stood out in the crowd in the lobby with his dark blond hair, his broad shoulders and his air of authority.

Why did she have such an intense response to him? She had from the first moment she met him. He took her breath away and dazzled her without really doing anything except being himself.

He spotted her and her excitement jumped a notch. She felt locked into gazing into his eyes, eyes the color of caramel. She could barely get her breath; realizing how intensely she reacted to him, she made an effort to break the eye contact.

When she looked again, he was still watching her as he approached.

"You look great. No one would ever guess you've been working since before dawn this morning."

"Thank you," she answered, thinking he was just being polite. Nobody ever told her she looked great or gorgeous, or said things she heard guys say to women. She was accustomed to not catching men's attention so she didn't give it much thought.

"I have a table in the dining room," he said, taking her arm. The room had been transformed since they'd left it. Lights had been turned low, the tables covered in white linen tablecloths. Tiny pots wrapped in red foil and tied with bright green satin bows held dwarf red poinsettias sprinkled with glitter, adding to the festive Christmas atmosphere.

A piano player played softly at one end of the room in front of a tiny dance floor where three couples danced to a familiar Christmas song. Near the piano was a fully decorated Christmas tree with twinkling lights.

Aaron held her chair and then sat across from her, moving the poinsettia to one side even though they could both see over it.

"I haven't seen many Christmas trees this season," she said. "It's easy to even forget the holiday season is here when so many are hurting and so much is damaged."

"Will you be with your family for Christmas?"

"No. My parents don't pay any attention to Christmas. They're divorced and Christmas was never a fun time at our house because of the anger between them. It was a relief when they finally ended their marriage."

"Sorry. I know we talked about families before. Earlier today you said you are going to see your sister in Austin tomorrow. Do you see her at Christmas?"

"Some years I spend Christmas at her house. Some years I go back and forth between my parents and my sister. Mom has moved to Fort Worth. She's a high school principal there. After the divorce my dad moved his insurance business to Dallas because he had so many customers in the area. I see him some, but not as much as my mom. My grandmother lives with her and my grandfather is deceased."

"So this year what will you do at Christmastime?"

"I plan to stay here and keep trying to help where I can until the afternoon of Christmas Eve. Then I'll fly to Austin to be at my sister's. I have a feeling the holidays will be extremely difficult here for some people. I'm coming back Christmas afternoon and I've asked people here who are alone to come over that evening—just a casual dinner. So far there are about five people coming."

"That's nice, Stella," Aaron said, sounding sincere with a warmth in his gaze that wrapped her in its glow.

"What about you, Aaron? Where will you spend Christmas? You know more about my family than I do about yours."

For an instant he had a shuttered look that made her feel as if she had intruded with her question. Then he shrugged and looked at her. "My parents moved to Paris and I usually go see them during the holidays. My brother is in Dallas and I'll be with him part of the time, although he's going to Paris this year. I like to ski, and some years I ski. This year I'll see if I can help out around here. You're right. A holiday can hurt badly if someone has lost his home or a loved one. After losing his brother, Cole will need my support. So I'm going to spend the holidays in Royal."

As he spoke quietly, there was a glacial look in his eyes that made her feel shut out. She wondered about his past. More and more she realized how little she knew about him.

Their waiter appeared to take their drink order, and Aaron looked at her, his brown eyes warm and friendly again. "The last time we were together you preferred a glass of red wine. Is that what you'd like now?"

She shook her head. "No, thank you. I would prefer a glass of ice water. Maybe later I'll have something else," she said, surprised that he remembered what she had ordered before. She didn't want to drink anything alcoholic and she also didn't care to do anything to cause him to talk about the last time they were together.

"Very well. Water for the lady, please, and I'll have a beer," he said to the waiter.

As soon as they were alone, Aaron turned to her. "Let's dance at least one time and then we'll come back to place our order. Do you already know what you want? I remember last time it was grilled trout, which is also on this menu here."

"I don't know what I want and I need to read the menu. I'll select something and then we'll dance," she said, trying to postpone being in his arms. If she could gracefully skip dancing, she would, but he knew from the last time that she loved to dance. He was remembering that last time together with surprising clarity. She figured he had other women in his life and had forgotten all about her.

"Let's see what we want. When he brings drinks, we can order dinner. I remember how much you like to dance."

"You have a good memory."

"For what interests me," he said, studying her.

"What?" she asked, curious about the intent way he looked at her.

"You're different from last time. Far more serious."

Her breath caught in her throat. "You notice too much, Aaron. It's the storm and all the problems. There are so many things to do. How can I look or feel or even be the same person after the event that has touched each person who lives here," she said, realizing she needed to lighten the situation a bit so he would stop studying her and trying to guess what had changed and what was wrong.

"C'mon. One dance. You need to get your mind off Royal for just a few minutes at least. We can order dinner after a dance. You're not going to faint on the dance floor from hunger. Let it go for a minute, Stella. You've got the burden of the world on your shoulders."

She laughed and shook her head. "I don't think it's that bad. Very well, you win," she said. By trying to stay remote and all-business, she was drawing more attention instead of less, which wasn't what she wanted.

"That's more like it," he said, smiling. "What time do you leave in the morning?" he asked.

"I'll fly the eight-o'clock commuter plane from here to Dallas and change planes for Austin."

They reached the dance floor as the music changed to an old-time fast beat. She was caught in Aaron's direct look as they danced, and his brown eyes had darkened slightly. Desire was evident in his expression. Her insides clenched while memories of making love with him bombarded her.

His hot gaze raked over her and she could barely get her breath. How could she resist him? He was going to interfere in her work in Royal, interfere in her life, stir up trouble and make her want him. The last part scared her. She didn't want Aaron involved too soon because he was a man who was accustomed to taking charge and to having things his way.

Watching him, she gave herself to dancing around the floor with him, to looking into brown eyes that held desire and a promise of kisses, to doing what he said—having fun and forgetting the problems for just a few minutes. The problems wouldn't go away, but she could close her mind to them long enough to dance with Aaron and have a relaxing evening.

As they danced the beat quickened. Smiling, she shut her mind to everything except dancing and music and a drumming beat that seemed to match her heartbeat. The problems would be waiting, but for a few minutes, she pushed them aside.

Her gaze lowered to Aaron's mouth and her own lips parted. Having him close at hand stirred up memories she had been trying to forget. If only she could go back and undo that night with him, to stop short at kissing him.

The dance ended and when a ballad began he held her hand to draw her closer.

"Aaron, I thought we were going to have one dance and then go order dinner," she said, catching her breath.

"I can't resist this. I've been wanting to dance with you and hold you close."

The words thrilled her, scared her and tormented her. They danced together and she was aware of pressing lightly against him and moving in step with him. Memories of being in his arms became more vivid. His aftershave was faint but she recalled it from before. Too many things about him were etched clearly in her memory, which hadn't faded any in spite of her efforts to try to avoid thinking about him.

The minute the song ended, she stepped away and smiled. "Now, we've danced. Let's go order so we get dinner tonight."

"There, that's good to see you relax a little and laugh and smile. That's more the way I remember you."

"I think you just wanted to get your way."

"No. If I just wanted to get my way, we wouldn't be here right now. We'd be upstairs in my room."

She laughed and shook her head, trying to make light of his flirting and pay no attention to it.

At their table she looked over the menu. She selected grilled salmon this time and sipped her cold water while Aaron drank a beer.

"See, it's good to let go of the problems for at least a brief time. You'll be more help to others if you can view things with a fresh perspective."

"I haven't done much of this. The calls for help have been steady although it's not like it was at first. We've had some really good moments when families found each other. That's a triumph and joy everyone can celebrate. And it's touching when pets and owners are reunited. Those are the good moments. Frankly, I'll be ready to have my peace and quiet back."

Her phone dinged and she took it out. "Excuse me," she said as she read the text message and answered it.

Their dinner came and they talked about the houses that were being rebuilt by his company and the families who would eventually occupy them. With Aaron she had a bubbling excitement that took away her appetite. She didn't want him to notice, so she kept eating small bites slowly. Before she was half-through, she got a call on her phone.

"Aaron—" She shrugged.

"Take the call. I don't mind."

She talked briefly and then ended the call. "That's Mildred Payne. She's elderly and lives alone. Her family lives in Waco. Her best friend was one of the casualties of the storm. She just called me because her little dog got out and is lost. Mildred's crying and phoned me because I've helped her before. I'm sorry, Aaron, but I have to go help her find her dog."

He smiled. "Come on. I'll get the waiter and then I'll take you and we'll find the dog."

"You don't have to."

"I know I don't have to. I want to be with you and maybe I can help."

"I need to run to my suite and get my coat."

"I'll meet you in the lobby near the front door in five minutes."

"Thanks."

"Wouldn't miss a dog hunt with you for anything," he said as they parted.

She laughed and rushed to get her coat. When she came back to the lobby, Aaron was standing by the door. He had on a black leather bomber jacket and once again just the sight of him made her breathless.

His car was waiting outside and a doorman held the door for her as Aaron went around to slide behind the wheel. She told him the address and gave him directions. "You're turning out to be a reliable guy," she said. "I appreciate this."

"You don't know the half about me," he said in an exaggerated drawl, and she smiled.

"To be truthful, I'm glad I don't have to hunt for the dog by myself. I do know the dog. It's a Jack Russell terrier named Dobbin. If you'll stop at a grocery I'll run in and get a bag of treats because he'll come for a doggie treat."

"I'll stop, but if we were home and I was in my own car, we wouldn't have to. My brother has a dog and I keep a bag of treats in the trunk of my car. That dog loves me."

"Well, so do I," she said playfully. "You're willing to hunt for Dobbin."

"When we find Dobbin, we'll go back to the Cozy Inn and I'll show you treats for someone with big blue eyes and long brown hair—"

"Whoa. You just find Dobbin and we'll all be happy,"

she said, laughing. "Seriously, Aaron, I appreciate you volunteering to help. It's cold and it's dark out. I don't relish hunting for a dog, and Dobbin is playful."

"So am I if you'll give me half a chance," he said. She shook her head.

"I'm not giving you a chance at all. Just concentrate on Dobbin."

"I'll only be a minute," he said, pulling into the brightly lit parking lot of a convenience store. He left the engine running with the heater on while he hurried inside. She watched him come out with a bag of treats.

"Thanks again," she said.

"Hopefully, Dobbin will be back home before we get there. You must get calls for all kinds of problems."

"I'm glad to help when I can. I'm lucky that my house didn't have a lot of damage and I wasn't hurt. Mildred had damage to her house. She's already had a new roof put on and windows replaced. She has a back room that has to be rebuilt, but she was one of the fortunate ones who got help from her insurance company and had a construction company she'd worked with on other jobs, so she called them right after the storm."

"That's the best way. Make the insurance call as soon as possible."

"It worked for Mildred." They drove into a neighborhood that had damage but not the massive destruction that had occurred in the western part of Royal. Houses were older, smaller, set back on tree-filled lots. Stella saw the bright beacon of a porch light. "There's her house where the porch light is on. Mildred is in a block where power got restored within days after the storm. Another help. There she is, waiting for us and probably calling Dobbin."

"He could be miles away. It's a cold night and she's elderly. Get her in where it's warm and I'll drive around looking for Dobbin. Hopefully, he loves treats."

When they reached the house, Aaron turned up the narrow drive. A tall, thin woman with a winter coat pulled around her stood on the porch. She held a sack of dog treats in her hand.

"Thanks again, Aaron. You didn't know what you were in for when you asked me to eat dinner with you. I'll get her settled inside and then I'll probably walk around the block and look. She said he hadn't been gone long when she called."

"That's good because a dog can cover a lot of ground. I have my phone with me. My number is 555-4378."

"And mine—"

"Is 555-6294," he said, startling her. "I started to call you a couple of times, but you said you wanted to say goodbye, so I didn't call," he said.

That gave her a bigger surprise. She figured he had all but forgotten the night they were together. It was amazing to learn that not only had he thought about calling her, he even knew her phone number from memory. He had wanted to see her again. The discovery made her heart beat faster.

"Stella—"

Startled, she looked around. He had parked and was letting the motor idle. She was so lost in her thoughts, for a moment she had forgotten her surroundings or why they were there. "I'll see about Mildred," she said, stepping out and hurrying to the porch as Aaron backed out of the drive.

"Hi, Mildred. I came as quickly as I could."

"Thank you, Stella. I just knew you would be willing to help."

"I'm with Aaron Nichols, who is Cole Richardson's partner. They own one of the companies that has helped so much in rebuilding Royal. Aaron will drive around to search for Dobbin."

"I appreciate this. He's little and not accustomed to being out at night."

"Don't worry. We'll find him," Stella said, trying to sound positive and cheerful and hoping they could live up to what she promised. "Let's go inside where it's warm and I'll go look, too. You should get in out of the cold."

"You're such a help to everyone and I didn't know who else to turn to. There was George, my neighbor, but their house is gone now and he and his family are living with his sister."

They went inside a warm living room with lights turned on.

"You get comfortable and let us look for Dobbin. Just stay in where it's warm. May I take the bag of treats with me?"

"Of course. Here it is." Mildred wiped her eyes. "It's cold for him to be out." Gray hair framed her long face. She hung her coat in the hall closet and stepped back into the living room.

"I'm going to walk around the block and see if I can find him. Aaron is looking now. We'll be back in a little while."

Mildred nodded and followed Stella to the door.

"This is nice of you, Stella. Dobbin is such company for me. I don't want to lose him."

"Don't worry." She left, closing the door and hurrying down the porch steps. "Dobbin. Here, Dobbin," she called, rattling the treat sack and feeling silly, thinking Dobbin could be out of Royal by now. She prayed he was close and would come home. No one in Royal needed another loss at a time like this.

"Dobbin?" she called, and whistled, walking past Mildred's and the lot next door where a damaged house stood dark and empty. The roof was half-gone and a large elm had fallen on the front porch. Away from the lights the area was grim and cold. She made a mental note to check tomorrow about Mildred's block because she thought this section of town had already had the fallen trees cleared away.

"Dobbin," she called again, her voice sounding eerie in the silent darkness.

A car came around the corner, headlights bright as it drove toward her. The car slowed when it pulled alongside her and she recognized Aaron's rental car. He held up a terrier. Thrilled, she ran toward the car. "You have Dobbin?"

"Dobbin is my buddy now. He's waiting for another treat."

"Hi, Dobbin," she said, petting the dog. "Aaron, you're a miracle man. I'll meet you on Mildred's porch."

"Get in and ride up the drive with me. I'll hold Dobbin so he doesn't escape."

She laughed, thinking it was becoming more and more difficult to try to keep a wall up between them. All afternoon and this evening he had done things to make her appreciate and like him more.

She climbed into the warm car. "I'll hold Dobbin," she said. When Aaron released the terrier, he jumped into her lap. Aaron drove up the drive and parked.

"Come in and meet Mildred because she'll want to thank you."

"Here, you might as well give Mildred the bag of treats. I'll carry Dobbin until we get to the door," Aaron said, taking the dog from her.

On the porch Aaron rang the bell. In seconds the door opened and Mildred smiled. "You found him. Thank you, thank you." She took the dog from Aaron and the bags of treats from Stella. "Please come in. I'm going to put him in my room and I'll be right back. Please have a seat."

When she came back, Stella introduced everyone. "Mildred, this is Aaron Nichols. Aaron, meet Mildred Payne."

"Nice to meet you, ma'am. Dobbin was in the next block, sitting on a porch of a darkened, vacant home as if waiting for a ride home. I had a bag of treats, so he came right to me."

"Good. He doesn't like everybody."

"Mildred, we're going back. It's been a long day and I still have some things to do."

"I wish you could stay. I have cookies and milk."

"Thanks, but we should go," Stella said. Mildred followed them onto the porch, thanking them as they left and still thanking them when they got into the car.

"Now you've done your good deed for today," Stella said when he backed down the drive. "It was appreciated."

"It was easy. I think you've become essential to this town."

"No. I'm just happy to help where help is needed. And I'm just one of many helping out. The Texas Cattleman's Club has been particularly helpful, and you and Cole have certainly done more than your fair share."

"Your life may have changed forever because of the storm. I'm surprised you haven't had job offers from people who saw you on television."

"Actually, I have from two places. The attorney general's office in San Angelo has an opening for an administrative assistant and another was a mayor's office in Tyler that has a position that would have the title of office manager."

"Are you interested in either one?"

"No, I thanked them and turned them down. My friends are in Royal and I've grown up here so I want to stay. Besides, they need me here now."

"Amen to that. I'm glad you're staying here because

we'll be working together and maybe seeing each other a little more since we're both at the Cozy Inn."

"Did you get your suite changed to the sixth floor?"

"Indeed, I did," he said. "I'll show you."

"I'll take a rain check."

"Oh, well, it's still early. Let's go have a drink and a dance or two."

She hesitated for just a moment, torn between what she should do and what she wanted to do.

"You're having some kind of internal debate, so I'll solve it. You'll come with me and we'll have a drink. There—problem solved. You think you'll be back in Royal tomorrow night?"

"Yes," she said, smiling at him.

When they got back to the hotel, Aaron headed for a booth in the bar. The room was darker and cozier than the dining room. There was a small band playing and a smattering of dancers.

Over a chocolate milk shake, she talked to Aaron. They became enveloped in conversation, first about the town and the storm and then a variety of topics. When he asked her to dance, she put him off until later, relieved that it did not come up again.

"Our Texas Cattleman's Club friends want an update on the progress here. Cole is good about keeping in touch with both groups."

"I think you'll be surprised by how much they have rebuilt and repaired," she replied.

"Good. I'm anxious to see for myself what's been done."

"You'll be surprised by changes all over town."

Later, she glanced at her watch and saw it was almost one, she picked up her purse. "Aaron, I have to fly out early in the morning. I didn't know it was so late. I never intended to stay this late."

"But you were having such a good time you just couldn't tear yourself away," he teased, and she smiled at him.

"Actually, it has been a good time and the first evening in a while that has had nothing to do with the storm."

They headed out to the elevator and rode to the sixth floor. The hallway was empty and quiet as Aaron walked her to her door.

"Let me take you to the airport in the morning and we can get breakfast there."

"No, thank you. It's way too early."

"I'll be up early. It'll save you trouble and we can talk some more. All good reasons—okay?"

She stopped at her door, getting her card from her purse. "I know you'll get your way in this conversation, too, Aaron. See you in the lobby at six o'clock. Thanks for dinner tonight and a million thanks for finding Dobbin. That made Mildred happy."

"It was fun. Mostly it was fun to be with you and see you again. Before we say good-night, there's something I've been wanting to do since the last time we were together."

"Do I dare ask—what have you been wanting to do?"

"Actually, maybe two or three things," he said softly. "First, I want to kiss you again," he said, moving close and slipping his arm around her waist. Her heart thudded as she looked up at him. She should step back, say no, stop him now, but what harm was there in a kiss? She gazed into his light brown eyes and there was no way to stop. Her heartbeat raced and her lips tingled. She leaned closer and then his mouth covered hers. His arms tightened around her and he pulled her against him.

She wrapped her arms around him to return his kiss, wanting more than kisses. She felt on fire, memories of being in his arms and making love tugging at her.

He leaned over her while he kissed her, his tongue going

deep, touching, stroking, building desire. She barely felt his fingers in her hair, but in minutes her hair fell over her shoulders.

She had to stop, to say no. She couldn't have another night like the last one with him.

"Aaron, wait," she whispered.

He looked down at her. His brown eyes had darkened with passion. "I've dreamed of you in my arms, Stella," he whispered. "I want to kiss you and make love."

"Aaron, that night was so unlike me."

"That night was fantastic." He held long strands of her hair in his fingers. "Your hair is pretty."

She shook her head. "I have to go in," she whispered. "Thank you for dinner, and especially for finding the dog."

She opened her door with her card.

"Stella," he said. His voice was hoarse. She paused to look at him.

"I'll meet you in the lobby at six in the morning. I'll take you to the airport."

She nodded. "Thanks," she said, and stepped into her entryway and closed the door. The lock clicked in place. She rested her forehead against the door and took a deep breath. She didn't intend to get entangled with him at this point in time. Not until she had a definite answer about whether she was pregnant.

At six the next morning Aaron stood waiting. He saw her step off the elevator. She wore a gray coat and a knitted gray scarf around her neck. Her hair was back in a bun. She was plain—men didn't turn to look at her as she walked past, yet she stirred desire in him. She was responsive, quick-witted, kind, helpful, reliable. She was bright and capable and—he knew from firsthand experience—sexy.

He drew a deep breath and tried to focus on other things.

But he was already thinking about how long she would be gone and when he would see her again. He hoped that would happen as soon as she returned to Royal. Maybe she would let him pick her up at the airport.

He needed to step back and get a grip. If anyone would be serious in a relationship, it would be Stella. She would want wedding bells, which was reason enough that he should leave her alone. He didn't want a long-term relationship. But she might be one of those women who couldn't deal with a casual affair.

"Good morning," he said as she walked up.

"I'm ready to catch a plane," she said, smiling at him and looking fresh. Beneath the coat he saw a white tailored blouse, tan slacks and brown loafers. Always practical and neat, so what was it about her that made his pulse jump when he saw her?

"You look as if you don't have a care in the world and as if you had a good night's sleep."

"Well, I'm glad I look that way. By the end of some of the days I've spent dealing with all the storm problems, I feel bedraggled."

"I think we can do something about that," he said, flirting with her and wanting to touch her if only just to hold her hand.

"I pass on hearing your suggestions. Let's concentrate on getting to the plane."

"The car is waiting."

As soon as they were headed to the Royal airport, Aaron settled back to drive. "Cole left a list of what we're working on and I have the list we made yesterday of more places where we can help. I'll spend the day visiting the sites, including the Cattleman's Club. When Cole gets back, I want to be able to talk to him about what I can do to help."

"If you have any questions, I'll have my phone, although some of the time it may be turned off."

"I'll manage," he said.

She chuckled. "I'm sure you will."

"You should be able to get away a day without a barrage of phone calls from Royal. Maybe we should think about a weekend away and really give you a break."

She laughed again. "No weekend getaways, Aaron. For more than one reason. You can forget that one. I'll manage without a weekend break."

"Can't blame me for trying," he said, giving her a quick grin. "I'll miss you today," he said.

"No, you won't. You'll be busy. Once people find out who you are and that you're here in Royal, you'll be busy all day long with questions and requests and just listening to problems. I can promise you—get ready to be in high demand."

"Is that the way it's been for Cole? If it has, it probably is good for him because it takes his mind off his loss."

"I'm sure it's what he deals with constantly. We've come a long way, but we still have so far to go to ever recover from all the devastation."

He turned into the small airport and let her out, then parked and came back to join her for breakfast. All too soon she was called to board. He stood watching until she disappeared from sight and then he headed back to town. At least she had agreed to let him pick her up when she returned later today. He was already looking forward to being with her again, something that surprised him. Since losing Paula and Blake, he hadn't been this excited about any woman. Far from it. He felt better staying home by himself than trying to go out with someone and fake having a good time.

That had all changed with Stella—which surprised and puzzled him, because she was so unlike anyone who had ever attracted him before.

Three

Stella left the doctor's office in a daze. The home pregnancy test had been accurate. She was carrying Aaron's baby. Why, oh, why had she gotten into this predicament?

She climbed inside her rental car and locked the doors, relieved to be shut away from everyone else while she tried to adjust to the news.

To make matters worse, now Aaron was not only in Royal, but staying in the neighboring sixth floor suite at the Cozy Inn. He wanted to be with her, to dance with her. She did not want him to know yet. She wished he would go back to Dallas to R&N headquarters and give her time to think things through. She had to decide how much and when she would tell him.

She groaned aloud and put her forehead against the steering wheel. Aaron was a good guy. He had military training, was caring and family oriented, from what little she knew. She could guess his reaction right now. He would instantly propose.

She groaned again and rubbed her temples with her fingertips. "Oh, my," she whispered to the empty car.

She couldn't let Aaron know yet. She would have to get so busy she couldn't go out with him. Her spirits sank lower. He had a suite next to hers—there wasn't going to be any way to avoid him.

He was a take-charge guy and he would definitely want to take charge of her situation.

He would want to marry her. She was as certain of that as she was that she was breathing air and sitting in Austin.

Glancing at her watch, she saw she would be late meeting her sister for lunch. Trying to focus, she started the car and drove to the restaurant they'd agreed on earlier.

At the restaurant, she saw that her sister was already seated. When Stella sat down at the table, her sister's smile faded. "You've had bad news."

"Linda, I just can't believe the truth," Stella said, tears threatening, which was totally unlike her. "I'm pregnant. The test was correct."

"Oh, my, of all people. Stella, I can't believe it. I'll tell you something right now. I know you—you're a wonderful aunt to my children. You're going to love this baby beyond your wildest imaginings. You'll see. I know I'm right."

"That will come, but at the moment this is going to complicate my life. This shouldn't have happened."

"Here comes the waiter."

"I've lost my appetite. There's no way I can eat now."

"Eat something. You'll be sorry later if you don't."

Linda ordered a salad and Stella ordered chicken soup.

As soon as they were alone, Linda turned to Stella. "Look, I'll help any way I can, anytime. When the baby is due, you can stay here and I'll be with you."

"Thank you," Stella said, smiling at her sister. "I can't believe this is happening."

"You've said the dad is a nice guy. Tell him."

"I'll have to think about what I'm going to do first and make some decisions. I know I have to tell him eventually, but not yet. The minute he finds out, I'm sure he'll propose."

"That may solve your problem. Marry him. Accept his

proposal. You've already been attracted to each other or you wouldn't be pregnant. There's your solution."

"It's not that simple. Aaron and I are not in love. Look at our parents. That's marriage without love and it was horrible for them and for us. I don't want that. And I feel like there are moments Aaron shuts himself off. He doesn't share much of himself."

"You may be imagining that. Marry him and if he's nice and you've been attracted to each other, you'll probably begin to love him."

"I'm not falling into that trap. Linda, when you married, you and Zane were so in love. That's the way I want it to be if I marry. I couldn't bear to do it otherwise. And it will be a sense of duty for Aaron. He won't give it one second's thought. I'm just sure."

"I'm telling you—if he proposes, marry him. You'll fall in love later."

"Think back to our childhood and the fights that our parents had—the yelling and Mom throwing things and Dad swearing and storming around slamming doors. Oh, no. You can forget the marriage thing. I'll work this out. It's just takes some getting used to and careful planning."

"At least consider what I'm saying. If this man is such a nice guy, that's different from Mom and Dad."

"You know Dad can be a nice guy when he wants to. Mom just goads him. And vice versa. Here comes lunch."

"Try to eat a little. You'll need it."

"It helps to have someone to talk to about it."

"Do you have anyone in Royal?"

"Of course. You should remember Edie. We're close enough that I can talk to her about it. She'll understand, too. Actually, I can probably talk to Lark Taylor."

"I know Lark, but not as well as you do since you're

both the same age. She's not the friendliest person until you get to know her."

"In this storm, believe me, we got to know each other. She and the other nurses from the hospital were out there every day trying to help. So were others that I feel are life-long friends now. Megan Maguire, the shelter director. I feel much closer to some of the people I've worked with since the tornado. I can talk to them if I want."

"Is he good-looking?"

"I think so."

"Well, then you'll have a good-looking baby."

"Frankly, I hope this baby doesn't look *exactly* like him." Stella smiled. "I'm teasing. I'll think about what you've said. Actually, Aaron is in Royal. I'm having dinner with him tonight."

"There," Linda said, sounding satisfied, as if the whole problem was solved. "Go out with him some before you tell him. Give love a chance to happen. You're obviously attracted to each other."

"I might try, Linda. It's a possibility. But that's enough about me. How are the kids?"

They talked about Linda's three children, their parents, progress in rebuilding Royal and finished their lunch.

As they stood in the sunshine on the sidewalk saying their goodbyes, Linda asked, "You're coming for Christmas, aren't you?"

"Yes. I'll fly in late afternoon Christmas Eve and then back home Christmas afternoon."

"Think about what I've said about marrying the dad. That might turn out a lot better than it did for Mom and Dad."

"I'll think about that one. You take care. See you next time." She turned and hurried to the rental car.

She paused to do a search on her phone and located the

nearest bookshop, which was only two blocks away. She drove over and went inside. It took a few minutes to find a book on pregnancy and what to expect with a first baby but before she knew it, she was back in the car, headed to the airport.

All the way to Dallas on the plane she read her new book. She would have to find a doctor in Royal. She was certain Lark could help her there. She knew of two who were popular with women her age.

When she changed planes for Royal, she tucked her new book into her purse and tossed away the shopping bag in the airport.

As she flew to Royal her dread increased by the minute. She felt as if she had gained ten pounds and her waist had expanded on this trip. She felt uncomfortable in her own skin.

When she stepped off the plane, Aaron was waiting. He had on jeans and a navy sweatshirt. There was no way to stop the warmth that flowed over her at the sight of him and his big smile. She had mixed reactions just as she always had with him.

"Hi," he said, walking up and draping his arm across her shoulders to give her a slight hug as they headed for the main door leading to the parking lot. His brown-eyed gaze swept over her. He saw too much all the time. How long did she have before he could tell she was expecting?

"How's your sister?"

"She's fine. I enjoyed seeing her and all is well."

"Good. I hope you had a restful day."

"I did. How was it here?"

"I imagine if you'd been here, you would answer, 'The usual.' I saw a great deal of the construction and talked to a lot of people. I've been at the Texas Cattleman's Club most of the day. Repairs have begun on the clubhouse.

They didn't have total destruction, so it should be done before too long. Actually, I helped some with the work there today." They reached his car and he held the door for her. She watched him walk around the car and slide behind the wheel.

As soon as they were on the freeway, he said, "Let me take you to dinner again. We'll eat at the Cozy Inn if you prefer."

"Thanks, Aaron, I would like that. There's still time for me to go by the hospital this afternoon. By the end of the day, all I'll be up for is the Cozy Inn for dinner. Right now I want to go back to my suite and catch up on emails."

"You may regret doing that. What if you have over a hundred emails waiting? You might have to go look for another lost dog."

She smiled, feeling better.

"I'll tell you one thing," he said, "people are really grateful to you for all you've done. I've had a lot of people out of the blue mention your name. I guess they assume everyone knows who you are and they'll just start talking about 'Stella did this' or 'Stella did that.'"

"I'm always happy to help."

"A lot of people are also talking about Royal needing an acting mayor because it's obvious now that the mayor can't return to work anytime soon. And people I talked to are mentioning your name in the same breath they talk about needing an acting mayor."

"Aaron, I'm an administrative assistant. A lot of us are helping others."

"You've been a big help to lots of people and they appreciate it."

She shook her head and didn't answer him as he pulled to a stop at the front door of the Cozy Inn.

"I'm letting you out here and heading back to the club. I'll see you at seven."

"Let's just meet in the lobby in case I get delayed."

"Sure," he said as a doorman opened her door and she stepped out. She walked into the inn without looking back.

In her room she went straight to her mirror to study her figure. She didn't look one bit different from when she had checked earlier, but she felt different. For one minute she gave herself over to thinking *if only*—if she were married to Aaron this would be one of the most joyous occasions for her.

With a long sigh, she stopped thinking about being married to Aaron and faced the reality that Aaron was in his thirties and still single. She thought back to the night she had met him after the storm. She had been comforting Paige Richardson whose husband, Craig, had died in the tornado. Others had come to call on Paige and someone introduced Stella to Aaron. He was staying in a motel on the edge of Royal, but he offered to take Stella back to the Cozy Inn. They had talked and one thing had led to another until they were in bed together—a rare event to her.

The next morning, when she told Aaron the night was totally uncharacteristic of her and she wanted to avoid further contact, he had agreed to do whatever she wanted and also told her he wasn't in for long-term relationships. She really didn't know much about him. That night they had had fun and lots of laughter, lots of talking, but she was beginning to realize that none of their conversation was about anything serious or important. Last night with him could be described the same way. She knew almost nothing about him and he hadn't questioned her very much about her background. Aaron Nichols would be the father of her child, and it was time she found out more about him. Whether he hated or loved becoming a dad, that was what had happened and they both would have to adjust to the reality of parenthood.

She went to her laptop to read her emails, answering what she needed to, and then left for Royal Memorial Hospital.

The west side of town had taken the brunt of the F4 tornado. Town hall where she had worked was mostly reduced to debris. Almost all three stories of the building had been leveled. The only thing left standing was part of the clock tower—the clock stuck at 4:14 p.m., a permanent reminder of the storm. She couldn't pass it without shivering and getting goose bumps as she recalled the first terrifying moments.

Approaching the hospital, she saw the ripped and shattered west wing. As far as she could tell, rebuilding had not yet begun.

As soon as she went inside the building, outside sounds of traffic and people were shut out. She stepped into an elevator. A nurse had already boarded and Stella realized it was Lark Taylor. They had known each other since childhood, but had become closer in the weeks after the storm. Some accused the ICU nurse of being unfriendly, but Stella couldn't imagine how anyone could feel that way.

"Here to see the mayor's family?" Lark asked.

"Yes. I try to stop by every few days. The changes are slow, but I want to keep up with how he's doing. How's Skye?" As she asked about Lark's sister, Stella gazed into Lark's green eyes and saw her solemn look.

"No change, but thank you for asking about her." Skye had sustained head injuries during the tornado and had been in a medically induced coma ever since. Stella knew Lark was worried about her sister and the baby and it hadn't helped that no one knew who the baby's father was.

"And how's her baby?"

"She's doing well," Lark answered, her voice filling with relief. "I'm so thankful to work here so I can be closer to them."

"I'm glad Skye is doing well," Stella said, happy to hear good news about Skye's tiny baby, who came into the world two months prematurely after her mother was injured during the storm. "Every storm survivor is wonderful," Stella said.

"Right now, we're looking for Jacob Holt." Stella remembered the gossip four years earlier when Jacob had run away with Skye.

"You think he's in Royal?"

"No. If he was here in Royal, I think, in a town this size someone would know. But they're trying to find him. His brother is looking."

"If Keaton doesn't know where Jacob is, I doubt if anyone else does."

"You know so many people—have you heard anything about him?"

"No, nothing. If I do, I'll let you know."

When the elevator stopped on Lark's floor, she stepped into the doorway and turned back.

"If you do hear about him, please let me know. Skye can't tell us anything, and her baby certainly can't. We need to talk to Jacob. With him missing and Skye in a coma, Keaton wants to test the baby's DNA to see if she's a Holt." Lark shook her head. "If you hear anything at all about Jacob, please call me. You have my cell number. Just call or text."

Stella nodded. "I will."

The doors closed and Stella thought about Skye. So many people had been hurt by the storm. But Stella was happy to hear the joy in Lark's voice when she said the little preemie was doing well.

The elevator stopped on Mayor Richard Vance's floor. When she went to the nurse's station, she was told the mayor's wife was in the waiting room.

It was an hour later when Stella left the hospital and hurried to her car. Before she left downtown she stopped at a drugstore to pick up a few things she needed at the Cozy Inn. When she went inside, she recognized the tall, auburn-haired woman she had known for so long because their families were friends. She walked over to say hello to Paige Richardson.

At her greeting Paige turned and briefly smiled. Stella gazed into her friend's gray eyes.

"How are you? How's the Double R, Paige?" she asked about Paige's ranch, which she now had to run without her husband.

"Still picking up the pieces," Paige said. "I heard Aaron Nichols is here again to help. Are you working with Cole and Aaron?"

"A little. A lot of their paperwork comes through the mayor's office. Cole is out at a friend's ranch now—Henry Markham, who lost his brother, too, in the storm."

"His ranch was badly damaged. Cole's probably helping him."

"The storm was hard on everybody. I'm sure you keep busy with the Double R."

"Some days I'm too busy to think about anything else. Is Cole staying very long with Henry?"

"It should be four or five more days."

"How's the mayor?" Paige asked. "I'm sure you're keeping up with his condition."

"It's a slow healing process, but each time I check, he's holding his own or getting better."

"It's been nice to talk to you because you have some

good news. Sometimes I dread coming to town because of more bad news," Paige said.

"This week I've gotten some hopeful reports. It's been great to see you, and you take care of yourself."

"Thanks," Paige replied with another faint smile. "You take care of yourself."

Stella left Paige and greeted other people in the store while she got the things she needed, paid for them and left. Outside she ran into two more people she hadn't seen for a few weeks. They talked briefly and she finally started back to the hotel. Her thoughts shifted from the people she had seen to being with Aaron shortly.

At the Cozy Inn, she walked through to her bedroom and went straight to a mirror to study herself and how she looked. So far, she didn't think she showed no matter which way she stood. She felt fine. The baby should be due next summer. Her baby and Aaron's. She felt weak in the knees whenever she thought about having his baby.

Did she want to go out with him, keep quiet and hope they both fell in love before she had to confess that she was pregnant?

She didn't think that was the way it would work out. She pulled out a navy skirt and a white cotton blouse from the dresser, then put on a navy sweater over the blouse. Once again she brushed and pinned up her hair. She saw she just had a few minutes to get to the lobby to meet Aaron.

If anything, when she spotted him standing near the door of the main restaurant, her excited response resonated deeper than it had the night before. At the same time, she had a curl of apprehension. How would she tell him? When would she? How long could she wait until she did?

Wearing a navy sweater, navy slacks and black cowboy boots, he stood near a potted palm while he waited. She crossed the lobby with its ranch-style plank floor scattered with area rugs. Hotel guests sat in clusters and chatted with each other. The piano music from the restaurant drifted into the lobby. So many local hotels had become temporary homes for the folks displaced by the tornado; whole families were staying and becoming friends.

When she approached, she saw a look in Aaron's brown eyes that made her tingle inside. "I've been looking forward to this all day," he said in greeting.

"So have I," she said. "I haven't had many leisurely dinners with a friend since the storm hit and I hope we can have one tonight."

"We're going to try. You know you can turn that phone off."

She shook her head. "This from the man who would never turn down helping someone. There are too many real emergencies. Later, when everyone calms down and is back on an even keel, I'll think about turning it off, but not yet."

Once they had settled at their table and their drinks arrived—water for her and beer for Aaron—she listened to him describe his work at the Cattleman's Club that day.

"How's your sister?" Aaron asked when he was done.

"She's fine. We had a nice time and had lunch together before I left. We don't see each other much, just the two of us."

"Any change with Mayor Vance?"

She shook her head. "No. But his wife told me he's stable. He's had a very rough time. I talked to Lark Taylor briefly. Her sister Skye is still in a medically induced coma, which sounds terrible to me, but I know it's necessary sometimes. I didn't ask further and, of course, she can't tell me details."

"How is Skye's baby? Still in NICU?"

"Yes, but Lark said Skye's baby is doing well."

"That's good," he said. He tilted his head to look at her. "What?" he asked. "You look puzzled."

"Most single men don't have much to say about a preemie baby in NICU."

He gave her that shuttered look he got occasionally. She seemed to have hit a nerve, but she didn't know why. She didn't pry into other's lives. If Aaron wanted to share something with her, he would.

Their dinners came, and once again her appetite fled even though the baked chicken looked delicious.

About halfway through dinner, Aaron noticed. "No appetite?"

"We had a big lunch just before I went to the airport."

She didn't like looking into his probing brown eyes that saw too much. Aaron was perceptive and an excellent listener, so between the two qualities, he guessed or understood things sooner than some people she had known better and longer.

"One thing I didn't mention," she said, to get his attention off her. "Lark said they were searching for Jacob Holt."

"Cole told me something about that. I imagine they are, with Skye in a coma and a new baby no one knows anything about. It's tough. The Holts must be anxious to know if the child is Jacob's."

"You can't blame him. Most people who've lived here long know about the Holt-Taylor feud."

"From what Cole told me, that feud goes back at least fifty years. What I've always heard is that it was over a land dispute."

"There are other things, too. A creek runs across both ranches, so they've fought over water rights," Stella said.

"There's been enough publicity, even nationally, over the tornado, I'd think Jacob Holt would have heard."

"I can't imagine he's anywhere on earth where he wouldn't hear something about it," she said.

"If the baby is Jacob's, she will be both a Taylor and a Holt and it might diminish the feud."

"High time that old feud died. I wonder if Jacob will ever come back to Royal."

"One more of those mysteries raised by the storm." He smiled at her. "Now speaking of the storm—I have a surprise for you."

Startled, she focused intently on him, unable to imagine what kind of surprise he had.

"I have made arrangements for you to speak to a men's group in Lubbock to raise funds for Royal to help in the rebuilding."

Her surprise increased, along with her dread. "Aaron, thank you for setting up an opportunity to raise funds, but I'm not the one to do it. You didn't even ask me. I'm not a public speaker or the type to talk a group of people into giving money for a cause," she said, feeling a momentary panic.

"You've done this countless times since the storm—you've been the town hall spokesperson really. With Mayor Vance critically ill and Deputy Mayor Rothschild killed in the storm, someone had to step forward and you did. You've done a fantastic job getting people to help out and donate. That's all you've been doing since the storm hit," he said, looking at her intently.

"That's so different," she said, wondering why he couldn't see it. "I did those things in an emergency situation. I was talking to people I knew and it was necessary. Someone had to step in. I was helping, not trying to persuade total strangers to donate to a cause. I'm not the person for that job. I'm not a public speaker and I'm not persuasive. I'm no salesperson or entertainer. A group like that will want to be entertained." Her panic grew because what Aaron expected was something she had never done. "Aaron, I can't persuade people to give money."

"I'm not sure I'm hearing right," he said. "You've persuaded, ordered and convinced people to do all sorts of things since the afternoon the storm hit."

"What I've been doing is so different. I told you, I stepped in when someone had to and the mayor couldn't. Of course people listened to me. They were hurt, desperate—what you've set me up to do is to entertain a group of businessmen in a club that meets once a month with a guest speaker. They're used to a fun speaker and then they go back to work. If I'm to walk in and convince them they should contribute money to Royal, I can't do it." Her old fears of public speaking, of having to try to deal with an audience—those qualms came rushing back.

"When you get there, you'll be fine," he said, as if dismissing her concerns as foolish. "When you meet and talk to them, you'll see they're just like people here. I'll go with you. I think once you start, it'll be just like it is when you're here. Relax, Stella, and be yourself. You've done a great job on national television and state and local news." He smiled at her and she could tell he didn't have any idea about her limitations.

"When I had interviews that first afternoon and the day after the tornado, I didn't have time to think about being on national television. I just answered questions and went right back to wherever I was needed."

"This isn't going to be different, Stella. You'll see. You'll be great."

"You may be surprised," she said, feeling glum and scared. "Really, Aaron, I don't know why you think I can do this. So when is this taking place?"

"Day after tomorrow. They have a program that day, so

you're not the only one to talk to them if that makes you feel better."

"It makes me feel infinitely better. Day after tomorrow. Next time run this past me, please, before you commit me to going."

"Sure. Stella, it never occurred to me that you wouldn't want to do this. It'll be so easy for you. I have great faith in you. This will help raise funds for Royal. People will know you're sincere in what you say, which will help."

She shook her head in exasperation. "That's what keeps me from flat-out telling you I refuse. I know it will help Royal. I just think someone else might make a better pitch. Thanks, Aaron, but you just don't get it," she said.

"Sure I do and I'm certain it will be easy for you. But all that is in the future. Right now, in our immediate future, I think it's time to dance," he said, holding out his hand.

She went to the dance floor with him, but her thoughts were on the group in Lubbock. She wanted to ask how many people would be in the audience, but she had already made a big issue of it and she couldn't back out now. It was a chance to raise funds and awareness for Royal, so she had to get over her fears and help. She wanted to help her town so maybe she should start planning what to say.

They danced three fast numbers that relaxed her and made her forget the rest of the week. Next, the piano player began an old ballad and Aaron drew her into his arms.

For a moment she relished just being held so close and dancing with him.

They danced one more song and then sat down and talked. Later, he ordered hot cocoa and they talked longer until she looked at her watch and saw it was after one in the morning.

"Aaron, I lost track of time. I do that too much with

you. I need to go to my suite. It's been a long day. I'm exhausted," she said as she stood up.

"I'm glad you lost track of time," he said, standing and draping his arm across her shoulders to draw her close to him.

When she reached for her purse, it fell out of her hands. As the purse hit the floor, Aaron bent down instantly to pick it up for her. A coin purse, a small box of business cards and a book fell out.

Horrified, she realized she had not taken the book she had bought earlier out of her purse. She tried to grab it, but Aaron had it in his hand and was staring at the cover with its picture of a smiling baby. For a moment her head spun and she felt as if she would faint, because in his hands that tiny book was about to change their future.

Four

Your Pregnancy and Your First Baby. The title jumped out at Aaron. Stella grabbed the book and dropped it into her purse.

When he looked up at her, all color had drained from her face. She stared, round eyed, looking as if disaster had befallen her.

He felt as if a fist slammed into his chest. Was she pregnant from their night together? She couldn't be, because he'd used protection. Gazing into her eyes, he had his answer that the impossible had happened—apparently the protection they'd used wasn't foolproof after all. Her wide blue eyes looked stricken. Shivering, she clutched her purse in both hands.

"I need to go to my suite," she said in almost a whisper. "We can talk tomorrow."

She brushed past him and for one stunned moment he let her go. Then he realized she would be gone in another minute and went after her. He caught up with her at the elevators and stepped on with her. Another couple joined them and they couldn't talk, so they rode in silence to the fourth floor, where the couple got off.

Aaron looked at her profile. Color had come back into her flushed cheeks. She looked panicked. It had to be because she was carrying his child.

Stunned, he couldn't believe what had happened. She might as well shout at him that he had gotten her pregnant. Her stiff demeanor, terrified expression and averted eyes were solid proof.

He felt as cold as ice, chilled to the bone, while his gaze raked over her. Her sweater hid her waist, but he had seen her waist yesterday and she was as tiny as ever, her stomach as flat as when they had met.

He took a deep breath and followed her out of the elevator.

At her door she turned to face him. "Thank you for dinner. Can we talk tomorrow?"

"Are you really going to go into your suite, get in bed and go to sleep right now?" he asked. His own head spun with the discovery, which explained why she had been so cool the other day when she had first seen him again. Shock hit him in waves and just wouldn't stop. She was pregnant with his baby. He would be a father. He had no choice now in the situation. He had made his choice the night he seduced her and he couldn't undo it now. "You're not going in there and going to sleep."

She met his gaze. "No, I guess I'm not," she replied in a whisper. "Come in."

There was only one thing for him to do. She carried his baby. He had gotten her pregnant. He had taken precautions and both of them thought they had been safe when in reality they had not been. It was done and could not be undone. As far as he could see there was no question about what he needed to do.

She unlocked her door and he closed and locked it behind them, following her into a spacious living area with beige-and-white decor that was similar to the suite he had. The entire inn had a homey appearance with maple furniture, old-fashioned pictures, needlepoint-covered throw pillows, rocking chairs in the living areas and fireplaces with gas logs.

"Have a seat, please. Do you want anything to drink?" she asked.

"Oh, yeah. Have any whiskey?"

"No. There's a bottle of wine," she replied, her voice cold and grim.

"That's okay. I'll pass. Have you been to a doctor yet?"

"Yes. That's where I went today," she said, her voice barely above a whisper. "I couldn't go to a doctor here in Royal where I know everybody and they know me. If they don't know me, a lot of people recognize me now from seeing me on television."

She sat perched on the edge of a wing chair that seemed to dwarf her. He studied her in silence and she gazed back. Her hands were knotted together, her knuckles white; once again she had lost her color. He suspected if he touched her she would be ice-cold.

He was in such shock he couldn't even think. This was the last possible thing he thought would happen to him. Actually, he'd thought it was impossible.

"You're certain you're pregnant?"

"Yes, Aaron, I am. There isn't really much to talk about right now. It's probably best you think about it before you start talking to me. I know this is a shock."

He stared at her. She was right in that he needed to think, to adjust to what had happened. It was a huge upheaval, bigger even than the storm, where he had merely come in afterward to try to help. Now he had his own storm in his life and he wondered if he could ever pick up the pieces.

She looked determined. Her chin was tilted up and she had a defiant gleam in her eyes. He realized he had been entirely focused on himself and the shock of discovering that he would be a father. He needed to consider Stella.

He crossed the room and pulled her to her feet, wrapping his arms around her. She stood stiffly in his embrace and gazed up at him.

"Stella, one thing I don't have to think about—I'm here for you. I know it's going to be hard, but let's try to reason this out and avoid worry. First, you're not alone. I want—"

She placed her finger on his lips. "Do not make any kind of commitment tonight. Not even a tiny one. You've had a shock, just as I had, and it takes a bit of time to adjust to this. Don't do something foolish on the spur of the moment. Don't do something foolish because of honor. I know you're a man of honor—Cole has said that and he knows you well. It shows, too, in things you've done to help the people here."

"You've had a head start on thinking about this and the future," he said, listening to her speech. "Stella, I don't have to think about this all night. It seems pretty simple and straightforward. We were drawn to each other enough for a baby to happen."

He took her cold hands in his. Her icy hands indicated her feelings and he wanted to reassure her. He saw no choice here.

"Stella, this is my responsibility. I want to marry you."

She closed her eyes for a moment as if he had given her terrible news. When she opened them to look up at him, she shook her head.

"Thank you, but no, we will not get married. I didn't want you to know until I decided what I would do. I knew you would propose the minute you learned about my pregnancy."

"I don't see anything wrong with that. Some women would be happy to get a proposal," he said, wondering if she was thinking this through. "I'm not exactly repulsive to you or poor husband material, am I?"

"Don't be absurd. There's something huge that's wrong with proposing tonight—within the hour you've discovered you'll be a father. We're not in love, Aaron. Neither one of us has ever said 'I love you' to the other."

"That doesn't mean we can't fall in love."

She frowned and her lips firmed as she stared at him and shook her head. "There was no love between my parents. I don't think there ever was," she said. "They had the most miserable, awful marriage. There was no physical abuse or anything like that. There were just tantrums, constant bickering, tearing each other down verbally. My sister and I grew up in a tense, unhappy household. I don't ever want to be in that situation. I'll have to be wildly in love to marry someone. My sister and her husband are, and it's a joy to be around them. They love each other and have a happy family. I couldn't bear a marriage without love and I don't want you to be in that situation, either. We're not in love. We barely know each other. We'll work this out, but marriage isn't the way."

He pulled her close against him to hold her while they stood there quietly. "Look, Stella, we're not your parents. I can't imagine either one of us treating the other person in such a manner."

She stood stiffly in his arms and he felt he couldn't reach her. He'd had his second shock when she turned down his offer of marriage. It didn't occur to him that she wouldn't marry him. Now there were two shocks tonight that hit him and left him reeling.

"You got pregnant when we were together in October," he said.

"Yes," she whispered.

He tilted her face up to look into her eyes. He caressed her throat, letting his fingers drift down her cheek and around to her nape. He felt the moment she relaxed against him. The stiffness left her and he heard her soft sigh.

"I didn't want you to know yet," she whispered.

"Maybe it's best I do. We'll work through this together," he said.

As he looked into her wide blue eyes, he became more aware of her soft curves pressed against him. His gaze lowered to her lips and his heart beat faster as desire kindled.

"Stella," he whispered, leaning closer. When his lips brushed hers, she closed her eyes.

He wrapped his arms more tightly around her, pulling her closer against him as he kissed her. It started as a tender kiss of reassurance. But then his mouth pressed more firmly against hers as his kiss became passionate. He wound his fingers in the bun at the back of her head and combed it out, letting the pins fall.

He wanted her. As far as he was concerned, their problem had a solution and it would only be a matter of time until she would see it. The moment that thought came to him, he remembered her strength in tough situations. If she said no to him, she might mean it and stick by it no matter what else happened.

She opened her eyes, stepping back. "Aaron, when we make love, I want it to be out of joy, not because of worry and concerns. Tonight's not the night."

Her hair had partially spilled over her shoulders and hung halfway down her back. A few strands were still caught up behind her head. Her lips had reddened from his kisses. Her disheveled appearance appealed to him and he wanted to draw her back into his embrace. Instead, he rested his hands lightly on her shoulders.

"You don't have to be burdened with worry and concerns tonight," he said. "We're in this together."

"Aaron, has anything ever set you back in your life?"

Her question was like a blow to his heart. She still hadn't heard about Paula and Blake, and he still didn't want to talk about them or his loss. Over the years, the pain had dulled, but it would never go away. Everyone had setbacks in life. Why would she think he had never had any? "All right, Stella. You want to be alone. I'll leave you alone," he said, turning to go. He had tried to do the right thing and been rebuffed for it.

"Aaron," she said, catching up with him, "I know you're trying to help me. I appreciate it. A lot of men would not have proposed. You're one of the good guys."

Realizing she needed time to think things through, he gazed at her. "I'm the dad. I'm not proposing just for your sake. It's for mine, too. Stella, this baby coming into my life is a gift, not an obligation," he said.

Her eyes widened with a startled expression and he realized she hadn't looked at it from his perspective, other than to expect him to propose.

"We can do better than this," he said, pulling her into his arms to kiss her again, passionately determined to get past her worries and fears.

For only a few seconds she stood stiffly in his arms and then she wrapped her arms around him, pressing against him and kissing him back until he felt she was more herself again and their problems were falling into a better perspective.

As their kiss deepened, his temperature jumped. He forgot everything except Stella in his arms while desire blazed hotly.

Leaning back slightly, he caressed her throat, his hands sliding down over her cotton blouse. He didn't think she could even feel his touch through the blouse, but she took a deep breath and her eyes closed as she held his forearms. Her reaction made him want to peel away the blouse, but he was certain she would stop him. He slipped his hand to the top button while he caressed her with his other hand. As he twisted the button free, she clutched his wrist.

"Wait, Aaron," she whispered.

He kissed away her protest, which had sounded faint and halfhearted anyway. He ran his fingers through her hair, combing it out, feeling more pins falling as the locks tumbled down her back.

"You look pretty with your hair down," he whispered.

She turned, maybe to answer. Instead, he kissed her and stopped any conversation.

"I want to love you all night. I will soon, Stella. I want to kiss and hold you," he whispered when the kiss subsided.

She moaned softly as he twisted free another button, his hand sliding beneath her blouse to cup her breast.

She gasped, kissing him, clinging to him. He wanted to pick her up, carry her to bed, but he suspected she would end their kisses and tell him good-night.

She finally stepped back. "We were headed to the door."

He combed long strands of brown hair from her face. "I'll go, but sometime soon, you'll want me to stay. I'll see you in the morning." He started out the door and turned back. "Don't worry. If you can't sleep, call me and we'll talk."

She smiled. "Thanks, Aaron. Thanks for being you."

He studied her, wondering about her feelings, wondering where they were headed, because he could imagine her sticking to the decisions she had already made involving their future. "Just don't forget I'm half the parent equation."

"I couldn't possibly forget," she said, standing in the open doorway with him.

"Good night," he said, brushing a light kiss on her lips and going to his suite.

When he got there, he went straight to the kitchen and

poured himself a glass of whiskey. Setting the bottle and his drink on the kitchen table, he pulled out his billfold. As he sat, he took a long drink. He opened the wallet and looked at a picture of Paula holding Blake. Aaron's insides knotted.

"I love you," he whispered. "I miss you. I'm going to be a dad again. I never thought that would happen. It doesn't take away one bit of love from either of you. That's the thing about love—there's always more."

He felt the dull pain that had been a part of him since losing Paula and Blake. "This isn't the way it was supposed to be. I know, if you were here, you'd tell me to snap out of it, to marry her and be the best dad possible." He paused a moment and stared at the photo. "Paula, Blake, I love you both. I miss you."

He dropped his billfold and put his head in his hands, closing his eyes tightly against the hurt. He got a grip on his emotions, wiped his eyes and took a deep breath. He was going to be a dad again. In spite of all the tangled emotions and Stella's rejection of his proposal, he felt a kernel of excitement. He would be a dad—it was a small miracle. A second baby of his own. How would he ever persuade Stella to marry him? She wanted love and marriage.

He could give her marriage. He would have to try to persuade her to settle for that. Just marriage. A lot of women would jump at such a chance. One corner of his mouth lifted in a grin and he held up his drink in a toast to an imaginary companion. "Here's to you, Stella, on sticking to your convictions and placing a premium on old-fashioned love. You'll be a good mother for our child."

So far, in working with her, Stella had proved to be levelheaded, practical and very intelligent. That gave him hope.

He finished his drink and poured one more, capping the bottle. Then he stood up and put it away. He started to pocket his billfold, but he paused to open it and look once more at the picture of his baby son. As always, he felt a hollow emptiness, as if his insides had been ripped out. Now he was going to have another baby—another little child, his child. It was a miracle to him, thrilling.

Stella had to let him be a part of his child's life. It was a chance to be a dad again, to have a little one, a son or daughter to raise. In that moment, he cared. He wanted Stella to marry him or let him into the life of his child in some way. He wasn't giving up a second child of his. One loss was too many. He sure as hell didn't plan to lose the second baby. He would have to court Stella until she just couldn't say no. He had to try to win her love.

As much as he hurt, he still had to smile. Stella wouldn't go for any insincere attempt to fake love or conjure it up where it didn't exist.

He had to make her fall in love with him and that might not be so easy when he didn't know whether he could ever really love her in return.

The next morning Stella was supposed to have breakfast with Aaron, but he called and told her to go ahead because he'd be late. A few minutes after she'd settled in and ordered, she watched him cross the dining room to her table. He was dressed for a day of helping the cleanup effort in jeans, an R&N sweatshirt and cowboy boots. Even in the ordinary clothes, he looked handsome and her heart began racing at her first glimpse of him. The father of her baby. She was beginning to adjust to the idea of being pregnant even though she had slept little last night.

"Sorry. You shouldn't have waited. Did you order from the menu or are you going with the buffet?"

"I've ordered from the menu and I didn't wait," she said, smiling.

"I'll get the buffet and be right back."

While they ate, Aaron sipped his coffee. "So, did you sleep well last night?" he asked.

"Fine," she replied, taking a dainty bite of yellow pineapple.

"Shall I try again? Did you get any sleep last night?"

She stared at him. "How do you know I didn't?"

"You're a scrupulously honest person so prevarication isn't like you. You were a little too upset to sleep well."

"If you must know, I didn't sleep well. Did you?"

"Actually, pretty good after I thought things through."

"I'm glad. By the way, today after work, I'll try to get something together for the presentation in Lubbock tomorrow. Please tell me this is a small group."

"This is a small group," he said, echoing her words.

She wasn't convinced. "Aaron, is this a large or small group?"

"It's what I'd call in-between."

"That's a real help," she said. He grinned and took her hand in his to squeeze it lightly.

"All you need is an opening line and a closing line. You know the stuff in between. You'll be fine. I know what I'm talking about. And so will you, so just relax," he said, his eyes warm and friendly. She would be glad to have his support for the afternoon.

When they finished breakfast and stood to go, she caught him studying her waist. She wore a tan skirt and matching blouse that was tucked in. She knew from looking intently in her mirror before she came down for breakfast, that her pregnancy still didn't show in her waist and that her stomach was as flat as ever.

His gaze flew up to meet hers. "You don't look it," he said quietly.

"Not yet. I will," she replied, and he nodded.

They walked out together and climbed into Aaron's car. He dropped her off at the temporary headquarters for town hall and drove away to go to the Cattleman's Club. Today she would be overseeing the effort to sort records that had been scattered by the storm. She wondered how many months—or worse, years—of vital records they would find. She hoped no one's life changed for the worse because of these lost records.

Stella entered the makeshift office that had been set up for recovered documents. The room held long tables covered with boxes labeled for various types of documents. As Stella put her purse away, Polly Hadley appeared with a box filled with papers that she placed on a cleared space on a desk.

"Good morning, Stella. You're just in time," her fellow administrative assistant said. "Here's another box of papers to sort through. I glanced at a few of these when I found them. What I saw was important," Polly said.

"I'm thankful for each record we find."

"Most of these papers were beneath part of a stockade fence."

"Heaven knows where the fence came from," Stella said.

"I don't want to think about how long we'll be searching for files, papers, records. Some of these were never stored electronically."

"Some records that were stored electronically are destroyed now," Stella stated as she pulled the box closer. "We'll just do the best we can. Thank goodness so many people are helping us."

"I'll be back with more." Polly smiled as she left the makeshift office.

Stella picked up a smudged stack of stapled papers from the top of the pile and looked at them, sighing when she saw they were adoption papers. A chill slithered down her spine as she thought again of important documents they might not ever find. She smoothed the wrinkled papers and placed them in a box of other papers relating to adoptions. She picked up the next set of papers and brushed away smudges of dirt as she read, her thoughts momentarily jumping back to breakfast with Aaron. In some ways it was a relief to have him know the truth. If only he would give her room to make decisions—that was a big worry. As for dinner with him tonight—she just hoped he didn't persist about marriage.

That evening as they ate, she made plans with Aaron to go to Lubbock the next day. She tried to be positive about it, but she had butterflies in her stomach just thinking about it.

She had finished eating and sat talking to Aaron while he sipped a beer when her phone rang. She listened to the caller, then stood up and gave instructions. When she hung up, she turned to Aaron.

"I heard some of that call. Your part," he said.

"We can talk as we walk to the car. That was Leonard Sherman. He's fallen and his daughter is out of town. He can't get up and he needs someone to help him. He hit his head. I told him that I would call an ambulance."

Aaron waited quietly while she made the call. As soon as she finished, she turned to him. "I need to go to his house to lock up for him when the ambulance picks him up. He lives alone near his daughter. He said his neighbor isn't home, either."

"Does everyone in town call you when they have an emergency?"

Smiling, she shook her head. "Of course not, but some of these people have gotten so they feel we're friends and

I'll help, which I'm glad to do. It's nice they feel that way. I'm happy to help when I can."

"I'll take you."

A valet brought Aaron's car to the door of the inn. As they drove away, she finished making her calls.

"You don't need to speed," she said. "I don't think he's hurt badly."

"You wanted to get there before they took him in the ambulance, so we will."

In minutes Aaron pulled into Leonard Sherman's driveway. She stepped out of the car and hurried inside while Aaron locked up and followed.

The ambulance arrived only minutes later and soon they had their patient loaded into the back and ready to go to the hospital. As the paramedics carefully pulled away from the curb, Stella locked up Leonard's house, pocketed the key and walked back to the car with Aaron.

"You don't have to go to the hospital with me. I'll call his daughter and she'll probably want to talk to the doctor. He said she's coming back tonight, so hopefully, she'll be home soon."

"I'll go with you. These evenings are getting interesting."

She laughed. "I told you that you don't have to come."

"You amaze me," Aaron said. "I've never told you any news I get about anyone in Royal that you don't already know. People tell you everything. I'll bet you know all sorts of secrets."

"I'm just friendly and interested."

"People trust you and you're a good listener. They call you for help. Mayor Vance doesn't do all this."

Stella watched him drive, thinking he was one person who didn't tell her everything. She always had a feeling that Aaron held personal things back. There were parts of his life closed to her. A lot of parts. She still knew little about him. She suspected Cole knew much more.

She called Leonard's daughter and, to her relief, heard her answer.

When Stella was done with the call, she turned to Aaron. "I'll go to Memorial Hospital to give her the key to his house, but his daughter is back and she'll be at the hospital, so we don't need to stay."

"Good. You said you wanted to get ready for tomorrow, so now you'll have a chance unless calamity befalls someone else in this town tonight."

"It's not that bad," she said.

"I had other plans for us this evening. We're incredibly off the mark."

"That's probably for the better, Aaron," she said.

"You don't have to do everything for everyone. Learn to delegate, Stella."

"Some things are too personal to delegate. People are frightened and hurting still. I'm happy to help however I can if it makes things even the smallest bit better."

He squeezed her hand. "Remind me to keep you around for emergencies," he said lightly, but she again wondered about what he kept bottled up and how he had been hurt. He might want them to be alone tonight, but she had to respond when someone called.

And she stuck to her guns. When they got back to the hotel, she told Aaron good-night early in the evening so she could get ready to leave for Lubbock with him the next morning.

As soon as she was alone in her suite, she went over her notes for the next day, but her thoughts kept jumping to Aaron. Every hour they spent together bound her a little more to him, making his friendship a bit more important to her. Now she was counting on him for moral support tomorrow.

The next morning, when she went to the lobby to meet Aaron and head for Lubbock, she saw him the minute she emerged from the elevator. The sight of him in a flawless navy suit with a red tie took her breath away and made her forget her worries about speaking. He looked incredibly handsome, so handsome, she wondered what he saw in her. She was plain from head to toe. Plain clothes, plain hair, no makeup. This handsome man wanted to marry her and she had turned him down. Her insides fluttered and a cold fear gripped her. Was she willing to let him go and marry someone else? The answer still came up the same. She couldn't marry without love. Yet Aaron was special, so she hoped she wasn't making a big mistake

This baby coming into my life is a gift, not an obligation. She remembered his words from the night before last. How many single men who had just been surprised to learn they would be a dad would have that attitude? Was she rejecting a very special man?

He saw her and she smiled, resisting the temptation to raise her hand to smooth her hair.

She was aware of her plain brown suit, her skirt ending midcalf. She wore a tan blouse with a round neck beneath her jacket. Her low-heeled brown pumps were practical and her hair was in its usual bun. When she crossed the lobby, no heads would turn, but she didn't mind because it had been that way all her life.

When she walked up to him, he took her arm. "The car is waiting," he said. "You look pretty."

"Thank you. Sometimes I wonder if you need to get your eyes checked."

He smiled. "The last time I was tested in the air force, I had excellent eyesight," he remarked. "You sell yourself short, Stella. Both on giving this talk and on how you look."

She didn't tell him that men rarely told her she was pretty. They thanked her for her help or asked her about their problems, just as boys had in school, but they didn't tell her how pretty she looked.

In minutes they were on the highway. She pulled out a notebook and a small stack of cards wrapped with a rubber band. "These are my notes. I have a slide presentation. I think the pictures may speak for themselves. People are stunned when they see these."

When she walked into the private meeting room in a country club, her knees felt weak and the butterflies in her stomach changed to ice. The room was filled with men and women in business suits—mostly men. It was a business club and she couldn't imagine talking to them. She glanced at Aaron.

"Aaron, I can't do this."

"Of course you can. Here comes Boyce Johnson, my friend who is president," he said, and she saw a smiling, brown-haired man approaching them. He extended his hand to Aaron, who made introductions that she didn't even hear as she smiled and went through the motions.

All too soon, Boyce called the group to order and someone made an introduction that Aaron must have written, telling about how she had helped after the storm hit Royal. And then she was left facing the forty or so people who filled the room, all looking at her and waiting for her to begin.

Smiling and hoping his presence would reassure her, Aaron sat listening to Stella make her presentation, showing pictures of the devastation in the first few hours after the storm hit Royal. That alone would make people want to contribute. After her slide presentation, Stella talked. She was nervous and it showed. He realized that right after the storm, adrenaline—and the sheer necessity for someone to take charge with Mayor Vance critically injured and the deputy mayor killed—had kept her going. Now that life in Royal was beginning to settle back into a routine, she could do it again, but she had to have faith in herself.

He thought of contacts he had and realized he could help her raise funds for the town. Her slide presentation had been excellent, touching, awesome in showing the storm's fury and giving the facts about the F4 tornado.

He sat looking at her as she talked and realized she might like a makeover in a Dallas salon. She could catch people's attention more. The men today were polite and attentive and she was giving facts that would hold their interest, but if she had a makeover, she might do even better. It should bolster her self-confidence.

She had done interviews and brief appearances almost since the day of the storm. Maybe it was time she had some help. He had statewide contacts, people in Dallas who were good about contributing to worthwhile causes. While she talked, he sent a text to a Dallas Texas Cattleman's Club member. In minutes he got a reply.

He sent a text to a Dallas salon, and shortly after, had an appointment for her.

He hoped she wouldn't balk at changing her hair. She clung to having it up in a bun almost as if she wanted to fade into the background, but hopefully, the makeover in the salon might cause her to be willing to change.

When she finished her speech and opened up the floor to questions, she seemed more poised and relaxed. She gave accurate facts and figures and did a good job of conveying the situation in Royal. Finally, there were no more questions. Boyce thanked her and Aaron for coming. He asked if anyone would like to make a motion to give a check to Stella to take back to Royal now because they seemed to need help as soon as they could possibly get it.

Boyce turned to ask their treasurer how much they had available in their treasury at present and was told there was $6,000.

One of the women made a motion immediately to donate $5,000. It was seconded and passed. A man stood and said he would like to contribute $1,000 in addition to the money from the treasury.

Aaron felt a flash of satisfaction, happy that they could take these donations back to Royal and happy that he had proved to Stella she could get out and lead the recovery effort now, just as she had right after the storm.

By the time the meeting was over, they had several checks totaling $12,000. Stella's cheeks were once again rosy and a sparkle was back in her blue eyes and he felt a warm glow inside because she was happy over the results.

With the help he planned to give her, he expected her to do even better. As he waited while people still talked to her, he received a text from the TCC member he had contacted. Smiling, he read the text swiftly and saw that his friend had made some contacts and it looked hopeful for an interview on a Fort Worth television station. Aaron sent a quick thank-you, hoping if it worked out Stella would accept.

It was almost four when they finally said goodbye and went to his car. When he sat behind the wheel, he turned to her, taking her into his arms. His mouth came down on hers as he kissed her thoroughly. Finally he leaned away a fraction to look at her.

"You did a great job. See, you can do this. You've raised $12,000 for Royal. That's fantastic, Stella."

She smiled. "My knees were shaking. Thank heavens you were there and I could look at your smiling face. They were nice and generous. I couldn't believe they would take all that out of their treasury and donate it at Christmastime."

"It's a Christmas present for Royal, thanks to you. That's what that club does. It's usually to help Lubbock, but Royal is a Texas town that is in desperate need of help. You did a great job and I think I can help you do an even bigger and better one," he said.

She laughed. "Aaron, please don't set me up to talk to another group of businesspeople. I'm an administrative assistant, not the mayor."

"You did fine today and I promise you, I think I can help you do a bit better if you'll let me."

"Of course, I'll let you, but I keep telling you, this is not my deal."

"You're taking $12,000 back to Royal. I think you can make a lot more and help people so much."

"When you put it that way—what do you have in mind?"

"I have lots of contacts in Dallas and across the state. Let me set up some meetings. Not necessarily a group thing like today—what I have in mind is meeting one-on-one or with just two or three company heads who might make some big donations. You can also make presentations to agencies that would be good contacts and can help even more."

"All right."

"Good. After your talk today I went ahead and contacted a close friend in Dallas. Through him you may get a brief interview on a local TV show in Fort Worth. Can I say you'll do it?"

"Yes," she answered, laughing. "You're taking charge again, Aaron."

"Also, if you'll let me contact them, I think I can get meetings in Dallas with oil and gas and TV executives, as well as some storm recovery experts. The television people will help get out the message that Royal needs help. The oil and gas people may actually make monetary donations. How's that sound?"

"Terrifying," she said, and smiled. "Well, maybe not so bad."

"So I can try to set up the meetings with the various executives?"

She stared at him a moment while she seemed to give thought to his question. "Yes. We need all the help we can get for the people at home."

"Good," he said, kissing her lightly.

"Let's take some time and talk about dealing with the press and interviews. We can talk over dinner. The press is important."

"I'll be happy to talk about interviews, but I don't think that I'll be giving many more."

"It's better to be ready just in case," he said, gazing into her wide blue eyes.

"Also I sent a text and asked for a salon makeover in Dallas for you. It's a very nice salon that will really pamper you. Would you object to that?" he asked, thinking he had never known a woman before that would have had to be given a sales pitch to get her to consent to a day at an exclusive Dallas salon.

She laughed. "Aaron, that seems ridiculous. I'm not going into show business. Mercy me. I don't think I need to go to Dallas to have a makeover and then return to Royal to help clean up debris and hunt through rubble for lost documents at town hall. That seems ridiculous."

"Stella, we can raise some money for Royal. A lot more than you did today. Trust me on this," he said, holding back a grin. "I told you that it's a very nice salon."

Shaking her head, she laughed again. "All right, Aaron. I can arrange to get away to go to Dallas. When is this makeover?"

"Someone canceled and they have an opening next Wednesday and I told them to hold it. Or they can take you in January. With the holidays coming, they're booked."

"How long does this take? I'll have to get to Dallas," she said, sounding as if he had asked her to do a task she really didn't relish.

"Cole and I have a company plane. We can fly to Dallas early Tuesday morning and be there in time for you to spend the day. I'll get you to the Fort Worth interview and I'll try to set up a dinner in Dallas that night. Afterward, we can stay at my house. I have lots of room and you can have your own suite there."

She smiled at him. "Very well. I can go to the salon Wednesday and get this over with. Thank you, Aaron," she said politely.

"Good deal," he said, amused at the reluctance clearly in her voice. "Take a dress along to go out to dinner. The next convenient stop, I'm pulling over to text the salon about Wednesday."

"I think this is going to be expensive for you and a waste of your money. People can't change in a few hours with a makeover. I really don't expect to do many more appearances or interviews."

"Just wait and see," he said.

"While we're on the subject of doing something for Royal, I've been thinking about Christmas. There are so many people who lost everything. We've talked about Christmas being tough for some of them. I want to organize a Christmas drive to get gifts for those who lost their homes or have no income because of their business losses. I want to make sure all the little children in those families have presents."

"That's a great idea, Stella. I'll help any way I can."

"I'm sure others will help. I'll call some of the women I

know and get this started. It's late—we should have started before now, but it's not too late to do this."

"Not at all. I think everyone will pitch in on this one. You're doing a great job for Royal."

"Thanks, Aaron. I'd feel better knowing that everyone has presents. We have a list now of all those who were hurt in some way by the storm. It's fairly detailed, so we know who lost homes and who is in the hospital and who lost loved ones or pets—all that sort of thing, and I can use it to compile a list for the Christmas gifts."

With a quick glance he reached over to take her hand. As he looked back at the highway, he squeezed her hand lightly. "Royal is lucky to have you," he said.

She laughed. "And you. And Cole and Lark and Megan and so many other people who are helping." He signaled a turn. "There's a farm road. We're stopping so I can send the text."

As soon as he stopped he unbuckled his seat belt and reached over to wrap his arms around her and pull her toward him.

"Aaron, what are you doing?"

"Kissing you. I think you're great, Stella," he said. As she started to reply, his mouth covered hers. It was as if he had waited years to kiss her. Startled, she didn't move for a second. Then she wrapped her arm around his neck to hold him while she kissed him in return.

What started out fun and rewarding changed as their desire blossomed. She wound her fingers in his hair, suddenly wanting to be in his arms and have all the constraints out of her way. She wanted Aaron with a need that overwhelmed her. The kiss deepened, became more passionate. She wanted to be in his arms, in his bed, making love. Would it give them a chance to fall in love?

She moaned softly, losing herself in their kiss, running

one hand over his muscled shoulder, holding him with her other arm.

She realized how intense this had become and finally leaned away a fraction. Her breathing was ragged. His light brown eyes had darkened with his passion. Desire was blatant in their depths, a hungry look that fanned the fires of her own longing.

"You did well today. You're taking back another check to help people," he said, his gaze drifting over her face. "When we get back we'll go to dinner and celebrate."

"I'm glad you went with me."

He moved away and she watched as he sent a text. He lowered his phone. "I want to wait a minute in case they answer right away."

His phone beeped and he scanned the message. "You're set for Wednesday," he said, putting away his phone. "We'll go home now."

She had a tingling excitement. Part of it was relief that the talk was over and she had been able to raise some money for Royal. Part of it was wanting Aaron and knowing they would be together longer.

They met again for dinner in the dining room at the inn. Both had changed to sweaters and slacks. Throughout dinner Stella still felt bubbly excitement and when Aaron finally escorted her back to her suite, she paused at her door to put her arms around him and kiss him.

For one startled moment he stood still, but then his arm circled her waist and he kissed her in return. Without breaking the kiss, he took her key card from her, unlocked her door and stepped inside. He picked her up and let the door swing shut while she reached out to hit the light switch.

Relishing being in his arms, she let go of all the problems for a few minutes while they kissed. Their kisses were becoming more passionate, demanding. He set her on her feet and then his hands were in her hair. The long locks tumbled down as the pins dropped away. As he kissed her, his hand slipped beneath her sweater to cup her breast and then lightly caress her.

She moaned, clinging to him, on fire with wanting him. He stepped back, pulling her blue sweater over her head and tossing it aside. He unfastened her bra and cupped her full breasts lightly in his hands. "You're soft," he whispered, leaning down to kiss her and stroke her with his tongue.

She gasped with pleasure, clinging to him, wanting him with her whole being but finally stopping him and picking up her sweater to slip it over her head again.

"Aaron, I need to sort things out before we get more deeply involved, and if we make love, I'll be more involved emotionally."

"I think we're in about as deep as it gets without marriage or a permanent commitment," he said solemnly. His voice was hoarse with passion. "You can 'sort' things out. I want you, Stella. I want you in my arms, in my bed. I want to make love all night."

Every word he said made her want to walk back into his arms, but she stood still, trying to take her time the way she should have when she first met him, before she made a physical commitment. Could they fall in love if she just let go and agreed to marry him? Or would she be the only one to fall in love while Aaron still stayed coolly removed from emotional involvement or commitment?

"Aaron, we really don't know a lot about each other," she said, and that shuttered look came over his expression. A muscle worked in his jaw as he stared at her in silence.

"What would you like to know?" he asked stiffly.

"I don't know enough to ask. I just think we should get to really know each other."

He nodded. "All right, Stella. Whatever you want. Let's eat breakfast together. The more we're together, the better we'll know each other."

"I'll see you at breakfast. Thanks again for today. It was nice to raise the money for people here and to have your moral support in Lubbock today."

"Good. See you at seven in the morning."

"Sure," she said, following him to the door. He turned to look at her and she gazed into his eyes, her heart beginning to drum again as her gaze lowered to his mouth. She wanted his kisses, wanted to stop being cautious, but that's how she had gotten pregnant. Now if she let go, she might fall in love when he wouldn't. Yet, was she going to lose a chance on winning his love because of her caution? She couldn't see any future for them the way things were.

Five

The next morning after breakfast with Stella, Aaron sent text messages to three more Texas Cattleman's Club members in Dallas. Stella had given him permission to plan two meetings, so he wanted to get them arranged as soon as possible.

Next, he drove to the temporary office R&N Builders had set up in Royal. It was a flimsy, hastily built building on a back street. He saw Cole's truck already there and was surprised his partner had returned a little earlier than he had planned.

Seated at one of the small tables that served as a desk, Cole was in his usual boots, jeans and R&N Builders T-shirt. His broad-brimmed black Resistol hung on the hat rack along with his jacket.

"How's Henry?" Aaron asked in greeting.

"He's getting along, but he needs help and he still has a lot of repairs to make. He had appointments with insurance people and an attorney about his brother's estate, so I came back here."

"I'm sorry to hear he still has a lot to do. That's tough. In the best of times there's no end to the work on a ranch."

"You got that right. And he's having a tough time about losing his brother. I figure I'm a good one to stay and give him a hand."

"I'm sure he'll appreciate it. I think a lot of people are glad to have you back in Royal. You didn't go home much before the storm."

"I've avoided being here with Craig and Paige since their marriage. I've gone home occasionally for holidays, but never was real comfortable about it since Craig and I both dated Paige in high school," Cole said, gazing into space. Aaron wondered if Cole still had feelings for Paige or if he had been in love with her when she'd married Craig.

"When the folks died, I came even less often." He turned to look at Aaron. "I'm ready to leave for the TCC. Want to ride with me?"

"I'll drive one of the trucks because I'm going to see Stella for lunch. She raised $12,000 from people in Lubbock yesterday afternoon."

"That's good news. Royal needs whatever we can get. There's still so much to be done."

"Cole, she has an idea—she's worried about Christmas and the people who lost everything, the people with little kids who are having a hard time. She wants to have a Christmas drive to get presents."

"She's right. Those people need help. Christmas is going to be tough."

"She's getting some women together to organize it. Meanwhile TCC has its Christmas festival coming up. Sure, you and I are members of the Dallas TCC, so I don't want to come in and start asking for favors, but I'm going to this time. I thought about talking to Gil and Nathan and a few other members. It might be nice to tie this Christmas present drive to the festival and invite all those people and let them pick up their presents then. What do you think?"

"I think that's a great idea. I'd say do it."

"Also, I think we should ask the Dallas TCC to make a

Christmas contribution to Royal. We could invite Dallas members to the Royal TCC Christmas Festival."

"Another good idea. We know some guys who would be willing to help and are usually generous when it's a good cause. I hope the whole town is invited this year. Everyone needs a party."

"I agree. We can talk to Gil."

"I'd be glad to," Cole replied, standing to get his jacket and hat. "I'll see you at the Cattleman's Club."

Aaron waved as he put his phone to his ear to make a call. When he was done, he stuffed some notes into his jacket pocket and locked up to go to the TCC.

When he arrived at the club, he glanced at the damage to the rambling stone and dark wood structure. Part of the slate roof of the main building had been torn off, but that had already been replaced. Trees had fallen on outbuildings, and many windows had to be replaced. A lot of the water damage had been taken care of early while the outbuildings were still in need of repair.

Aaron knew that repairs had started right away. The sound of hammers and chainsaws had become a fixture in Royal as much as the sight of wrecking trucks hauling away debris. As Aaron parked the R&N truck and climbed out, he saw Cole talking to Nathan Battle. Cole motioned to Aaron to join them.

The tall, brown-haired sheriff shook hands with Aaron. "Glad you're here. Work keeps progressing. We have the windows replaced now and that's a relief. You get tired of looking through plastic and hearing it flap in the wind."

"I told Nathan about Stella's idea for the Christmas drive and how it might be nice to combine it with the TCC Christmas festival," Cole said.

"I think it would be great. It'll add to the festivities. The holidays can be hard enough, as both of you know too well," Nathan said. "This will be a nice way to cheer people up."

"When will Gil be here?" Aaron asked.

"He's inside now," Nathan replied. "Let's go find him. We need the president's approval before you take it to a meeting."

Aaron worked through the morning, sitting in one of the empty meeting rooms. He did take time to make some calls to set up more appointments for Stella. He grinned to himself. She might not like all the appointments he planned to get for her, but he was certain she would rise to the occasion and he would help her.

Hopefully, the makeover might help her self-confidence a little. He would talk to her about dealing with the press and interviews and then see what kind of meetings he could help her get with people who would be willing to contribute to rebuilding Royal.

He had heard people mention her for the role of acting mayor if Mayor Vance didn't recover and someone was needed to step in. He wondered whether she had heard those remarks. He suspected if she had, Stella would dismiss them as ridiculous. She had been too busy to take time to realize that she was already fulfilling the position of acting mayor.

He had to admire her in so many ways. And in private— she was about to become a lot more important to him.

He leaned back in his chair, stretching his legs. Stella was going to have his baby. The thought still shocked him. He wanted this baby to be part of his life. He had lost one child. He didn't want to lose this one. And Stella was the mother of his child. He needed to forget shock and do something nice for her right now. Neither of them were in love, but they liked being together. As he thought about it, he was startled to realize she was the first woman he had truly enjoyed being with since his wife.

That was good enough to build a relationship as far as he was concerned, and Stella was a solid, super person who was appealing and intelligent. She deserved better from him. He glanced at his watch, told Cole he was going to run an errand and left the club to head to the shops in town. He intended to do something for Stella soon. Even if he couldn't give her love, he could help her and be there for her.

Stella decided to start with Paige. They agreed to meet briefly in the small café in the Cozy Inn midmorning over coffee. Stella arrived first and waved when she saw Paige step into the wide doorway. Dressed in jeans, a navy sweater, Western boots and a denim jacket, she crossed the room and sat at the small table across from Stella.

"What's up?"

"Thanks for taking time out of your busy day. I want to ask you a favor. I'm concerned about how hard Christmas will be on the people who lost so much in the storm," she said. "Christmas—any holiday—is a tough time when you've lost loved ones, your home, everything. I know you suffered a devastating loss, so if it upsets you to deal with this, Paige, say so and bow out. I'll understand."

"No. The holiday is going to be hard for a lot of people."

"Well, there are some people here who can't afford to have any kind of Christmas after all they lost. It's another hurt on top of a hurt. This is about the people who can't afford to get presents for their kids, for their families, who'll be alone and don't have much, that sort of thing."

"They should have help. What did you have in mind?"

"A Christmas drive with gifts and maybe monetary donations for them so they can buy things."

"Stella, I think that's grand. Thank goodness we can afford to do things at Christmas. But you're right about some of these people who have been hurt in every sort of way including financially. I think a Christmas drive to get presents would be wonderful. I'm so glad you thought about that."

"Well, what I really want— I need a cochair and you would be perfect if you'd do it. I know you're busy—"

Shaking her auburn hair away from her face, Paige smiled. "Stop there. I think it's a good cause so, yes, I'll cochair this project."

"That's so awesome," Stella said, smiling at her friend. "I can always count on you. I'm going to call some others to be on our committee."

"If you need my help, I can ask some friends for you."

"Here's my list. I've already sent a text to Lark and I left a message. I'll call Megan and my friend Edie."

"I can talk to Beth and Julie. I know Amanda Battle and I think she would help."

"I have my lists. We'll have a Christmas tree in the temporary town hall or I can get some of the merchants to take tags and hang them in their windows. We can make little paper ornaments and hang them on merchant's Christmas trees. Each ornament will match up with a person who will receive a gift. The recipients can choose an ornament and take it home. They'll match up with our master list, so we can tell who gets what present and we won't have to use names. So, for instance, the ornament could read, 'Boy—eight years old' plus a number to match our list and suggested gift ideas. We'll need to have gifts for the adults, too."

"Sounds good to me. We'll need to set up a Christmas-drive fund at one of the banks, so people can get tax credit for their donations," Paige said.

"I can deal with that because I'll be going by the bank anyway," Stella said.

"Fine. You take care of setting up the bank account."

"Paige, I appreciate this so much. I talked to Aaron about it and he'll run it past Cole and the TCC guys. I have a list of people who will probably participate in the drive. I'll email it to you."

"Good. I better run."

"Thanks again. I'll walk out with you. I'm going to the office—our temporary one. I think town hall will be one of the last places to get back to normal."

"There are so many places that still need to get fixed, including the Double R," she said.

"How're you doing running that ranch by yourself?"

"I run it in Craig's place, but not by myself. Our hands have been wonderful. They've really pitched in and gone the extra mile."

"I'm glad. See you soon."

They parted and Stella drove to town hall, trying to focus on work there and stop thinking about Aaron.

It was seven when she went down to meet Aaron in the Cozy Inn dining room, which had gotten to be a daily occurrence. She thought about how much she looked forward to being with him as she glanced once more at her reflection in the mirror in the elevator. Her hair was in a neat bun, every hair in place. She wore a thick pale yellow sweater and dark brown slacks with her practical shoes. The night air was chilly, although it was warm in the inn.

She stepped off the elevator and saw him only a few yards away.

Tonight he was in slacks, a thick navy sweater and Western boots. He looked sexy and appealing and she hoped he asked her to dance.

"You're not in your usual spot tonight. I thought maybe you decided not to come," she said.

"Never. And if something ever does interfere with my

meeting you when I said I would, believe me I'll call and let you know unless I've been knocked unconscious."

She laughed. "I hope not. I had a productive day, did you?"

"Oh, yes, I did. Let's get a table and I'll tell you all about it, because a lot of it concerns you. I'll bet they were pleased at town hall with the checks you got yesterday."

"Oh, my, yes. We have three families that are in a desperate situation and need money for a place to stay. Then some of it will go to buy more supplies where needed. Do you want me to keep going down the list?"

"No need." He paused to talk to the maître d', who led them to a table near the fireplace. Mesquite logs had been tossed in with the other logs and the pungent smell was inviting.

Stella ordered ice water again. When they were alone, she smiled at him. "I saw Paige Richardson today. She agreed to cochair my Christmas-drive committee."

"You didn't waste time getting that going."

"No, we need to as soon as possible. Actually, I kept $2,000 of the check from Lubbock to open a fund at the bank for the Christmas drive. She is recruiting some more members for the committee and I have Megan's and Julie's help."

"I talked to Cole about it and then we talked to Gil Addison and Nathan Battle and the TCC is willing to tie the Christmas drive in with their Christmas festival. They'll invite all the families and children to receive their gifts during the festival."

"That's wonderful, Aaron. Thank you. Paige was going to contact Amanda Battle and see if she will be on our committee."

"That's a good person to contact. So you're off to a roaring start there."

"Now tell me more about the Dallas trip."

"Here comes our waiter and then we'll talk."

They ordered and she waited expectantly. "Next week you have one little fifteen-minute spot on the noon news in Fort Worth. This will be your chance to kick off the Christmas drive and maybe get some donations for it."

"I'm looking forward to getting news out about the Christmas drive."

"Good. That night I have the oil and gas executives lined up. We will meet them for dinner and you can talk to them about the storm and what people need. I know you'll reach them emotionally because you have so many touching stories."

"Thank you. I'll be happy to do all of these things but I still say I wasn't meant to be a fund-raiser," she said, suspecting she wasn't changing his mind at all.

"You'll be great. You'll be fine. You've been doing this sort of thing since the storm. I've seen your interviews. I even taped one. You're a natural."

"Aaron, every cell in your body is filled with self-assurance. You can't possibly understand having butterflies or qualms."

"I have to admit, I'm not burdened with being afraid to talk to others about subjects I know."

Smiling, she shook her head. "I don't know everything about my subject."

"You know as much as anybody else in Royal and more about the storm than about ninety-eight percent of the population. You went through it, for heaven's sake. You were at town hall. You were there for all the nightmarish first hours after the storm and you've been there constantly ever since. I heard you crawled under debris and rescued someone. Is that right?"

"Yes. I could hear the cries. She was under a big slab of

concrete that was held up by rubble. Not fun, but we got her out. It was a twenty-year-old woman."

"That's impressive," he said, studying her as if he hadn't ever seen her before. "If you did that, you can talk to people in an interview. After we eat let's go up to your room or mine and go over ways you can handle the interview."

When their tossed green salads came, Aaron continued to talk. She realized he was giving her good advice on things to do and she soaked up every word, feeling she would do better the next appearance she made.

Aaron kept up his advice and encouragement throughout the meal, and when they were through dinner, Stella didn't want him to stop. "Aaron, why don't we go to my room now and you can continue coaching me?"

"Sure, but a couple of dances first," he said, standing and taking her hand. In minutes she was in his arms, moving with him on the dance floor, relishing dancing, being in his arms.

Aaron was becoming important to her. She was falling in love with him, but would he ever let go and fall in love with her? She felt he always held himself back and she still had that feeling with him. There couldn't be any real love between them until all barriers were gone.

Was she making a mistake by rejecting intimacy when Aaron obviously wanted it, as well as wanted to marry her? The question still constantly plagued her.

In the slow dances, their steps were in perfect unison as if they had danced together for years. Sometimes she felt she had known him well and for a long time. Other times she realized what strangers they were to each other. Sometimes when he got that shuttered look and she could feel him withdrawing, she was certain she should tell him goodbye and get him out of her life now. Yet with a baby between them, breaking off from seeing Aaron was impossible.

When the music ended they left and went to her suite. He got the tape of her interview.

"Want something to drink while we watch?" she asked. "Hot chocolate? Beer?"

"Hot chocolate sounds good. Go easy on the chocolate. I'll help."

They sat on the sofa and he put on the tape. While they watched, Aaron gave her pointers and when the tape ended, he talked about dealing with the press. Removing pins from her hair, he talked about doing interviews. As the first locks fell, she looked up at him.

"You don't need to keep your hair up all the time. You surely don't sleep all night this way."

"Of course not. It wouldn't stay thirty minutes."

"So, we'll just take it down a little early tonight," he said. "Now back to the press. Get their cards and get their names, learn their names when you meet them. They have all sorts of contacts and can open doors for you."

As she listened to him talk, she paid attention, but she was also aware of her hair falling over her back and shoulders, of Aaron's warm breath on her nape and his fingers brushing lightly against her. Every touch added a flame to the fires burning inside. Desire was hot, growing more intense the longer she sat with him. She wanted his kiss.

She should learn what he was telling her, but Aaron's kisses seemed more important. When the bun was completely undone, he placed the pins on a nearby table. He parted her hair, placing thick strands of it over each shoulder as he leaned closer to brush light kisses across her nape.

Catching her breath, she inhaled deeply. Desire built, a hungry need to turn and wrap her arms around him, to kiss him.

She felt his tongue on her nape, his kisses trailing on her skin. He picked her up, lifting her to his lap. She gazed into his brown eyes while her heart raced and she could barely get her breath.

"I want you, Aaron. You make me want you," she whispered. She leaned closer to kiss him, her tongue going deep. Her heartbeat raced as she wrapped her arms around his neck.

His hands slipped lightly beneath her sweater, sliding up to cup her breasts. In minutes he cupped each breast in his hands, caressing her. She moaned with pleasure and need, wanting more of him. She wanted to be alone with him. To make love and shut out the world and the future and just know tonight.

Would that bring him closer to her? Her to him? She couldn't marry him without love, but intimacy might be a way to love.

She tightened her arms, pressing against his solid warmth, holding him as they kissed. His fingers moved over her, touching lightly, caressing her, unfastening snaps, unfastening her bra.

His fingers trailed down over her ribs, down to her slacks. While they kissed, she felt his fingers twisting free buttons. Without breaking their kiss, he picked her up and carried her into her bedroom. Light spilled through the doorway from the front room, providing enough illumination to see. He stood her on her feet by the bed and continued to kiss her, leaning over her, holding her against him as his hand slipped down to take off her slacks.

She stepped out of them and kicked off her shoes, looking up at him for a moment as she gasped for breath.

Combing his fingers into her hair on either side of her face, he looked down at her. "I want you. I want to make love to you all night long."

"Aaron—"

He kissed her again, stopping any protest she might have made, but she wasn't protesting. She wanted him, this strong man who had been at her side for so much now, who was willing to do the honorable thing and marry her. She wanted his love. She wanted him with her, loving her. That might not ever happen if she kept pushing him away.

He tugged her sweater up, pulling it over her head and tossing it aside. Her unfastened bra slipped down and she let it fall to the floor. Cupping her breasts again, he trailed light kisses over her while she clung to him and gasped with pleasure. When he tossed away his sweater, she ran her hands across his chest, stroking his hard muscles, caressing him lightly.

Wanting to steal his heart, she kissed him.

It was an impossible, unreasonable fantasy. Yet she could love him until he found it difficult to resist her and impossible to walk away. Would she ensnare her own heart in trying to win his?

He placed his hands on her waist, stepping back to look at her, his gaze a burning brand. "You're beautiful, so soft," he whispered, and leaned forward to trail kisses over her breasts.

Desire continued to build, to be a fire she couldn't control. She wanted him now and there were no arguments about whether she should or shouldn't make love with him. She unfastened his slacks, letting them fall, and then removed his briefs. He pulled her close, their bare bodies pressed together, and even that wasn't enough. Again, he picked her up and turned to place her on the bed, kneeling and then stretching beside her to kiss her while his hands roamed over her to caress her.

She moaned softly, a sound taken by his kisses. Now union seemed necessary, urgent. Her hands drifted over him, down his smooth back, over his hard butt and along a muscled thigh.

He moved, kneeling beside her, looking at her as his hands played over her and then he trailed kisses over her knees, up the inside of her thighs, parting her legs, kissing and stroking her.

Arching beneath his touch, she wanted more of him. Her eyes were shut as he toyed with her, building need. One of his hands was between her thighs, the other tracing her breasts, light touches that drove her wild until she rose to her knees to kiss and stroke him.

His eyes were stormy, dark with desire. Need shook her because of his intensity. His groan was deep in his throat while his fingers locked in her hair and she held and kissed him, her tongue stroking him slowly. He gasped and slipped his hands beneath her arm to raise her.

He kissed her hard, one arm circling her waist, holding her close against him, his other hand running over her, caressing her and building need to a fever pitch.

She clung to him as she kissed him. "Aaron," she whispered. "Let's make love—"

They fell on the bed and he moved over her as she spread her legs for him and arched to meet him, wanting him physically as much as she wanted his love.

He entered her slowly, filling her, taking his time while he lowered himself, moving close to kiss her.

When he partially withdrew, she raised her hips, clinging to him to draw him back.

"Aaron, I want you," she whispered.

He slowly entered her again, and she gasped with pleasure, thrashing beneath him and running her hands over his back. He loved her with slow deliberation, maintaining control, trying to increase her pleasure as she moved beneath him and her need and desire built. Her pulse roared in her ears as his mouth covered hers again in another hungry kiss that increased her need.

Caught in a compelling desire that drove her beyond thought to just react to every stroke and touch and kiss from him, she tugged him closer, moving faster beneath him.

Beaded in sweat, he rocked with her until she reached a pinnacle and burst over it, rapture pouring over her while she moved wildly. When his control ended, he thrust deeply and fast.

Arching against him, she shuddered with another climax. Letting go, she slowed as ecstasy enveloped her.

"Aaron, love," she cried, without realizing what she had said.

Aaron groaned and finally slowed, his weight coming down partially on her. He turned his head to kiss her lightly.

While each gasped for breath, they lay wrapped in each other's arms. Gradually, their breathing slowed until it was deep and regular. He rolled to his side, keeping her with him.

She opened her eyes to look at him and he kissed her lightly again.

"I don't want to let go of you," he whispered.

"I don't want you to," she answered, trailing her fingers over his chest, feeling rock-solid muscles. She kept her mind closed to everything except the present moment and enjoying being in his arms and having made love with him.

"Stella, if you would marry me, we could have this all the time," he whispered, toying with a lock of her long hair.

She didn't feel like talking and she didn't care to argue, so she kept quiet, still stroking him.

They held each other in a silence that was comfortable for her. She suspected it was for him, too. She knew he wasn't asleep because he continued to play with strands of her hair. He had to know she was awake, because she still ran her fingers lightly over him, touching, caressing, loving him.

"Before I commit to marriage, I will have to be deeply in love and so will you. If that happens, we'll both know it and the rest of the world will know it. We're not at that point. We're not in love with each other," she said, the words sounding bleak to her.

"I still say it could come in marriage."

"I don't want to take that chance," she whispered, hoping she wasn't throwing away her future and her baby's future in a few glib sentences that were easy to say when she was being held close to his heart.

"Think about it. We're good together, Stella."

She raised herself slightly on her elbow, propping her head on her hand, and looked down at him. "You think about it. Do you want a marriage without love?"

Again, she got that look from him as if he had closed a door between them. She felt as if he had just gone away from her, almost as if he had left the room even though he was still right here beside her. An ache came to her heart. Aaron had closed himself off. There was a part of his life he wouldn't share, and with time it could become a wedge between them.

She thought about asking him what made him withdraw into a shell, but she suspected that would only make him do so more and make things worse.

"No, I suppose you're right. I don't want that," he answered, and she heard a note of steel in his voice.

"Maybe things will change if we keep seeing each other."

"I want to be in my child's life, so someday we'll have to work out how we're going to share our baby," he said in a different tone of voice. Why had he changed? Only minutes ago he hadn't been this way. She wondered whether they would ever be truly close, much less truly in love.

She lay down beside him again, her hair spreading on his shoulder as he pulled her close against him, leg against leg, thigh against thigh, her head on the indention between his chest and shoulder. He had proposed. He'd helped her. He wanted to be with her and take her out. What had happened in his life to cause him to let it get between him and someone else he would otherwise be close to in a relationship?

Would he ever feel close enough to her to share whatever he held back from her now?

Six

"Hey, why so solemn?" he asked, nuzzling her neck and making her giggle.

"That's better. Let's go shower and see what happens."

"Evidently you have plans," she said, amused and forgetting the serious life-changing decisions that loomed for her.

He stepped out of bed, scooped her up and carried her to the large bathroom, to stand her on her feet in the roomy tiled shower.

They played and splashed beneath the warm water until he looked at her and his smile faded, desire surfacing in his eyes. He reached out to caress her breasts and she inhaled, placing her hands on his hips and closing her eyes.

He was aroused, ready to love again, and she wanted him. She stroked him, stepping closer to kiss him and hold him. His lips were wet, his face wet, his body warm and wet against hers.

He turned off the water and moved from the shower, taking her hand as she stepped out. Aaron picked up a thick towel, shaking it out and lightly drying her in sensuous strokes that heightened desire. She picked up another fresh towel to dry him, excited by the look in his eyes that clearly revealed desire.

She rubbed the thick white towel over sculpted muscles, down over his flat belly, lightly drawing it across his thick staff.

He groaned, dropping his towel and grabbing hers to toss it away. He scooped her into his arms and carried her back to bed as he kissed her. Their legs were still wet, but she barely noticed and didn't care as she clung to him and kissed him.

He shifted between her legs and then rose up slightly, watching her as he entered her again. She cried out, arching to meet him, reaching for him to pull him back down into her embrace.

They made love frantically as if they never had before and she cried out with her climax.

He climaxed soon after, holding her as he pumped, finally lowering his weight and then rolling on his side to hold her against him.

"Fantastic, Aaron," she whispered, floating in euphoria. "Hot kisses and sexy loving."

"I'll have to agree," he said. "I want to hold you all night."

"No arguments from me on that one."

Once again they were silent and she ran her hand over him, thinking she would never tire of touching him. Aaron brought joy, help, fun, excitement, sex into her life. He was giving her his baby. If only he could give her his love.

"This has cut short all your help with giving interviews and dealing with the press."

"I'm still here and we'll continue. Besides, you're a fast learner."

"You don't really know that, but I'm trying. Aaron, when we fly to Dallas on Tuesday, I want to visit with my mom in Fort Worth. I called her and we made plans to have lunch. She's meeting me on her lunch hour and my grandmother has gone to Abilene to stay a week with my aunt. You're welcome to join us for lunch if you want, but you don't have to do that."

"I'll pass because you don't see her real often, so she may want to talk to you alone. I've got a limo for you—"

"A limo? Aaron, that's ridiculous. I can rent a car at the airport."

"No need. Cole and I have a limo service we use and two men who regularly drive for us. Sid will drive you Tuesday. He'll take you to Fort Worth for lunch and the interview and then he'll drive you back to a shop I recommend in Dallas where you can buy some new dresses. He'll either wait or give you a number and you can call him when you're ready to be picked up."

"I'm beginning to feel like your mistress."

Aaron laughed. "This is for Royal. I expect you to get a lot of donations for the town. Just keep thinking about the good we can do. Now if you would like to be my mistress—"

"Forget that one," she said, and he chuckled.

"We'll get back to talking about business tomorrow. Tonight I have other things on my mind. You don't have any morning sickness, do you?"

"Not a bit so far. I just can't eat as much and sometimes I get sleepy about two in the afternoon."

"Why don't you catch a few winks. The world won't stop spinning if you do. You're vital to Royal, Stella. You've done a superb job, but the world will go on without you for the time it takes you to get a good night's sleep."

"Thank you, Dr. Nichols. How much do I owe you for that advice?"

"About two dozen kisses," he said, and she laughed, pushing him on his back and rolling over on top of him.

"I'm going to pay you now."

"Best collection I'll ever make," he said, wrapping his arms around her.

Aaron stirred and rolled over to look at Stella. She lay on her back, one arm flung out, her hair spread over the pillow. She was covered to her chin by the sheet. Even in her sleep she stayed all covered, which amused him.

She continued to fill in for the mayor. It amazed him how people turned to her for help, everyone from the city treasurer to ordinary citizens. He didn't think Stella was even aware of the scope of what she was doing for the citizens of Royal. She was one of the key people in restoring the town and securing assistance for people. She was willing to accept his help and he could introduce her to so many people who would contribute to rebuilding Royal. He liked being with her. He liked making love with her. She excited him, and the more he got to know her, the more he enjoyed her. If she would agree to marriage, he thought, with time they would come to really love each other.

He thought of Paula and Blake, and the dull pain came as it always did.

Along with it came second thoughts. Maybe he was wrong about never being able to love someone else again. And maybe Stella was right—the only time to marry someone would be if he was as wildly in love as he had been with Paula. If he only married to give his baby a father, and wasn't really in love, that wouldn't be fair to Stella and might not ever be a happy arrangement.

He thought the fact that they got along well now and he liked being with her would be enough. The sex was fantastic. But there was more to life than that.

He sighed. He wanted to know this baby of his. He

wanted to be a dad for his child, to watch him or her grow up. Aaron wanted to be a part of that.

If he didn't marry her, she could marry someone else who would take her far away where Aaron wouldn't get to see his son or daughter often. Maybe he needed to contact one of his lawyers and get some advice. The one thing he was certain about—he did not want to lose his second child.

He lifted a strand of Stella's hair. She excited him and he liked being with her. She was levelheaded, practical. If he gave it a little more time and attention, maybe they could fall in love.

He had been a widower for seven years now. How likely was he to change?

If anyone could work a change, it would be Stella. She had already done some miracles in Royal. If Mayor Vance recovered, someone should tell him exactly how much Stella had stepped in and taken over.

Desire stirred. There might not be love, but there was a growing fiery attraction for both of them. He wanted to be with her and he was going to miss her when he returned to Dallas. Right now that wasn't going to happen—without her being beside him—until after the holidays. He would worry about that when it came time for them to part.

He leaned down to brush a kiss on her temple as he pushed the sheet lower to bare her breasts so he could caress her. Then he shifted to reach her so he could trail light kisses over her full breasts. Beneath those buttoned-up blouses she wore, there were some luscious curves.

She stirred, opened her eyes and blinked. Then she smiled and wrapped her arms around his neck, pulling him down so she could kiss him.

Forgetting his worries, Aaron wrapped his arms around her, drawing her close as he kissed her passionately.

* * *

It was Saturday, but still like a workday for her with all that needed to be done in Royal. She glanced at the clock and sat up, yanking the sheet beneath her arms. Alarmed, she glanced at Aaron. "Aaron, it's nine in the morning," she said, horrified how late they had slept. "Aaron."

He opened his eyes and reached up to pull her down. She wriggled away. "Oh, no, you don't. We've got to get out of this bed."

Looking amused, he drew her to him. "No, we don't. It's Saturday. Come here and let me show you the best possible way to start our weekend."

"Aaron, I work on Saturday. Royal needs all sorts of things. I have a list of things to do."

"Any appointments with people?"

"I don't think so, just things to do."

"Like finding Dobbin and locking up Mr. Sherman's house?"

"Maybe so, but I spend Saturdays doing those things. I don't lollygag in bed."

"Let me show you my way of lollygagging in bed." He pulled her closer.

"Aaron, look—"

He kissed away her words, his hand lightly fondling her, caressing her breast while he kissed her thoroughly. He raised up to roll over so he was above her as he kissed her.

She was stiff in his arms for about ten seconds and then she melted against him, knowing she was lost.

It was two hours later when she grabbed the sheet and stepped out of bed. "Aaron, I'm going to shower alone," she said emphatically. "There are things I think I should do today and if someone came looking for either one of us, I would be mortified."

He grinned. "You shouldn't be. First, it's none of anyone

else's business. Second—and most important—you're passing up a chance to spend a day in bed with me."

She had to laugh. "You do tempt me beyond belief, but I know there are things I can get done and sooner or later someone will ask me to help in some manner. I'm going to shower."

She heard him chuckle as she left the room. When she came out of the shower, he was nowhere around. As she looked through the suite, she realized he must have left.

She found a note and picked it up. In scrawling writing, she read, "Meet me in the dining room in twenty minutes."

"Twenty minutes from when?" she said aloud to no one. She shook her head and went to get dressed to go to the dining room and eat with him.

She spent the day running the errands on her list, making calls, going by the hospital again. At dinner she ate with Aaron, and for a short time after he talked to her more about dealing with the press, until she was in his lap, his kisses ending the coaching session on how to deal with the press.

They had grown more intimate, spent more time together, yet he still shut himself and his past off from her.

She could ask someone else about Aaron, but she wanted him to get close enough to her to stop keeping part of himself shut away. Moments still came when she could sense him emotionally withdrawing and at those times, she thought they would never really be close or deeply in love with each other. Not in love enough to marry.

Why was true intimacy so difficult for Aaron when he was so open about other aspects of his life?

The days leading up to the Dallas trip flew by.

Sunday morning Aaron went to church with her. After the service he stood to one side waiting as people greeted her and stopped to talk briefly.

When she finally joined him to go eat Sunday dinner, he smiled at her.

"What are you smiling about?"

"You. How can you lack one degree of confidence about talking to crowds? You had as long a line of people waiting to speak to you as the preacher did."

She laughed. "You're exaggerating. They were just saying good morning."

"Uh-huh. It looked like an earnest conversation three or four times."

"Maybe one or two had problems."

"Sure, Stella. Sometime today or tomorrow I'll bet you do something about those problems."

"Okay, you win. I still say helping people one-on-one is different from talking to a group of people I don't know and trying to get them to donate to the relief effort in Royal."

He grinned and squeezed her arm lightly. "Let's go eat. We missed breakfast."

By midafternoon she was in bed again with Aaron. She felt giddy, happy, and knew she was in love with him. She might have huge regrets later, but right now, she was having the time of her life with him.

Sunday night while she was in his arms in bed, she turned to look at him. "You should either go home now or plan to get up very early because Monday will be a busy day."

"I'll opt for the get-up-early choice," he drawled, toying with locks of her hair. "The more time with you, the better life is."

"I hope you mean that," she said, suddenly serious.

He shifted to hold her closer. "I mean it or I wouldn't have said it." He kissed her and their conversation ended.

Monday, after breakfast with Aaron, she got back on track with appointments and meetings. Later that afternoon, she had another brief meeting with Paige at the Cozy Inn café.

"Paige, we need to have a meeting with everyone who wants to be on this committee. I've talked to Megan Maguire, Gloria Holt, Keaton's mom, Lark Taylor, Edith Simms—they all volunteered to help us. I told Lark that Keaton's mom had volunteered and Lark said she still wanted to be a volunteer. I think it will all be harmonious."

"Great. I have Beth, Amanda Battle and Julie Kingston. This is such a good idea, Stella. It would have been dreadful if we'd ignored these people at this time of year."

"Someone would have thought of it if we hadn't. But it's especially nice to do this in conjunction with the TCC Christmas festival. Also, I intend to raise some money beyond what we'll need for getting presents. It'll be wonderful to have people bring presents for those who lost so much, but I also want them to get cash to spend as they want to. Everyone wants to give their children something they've selected. Donated presents are wonderful, but giving these families a chance to buy and wrap their own gifts is important, too."

"Another good idea, Stella. You're filled with them."

"'Tis the season. I'll be in Dallas tomorrow and gone for the rest of the week. Aaron has made appointments for me to meet people he thinks will be willing and able to help Royal."

"That's good. I'll take care of the Christmas drive while you're gone. You see if you can get some more donations."

"Thanks for all your help," Stella said, giving Paige's hand a squeeze, always sorry for Paige's losses.

After they parted, Stella went to the hospital. Mayor Vance was improving and now he could have visitors. She knocked lightly on the door and his wife called to come in.

The mayor was propped up in bed. His legs were in

casts and he was connected to machines with tubes on both sides of the bed.

"He's sitting up now and he's on the mend," his wife said.

"Mayor Vance, I am so happy to see you," Stella said, walking closer. He had always been thin, but now he was far thinner and pale, his dark brown hair a bigger contrast with his pale complexion. His brown eyes were lively and she was glad he was improving.

"Stella, it's good of you to come by. I've heard you've been a regular and I've heard so many good things about you. I could always count on you at the office."

"Thank you. The whole town has pulled together. Support for Royal has poured in—it amazes me and the donations to the Royal storm recovery fund grow steadily."

"That's so good to hear. It doesn't seem possible the tornado happened more than two months ago. It's almost mid-December and here I am still in the hospital."

"At least you're getting better," she said, smiling at him and his wife.

"I've talked with members of the town council. We need an acting mayor and I hope you'll be willing to do it."

"Mayor Vance, thank you for the vote of confidence, but I think there are more qualified people. I'm sure the town council has others in mind."

"I've heard all the things you've been doing and what you did the first twenty-four hours after the storm hit. You're the one, Stella. I'm pushing for you so don't let me down. From the sound of it, you're already doing the job."

"Well, I'll think about it," she said politely, wanting to avoid arguing with him in her first visit with him since the storm. "We've had so much help from other places that it's really wonderful."

She sat and visited a few more minutes and then left. His wife followed her into the hall.

"Stella, thanks again for coming. You've been good to check on him through all this."

"I'm glad to see he's getting better steadily."

"We're grateful. Come again. Think about what he said about filling in for him. He can't go back for a long time."

"I will," Stella said, maintaining a pleasant expression as she left and promptly dismissing the conversation.

Tuesday morning she flew to Dallas with Aaron. He picked up his car at an agency near the airport and they headed to his house in a gated suburb north of the city.

"We'll leave our things at my house. I've got the limo for you, and Sid will drive you to Fort Worth for lunch with your mother and next, to your interview at the Fort Worth TV station. After that he'll drive you back to Dallas to a dress shop while I go to the office. If you're having a makeover, you should have some new clothes. Get four or five dresses and a couple of suits."

"Seriously?" she asked, laughing. "Have you lost it, Aaron? I don't need one new thing, much less a bunch."

"Yes, you do for the people I'll introduce you to."

"When you tell me things like that, I get butterflies again."

"Ignore them and they'll vanish. Buy some new duds and shoes—the whole thing. This is an investment in Royal. Get something elegant, Stella."

She laughed again. "Aaron, you're talking to me, Stella. I don't need to look elegant to climb over debris in Royal."

"You need to look elegant to raise money so we can get rid of the debris in Royal."

She studied his profile, wondering what he was getting her into and if she could do what he wanted. Would it really help Royal? She thought about the money she had raised in Lubbock and took a deep breath. She would give it a try. "You're changing me," she said, thinking about how that was true in every way possible.

He picked up her hand to brush a kiss across her knuckles while he kept his attention on the highway. "Maybe you're changing me, too," he said.

Startled, she focused more intently on him. How had she made even the tiniest change in his life?

He remained focused on his driving, but he had sounded serious when he spoke. Was she really causing any changes in his life? Continually, ordinary things popped up that reminded her how little she really knew about him, and his last remark was just another one of them.

"Aaron, you and I don't really know each other. You don't talk about yourself much," she said, wondering how many times she had told him the same thing before.

"I think you should be grateful for that one. Also, I think we're getting to know each other rather well. We can work on that when we're home alone tonight."

"I didn't mean physically."

"Whoa—that's a letdown. You got me all excited there," he teased.

"Stop. Your imagination is running away with you," she said, and he grinned.

They finally arrived at his neighborhood and went through the security gate. Tall oaks lined the curving drive and she glimpsed an occasional mansion set back on landscaped lawns through the trees.

"This isn't where I pictured you living."

"I'm not sure I want to ask what you pictured."

"Just not this big." She looked at the immaculate lawns with multicolored flowerbeds. In many ways Aaron's everyday life was far removed from her own. Even so, he was doing so much for her, including all he had set up for today.

"Aaron, thanks for doing all this for me. The appointments, the opportunities to help Royal, the salon visit. I appreciate everything."

With a quick glance, he smiled at her. "I'm happy to help because you've been doing a great job."

"The mayor seemed happy with reports he's had of what's been happening and I'm glad. It would be terrible if he felt pressured to get out of the hospital and back to work."

"I'm sure he's getting good reports. I think he'll get more good reports from what you do today."

"You're an optimist, Aaron."

"It's easy where you're concerned," he said, and she smiled at him. "Earlier, I talked to Cecelia at the dress shop and she'll help you. We're friends and I've known her a long time. Pick several things so you have a choice. It'll go on my bill. You don't even have to take my credit card. If you don't choose something, I will, and I promise you, you won't like that."

She shook her head. "Very well, I won't argue with you, because you won't give up. Don't forget, I'm meeting my mom at half past eleven. You're welcome to join us."

"Thanks, but I have a lot of catching up to do at the office and you and your mom will enjoy being by yourselves. What I will do, if you want me to be there, is meet you at the television station for the interview."

"You don't need to drive to Fort Worth to hold my hand through an interview," she said, smiling. "I can do this one alone. Now tonight, you better join me."

"I'll be with you tonight."

"Buying more clothes and going to a salon will be a

whole new experience," she said. "Aaron, I think I can raise just as much money looking the way I already look."

"Humor me. We'll see. I think you can raise more and you'll be more at ease on television for interviews."

"I don't think clothes will make a bit of difference."

He grinned. "Clothes will make all kinds of difference. You go on television without any and you'll get so much money—"

"Aaron, you know what I mean," she interrupted, and they both laughed. She had fun with him and he was helpful to her. She gazed at him and wished she didn't still feel some kind of barrier between them, because he was growing more important to her daily. And she was falling more in love with him daily while she didn't think his feelings toward her had changed at all.

They passed through another set of iron gates after Aaron entered a code. When he drove up a winding drive to a sprawling three-story house, she was shocked at the size and obvious wealth it represented. "You have a magnificent home."

"I'm in the construction business, remember?"

She rode in silence, looking at the mansion that was far too big for one person. It was just another reminder of how little she knew about Aaron and how closed off he was about himself.

When he parked at the back of the house and came around the car to open the door for her, she stepped out. Stella stood quietly staring at him and he paused.

"What?" he asked. "Something's worrying you."

"I don't even know you."

He studied her a moment and then stepped forward, his arm going around her waist as he pulled her against him and kissed her. For a startled moment she was still and then she wrapped her arms around him to return the kiss.

"I'd say you know me," he said to her when he released her.

As she stepped back, she waved her hand at the house. "This is not what I envisioned."

"You'll get accustomed to it. C'mon, let me show you your room," he said, retrieving their bags from the back.

"We'll take a tour later," he said, walking through a kitchen that was big enough to hold her entire suite at the Cozy Inn. It had dark oak walls and some of the state-of-the-art appliances had a dark wood finish.

She walked beside him down a wide hallway, turning as hallways branched off in opposite directions. He stepped into the first open doorway. "How's this?" he asked, placing her bag on a suitcase stand.

She looked around a spacious, beautiful room with Queen Anne furniture, dark and light blue decor and thick area rugs.

"I'll get my mail and you can meet me in the kitchen. As soon as you're ready, we'll go to town. It'll give you more time to shop and I need to get to the office." He stepped closer, placing his hands on her shoulders and lowering his voice. "There are other things I'd rather do this morning, but with your appointments we better stick to business."

"I agree. You check your mail and I'll meet you."

He nodded and left.

Twenty minutes later, he stood waiting in the kitchen when she returned. "The limo's here. C'mon and I'll introduce you to Sid."

When they stepped outside, a brown-haired man who looked to be in his twenties waited by a white limo. He smiled as they walked up.

"Hi, Sid," Aaron said. "Stella, meet Sid Fryer. Sid, this is Ms. Daniels."

"Glad to meet you, Sid," she said.

"She's going to Cecelia's shop later and you can hang

around or give her a number and she'll call you. She'll be there two hours minimum," Aaron instructed.

Stella was surprised. She couldn't imagine spending that much time picking out dresses.

Sid held the limo door for her and she climbed inside, turning to the window as Aaron stepped away and waved.

Sid climbed behind the wheel and they left. When she glanced back, Aaron was already in his car.

"Sid—?"

He glanced at her in the rearview mirror. "Yes, ma'am?"

"Just call me Stella. Everyone does in my hometown of Royal. I just can't be that formal—we'll be together off and on all day."

She could see him grin in the rearview mirror. "Yes, ma'am. Whatever you say."

When Sid turned out of the gated area where Aaron lived, Stella looked behind them and saw Aaron turning the opposite way.

She met her mother in a coffee shop near the high school where her mother was principal. As Stella approached the booth where her mother sat looking at papers on the table, she realized where she got her plain way of dressing and living. Her mother's hair was in a roll, fastened on the back of her head. She wore a brown blouse and skirt, practical low-heel shoes and no makeup. Stella hadn't told her mother about the pregnancy yet and intended to today, but as she looked at her mother bent over her papers, she decided to wait a bit longer, until she had made more definite plans for raising the child. Her mother would probably want to step in and take charge, although she was deeply wrapped up in her job and, in the past few years, had interacted very little with either Stella or her sister.

Stella greeted her mother, gave her a slight hug and a

light kiss on the cheek and slid into the booth across from her. "How are you?" Stella asked.

"So busy with the end of the semester coming. I can only stay an hour because I have a stack of papers on my desk I have to deal with and three appointments with parents this afternoon. How are things in Royal?"

"Slowly improving."

"I've seen you in television clips. It looks as if you're busy. When will the mayor take over again so you won't have to do his job for him?"

"Mom, he was hurt badly and was on the critical list for a long time. The deputy mayor was killed."

"I'm glad I moved out of Royal. You should give it thought."

"I'll do that," she said, reminded again of why she was so much closer to her sister than her mother.

They talked over salads and then her mother gathered up papers and said she had to get back to her office. Stella kissed her goodbye and waited a few minutes before calling Sid for the limo—something she did not want to have to explain to her mother.

Sid drove her to the television station. Everyone she dealt with welcomed her and was so friendly that she was at ease immediately. A smiling receptionist let the host know Stella had arrived and in minutes a smiling blonde appeared and extended her hand.

"Welcome. I'm Natalia Higgens and we're delighted to have you on the show."

"Thank you," Stella said, shaking the woman's hand and relaxing. "I hope this does some good for my hometown."

"We're happy to have you and sorry about Royal. The tornado was dreadful. I think our viewers will be interested and I think you'll get some support. We'll show a short video one of our reporters made after the storm. I'll have some questions for you. People are responsive when someone has been hurt and you have a town filled with people who have been hurt."

"I really appreciate this opportunity to try to get help for Royal."

"We're glad to air your story. If you'll come with me."

Fifteen minutes later, Natalia Higgens made her brief introduction, looking at the camera. "The F4 tornado struck at 4:14 p.m. on October 6th, a Monday." The camera cut to the video the studio had taken after the storm. As soon as the video ended, Natalia turned to ask Stella about Royal.

From the beginning of the interview, Natalia's friendliness put Stella at ease. She answered questions about the storm and the people in Royal, listing places that were badly damaged, giving facts and figures of families hit, the people who died in the storm and the enormous cost of the cleanup.

"If people would like to help, do you have an address?" Natalia asked.

"Yes," Stella replied, giving the address of the bank in Royal where the account had been set up for donations. "Also, the Texas Cattleman's Club of Royal will have a Christmas festival and we hope to be able to provide toys for all the children of families who were so badly hurt by the storm. Some families lost everything—their homes, their livestock, their livelihoods—and we want to help them have a happy holiday," Stella said, smiling into the camera before turning to Natalia.

Before Stella knew it, her fifteen-minute segment was finished.

When the show ended, Natalia turned to Stella. "Thank you. You gave a wonderful presentation today that should get a big response."

"I enjoyed having a chance to do the show and to tell

about our Christmas festival. I'm very excited about that and the joy it will bring."

"Maybe we can have someone from the Royal and the Dallas TCC be on our show soon to mention it again."

"That would be wonderful," Stella said.

Natalia got a text, which she scanned quickly. "We're getting donations. Your bank will be able to total them up and let you know. Congratulations on getting more help for Royal."

Stella smiled broadly, happy that the interview went well, hoping they did get a big response.

After thanking them, telling them goodbye and making arrangements to get a video of the interview, she was ready to go back to Dallas.

As she left the station, people who worked there stopped to greet her and wish her success in helping her town.

Exhilarated, she saw Sid holding the door of the limo as she emerged from the building.

"I watched your interview in the bar down the block and two guys there said they would send some money to Royal. Way to go," he said, and she laughed, giving Sid a high five, which after one startled moment, he returned.

Sid drove to an upscale shopping area in that city. He parked in front of a redbrick shop with an ornate dark wood front door flanked by two huge white pots of red hibiscus and green sweet potato vines that trailed over the sides of the pots. To one side of the door a large window revealed an interior of subdued lighting and white and red furniture. The only identifying sign was on the window near the door. Small gold letters spelled out the name, Chez Cecilia.

Sid hopped out to open her door. "Here's my number. Just give me a call a few minutes before you want to be picked up and I'll be right here."

"Thanks, Sid," she said, wondering what Aaron had gotten her into. She went inside the shop—which had soft music playing in the background, thick area rugs, contemporary oil paintings on the walls and ornately framed floor-to-ceiling mirrors—and asked for Cecelia.

A tall, slender brunette appeared, smiling and extending her hand. "You must be Stella. I'm happy to meet you. Let me take your coat," she said, taking Stella's jacket and hanging it up. "Aaron has told me about you."

"That surprises me," Stella said, curious how Aaron knew Cecelia and the dress shop but not wanting to pry. She'd rather Aaron would tell her the things he wanted her to know.

"Surprised me, too. Aaron keeps his world to himself. From what he told me, I think I know what we should show you. Let's get you comfortable. I have a few things picked out. He said you have a dinner date tonight with some people who want to hear about Royal and the storm and how they can help."

"You're right."

"Now make yourself comfortable. Can I get you a soft drink? Coffee or tea? Ice water?"

"Ice water please," she said, thinking this whole excursion was ridiculous, a feeling that changed to dismay when Cecelia began to bring clothes out to show her.

"Just tell me what appeals to you and we'll set it aside for you to try on if you'd like."

Within minutes Stella felt in a daze. Nothing Cecelia brought out looked like anything Stella had ever worn. Necklines were lower; hemlines were higher. Skirts were tighter and material was softer. "Cecelia, I can't imagine myself in these," she said, looking at a green dress of clinging material that had a low-cut cowl neckline and a tight, straight skirt with a slit on one side. "These are so unlike me."

"You may be surprised how nice they'll look on you. These are comfortable dresses, too."

Her dazed feeling increased when she tried on the dresses she selected, yet when she looked in the mirror, she couldn't keep from liking them.

When she tried to stop shopping, Cecilia shook her head. "You need to select an elegant dress for evening. You need two suits. You should have a business dress. Aaron made this very clear and he'll come down and pick something out himself if you don't. You will not want him to do that. Aaron is not into shopping for dresses. Our clothing is tasteful and lovely, but he doesn't select what's appropriate for business unless I help him. Fortunately, he'll listen."

Even as Stella laughed, she was surprised and wondered how Cecelia knew this about Aaron. It hinted at more mysteries in his life before she knew him.

Stella tried on a red silk wool sleeveless dress with a low V-neck that she would have to grow accustomed to because she hadn't worn a dress like this one ever. "Cecilia, this isn't me."

"That's the point, Stella. Aaron wants you to have dresses that will help you present a certain image. From what Aaron has said, you're trying to get help for your town. Believe me, that dress will help you get people's attention. It's beautiful on you."

Stella laughed and shook her head. "Thank you. I feel as if I'm only half-dressed."

"Not at all. You look wonderful."

Stella shook her head and studied her image, which she barely recognized.

"Try it," Cecilia urged. "You don't want Aaron shopping for you."

"No, I don't." She sighed. "I'll take this one."

The next two were far too revealing and she refused. "I

would never feel comfortable even though these are beautiful dresses."

The next was a black dress that had a high neck in front, but was backless as well as sleeveless.

She had to agree with Cecilia that she looked pretty in the dress, but she wondered whether she would ever really wear it.

"You should have this. It's lovely on you," Cecilia said. "I know Aaron would definitely like this one."

She felt like telling Cecilia that she was not buying the dresses to please Aaron, but she wondered if she would be fooling herself in saying that. She finally nodded and agreed to take it, because she had to agree that she looked nice in it.

Not until the business suits was she comfortable in the clothes she tried on. The tailored dark blue and black suits were plain and her type of clothing. Until she tried on blouses to go with them. Once again, it was low necklines, soft, clinging material—so different from her usual button-down collars and cotton shirts.

Finally she was finished and had all her purchases bagged and boxed. She was shocked to look at her watch and see that it was almost four.

Sid came in to pick her purchases up and load them into the limo as Stella thanked Cecilia and the two other women who worked in the shop. Finally she climbed into the limo to return to Aaron's to get ready for dinner with the oil and gas executives who were potential donors.

When she arrived, Aaron was waiting on the drive. After she stepped out of the limo, Aaron and Sid carried her purchases into the house.

When Sid left them, Aaron closed the back door and turned to take her into his arms. "We're supposed to meet the people we're having dinner with in less than two hours. These are the oil and gas executives I told you about."

"Thanks, for setting this up, Aaron."

"I'm glad to, and Cole has made some appointments with potential donors, as well. How was your mother?"

"Busy with her own life."

"Have you told her about your pregnancy?"

"No. She was very unhappy to learn she was going to be a grandmother when my sister had her first baby. I think Mom thought it aged her to suddenly become a grandmother. She's not close to her grandchildren and doesn't really like children in general. My mother is in her own world. To her, my news will not be good news."

"Thank heavens you don't take after her. She's missing out on one of the best parts of life," he said, surprising her that a single guy would express it that way.

"It'll take over half an hour to drive to the restaurant," he continued after a pause. "We better start getting ready. I need to shower and shave."

"In other words, I need to start getting ready now," she said, "because I want to shower."

"We can shower together."

"If we don't leave the house tonight," she said.

He smiled. "We can't afford to stand these people up so we'll get ready and shower separately. Maybe tomorrow we can be together. Cecelia said she thinks I'll like what you bought."

"I don't know myself when I look in the mirror. In those dresses the reflection doesn't look like me, but hopefully, we'll achieve the effect you expect. If not, you wasted a lot of money."

"I think it'll be worth every penny."

"So you better run along and let me get ready."

He nodded, his eyes focused intently on her as he looked

at her mouth. She stepped away. "Bye, Aaron. See you shortly."

"Come here," he said, taking her hand and leading her out to the central hall. "See that first open door on the left? When you're ready, meet me there. I'll wait for you in the library."

"The library. Fine," she said.

"See you soon," he said, brushing a light kiss on her lips and leaving her. She went back to shower and dress in the tailored black suit she had bought earlier with an old blouse that had a high collar—an outfit that she could relax in and be comfortable.

When she was ready, she went to the library to meet Aaron, who was already there waiting. Dressed in a brown suit and dark brown tie, he looked as handsome as he always did. His gaze raked over her and he smiled.

"You look pretty," he said, crossing the room to her. "We have to go, but I know what I'd prefer doing."

"I definitely feel the same, but you're right about having to go."

"Before we do, there's something I want you to have," he said, turning to walk to a chair and pick up a gift that she hadn't noticed before. Wrapped in silver paper, it had a blue silk ribbon tied around it and a big silk bow on top. "This is for you."

Surprised, she looked up at him. "It's not my birthday," she said quietly, startled he was giving her a present.

"You're carrying my baby. That's very special and I want to give you something that you'll always have to celebrate the occasion."

"Aaron, that is so sweet," she said, hugging and kissing him. She wondered about the depth of his feelings for her. He had to care to give her such gifts and do so much for her. As quickly as that thought came and went, another occurred to her—that the makeover and clothes benefited Royal. Was she just a means to an end with him? She looked at the present in her hands. This one was purely for her because of the baby—a sweet gesture, but it still didn't mean he had special feelings for her beyond her motherhood.

Finally she raised her head. "Thank you," she whispered.

"Look at your present," he said. "You don't even know what I'm giving you."

Smiling, she untied the bow and carefully peeled away the paper. She raised the lid to find a black velvet box. She removed it from the gift box, opened it and gasped. "Aaron!" she exclaimed as she looked at a necklace made of gold in the shape of small delicate oak leaves, each with a small diamond for a stem. There was a golden leaf and diamond bracelet to match. "These are beautiful." She looked up at him. "These are so gorgeous. Thank you." She stepped forward to kiss him. He held her in one strong arm and kissed her. In seconds the other arm circled her waist and he leaned over her, still kissing her.

"Want to wear them tonight?"

She looked at her suit. "Yes, I'd love to."

"I tried to get something that you can wear whether it's day or night—in other words, all the time."

"I love this necklace and bracelet. I love that you thought of me and wanted to do this," she said, smiling at him.

"Let me put it on you," he said, and she nodded.

In seconds he stepped back. "Hold out your wrist." When she did, he fastened the bracelet on her slender wrist and kissed her lightly. "We'll celebrate more tonight when we get back home. Stella, a baby is precious. It is a celebration and this is just a tiny token."

"It's more than a token and I'll treasure it always, Aaron. It's absolutely beautiful," she said, thrilled that he was that happy about the baby.

"I'm glad you feel that way."

She nodded. Touched, wishing things were different, she felt her emotions getting out of hand. Tears stung her eyes.

"Ready? Sid's waiting."

"Yes," she answered, turning toward the door. She wanted to wipe her eyes but didn't want Aaron to know she was crying. If only he loved her—then his gift would hold a deeper meaning for her.

Seven

That evening, Stella really wowed her dinner companions. She gave a talk similar to the one in Lubbock, showing pictures of the devastation in Royal, which she had on her iPad. By the time the evening was over, it looked promising that the oil and gas executives were going to publicize Royal's need for financial help and make a large donation. As she and Aaron left the restaurant, she breathed a sigh of relief that her efforts for the town were paying off.

Then they went back to Aaron's house to make love through the night. They were in the big bed in the guest bedroom where she was staying. She wore her necklace and bracelet through the night, but in the morning as Aaron held her in his arms, he touched the necklace lightly. "Put your necklace and bracelet away today. Just leave them here instead of taking them to the salon."

"Sure," she answered, smiling at him.

"Sid has the limo waiting," Aaron said. "Tonight, we're meeting television executives from here in Dallas. These people can do a lot, Stella. Tomorrow we'll fly to Austin. You have a lunch, an interview and a dinner there and then we fly back to Dallas for one more interview at noon on Friday."

"Don't say another word. You'll just stir up my nerves more than ever."

"You're doing great. I'll tell you again, relax and enjoy your day at the salon. You better go now. I'm going to the office and I'll see you tonight. It'll take all day at the salon and, afterward, Sid will take you to the restaurant. Just call me when you're on the way. I'll try to get there before you do. That way we'll be ahead of the people we're meeting, so we can just sit and talk until they get there."

"You're getting me into more things," she said, holding a bag with her new dress and clothes that she would wear to dinner. Aaron grinned.

"You'll look back on all of this and be glad. I promise." He took her arm and they left, pausing while he locked up.

When they greeted her at the salon, she couldn't believe her day was turning out this way. It commenced with a massage. As she relaxed, she thought of the contrast with her life the first night after the tornado and how she had fallen into bed about four in the morning and slept two hours to get up and go back to work helping people.

She had her first manicure and first pedicure, which both seemed unnecessary. In the afternoon she had a facial. Following the facial, a salon attendant washed her hair and passed her over to the stylist to cut and blow-dry her hair. By the time she was done, Stella felt like a different woman. Instead of straight brown hair that fell halfway down her back, her hair was now just inches above shoulder length. It fell in a silky curtain that curled under, with slight bangs that were brushed to one side.

Next, a professional did her makeup and took time to show Stella how to apply it herself.

By late afternoon when she looked in the mirror, Stella couldn't recognize herself. She realized that she had so rarely ever tried makeup and then only lipstick that it gave her an entirely different appearance, although the biggest change was her hair.

The salon women gushed over the transformation that was amazing to her. Finally, she dressed for the evening.

"I really don't even know myself," she told the tall blonde named Gretchen at the reception desk.

"You look gorgeous. Perfect. The dress you brought is also perfect. We hope you love everything—your makeup, your hair and your nails."

She smiled at Gretchen. "I'll admit that I do," she said, pleased by the result and wondering what Aaron would think. "I've had the same hairdo since I was in college. It became a habit and it was easy. It's amazing how different I look," she said, turning slightly to look at herself in the mirror. The red silk dress fit her changing waistline; her old clothes were beginning to feel slightly tight in the waist because of her pregnancy.

She still wore her black wool coat and couldn't see any reason for a new coat. When she thanked them and left, Sid smiled at her as he held the limo door.

"You look great," he said appreciatively. "Mr. Nichols isn't going to know you."

"Thanks, Sid. I don't feel quite like me."

"Might as well make the most of it," he said, and grinned. "You'll turn heads tonight."

"You think? Sid, that would be a first," she admitted, laughing as she climbed into the limo and he closed the door.

Midafternoon Aaron went home to shower and change into a charcoal suit, a custom-made white dress shirt and a red tie. He returned to the office to spend the rest of the day catching up on paperwork. Just as he was ready to leave, he was delayed by a phone call. It only took a few minutes, but he guessed he might not get to the restaurant ahead of Stella, so he sent her a text.

He had received a call from the businessmen who'd had dinner with them last night, and they wanted to donate $20,000 to Royal's relief efforts, which he thought would be another boost to Stella's self-confidence. Aaron knew Stella hadn't faced the fact that she was filling in for the mayor as Royal's representative to the outside world even if it wasn't official. She was filling in and getting better at it all the time.

When he arrived at the restaurant, Aaron parked and hurried across the lot. He wanted to see what transformations they had made at the salon. Whatever they had done, he hoped the bun had disappeared for the evening.

The only people in the lobby besides restaurant employees in black uniforms were a couple standing, looking at a picture of a celebrity who had eaten at the restaurant. He didn't see any sign of Stella. The couple consisted of a tall, black-haired man and a beautiful woman half-turned toward him as she looked at the photograph.

He saw the maître d' and motioned to him to ask him about Stella. As the maître d' approached, Aaron glanced again at the woman. The man had walked away, and she was now standing alone. She was stunning in a red dress that ended at her knees, showing shapely long legs and trim ankles in high-heeled red pumps.

"Sir?" the maître d' asked.

"I'm supposed to meet someone here," he said. "Ms. Daniels."

"Aaron?"

He heard Stella's voice and looked up. The woman in red had turned to face him and he almost looked past her before he realized it was Stella. "She's here," he heard himself say to the maître d'. Aaron had expected a change, but not such a transformation that he didn't recognize her. Desire burst with white heat inside him as he walked over to her.

"I didn't even recognize you," he said, astounded and unable to stop staring at her. The temperature around him climbed. He tried to absorb the fact that this was Stella, because she had changed drastically. He was now looking at a stunning beauty.

"I told you long ago you might need to get your eyes checked," she said, smiling at him and making him feel weak in the knees. "Aaron, it's still me."

"You're going to knock them dead with your looks," he said without even thinking about it.

"I hope not," she said, laughing. "Aaron, you're staring."

"Damn straight, I'm staring. I can't recognize you."

"Get used to it. I'm really no different. I take it you like what you see," she prompted.

"Like? I'm bowled over. Stella, do you recognize yourself?"

"I'll admit it's quite a change. I have to get accustomed to my hair."

"You look fantastic. Wait right here," Aaron said and walked back to the maître d' to talk to him. After a moment, Aaron came back to take her arm. "Come with me," he said. The maître d' smiled at them and turned to lead the way.

"Aaron?" she asked, glancing at him.

"Just a moment, you'll see," he answered her unasked question.

The maître d' stopped to motion them through an open door. They entered an office with a desk covered by papers. The maître d' closed the door behind them.

"I asked where I could be alone with you for a few minutes. He's right outside the door should anyone want in this office."

"What on earth are we doing here?"

"I gave you a necklace and bracelet as a token of a celebration because you're carrying my baby, Stella. It's a relatively simple gold necklace and bracelet that you can wear in the daytime and wear often, which is what I wanted. To celebrate our baby, I also want you to have something very special, because this is a unique time in your life and mine. This present you can't wear as often, but you can wear it tonight," he said, handing her a flat package tied in another blue ribbon.

"You've given me a beautiful present. You didn't need to do this." Her blue eyes were wide as she studied him and then accepted the box. She untied the ribbon and opened the velvet box and gasped. "Aaron. Oh, my heavens. This is beautiful. It's magnificent."

He picked up a diamond necklace that sparkled in the light. "Turn around and I'll put it on," he said.

"I've never had anything like this. I feel as if I need a bodyguard to wear it." She turned and he fastened it around her slender throat, brushing a kiss on her nape, catching a scent that was exotic and new for Stella.

"You've got one—me. There," he said after a moment, turning her to face him, his gaze going over her features. Her blue eyes looked bigger than ever with thick lashes framing them. She didn't have on heavy makeup, just enough to alter her looks, but her hair was what had thrown him off.

And now her figure showed in the red dress, which fit a waistline that still was tiny. The diamonds glittered on her slender throat.

"You're beautiful, and that's an inadequate description. *Stunning* is more like it."

"Thank you. I'm glad you're pleased and thank you for doing this for me."

"Do you like the change?"

"After your reaction, yes, I do. It takes some getting used to. I sort of don't recognize myself, either."

They looked at each other and smiled. "I'd kiss you, but it would mess up that makeup."

"Wait until later."

"We better give the guy back his office. I just wanted a private moment to give the necklace to you."

"It's dazzling. I've never had anything like it."

He took her arm and they stepped out. "Thanks," Aaron said, slipping some folded bills to the maître d'. Then he turned to Stella and said, "Let's go meet your public. You'll wow them and get a bundle for Royal."

"Don't make me jittery," she said, but she sounded far more sure of herself than she had on that first drive to Lubbock.

"Also, I didn't tell you. I got a text from the guys last night. They're sending a check to the Royal storm recovery fund for $20,000."

She turned to gaze at him with wide eyes. "Mercy, Aaron. That's a big amount."

"You just wait and see what you can do for your hometown." He glanced at the maître d'. "We're ready for our table now and you can show the others in when they arrive."

Aaron introduced her to two men and a woman, all executives of a television station. Through salads and dinner Stella told them stories of people affected by the storm. Over dessert, and after-dinner drinks for everyone except Stella, she showed them her presentation on her iPad.

"Stella has suggested a Christmas drive," Aaron said, "to get presents for those who lost everything, for families with children and people still in the hospital."

"That's a wonderful idea," the woman, Molly Vandergrift, said. "I think that would be a great general-interest story. Would you like to appear on our news show and talk about this?"

"I'd love to," Stella replied, meaning it, realizing she was losing the butterflies in her stomach. Along with the change in her appearance and the money that she had already raised, she was gaining more confidence in her ability to talk to people about Royal. And tonight, the three television executives were so friendly, enthusiastic and receptive that she felt even better.

"We're going to try to tie it into the Texas Cattleman's Club Christmas festival in Royal this year," she added.

"That'll be good to have on a show. I know Lars West with the Dallas TCC. We could get him to come on, too, with Stella. Are the TCC here doing anything?"

"They will," Aaron replied. "I've just started talking to them."

"I'm sure the sooner you can do this, the better. I'll send a text now," Molly said, "and see if we can get you on the Friday show."

"That would be grand," Stella answered. "Everyone in Royal will appreciate what you're doing to help." She was aware Aaron had been quieter all evening than he had been in Lubbock, letting her do most of the talking. When she glanced at him, he looked pleased.

Excitement hummed in her because she was going to get so much support for Royal. As the evening wore on, she was even more pleased with her makeover, relieved that she could begin to relax talking to people and enjoy meeting them.

They didn't break up until after ten o'clock. She and Aaron told them goodbye outside as valets brought the cars to the door.

Finally she was alone in Aaron's car with him. He drove out of the lot, but on the drive back, he pulled off the road slightly, put the car in Park and turned to kiss and hug her.

Then he leaned away. "You were fantastic tonight. No butterflies either—right?"

"I think they're gone," she said.

"They'll never come back, either. Awesome evening. You did a whiz-bang job. Watch. The television show will be wonderful for Royal."

"I think so, too," she said, feeling bubbly and excited. "Thanks, Aaron, for all you've done for me. And thank you again for this fabulous necklace that I was aware of all evening."

"You're welcome. Stella, you'll be able to do more and more for Royal."

"I hope so." As he drove home they discussed the evening and what they would do Friday.

The minute they were in the kitchen of his house, Aaron turned her. "You take my breath away," he said.

Her heart skipped a beat as she gazed at him. "Thank you again for the diamonds. They're beautiful."

"That's why I didn't want you to take your gold necklace for tonight. I had something else in mind." He slipped his arms around her and kissed her, his tongue thrusting deeply as he held her. After a while he raised his head. "Go with me to the TCC Christmas festival. Will you?"

"I'd be delighted, thank you," she replied.

He kissed her again, picking her up to carry her to the guest bedroom where she was staying. Still kissing her, he stood her on her feet by the bed. "I can't stop looking at you," he whispered. He drew her to him to kiss her. When he released her, he slid the zipper down the back of her dress and pushed it off her shoulders. As it fell around her feet, he leaned back to look at her. "You changed everything," he said.

"I bought the underwear when I purchased the dress," she said as he unfastened the clasp of the lacy red bra that was a wisp of material and so different from her usual practical cotton underwear.

He placed his hands on her hips and inhaled deeply. "You're gorgeous," he whispered, his eyes raking over her lacy panties down to her thigh-high stockings. She was still in her red pumps.

As he looked at her she unfastened the buttons of his shirt and pushed it off his shoulders. Her hands worked to loosen his belt and then his suit trousers and finally they fell away and she pushed down his briefs to free him.

She stroked him lightly and he inhaled, picking her up. She kicked off her pumps, and he placed her on the bed, switching on a small bedside light before kneeling beside her to shower her with kisses.

As she wound her arms around his neck, she rose up slightly, pulling him to her to kiss him. "Aaron, this is so good," she whispered.

He moved over her, kissing her passionately while she clung to him.

Later, she lay in his arms, held closely against him. "Aaron, you're changing my life."

He shifted on his side to face her, toying with locks of her hair. "You're changing mine, too, you know."

"I suppose," she said, gazing solemnly into his eyes. "I hadn't thought about that, but I guess a baby will change both of us. Even just knowing we'll have a baby will bring changes. I was talking about this week and my makeover, my new clothes, meeting so many people and persuading them to help. Of course, I have the pictures and figures to persuade them."

"You're the cause, more than pictures and numbers. The mayor couldn't have had anyone do a better job." Aaron wound his fingers in her hair.

"It's a long time from now, but do you think you'll be present when our baby is born?"

"I want to be and I hope you want me to be there," he said.

"Yes, I do," she answered, hurting, wishing she had his love. "I want you to be there very much."

He hugged her again. "Then that's decided. I'll be there." They became silent and she wondered if he would still feel the same way when their baby came into the world.

"You're beautiful, Stella," Aaron said hoarsely. He drew her closer against him. "I don't want to let you go," he whispered as his arms tightened around her.

Her face was pressed against his chest and she hugged him in return. "I don't want you to let me go ever," she whispered, certain it was so soft, he couldn't hear her. "Tonight we have each other," she said. "Tomorrow we go home and back to the problems."

When they flew back to Royal on Saturday afternoon, she had eight more big checks to deposit in the Royal storm recovery fund. As they sat in the plane, she was aware of Aaron studying her. "What?" she asked. "You're staring."

"I'm thinking about all the changes in you. Now you'll be the talk of Royal with your makeover, plus the money you're bringing in to help everyone."

She laughed. "I'll be the talk of Royal maybe for five minutes. But the checks will last for quite a while. Aaron, I'm so thrilled over the money. People have been really generous. Thank for your introductions."

"Thanks, Stella, for talking to all of them. You're doing a fantastic job. As for the talk of the town—it'll be longer than five minutes. I suspect some guys are going to ask you out. I think I should make my presence known."

She was tempted to fling *What do you care?* at him.

How much did he care? He acted as if he wanted to be with her. He had done so much for her—in the long run, the results had been for Royal, so she didn't know how much of his motivation came from feelings for her or if it was for the town. Even the jewelry had been for her because she was having his baby—not necessarily because he loved her for herself.

She didn't know any more about what he felt now than she had after their first night together.

The sex was fabulous, but did it mean deeper feelings were taking root with Aaron or was it still simply lust and a good time?.

Aaron would talk to Cole Saturday or Sunday and then she would know if the TCC had made any more decisions about the Christmas festival. It could be so much fun for everyone if they opened it up for all to attend.

She hoped to get into her town house soon and have her own little Christmas tree. Each day she was in Royal, she noticed more trees going up in various places in town. Some Christmases they had had a decorated tree on the lawn of the town hall. She wanted to ask about putting up a Christmas tree on the town-hall lawn this year because she hated for the storm to destroy any customs they had.

"You have appointments for us starting Monday with a lunch in Austin and dinner that night. The next day we go to Houston and Wednesday, we have a noon meeting in Dallas. We won't be back to Royal until after lunch Wednesday. No more until after Christmas, Aaron. I need to be in Royal so I can focus on the Christmas gift drive."

"You'll be back Wednesday afternoon. Then you can start catching up."

After landing she ate with Aaron at the Cozy Inn, sitting and talking until after ten. At the door to her suite, she glanced at him as she inserted the card in the slot. "Want to come in?"

"I thought you'd never ask," he said. He held the door for her and she entered.

She turned to face him. "Want something to drink?"

He walked up to her and pulled her close. "No, thank you. I want you in my arms."

She kissed him, wrapping her arms around his narrow waist, holding him, wondering if they were forging any kind of lasting bond at all.

After appearing in Austin for a TV interview on Monday, they flew to Houston on Tuesday. During the flight, Stella turned to Aaron. He was dressed to meet people as soon as they landed. He had shed his navy suit jacket and loosened his matching tie. He sat across from her with his long legs stretched out in the roomy private jet.

She was comfortable in her new navy suit and matching silk blouse. She, too, had shed her suit jacket.

"Still no morning sickness?" he asked.

"Not at all," she said. "Aaron, I've had three job offers this week."

His eyebrows arched. "Oh? Who wants to hire you?"

"The Barlow Group in Houston. They want me for vice president of public relations. It's a prestigious Texas foundation that raises money for good causes."

"I know who you're talking about. I have a friend on their board. Who else has made an offer?" he asked, frowning slightly as he waited.

"A Dallas charity—Thompkins Charities, Ltd. They also want me for director of public relations."

"Another prestigious group that does a lot of good. That's old oil money. I have several friends there."

"The third one is No Hungry Children in Dallas who

want me for a coordinator-of-services position. The only one I'm considering is the Barlow Group in Houston. I'm seriously thinking about taking that job. It pays more than I make now. It would be in Houston, which would be nice. I can help a lot of people—that would be my dream career."

"Congratulations on the offers. Frankly, you're needed in Royal, though."

"Royal is beginning to mend. They can get along without me."

"People have talked to me and I think the whole town wants you to step in and become acting mayor."

"I definitely don't think it's the whole town. The town council would be the ones to select someone and they haven't said a word to me. I can't imagine the town really wanting me for that role."

"Wednesday we're going back to Royal. Are you moving out of the Cozy Inn Friday?"

"Yes. My town house is all fixed up, so I'm going home. Friday or Saturday I'm getting a Christmas tree and decorating it."

"I have appointments Thursday in Royal and Friday I have to go to Dallas. I hate to leave now, but this is a deal I've worked on since before the storm hit. A wealthy family from back east wants to move to Dallas and build a new home. He was a college buddy, so there is a personal interest. I made a bid for R&N on building it. Now they've finally decided to go with R&N Builders. It's a five-million-dollar house, so I have to see them and be there to sign the contract. Cole could, but that would take him away from Royal and this is really something I've dealt with and I know the family."

"Aaron, go to Dallas," she said, smiling. "That's simple enough."

"That's what I have to do. I just wanted you to know

why. I still can move you in early Friday morning before I go to Dallas. Also, I'll help you get a tree on Saturday if you'd like."

"I'd like your help on the tree," she said, smiling at him. "I don't have a lot to move, so I can move home all by myself. Will you stay in Royal through Christmas and New Year's?"

"Yes. Probably about January 3, I'll go back to Dallas for a little while. I'll still be back and forth."

That thought hurt. She would miss him, but she had known that day was inevitable.

Sadness gripped her and she tightened her fist in her lap. "Next week is the TCC Christmas festival. It should be so much fun, Aaron. We're getting lots of presents and I haven't been there this week, but I've had texts from Lark, from Paige and from Megan Maguire."

"You're right—it will be fun. You'll be shocked by the number of presents that are coming into the TCC. That doesn't count the ones dropped off at businesses, fire stations, all over town."

"We have envelopes with checks for individuals and families that are on our list. I'm so grateful we've been able to do this."

"The Christmas drive is a great idea," he said.

She smiled. "Right now I'm excited over the Christmas festival," she said, thinking it would be another chance for her to spend time with Aaron. When January came and he returned to Dallas, it was going to be hard on her without him. She knew that, but she pushed aside her fears. Friday she would move out of the Cozy Inn. She would never again see it without thinking of Aaron.

Their pilot announced they were approaching the Houston area.

"This is exciting, Aaron. I hope we can raise a lot of money and get more help for Royal," she said, slipping into her suit jacket.

By Wednesday afternoon they had finished the interviews, the dinners, the talks to groups, and were flying back to Royal. Aaron knew some money had been sent directly to Royal, some checks had been given to Stella and some to him. He sat with a pen and pad in hand figuring out a rough total. She remained quiet.

When he raised his head, he smiled. "You've done a wonderful job, Stella. As far as the money, the checks that have been promised and the ones we're taking back with us total approximately a quarter of a million dollars. That's tremendous. I don't think the mayor himself could have done any better."

"I'm just astounded by the help we've received. Some of it was from out-of-state people seeing interviews that got picked up and broadcast nationally. I can't believe I've had three more offers to go on television news and local interest shows after the first of the year."

"You look good on camera."

She laughed. "Don't be ridiculous. That isn't why I'm asked."

"I think that's a big part of it."

"I'm sure that it's much more because Royal has some touching stories."

"They do, but it helps to have a pretty lady tell them."

Shaking her head at him, she changed the topic. "I'm hungry and ready to get my feet on the ground in Royal and have dinner."

"That's easy. Where would you like to eat? I'll take you wherever you'd like to go?"

"After being gone this week, I'm happy to eat at the inn."

"That suits me."

"Good," she answered, certain their lives would change and wondering if Aaron would leave hers.

"We'll be on the ground now in about thirty minutes," he said, and she looked out the window, glad to get back to Royal and home.

"It'll be my last two nights in the Cozy Inn," she said, thinking how soon Aaron would be leaving the hotel, too.

"Stella, would you like for me to go with you to a doctor's appointment?"

"I've got to find a doctor in Royal. I went to Houston to my sister's doctor, but I want a doctor here."

"Definitely. I'd like to go with you and meet the doctor."

"I think that would be nice. I'll ask about a pediatrician here, too. I don't want to drive to Dallas each time I need to see the doctor."

"No, you shouldn't. I'll make arrangements for our plane to take you to Dallas when you need to go, but I think you should have a doctor here."

"Thanks, Aaron. I'm glad you're interested."

"Stella, you'd be surprised if you knew how deep my interest runs. You and this baby are important to me," he said in a serious tone and with a somber look in his brown eyes. Her heart skipped. How much did he really mean that? He had included her with the baby. She figured that he had an interest in his child, but she had no idea of the depth of his feelings for her.

How important was she to him?

Stella went by the hospital Thursday. A doctor was with Mayor Vance, so she couldn't see him. She talked briefly with his wife and found out he was still improving, so Stella said she would come back in a few days. She called on others and talked to Lark briefly about the Christmas drive.

Lark smiled at her. "Stella, I really didn't recognize you at first. Your hair is so different and it changes your whole appearance. I saw you on a Dallas TV show. You were great and you took our case to a big audience. It's wonderful for people here to find out about these agencies and how to access them."

"Some of those agencies were new to me. I didn't know all that help was available."

"The shows should do a lot for us. You got in a plug for the Christmas drive also, which was nice. Speaking of the drive, I think there will be some big presents for people this Christmas."

"I hope so. Some of the stores are donating new TV sets for each family on our list. That'll be a fun present. Other stores are sending enough iPads for each family to have one. It makes me feel good to be able to help. I hope Skye and the baby are getting along."

"We just take everything one day at a time for both of them. There's still no word on Jacob Holt. If you hear anything, please call."

"I will, I promise. I'm home to stay now until Christmas Eve day when I'll go to my sister's."

"You just look beautiful. I love your hair."

"Thanks. You're nice."

"I have a feeling your quiet nights at home that you talk about are over," Lark said, smiling at her.

Stella laughed. "I'll keep in touch on the Christmas drive."

As she left the hospital, outside on the sidewalk, she heard someone call her name. She turned to see Cole headed her way.

"Hey, you look great."

"Thanks, Cole." To her surprise, he smiled at her. Since the storm she had rarely seen Cole smile.

"You're doing a bang-up job for the town. Aaron has let me know. Excellent job."

"Thanks. I'm glad to and I'm thrilled by people's generosity and finding specific agencies that can meet people's needs."

"I just wanted to thank you. See you around."

"That's nice, Cole."

He headed toward the hospital entrance and she wondered whom he was going to see. There were still too many in the hospital because of the storm over two months later.

"Stella, wait up."

She turned to see Lance Higgens, a rancher from the next county and someone she had known most of her life. She smiled at him, feeling kindly because the afternoon of the tornado he had come to Royal to help and that night he had made a $1,000 donation to the relief effort.

"I saw you on television yesterday."

"Good. I guess a lot of people caught that show around here."

"I didn't recognize you until they introduced you. You look great and you did a great job getting attention for Royal. I'd guess you'll get some donations."

"We did, Lance," she said. "We received one right away."

"Good. Listen, there's a barn dance at our town center next Saturday night. Would you like to go with me?"

Startled, she smiled at him. "I'm sorry, I'm going to a dinner that night, but thanks for asking me, Lance. That's very nice."

"Sure. Maybe some other time," he said. "Better go. Good to see you, Stella."

"Good to see you, too," she said, wanting to laugh. He had never looked at her twice before, never asked her to anything even though they had gone through high school together.

Her next stop was the drugstore where she ran into Paige. "Stella!" Paige called, and caught up with her.

"You never come to town. What are you doing here again?" Stella asked, smiling at her friend.

"I didn't plan well for anything this week. I saw you on television yesterday. Word went around that you'd be on— probably thanks to Aaron. You look fantastic and you did a great job. I love your makeover except I hardly know you."

"Thanks. It's the same me."

"Actually, I didn't even recognize you at first glimpse."

"Frankly, I barely recognize myself. The makeover has been fun and brought a bit of attention."

Paige's eyes narrowed. "I'll bet you're getting asked out by guys who never have asked you before."

Stella could feel her cheeks grow hot. "A little," she admitted. "I suppose looks are important to guys."

"Stella, most girls come to that conclusion before they're five years old," Paige remarked, and they both laughed. "We need a brief meeting soon for our Christmas drive to figure out how to coordinate the last-minute details. It's almost here."

"If you have a few minutes," Stella said, "we can go across the street to the café and talk about the drive now."

"Sure. Now's as good a time as any," Paige said. "We're running out of time. Christmas is one week away and the TCC festival is next Tuesday."

They walked to Stella's car, where she picked up her notebook. Then they crossed the street to a new café that had opened since the storm. As soon as they were seated, Stella opened the binder with notes and lists.

"Presents and donations are pouring in and I can add to them with checks I brought back from my talks this week."

"That's fantastic. I'll be there that night and I'll check with the others so we can help pass out envelopes with checks and help people get their presents. I'm sure some of the TCC guys will pitch in."

"I really appreciate all you're doing. I think we've contacted everyone we should and there's been enough publicity that no one will be overlooked. We'll have money or gifts for all the people who've lost so much and lost a loved one— I'm sorry, Paige, to bring that up with you," Stella said.

"It's the reality of life. So many of us live with loss. Lark's sister in a coma, Cole's lost his brother, Henry Markham lost a brother—you know the list. Holidays are tough for people with any big loss—that doesn't have to be because of the tornado—people like Aaron. I suppose that's why he's so sympathetic toward Cole."

"Aaron?"

Paige's gray eyes widened. "Aaron's wife and child."

Stella stared at Paige. "Aaron lost a wife and child?" she repeated, not thinking about how shocked she sounded.

"Aaron hasn't told you? You didn't know that?" Paige asked, frowning. "I thought that was general knowledge. It happened years ago. Maybe I know more about Aaron because of his connection to Cole and Craig."

Stella stared into space, stunned by Paige's revelation. "He's never told me," she said, talking more to herself than Paige. She realized Paige had asked her a question and looked at her. "I'm sorry. What did you say?"

"I'm surprised he hasn't told you. I've always known— Cole and I went to the service. A lot of people in Royal knew. I think his baby was a little over a year old. The little boy and Aaron's wife were killed in a traffic accident. It was sudden—one of those really bad things. He's been single since then. It was six or seven years ago. A long time. I don't think he's dated much since, but I know the two of you have been together. I figured that's because of the storm."

"He doesn't talk about his private life or his past and I don't ask. I figure he'll tell me what he wants me to know."

"Men don't talk about private things as much. Aaron may be one of those who doesn't talk at all. I know at one point Craig said Aaron was having a tough time dealing with his loss."

"Paige, I just stayed at his house in Dallas this week. I didn't see any pictures of a wife and child."

"He may not have any. That wouldn't occur to some men."

"Maybe. I also wasn't all over the house. I was just in the back part and the guest bedroom. We didn't even eat there."

"Well, then, it would be easy to not see any pictures. Especially if he has a big house like Cole. Sorry if finding out about his wife and child upset you."

"Oh, don't be silly. It's common knowledge as you said. I'm glad to know. He's just never talked to me about it. It does explain some things about him. Well, back to this Christmas drive—" Stella said, trying for now to put Aaron and his past out of her thoughts and concentrate on working out last-minute details of the event with Paige.

They worked another fifteen minutes before saying goodbye. Stella watched Paige walk away, a slender, willowy figure with sunlight glinting on her auburn hair, highlighting red strands.

Stella sat in the car, still stunned over Aaron's never mentioning his loss. Now she had the explanation for the barrier he kept between himself and others, the door he closed off when conversations or situations became too personal.

No wonder he held back about personal relationships—he was still in love with his late wife. And he'd lost his baby son. That's why babies were so special to him. Stella was unaware of the tears running down her cheeks. She had to stop seeing so much of Aaron. She couldn't cut him out of her life completely because of their baby, but she saw no future in going out with him. She didn't want to keep dating, because she was falling more deeply in love with him all the time while his emotions, love and loyalties were still back with the wife and child he had lost. She was glad he loved them, but he should have leveled with her.

Tears fell on the back of her hand and she realized she was crying. "Aaron, why didn't you tell me?" she whispered. If he really loved her, he would have shared this hurt with her, shared that very private bit of himself. Love didn't cut someone off and shut them out.

She wiped her hand and got a tissue to dry her eyes and her cheeks. Knowing she would have to pay attention to her driving, she focused on the car lot as she turned the key in the ignition.

She drove to the Cozy Inn and stepped out of the car, gathering packages to take inside. She hoped she didn't see Aaron before she reached her suite. She wanted to compose herself, think about what she would say.

She would have to make some decisions about her life with Aaron.

She would see him tonight at dinner. Once again her life was about to change. The sad part was that she would have to start to cut Aaron out of it and see far less of him.

Stella was tempted to confront him with the information she'd learned and ask why he hadn't told her, but instead she wanted him to tell her voluntarily without her asking about it. There was no way she would accept his marriage proposal when he didn't even trust her enough to tell her something that vital. And if he still loved his first wife with all his heart, Stella didn't want to marry him.

Sadly, he wasn't ready to marry again—at least not for love. He had to love his late wife and child enormously still, maybe to the point of being unable to let go and face that they had gone out of his life forever.

Deep inside, her feelings for him crashed and shattered.

Eight

For their dinner tonight, Stella wore one of her new sweaters—a pale blue V-neck—and black slacks. She wore his gold-leaf necklace and bracelet but fought tears when she put the jewelry on.

She went to meet him, her body tingling at the sight of him while eagerness tinged with sadness gripped her as she crossed the Cozy Inn lobby. Aaron was in a black sweater, jeans and boots. She really just wanted to walk into his embrace, but she had to get over even wanting to do so.

"You're gorgeous, Stella. I've missed seeing you all day."

She smiled at him as he took her arm. As soon as they were seated, she picked up a menu.

After they ordered and were alone, he looked at her intently, his gaze slowly traveling over her. "I can't get used to the change in you. I've seen women change hairdos, men shave their heads and grow mustaches, a lot of things that transform appearances, but yours is the biggest change I've ever seen. I never expected you to change this much. It's fabulous."

"Thank you," she said, beginning to wonder if he would lose interest if she returned to looking the way she always had. The minute she thought about it, she remembered that it wouldn't matter because she was going to see him less often.

"Several people have called to thank me for getting you on television because they've found the agency they need for help."

"Good," she said. It was the first bright bit of news since she had sat down to dinner with him.

"Club members have been getting word out that the entire town is invited to the TCC Christmas festival, so I think we will have a big turnout."

"That is wonderful," she said. "It should be a happy time for people," she said. "For a little while that evening, maybe they can all forget their losses and celebrate the season. I know it's fleeting, but it's better than nothing."

"It's a lot better than nothing. It will help people so much and kids will have a great time. Some of the women are beginning to plan games and things they can do for the kids. It'll be an evening to look back on when we all pulled together and had a great time."

"That's good," she said, and then thought of his loss, sorry that Christmas was probably a bad time for Aaron.

She felt responsible for him staying in Royal for the holidays. She didn't think he would be if she hadn't talked about how it would help others if he would stay and do things for people who needed something at holiday time.

She didn't want to deliberately hurt him. But it had ended between them as far as she was concerned. She had to get over him even though she had fallen in love with him.

How long would it take her to get over Aaron?

"Did you buy a dress for the Christmas festival?" he asked.

"Aaron, I already had a dress," she said, beginning to wonder if he was wound up in her new persona and really didn't have that much interest in the former plain Jane that she was. It was a little annoying. Was he not going to like her if she reverted to her former self? She suspected it didn't matter, because after the Christmas festival she didn't expect to continue the intimate relationship they had. She would see him because of their baby, but it would be a parental relationship and not what they had now. She might be with him a lot where their child was concerned, but they wouldn't be having an affair and she wasn't going to marry a man who was still in love with his deceased wife. Aaron couldn't even talk to her about his wife and baby, so he hadn't let go at all.

"I think you should have something new and special," he said, breaking into her thoughts.

"Don't go shopping for a dress for me," she said. "I have a new dress for the festival I got at Cecilia's shop."

Three people stopped by their table to talk to her and tell her what a great job she had done on television Saturday. As the third one walked away, Aaron smiled at her. "I can see the butterflies are completely gone to another home."

"Yes, they are. Thanks to you."

"No, Stella. You did that yourself. You're the one who's developed poise to deal with people. You're the one who's talking to people, telling them what happened, telling people here how to get help. Oh, no. This isn't me. It's you. You have more confidence now and you're handling things with more certainty. You've brought about the changes in yourself. Maybe not hair and makeup, but confidence and self-assurance, making some of the tough decisions that have to be made about who gets help first. No, this is something you've done yourself."

"Thanks for the vote of confidence."

"I've had several people ask me if I would talk to you about stepping in as acting mayor. They're going to have to find someone soon."

"Now *that* position I'm not qualified for," she said firmly.

"Of course, you are. You're already doing the job. Take

a long look at yourself," he said, and his expression was serious, not the cocky friendliness that he usually exhibited.

"I see an administrative assistant."

"Look again, Stella. The administrative assistant disappeared the afternoon of the storm. You're all but doing Mayor Vance's job now. And I checked. The role will end before you have your baby next summer, so that won't be a problem."

She was thinking half about the job and half about Aaron, who looked incredible. How was she going to break things off with him?

All she had to do was remember than he had not recovered from his loss enough to even talk about it. He could not love anyone else and she hadn't changed her views of marrying without love. She wasn't going to do it.

They ate quietly. She listened to him talk about Royal and the things that had happened in the past few days. Finally, he leaned back in his chair, setting down his glass of water while he gazed at her.

"You're quiet. You've hardly said two words through dinner."

"Part of it was simply listening to you and learning what happened while we were in Dallas. I'm worn-out from the whirlwind week coming on top of everything else I've been doing."

"I think it's more than that. You weren't this quiet yesterday."

They stared at each other and she then looked down at her lap. "Aaron, tomorrow I move back to my town house. We have the festival coming up and we're going together. I want to get through that without any big upsets in my life."

"Why do I feel I'm part of what might be a big upset in your life? I don't see how I can be, but I don't think you'd be so quiet with me if I wasn't."

"I think it would be better if we talk when we're upstairs. This really isn't the place."

"I'd say that's incentive to get going," he said. "Are you ready?"

"Yes," she said. When she stood up, he held her arm lightly and led her from the dining room, stopping to say something to the maître d' and then rejoining her.

At her door to her suite, she invited him inside. When they were in the living room, she turned to face him. "What would you like to drink?"

He shook his head as he closed the space between them. He drew her close to kiss her. She melted into his arms, her heart thudding as she kissed him. She wound her arms around him to hold him close, kissing him in return, her resolutions nagging while she ignored them to kiss him.

She ran her fingers in his short, thick hair at the back of his head. She didn't want to stop kissing. She wanted him in her bed all night long. She thought about his loss and knew she couldn't keep spending days and nights with him or she would be so hopelessly in love she would be unable to say no to him.

Finally she stepped back. Both of them were breathing hard. She felt a tight pang and wanted him badly. Just one more night—the thought taunted her. It was tempting to give in, to step back into his arms and kiss him and forget all the problems.

In the long run, it would be better to break it off right now. She wouldn't be hurt as much. She didn't think he would ever love anyone except the first wife. It had been long enough for him to adjust to his loss better than he had. No one ever got over it, they just learned to deal with it and go on with life.

She could imagine how desperately he wanted this baby after losing his first one. She suspected before long he would start showering her with more presents and pressuring her to marry him—and it would be because of their baby.

She would be glad to have him in their baby's life, but that was where it would have to stop. She couldn't go into a loveless marriage just to please Aaron.

She stared at him, making sure she had his attention and he wasn't thinking about kissing her again. "I can't do this, Aaron. We're not wildly in love. I think this is a purely physical relationship. Frankly, it's lust. If we keep it up, I might fall in love with you."

"So what's wrong with that picture," he said, frowning and placing one hand on his hip.

"Because I don't think you're going to fall in love. This is a physically satisfying relationship that you can walk away from at any point in time. Emotionally, you're not in it. I don't want that. I don't want to be in love with a man who isn't in love with me in return."

"I might fall in love and I think we've been good together, and I think I've been good with you and to you, Stella."

"You've been fantastic and so very good to me. I don't want to stop seeing you, I just want to back off and take a breather from the heavy sex. That isn't like me and I can't do that without my emotions getting all entangled."

His frown disappeared and he stepped closer to place one hand lightly on her hip. "I can back off. Are you going to still let me kiss you?"

His question made her feel ridiculous. "As if I could stop you."

"I don't use force," he said as he leaned forward to brush a light kiss on her lips. "Okay, so we don't go to bed together. You'll set the parameters and send me home when you want me to go. In the meantime, kisses are good. Don't cut me off to the point where we don't even have a chance to fall in love," he whispered as he brushed kisses on her throat, her ear, the corner of her mouth.

She should have been more firm with him, but when he started talking, standing so close, his eyes filled with desire, his voice lowering, coaxing—she couldn't say no or tell him to leave. She would have to sometime during the night, but not for a few minutes. There wasn't any point in ending seeing him before Christmas, because they were going to be thrown together constantly and she didn't want a pall hanging over them.

And she couldn't ever end it entirely because of their baby.

His kiss deepened as his arms tightened around her, holding her against him. He was aroused, kissing her passionately, and she stopped thinking and kissed him in return.

Finally he picked her up. She was about to protest when he sat in the closest chair and held her on his lap, but ended up forgetting her protest and wrapping her arms around his neck to continue kissing him. How was she going to protect her heart?

His hand went beneath her sweater to caress her and in minutes he had both hands on her. When he slipped her sweater over her head, she caught his wrists, taking her sweater from him to pull it on again and slide off his lap.

"Aaron, let's say good-night," she said, facing him as she straightened her sweater.

"This is really what you want?" he asked.

"Tonight, it is. I need some space to think and sort out things."

He nodded. "Sure. Maybe you just need some time off. It's been a great week, Stella. You've done so much. You've been a great representative for Royal."

"Thanks. Thanks for everything," she whispered, scared she would cry or tell him to stay for the night or, worse, walk back into his arms, which was what she wanted.

"See you in the morning, hon," he said, brushing a kiss on her cheek and leaving.

She closed the door behind him and touched her cheek with her hand while tears spilled over. She loved him and this was going to be hard. After Christmas she would break up with him. But she wasn't ruining Christmas for either one of them. Suppose she had a little boy who looked like Aaron and was a reminder of his daddy every day of his life?

She had expected Christmas to be so wonderful. Instead, she was beginning to wonder how she would get through it

"Aaron," she whispered, knowing she was in love. He had been so good to her, helping her in multiple ways, changing her life, really. He was a good guy, honorable, loyal, fun to be with, sexy, loving. Was she making a mistake sending him away? Should she live with him and hope that someday he would love her? Was not telling her about his family an oversight—did he think she already knew because so many did?

She doubted it. She thought it was what gave him the shuttered look, what caused him to throw up an invisible barrier. He still had his heart shut away in memories and loss and she couldn't reach it, much less ever have his love.

Aaron lay in bed in the dark, tossing and turning, his thoughts stormy. He missed Stella. He wanted to make love to her, wanted just to be with her. It was obvious something was bothering her. Why wouldn't she just tell him and let them work it out?

Had it been the gifts? Did she want an engagement ring, instead?

He had proposed that first night he learned she was pregnant, but she had turned him down and she would until he declared he loved her and made a commitment to her with his whole heart. Without talking about it, he knew she was bothered and scared she was falling in love and he wouldn't love her in return.

He liked her and maybe there was love up to a point, but he wasn't into making a total commitment to her. He couldn't tell her he loved her with his whole heart and that was what she wanted to hear. They hadn't talked about it, but he felt he was right.

He enjoyed being with her more than any other woman since Paula. It surprised him to realize he wasn't thinking as often of Paula. He would always love her and Blake and always miss them. He knew every time February 5 came around that it would have been Blake's birthday. It always hurt and it always would.

All the more reason he wanted Stella in his life—because this baby was his and he wasn't losing his second child. All he had to do was tell Stella he loved her with his whole heart. But he couldn't; he had to be truthful about it. He was trying to back off and give her room, let her think things through. Why wouldn't she settle for what they had, which was very good. They might fall in love in time and he might be able to handle his loss better. But that wasn't good enough for Stella, because she wouldn't take a chance on falling in love later.

Stella had some strong beliefs and held to them firmly.

Tossing back the covers, he got out of bed. This was his first night away from her for a little while, and he was miserable. What would he feel like in January when they parted for maybe months at a time?

Aaron felt caged in the small suite at the Cozy Inn. At home he would just go to his gym and work out hard enough that he had to concentrate on what he was doing until he was so exhausted he would welcome bed and sleep. Even without her. He couldn't do that here. Knowledge that she was sleeping nearby disturbed him. He could go to her easily, but she would just say no.

Stella was intelligent. He figured at some point she would see they were compatible, the sex was fantastic and she surely would see that, hands down, it would be best for her baby to have a daddy—a daddy who would love him or her and be able to provide well for all of them.

Then he thought about Stella's makeover. He had heard enough talk—guys in Royal had asked her out since she had been back in town after their first trip to Dallas. Trey Kramer had even asked Aaron if they were dating because he wanted to ask her out if she wasn't committed. That didn't thrill him. He had told Trey that he was dating Stella, but when he returned to work in Dallas in January, Aaron expected her to be asked out often by several men.

The thought annoyed him. He didn't want to think about her with other men and he didn't want the mother of his child marrying another man. He realized on the latter point, he was being selfish. If he couldn't make a real commitment to her, he needed to let her go.

He suspected she was going to walk out of his life if he didn't do something. The notion hurt and depressed him.

He paced the suite, hoping he didn't disturb people on the floor below. He tried to do some paperwork, but he couldn't stop thinking about Stella.

It was after four in the morning when he fell asleep. He woke at six when he heard his phone ring, indicating he'd received a text. Instantly awake, Aaron picked up his phone to read the message, which was from Stella.

I have very little to move. Mostly clothes. I've loaded my car and checked out. I won't need any help, but thanks anyway. I'll keep in touch and see you Tuesday evening when we go to the TCC Christmas festival.

She didn't want to see him until Tuesday evening for the party. He had a feeling that she was breaking up with him. The day after the festival would be Christmas Eve when she would fly out of Royal to go to her sister's in Austin. Aaron stared at her message. In effect, she was saying goodbye.

At least as much as she could say goodbye when she was pregnant with his baby. One thing was clear: she had moved on from spending nights with him. No more passion and lovemaking, maybe not even kisses.

He was hurt, but he could understand why she was acting this way. He should accept what she wanted. He needed to go on with his life and adjust to Stella not being a part of it.

He did some additional paperwork, then after a while picked up his phone again to make calls. Soon he had moved his Dallas appointment until later in the day so he didn't have to leave Royal as early. He showered, shaved and dressed, ordering room service for a quick breakfast while he made more calls.

He may have to tell Stella goodbye this week, but before that happened, there was one last thing he could do for her. Hurting, he picked up the phone to make another call.

As soon as the hospital allowed visitors that morning, Aaron went to see Mayor Vance.

After he finished his business in Dallas later that afternoon, Aaron went home to gather some things to take back to Royal with him. He paused to call Stella. He had tried several times during the day, but she had never answered and she didn't now.

He suspected she didn't want to talk to him, because

she kept her phone available constantly in case someone in Royal needed help.

Certain he wouldn't even see her, he decided to stay at home in Dallas Friday night and go back Saturday. He wouldn't have even gone then except he had appointments in Royal all day Saturday to talk to people about the up-coming appointment of an acting mayor.

He already missed Stella and felt as if he had been away from her for a long time when it really wasn't even twenty-four hours yet.

He wondered whether she was thinking seriously about taking the Houston job offer. It would be a good job, but Aaron knew so many people in Royal wanted her to take the acting mayor position—including the mayor, who had now talked to the town council about it.

That night Aaron couldn't get her on her phone. When she didn't answer at one in the morning, he gave up, but he wondered where she was and who she was with. He missed her. She had filled an empty place in his life. He sat thinking about her—beautiful, intelligent, fun to be with, sexy—she was all that he wanted in a woman. Had he fallen in love with her without realizing it?

The idea shook him. He went to his kitchen and got a beer and then walked back to the guest bedroom down-stairs where she had stayed when she had been at his house. He thought about being in bed with her, holding her in his arms.

He missed her terribly and he didn't want to tell her goodbye. It shocked him to think about it, and decided that he was in love with her. Why hadn't he seen it before now? He'd wanted to be with her day and night.

When he recognized that he loved Stella, he also saw he might be on the verge of losing her. She was a strong woman with her own standards and views and so far she had turned him down on marriage. Plus, she was considering accepting a very good position in Houston, which was a long way from Dallas.

He was in love with her and she was going to have his baby. He didn't want to lose her. He ran his hand over his short hair while he thought about what he could do to win her love. She'd accused him of proposing out of a sense of duty instead of love, which was exactly what he had done at the time. But he had spent a lot of time with her since then. There had been intimacy between them, hours together. They had worked together regarding Royal, had fun being together.

Why hadn't he seen that his feelings for her were growing stronger? He admired her; he respected and desired her. She was all the things he wanted in a woman. He had to win her love.

While he had never heard a declaration of love from Stella, she had to feel something for him. She acted as if she did. He was certain she would never have gone to bed with him with only casual feelings about him. That would be totally unlike her. Was she in love, too?

Had he already tossed away his chance with her?

He stood and moved impatiently to a window to gaze out at the lit grounds of his estate. If nothing else he would see her Tuesday night when he took her to the TCC Christmas festival. He wished he could move things up or go back to last week, but he couldn't.

He walked down the hall to his office. Crossing the room, he switched on a desk lamp and picked up a picture of his wife and child. "Paula, I've fallen in love. I think you'd approve. You'd like Stella and she would like you."

He realized that the pain of his loss had dulled slightly and he could look at Paula's picture and know that he loved

Stella also. He set the picture on the desk, picked up his beer and walked out of the room, switching off the light.

He wanted to see Stella, to kiss her, to tell her he loved her. This time when he proposed, he would try to do it right. Was she going to turn him down a second time?

Next Tuesday was the TCC Christmas festival, a special time. The town was getting ready to appoint an acting mayor and they wanted Stella, but she just didn't realize how many wanted her and how sincere they were about it.

If he had lost her love, there still was something good that he could do for her.

Saturday morning Stella selected a Christmas tree, getting one slightly taller than usual. As soon as she had set it up on a table by the window across the room from her fireplace, she got out her decorations. Her phone chimed and she glanced at it to see a call from Aaron. She didn't take it. She would talk to him soon enough Tuesday night; right now she still felt on a rocky edge. Aaron could get to her too easily. She wanted to be firm when she was with him. After Tuesday night, she really didn't expect to go out with him again except in the new year when she had to talk to him about their baby.

She placed her hand on her tummy, which was still flat. Her clothes had gotten just the slightest bit tighter in the waist, but otherwise, she was having an easy pregnancy so far.

She was excited about the Christmas drive, which was going even better than she had expected. The presents were piling up at the TCC. Paige had told her that each day now, TCC members picked up presents from drop-off points around town and took them to the club to place around the big Christmas tree.

She tried to avoid thinking about Aaron, but that was

impossible. She wasn't sleeping well, which wasn't good since she was pregnant. After Tuesday, maybe it would be easier to adjust because they wouldn't be in each other's lives as much.

She talked to her sister and learned their mother would be in Austin Christmas Eve, too. Stella checked again on her flight, scheduled to leave Christmas Eve and come back Christmas afternoon.

Aaron finally stopped calling on Monday and she heard nothing from him Tuesday. He must have caught on that she didn't want contact with him. She assumed he would still pick her up, but if he didn't show by six-thirty, she would go on her own. According to their earlier plans, he would come by for her at 6:15 p.m., which was early because the celebration did not begin until six-thirty. Her anticipation had dropped since she had parted with Aaron. She just wanted to get through the evening, leave the next day for Austin and try to pick up her life without Aaron.

For the first time in her life, Stella had her hair done at the Saint Tropez Salon. The salon was on the east side of town, which had escaped most of the storm damage.

As she dressed, a glimmer of the enthusiasm she had originally experienced for the night returned. It was exciting to have a party and to know it would be so good for so many people who had been hurt in the storm. It cheered her to know that all the families would have presents and money and hope for a nice Christmas.

On a personal level, she hoped things weren't tense all evening with Aaron, but she thought both of them would have enough friends around that they could set their worries aside and enjoy the party. And Aaron might not care as much as she did that they would be saying goodbye.

She guessed Aaron would ask about her job offers. She

still had not accepted the job offer in Houston. Every time she reached for the phone to talk to them, she pulled back.

Getting ready, she paused in front of the full-length mirror to look at herself. She wore the red dress she had worn before. One other new dress still hung in the closet, but the red dress was a Christmas color and it should be fine for the evening. When she put it on, the waist felt tighter. It was still comfortable, but she thought this was the last time she would wear the red dress until next winter.

Thinking it would be more appropriate for this party and also draw less attention, she wore the gold and diamond necklace. Once again, she wondered if Aaron was more interested in the person she had become after the makeover and all that had happened since, or the plain person she really was.

She made up her face as they had taught her at the salon, but when she started to put something on her lips, she stared at herself and put away the makeup, leaving her lips without any. She studied herself and was satisfied with her appearance.

She heard the buzzer and went to the door to meet Aaron. When sadness threatened to overwhelm her, she took a deep breath, thought of all the gifts people would be receiving tonight and opened the door with the certainty that this was the last time she would go out with Aaron Nichols.

Nine

Looking every inch the military man in civilian clothes, ready for a semiformal party, Aaron stood straight, handsome and neat with his short dark blond hair. Wearing a flawless navy suit and tie and a white shirt with gold cuff links, he made her heart beat faster.

"I've missed you," he said.

Her lips firmed and she tried to hang on to her emotions. "This is a night we've both looked forward to for a long time. Come in and I'll get my purse and coat."

"You're stunning, Stella," he said as he stepped inside and closed the door behind him. "I'm glad you wore your necklace."

"It's lovely, Aaron."

He studied her intently and she tilted her head, puzzled by his expression.

"So what are you thinking?"

"That you're the most gorgeous woman in the state of Texas."

His remark made her want to laugh and made her want to cry. It was a reminder of one of the reasons it was going to hurt so much to tell him goodbye. "A wee exaggeration, but thank you. I'm glad you think so."

"Tonight should be fun," he said. "Let's go enjoy the evening."

"We're early, but there may be things to do."

He pulled her close. "I don't want to mess up your makeup so I won't kiss you now, but I'm going to make up for it later."

She pulled his head down to kiss him for just a minute and then released him. "Nothing on my lips—see. I'm not messed up."

"No, you're hot, beautiful and I want you in my arms, Stella," he said in a husky voice with a solemn expression that might indicate he expected her to tell him goodbye tonight.

"C'mon, Aaron. We have a party to go to." He held her coat and then took her arm to go to his car.

When they arrived at the Texas Cattleman's Club, she was amazed to see the cars that had already filled the lot and were parked along the long drive all the way back down to the street.

"Aaron, it looks like most of the people in Royal are here. Wasn't this scheduled to start at six-thirty tonight?"

"It was. I can't believe they already have such a huge turnout."

"I never would have imagined it," she said. "I know the TCC invited everyone in Royal, but I never dreamed they would all come. Did you?"

"The town's pulled together since the storm—neighbor helping neighbor. I think everyone is interested."

"I'm surprised. This isn't what I expected."

"It's what I expected and hoped for." A valet opened the door for her and she stepped out. Aaron came around to take her arm. Once inside the clubhouse, she glanced around at the rich, dark wood, the animal heads that had been mounted long ago when it was strictly a men's club. Now women were members and there was a children's center that had a reputation for being one of the finest in Texas. They paused by a coatroom where Aaron checked their coats and then he turned to take her arm again.

They headed for the great room that served for parties, events, dances and other club-wide activities. The sound of voices grew louder as they walked down the hall.

When they stepped inside the great room, a cheer went up, followed by thunderous applause. Stunned, Stella froze, staring at the smiling crowd. Everywhere she looked, people held signs that read, Stella for Acting Mayor, We Want Stella, and Thanks, Stella.

The TCC president, Gil Addison, appeared at her side. "Welcome, Stella."

Dazed, she tried to fathom what this was all about. She looked at Gil.

"This little surprise is to show you the support you have from the entire town of Royal. We all want you to accept the position of acting mayor until an election can be held and a new mayor chosen."

"I'm speechless," she said, smiling and waving at people.

"Stella, I have a letter from the mayor that I want to read to you and to all," Gil said. "Let's go up to the front."

"Did you know about this?" she asked, turning to Aaron. He grinned and gave her a hug.

"A little," he said, and she realized that Aaron might have been behind organizing this gathering of townspeople.

Gil smiled. "Aaron, you come with us," Gil said, and led the way. There was an aisle cleared to the stage at the front of the room.

As she approached the stage, people greeted her and shook her hand and she smiled, thanking them. Dazed, she couldn't quell her surprise.

At the front as she climbed the three steps to the stage,

more people greeted her. She shook hands with the town council and other city dignitaries. The sheriff greeted her, and the heads of different agencies in town crowded around to say hello.

"Stella, Stella, Stella," several people in the audience began chanting and in seconds, the entire room was chanting her name. She saw her friends Paige and Edie in the front row, smiling and waving.

"Mercy, Aaron, what is all this?" Dazed, embarrassed, she turned to Gil. "Gil—" She gave up trying to talk with all the chanting. Smiling, she waved at everyone.

Gil stepped forward and held up his hands for quiet. "Thanks to all of you for coming out tonight. The Texas Cattleman's Club is happy to have nearly everyone in Royal come celebrate the Christmas season and the holidays. We have a bit of business we wanted to discuss before the partying begins."

The crowd had become silent and Gil had a lapel mike so it was easy to hear him. "We have some people onstage—I imagine everyone here knows them, but in case they don't, I want to briefly tell you who is here. Please save your applause until I finish. I'll start with our sheriff, Nathan Battle." Gil ran through the list, reeling off the names of the town council members and heads of various agencies, and when he was done, the audience applauded.

"Now as you know, Mayor Vance was critically injured by the tornado. He is off the critical list—" Gil paused while people clapped. "He is still in the hospital and unable to join us tonight, but he has sent a letter for me to read, which I will do now.

'To the residents of Royal,
I am still recovering from the storm and most deeply

grateful to be alive and that my family survived. My deepest sympathy goes out to those who lost their loved ones, their homes, their herds or crops. We were hurt in so many ways, but from the first moment after the storm, people have helped each other.

It was with deep regret that I learned that Deputy Mayor Max Rothschild was also killed by the tornado. Since I will not be able to return to this job for a few more months, Royal will temporarily need an acting mayor. I have talked to our city officials, agency heads and concerned citizens, and one name comes up often and we are all in agreement. I hope we can persuade Ms. Stella Daniels to accept this position.'"

Gil paused to let people applaud and cheer. The noise was making her ears ring. Just then, Aaron leaned close to whisper in her ear, "I told you everyone wants you."

She smiled and threw kisses and waved, then put her hand down, hoping Gil could calm the crowd. She was stunned by the turnout and the crowd's enthusiastic support—for the first time in her life, she felt accepted by everyone. She glanced at Aaron, who smiled and winked at her, and she was certain he was the one behind this crowd that had gathered.

Gil raised his hand for quiet. "Folks, there's more from Mayor Vance.

'Please persuade Ms. Stella Daniels to accept this position. Since the first moments after the storm Stella has been doing my job. Now that I have recovered enough to read the mail I receive, I have had texts, emails, letters and cards that mention Stella and all she is doing for Royal and its citizens. I urge

Stella to accept this position and I am heartily supported by the town council, other officials of Royal and by its citizens.

Merry Christmas. Best wishes for your holiday,

The Honorable Richard Vance, Mayor of Royal, Texas.'"

There was another round of cheers and applause and Gil motioned for quiet. "At this point, I'm turning the meeting over to Nathan Battle."

Nathan received applause and motioned for quiet. "Thanks. I volunteered to do this part of the program. Royal needs an acting mayor." Nathan turned to Stella. "Stella, I think you can see that Mayor Vance, the town council and the whole town of Royal would like you to accept this position that will end in a few months when Mayor Vance can return to work. Will you be acting mayor of Royal?"

Feeling even more dazed, she looked up at Nathan Battle's dark brown eyes. Taking a deep breath, she smiled at him. "Yes, I'll accept the job of acting mayor until Mayor Vance gets back to work."

Her last words were drowned out by cheers and applause. Nathan shook her hand as he smiled. "Congratulations," he shouted. He stepped back and applauded as she turned and Aaron gave her a brief hug.

Everyone onstage shook her hand and tried to say a few words to her. The audience still cheered so she waved her hands for quiet.

"I want to thank all of you for this show of support. I'm stunned and amazed. I'll try my best to do what I can for Royal, as so many of you are doing. Let's all work together and, hopefully, we can get this town back in shape far sooner than anyone expected. Thank you so very much."

As the crowd applauded, Gil stepped forward and motioned for quiet again. "One more thing at this time. We can go from here to the dining hall. There's a buffet with lots of tables of food. Everyone can eat and during dessert we'll have Stella perform her first task as acting mayor and make presentations of gifts. There will be singing of Christmas carols in the dining room and then dancing back in this room, games in other rooms and the children's center will be open for the little ones. We have staff to take care of the babies. Now let's adjourn to the dining hall."

They applauded and Stella started down the steps to shake hands with people and talk to them. She lost track of Aaron until he showed up at her side and handed her a glass of ice water.

Gratefully, she sipped it and continued moving through the crowd toward the dining room. "You did this," she said to him.

"All I did was tell people we would do this tonight. No one would have come tonight if they hadn't wanted you for acting mayor and hadn't wanted to thank and support you."

"Aaron, I don't know what to say. I'm still reeling in shock."

"Congratulations. Now you'll get paid a little more for what you've been doing anyway. That's the thing, Stella. You're already doing this job and you have been for the past two months."

"If people know I'm pregnant, they might not want me for the job."

"It's most likely only for a couple more months and you're doing great so far."

"How many more surprises do you have in store tonight, Aaron?"

"I'm working on that one," he said, and she rolled her

eyes. "The band is coming in now. Let's head to the dining room and nibble on something while they set up."

"I don't know how long I'm going to feel dazed."

"It'll wear off and life will go right back to normal. You'll see."

Cole suddenly appeared in front of her. "Congratulations, Stella. You deserve to have the official title since you're doing all the work that goes with it."

"Thank you for coming tonight, Cole. I appreciate everyone showing their support. I had no idea."

"Well, Aaron organized this and I'm glad to be here because you should have this position. Just keep up what you're doing," he said, smiling at her.

"Thanks so much," she said.

"I'm touched you came tonight, Cole. I'm really amazed."

"I wouldn't have missed this."

As they moved on, she leaned closer to Aaron. "I'll remember this night all my life. I'll go see Mayor Vance tomorrow and thank him. But I suppose my biggest thanks goes to you. You must have been really busy talking to everyone."

"It didn't take any persuasion on my part. Everyone thought you'd be the best person for the job."

"Well, I'm amazed and touched by that, too. I just did what needed to be done, like hundreds of other people in Royal."

Gil Addison appeared again. "Stella. As acting mayor you should take charge of the next event on tonight's schedule. We'd like to tell people to pick up their envelopes and their presents whenever they want. Some families have little children and they won't want to stay long. Also, as acting mayor, you really should be at the head of the food line."

"I don't want to cut in front of people," she said, laughing and shaking her head. "I'll just get in line."

"Enjoy the few little perks you get with this job," Gil said. "There won't be many."

As they headed toward the dining room, people continued to stop and congratulate her. Paige walked up while the Battles talked to Aaron.

"You look gorgeous," she said. "Your necklace and bracelet are beautiful."

"Thank you. Aaron gave them to me."

"Aaron? I'm surprised, but glad Aaron is coming out of his shell. All our lives are changing, some in major ways, some in tiny ones, but the storm was a major upheaval for all of us. At least it looks as if we're all pulling together."

"I'm astounded, but oh, so thrilled. Thanks, Paige, for your part in this evening."

"Whatever I can do, I'm glad to. After I eat, I'll be at the table with the envelopes we're giving out. Members of the TCC will help us and we're doing this in shifts."

"Great, thanks."

Paige moved on and Aaron took Stella's arm to walk to the dining room. Enticing smells of hot bread, turkey and ham filled the air, and the dining room had three lines of long tables laden with food. The rest of the room was filled with tables covered in red or green paper where people could sit. At the back of the room was a huge decorated Christmas tree. Presents surrounded it, spilling out in front of it, lining the wall behind it. There appeared to be hundreds of wrapped presents. Paige, Lark, Edie, Megan and four TCC members sat at two tables to hand out envelopes of money some families would be receiving.

Gil appeared again. "Stella, you're the guest of honor—you get to go to the head of the line."

"I feel ridiculous doing that."

"We need you to go anyway so you can make the announcement about the gifts. Aaron, you go with her. Everyone's waiting for you to start."

Aaron took her arm as they followed Gil to the head of a line.

She had little appetite, but she ate some of the catered food that was there in abundance—turkey, dressing, mashed potatoes and cream gravy, ham, roasts, barbecued ribs, hot biscuits, thick golden corn bread, pickled peaches, an endless variety.

When they finished, Gil excused himself and left the table. He was back in minutes to sit and lean closer to talk to Stella. "We're ready to start matching people up with their gifts. People can pick up their things all evening long until eleven-thirty. The volunteers will change shifts at regular intervals so no one has to spend the whole evening handing out presents. If you're ready, I'll announce you. Aaron, go onstage. You'll be next about the Dallas TCC."

"Sure," she said. "Excuse me," she said to Nathan Battle, who sat beside her.

At the front of the room, Gil called for everyone's attention. "As I think all of you know, some people in Royal lost everything in the storm. A good number of Royal residents have been badly hit. So many of us wanted to do something about that. This was Stella's idea and I'll let her tell you more about it—" He handed a mike to Stella.

"As you all know," Stella began, "we decided to do a Christmas drive to provide presents and support for the people who need it most. All the Texas Cattleman Club's members, along with the ladies from the Christmas-drive committee volunteered to help. Those who could do so, both from Royal and other parts of Texas have contributed generously so everyone in Royal can have a wonderful holiday.

"Each family receiving gifts tonight has been assigned a number. First, go over to the table where the volunteers are seated near the west wall and pick up the envelope that matches your number. That envelope is for you and your family. Also, there are gifts that correspond to those numbers under the Christmas tree and along the back wall. Just go see a volunteer, who will help you. You get both an envelope plus the wrapped gifts that correspond to your number.

"We want to give a huge thanks to all who contributed money, time and effort to this drive to make sure everyone has a merry Christmas. Thank you."

People applauded and Stella started to sit, but Gil appeared and motioned her to wait. He took the mike. "I have one more important announcement—some really good news for us. Aaron Nichols and Cole Richardson are members of the Dallas, Texas, Cattleman's Club, but they are spending so much time and money in Royal trying to help us rebuild the town that the Texas Cattleman's Club of Royal invited them to join, which they did. Aaron Nichols and Cole will tell you about the rest. Aaron," Gil said, and handed the mike to Aaron while everyone applauded.

"Thanks. We're glad to help. This is Cole's hometown and I feel like it's mine now, too, because I've been here so much and everyone is so friendly. We've talked to some of our TCC friends in Dallas. I'll let Cole finish this." Aaron handed the mike to Cole, who received applause.

"It's good to be home again." He received more applause and waved his hand for quiet as he smiled. "We have friends here tonight from the Dallas TCC. They told us today that they wanted to make a presentation tonight. I want to introduce Lars West, Sam Thompkins and Rod

Jenkins. C'mon, guys," he said as each man waved and smiled at the audience.

Tall with thick brown hair, Lars West stepped forward. "Thanks, Cole. We know the TCC suffered damage along with so much of Royal. We talked to our Dallas TCC and we want to present a check to the TCC here in Royal," he said, turning to Gil Addison. "We'd like the Royal TCC to have a check for two million dollars to use for Royal storm aid however the TCC here sees fit."

The last of his words were drowned out by applause as the audience came to their feet and gave him a standing ovation.

Aaron motioned to Stella to join him and he introduced her to the men from Dallas. "Thank you," she said. "That's an incredibly generous gift and will do so much good for Royal."

"We hope so. We wanted to do something," Sam said.

They talked a few more minutes and then left the stage while Cole lingered and turned to Stella.

"I was about to go home," Cole said. "I thought Aaron could do this by himself, but he talked me into staying for the presentation. There are other Dallas TCC members here for a fun night. These three guys insist on going back to Dallas tonight, so we're all leaving now," Cole told them as Gil shook hands and thanked the Dallas TCC members.

"Cole, again, thanks so much for coming out," Stella said.

"I want to thank you, too," Aaron added.

"I hope all of this tonight brightened everybody's Christmas," Cole said. He left the stage to join the TCC Dallas members, moving through the crowd. He passed near Paige Richardson, speaking to her, and she smiled, speaking in return, both of them looking cordial as they passed each other.

Gil left to put the check in a safe place. Aaron took Stella's arm to go back to the great room where a band played and people danced. People stopped to congratulate Stella, to thank her. Some thanked Aaron for the TCC Dallas contribution.

"I'm going to dance with you before we leave here," Aaron said.

"I just hope we didn't miss anyone tonight in terms of the presents and money we're giving to families."

"Everyone could sign up who felt the need and some people signed up friends who wouldn't come in and sign up themselves. I don't think anyone got overlooked, but there's no way to really know," he said. "And with that, let's close this chapter on Royal's recovery for tonight and concentrate on you and me."

Startled, Stella looked up at him.

"Let's dance," he said, taking her into his arms. "We can't leave early, Stella. All these people came for you and they'll expect you to stay and have a good time. They'll want to speak to you."

"Aaron, in some ways," she said as she danced with him, "all my life I've felt sort of like an outsider. I've always been plain—I grew up that way and my mother is that way. For the first time tonight, I feel really accepted by everyone."

"You're accepted, believe me. Stella, people are so grateful to you. I've talked to them, and they're grateful for all you've done. And as for plain—just look in the mirror."

"You did that for me," she said solemnly, thinking the evening would have been so wonderful if she'd had Aaron's love. It was a subject she had shut out of her mind over and over since their arrival at the club tonight. Tears threatened again and she no longer felt like dancing.

"Aaron, I need a moment," she said, stepping away from him. She knew the clubhouse from being there with members for various events and she hurried off the dance floor and out of the room, heading for one of the small clubrooms that would be empty on a night like this. Tears stung her eyes and she tried to control them, wiping them off her cheeks.

A hand closed on her arm and Aaron stopped her. He saw her tears and frowned.

"C'mon," he said, holding her arm and walking down the hall to enter a darkened meeting room. Hanging a sign, Meeting in Progress, on the outside knob and switching on a small lamp, he closed the door.

She wiped her eyes frantically and took deep breaths.

He turned to face her, walking to her and placing his hands on his hips. "I was going to wait until we went home tonight to talk to you, but I think we better talk right now. What started out to be a great, fun evening for you has turned sour in a big way."

"Aaron, we can't talk here."

"Yes, we can." He stepped close and slipped one arm around her waist. His other hand tilted her chin up as he gazed into her eyes. "This is long overdue, but as the old saying goes, sometimes you can't see the forest for the trees. I've missed you and I've been miserable without you. I love you, Stella."

Startled, she frowned as she stared at him. "You're saying that—I don't think you mean it. It's one of those nice and honorable things you do."

"No. I'm not saying it to be nice and not out of honor. It's out of love. After I lost Paula and Blake, I didn't think I would ever love again. I didn't think I could. I was wrong, because there's always room in the heart for love. I just couldn't even see that I had fallen in love with you."

Shocked, she stared at him. "Aaron, I didn't know about your wife and son until this past week."

He frowned. "I thought everyone around here knew that. I just didn't talk about it."

"That's been a barrier between us, hasn't it?"

"It was, but it's not now. I'm in love with you. I want to marry you and if you'd found out today that you're not really pregnant, I would still tell you the same thing. I love you. When I lost Paula and Blake, I didn't want to live, either. I hurt every minute of every day for so long. When I finally did go out with a woman, I think it was three or four years later and after the date, I just wanted to go home and be alone."

She hurt for him, but she remained silent because Aaron was opening himself up completely to her and gone was the shuttered look and the feeling that a wall had come between them.

"I finally began to socialize, but I just never got close to anyone until you came along. I soon realized that you were the first woman I'd enjoyed being around since Paula. I also noticed I didn't hurt as much and I didn't think about her as much.

"Stella, I will always love Paula and Blake. There's room in my heart for more love—for you, for our baby. I love you and I have been miserable without you and it's my own fault for shutting you out, but I just didn't even realize I was falling in love with you."

"Aaron," she said, her happiness spilling over.

He pulled her close, leaning down to kiss her, a hungry, passionate kiss as if he had been waiting years to do this.

Joyously she clung to him and kissed him. "I love you, Aaron. I missed you, but I want your love. I just want you to be able to share the good and the bad, the hurts, the happiness, everything in your life with me and me with you. That's love, Aaron."

He held her so tightly she could barely breathe. "You mean everything to me. I just couldn't even recognize what I felt until I saw I was losing you. Thank goodness I haven't."

"No, you haven't. You have my heart. I love you, Aaron. I've loved you almost from the very first."

"Stella, wait." He knelt on one knee and held her hand. "Stella Daniels, will you marry me?" he asked, pulling a box from his jacket pocket and holding it out to her.

"Aaron." She laughed, feeling giddy and bubbly. "Yes, I'll marry you, Aaron Nichols. For goodness' sake, get up," she said, taking the box from him. "What is this, Aaron?"

She opened the box and gasped. Aaron took out the ten-carat-diamond-and-emerald ring he had bought. He held her hand and slipped the ring onto her finger. "Perfect," he said, looking into her eyes. "Everything is perfect, Stella. I will tell you I love you so many times each day you'll grow tired of hearing it."

"Impossible," she said, looking at the dazzling ring. "Oh, Aaron, I'm overwhelmed. This is the most beautiful ring. I can't believe it's mine."

"It is definitely yours. Stella, I love you. Also, I'm going to love our baby so very much. This child is a gift and a blessing for me. The loss of my first child—I can't tell you how badly that hurt and I never dreamed I'd marry and have another baby."

"We'll both be blessed by this child. I'm so glad. From the first moment, I thought this would be the biggest thrill in my life if I had your love when I found out we would have a baby."

"You have my love," he said, hugging her and then kissing her. After a few minutes, he leaned away. "C'mon. I think it's time for an announcement."

She laughed again. "Aaron, I'm used to staying in the background, being quiet and unnoticed. My life is undergoing every kind of transformation. I don't even know myself anymore in so many ways.

"I'm announcing this engagement to keep the guys away from you. I've even had them ask me if I cared if they asked you out. Yes, I cared. I wanted to punch one of them."

She laughed, shaking her head as he took her hand.

"C'mon. I'm making an announcement and then all those guys will stay away from my fiancée."

When he said *my fiancée*, joy bubbled in her as she hurried beside him.

"Stella, let's get married soon."

"You need to meet my family. I should meet yours."

"You will. I'll take you to Paris soon to meet them. Either before or after the wedding, whichever you want."

"You're changing my life in every way."

In the great room, when the band stopped between pieces, Aaron found Gil. Stella couldn't believe what was happening, but Gil motioned to the band and hurried to talk to them.

He turned to the dancers and people seated at small tables around the edge of the room. There was a roll from the drummer and people became quiet. "Ladies and gentlemen," Gil said. "May I have your attention? We have a brief announcement."

Stella shook her head. "Aaron, you started this," she said, and he grinned.

Aaron stepped forward, but Stella moved quickly to take the mike from a surprised Gil. "Folks," she said, smiling at Aaron as he took her hand. "I'd like to make my first announcement as acting mayor. I'd like to announce my engagement to Aaron Nichols," she proclaimed, laughing and looking at Aaron.

As everyone applauded and cheered, Aaron turned to slip his arm around her and kiss her briefly, causing more applause and whistles.

When he released her, he took the mike. "Now we can all go back to partying! Merry Christmas, everybody!"

There was another round of applause as the band began to play.

"Thanks, Gil," Aaron said, handing back the mike. "Let's go dance," he said to Stella. "Two dances and then we start calling family."

It was a fast piece and she danced with Aaron, having a wonderful time. She wanted him and was certain they would go home and make love. When the number ended, people crowded around them to congratulate her and look at her ring. She left the dance floor to let them and remained talking to friends until Aaron rescued her a whole number later.

"Instead of dancing some more, how about going to your place?"

"I'll beat you to the door," she said, teasing him, and he laughed. "I have to get my purse and start thanking people."

"Everybody is partying. Save the thank-you for one you can write on a Christmas card or wedding announcement or something."

"You're right about everyone partying," she said. "You win. Let's go."

He took her hand and she got her purse. They stopped

to get their coats and then at the door they waited while a valet brought Aaron's car.

Everybody who passed them congratulated her on becoming acting mayor and on her engagement.

When they drove away from the club, she turned toward him slightly. It was quiet and cozy in his car. "Aaron, this has been the most wonderful night of my life," she said. "Thanks to you."

"I'm glad. Let's have this wedding soon."

"That's what I'd like."

"I don't care whether we have a large or small one."

"My parents will want no part of a large wedding. I got my plain way of life from my mother."

"If you prefer a large wedding, have it. I'll pay for it and help you."

She squeezed his knee lightly. "Thank you. That's very nice. What about you?"

"I don't care. Mom and Dad will do whatever we want. So will my brother."

"Probably a small wedding and maybe a large reception. After tonight, I feel I have to invite the entire town of Royal to the reception."

"I agree. That was nice of everyone. All the people I talked to were enthused, everybody wanted you to be acting mayor. Stella, I didn't find anyone who didn't want you. Mayor Vance definitely wanted you."

"That makes me feel so good. I can't tell you. In high school I was sort of left out of things socially. I guess I always have been."

"Not now. You'll never be left out of anything with me."

"I think you're speeding. I'd hate for the new acting mayor to get pulled over the first few hours I have the job."

"I want to get home to be alone with you," he said as he slowed.

In minutes they reached her town house. "My trunk is filled with Christmas gifts. I'm not carrying them in tonight. I'll get them in the morning," he said.

"I have to go shopping tomorrow. I've been so busy I haven't gotten all my presents and I don't have any for you yet. I really didn't expect to be with you Christmas."

"But now you will be if I can talk you into it. How disappointed will your sister be if you don't come this year and we spend Christmas here, just the two of us?"

"With three kids, she won't care. We can go sometime during the holidays. We can call her."

"We sure can, but later. I have other plans when I close the door."

"Do you really?" she teased.

He parked where she directed him to and came around to open her door. As soon as they stepped into her entryway, Aaron closed the door behind him and turned to pull her into his embrace, giving a kiss that was filled with love and longing.

Later Stella lay in his arms while he toyed with her hair. The covers were pulled up under her arms.

Aaron stretched out his arm to pick up his phone and get a calendar. "Let's set a date now."

"Aaron," she said, trailing her fingers along his jaw, "since I just accepted the job of acting mayor, I feel a responsibility for Royal. I'll have to live here until I'm no longer acting mayor."

"I'm here all the time anyway. I'll work from here and go to Dallas when I feel I need to. We can build a house here if you want. Remember, that is my business."

"Whatever you'd like. When my job ends, I don't mind moving to Dallas."

"We'll work it all out. I just want to be with you."

"Our honeymoon may have to come after baby is here," she said.

"Baby is here," he echoed. "Stella, I've told you before and I'll tell you again—I'm overjoyed about the baby. I lost Blake and he was one of the big loves of my life. I have a second chance here to be a dad. I'm thrilled and I hope you are."

"I am. Do you particularly want another little boy?"

"No, I don't care," he said, and she smiled, relieved and happy that he didn't have his heart set on having a boy.

"Just a baby. I can't tell you." His voice had gotten deep and she realized he was emotional about the baby he'd lost. She hugged him and rose up to kiss him, tasting a salty tear. His hurt caused her heart to ache. "Aaron, I'm so glad about this baby. And we can have more."

He pulled her down to kiss her hard. When he released her, she saw he had a better grip on his emotions. "For a tough, military-type guy, you're very tenderhearted," she said.

"I am thrilled beyond words to be a dad. That's why I got those necklaces for you. I love you, Stella."

"I love you," she responded.

"Now let's set a date for a wedding. How about a wedding between Christmas and New Year's? That's a quiet time. January won't be."

"You're right. I'd say a very quiet wedding after Christmas. Can you do that, Mr. Nichols?"

"I can. Want to fly to Dallas next week to get a wedding dress from Cecilia? That'll be a Christmas present to you."

She smiled. "Your love is my Christmas present. Your

love, your baby, this fabulous ring. Aaron, I love you with all my heart. I give you my love for Christmas." Joy filled her while she looked into his brown eyes.

"Merry, merry Christmas, darling," he said as he wrapped his arms around her and pulled her close to kiss her.

Happiness filled her heart and after a moment she looked up at him. "Your love is the best Christmas gift possible." She felt joyous to be in Aaron's strong arms and to know she had his love always.

* * * * *

TEXAS CATTLEMAN'S CLUB:
AFTER THE STORM
Don't miss a single story!

STRANDED WITH THE RANCHER
by Janice Maynard
SHELTERED BY THE MILLIONAIRE
by Catherine Mann
PREGNANT BY THE TEXAN
by Sara Orwig
BECAUSE OF THE BABY...
by Cat Schield
HIS LOST AND FOUND FAMILY
by Sarah M. Anderson
MORE THAN A CONVENIENT BRIDE
by Michelle Celmer
FOR HIS BROTHER'S WIFE
by Kathie DeNosky

"When were you going to tell me, Scarlett?"

"Tell you what?"

"That you're pregnant."

If Raiden had told her he was an alien, then flew around the room to prove it, she wouldn't have been more stunned.

Slowly, carefully, as if testing her voice for the first time, she said, "Never, I guess. Since I'm not."

His eyes suddenly took on a faraway look. "I *have* been feeling it in every inch of you. But I didn't reach the obvious conclusion because I thought you'd tell me if it was true. But you didn't." His eyes focused on hers again, something enormous roiling in their depths. "Why, Scarlett? Was it because you thought we'd say goodbye and I didn't have to know?"

* * *

Scandalously Expecting His Child
is part of The Billionaires of Black Castle series:
Only their dark pasts could lead these men
to the light of true love.

SCANDALOUSLY
EXPECTING
HIS CHILD

BY
OLIVIA GATES

Published in Great Britain 2014
by Mills & Boon, an imprint of Harlequin (UK) Limited,
Eton House, 18-24 Paradise Road, Richmond, Surrey, TW9 1SR

© 2014 Olivia Gates

ISBN: 978-0-263-91486-3

51-1214

Harlequin (UK) Limited's policy is to use papers that are natural, renewable and recyclable products and made from wood grown in sustainable forests. The logging and manufacturing processes conform to the legal environmental regulations of the country of origin.

Printed and bound in Spain
by CPI, Barcelona

Olivia Gates has always pursued creative passions such as singing and handicrafts. She still does, but only one of her passions grew gratifying enough, consuming enough, to become an ongoing career—writing.

She is most fulfilled when she is creating worlds and conflicts for her characters, then exploring and untangling them bit by bit, sharing her protagonists' every heart-wrenching heartache and hope, their every heart-pounding doubt and trial, until she leads them to an indisputably earned and gloriously satisfying happy ending.

When she's not writing, she is a doctor, a wife to her own alpha male and a mother to one brilliant girl and one demanding Angora cat. Visit Olivia at www.oliviagates.com.

To Stacy Boyd, my incredible editor, who's supported me throughout the toughest two years of my life.

One

Raiden Kuroshiro looked down at the woman standing beside him. Megumi was indeed her name. A beautiful blessing. With flawless white skin, gleaming raven hair and naturally red lips, she looked like a real live version of Snow White. And with her small, svelte body wrapped to perfection in that vivid blue dress, she did look like a fairy-tale princess. There was something regal about her bearing as she received everyone's congratulations on their engagement. Their wedding was exactly ten weeks from tonight.

And he felt absolutely nothing for her.

Thankfully, her feelings for him were as nonexistent.

Which was as it should be.

The reasons he was marrying Megumi, and the ones she had to marry him, didn't necessitate they even tolerated each other. Theirs would be a pure marriage of convenience.

Megumi looked up at him, ultrapoliteness playing on her dainty lips. Though smiling wasn't one of his usual activities, it was easy to answer her smile. Not that he had anything to do with it. Known as an angel, Megumi would get along with the devil himself. Which she did. Raiden was known as a fiend. He'd been called that during his years as a mercenary, and worse as he'd slashed his way to the top of the venture capitalism field and carved himself a permanent place there.

"I can join my mother if you like."

He barely heard Megumi over the traditional *gagaku* court music and the loud drone of the five hundred people filling the ballroom. It was the first time he'd been with that many members of Japanese society's upper crust in one place. It was his goal not only to belong to that class but to rule it. Megumi knew that, and she was thoughtfully offering to slip away so he could make the most of the event without her hindering presence.

Though it was a tempting offer, he shook his head. He was under said upper crust's microscope, and he knew it would be frowned upon to leave his bride-to-be in their first public appearance together, especially one dedicated to celebrating their impending union.

But at least he didn't have to play the besotted groom, as he would have had to in Western societies. It was a relief that in Japanese society prospective partners in traditionally arranged marriages demonstrated nothing more than utmost courtesy to each other. Which was easy with Megumi. He didn't have to feign gallantry with her.

Not that he liked her. He didn't like anyone. Apart from his Black Castle "brothers"—who were integral parts of his own being—he categorized people in limited roles. He had allies, subordinates and enemies. Megumi fell somewhere between the first two categories. He'd made her position in his life clear, and she seemed accepting of it.

Which she should. He was the wealthiest, most powerful husband and future father of her children she could have. Even if he weren't already the ultimate catch, as an obedient daughter, Megumi would have still married him. Her father wanted Raiden as family at any cost.

And *that* was the main reason he was marrying her. She was his only path to the one thing he'd dreamed of all his life, what he'd been working to achieve for the past ten years.

Reclaiming his birthright.

But though everything was going according to plan, one thing niggled at him. The other reason he was marrying Megumi was to have full-blooded Japanese heirs. Which meant he would have to…perform. He worried he wouldn't be able to. Not without falling back on what managed to thaw his deep-frozen libido. Fantasizing about *her.*

It was galling he'd have to resort to this measure to…rise to the occasion, but he was brutally pragmatic. He'd resort to whatever worked. Hopefully only once. With careful timing, it might be all it took to impregnate Megumi.

After conception, it was another major relief that most Japanese wives in arranged marriages mostly retreated to their own quarters, with their lives from then on revolving around their baby. From what he'd been hearing about the society that was still alien to him, in the kind of marriage he was entering, it was accepted that a husband's role was as a sperm donor and financier. His wife mostly relegated him to public social activities and appearances, with his intimacy sought again only when another baby was needed. Which was exactly the kind of marriage he wanted. The only kind he could stomach.

He looked at Megumi as she graciously smiled at another congratulator and wondered at his intense aversion to the idea of sex with her. If anyone knew he thought having sex with such a beauty was such a terrible fate, they'd question his virility. If they knew he'd have to invoke another woman's memory to go through with it, they'd think him pathetic. If they knew that woman had been a fraud, they'd question his judgment. But if they knew that not even finding out the truth about her had lessened her hold over him, it would totally decimate the uncompromising identity he presented to the world.

Not that anyone would ever learn of her. Or of any of his other dark secrets. He'd accumulated unspeakable ones during the twenty years when he'd been The Organization's slave. It was imperative the persona he'd built since his escape ten years ago remained unimpeachable. He wasn't letting anything threaten his chances of reclaiming his heritage.

To that end, he had to follow this society's rules until they became second nature to him. As they were to Megumi and her family. The family that had no idea *he* was one of them.

They'd never find out he was. But he would become one of them. He'd become a Hashimoto through marriage to—

Suddenly, a jolt speared through his body. It originated at his nape and forked down to his toes.

But the all-out alarm wasn't one of danger. He was versed in recognizing threats. This red alert was one of awareness.

Without any change in expression or posture, he threw the net of his senses out before yanking it back, eliminating everything but the source of the disturbance.

The next second, Megumi gripped his forearm.

He frowned. Megumi never touched him. So had his reaction been in anticipation of her touch? But why would she suddenly wring such a jarring response from him?

Turning his gaze down to her, he was relieved to feel no reaction to her sight and now touch, as usual. But the awareness searing through him was intensifying. It took all his control not to look around for its origin.

"Matsuyama-san is approaching."

So that was why she'd grabbed him so urgently—to draw his attention to the approach of their host. Hiro Matsuyama. The man who'd gone all-out holding this ball in his mansion. And his bitterest business rival in Japan.

It still felt weird being honored by an adversary. But that was an expected ritual in Japan. A necessary one even. Tradition and decorum were valued above all in business as in society. It would take him a while to get used to that, along with everything else, as he hadn't been raised Japanese.

But then, he hadn't been raised at all. From the age of four years old, he'd been forged. Into a lethal weapon.

He let adversaries glimpse that side of him to keep them in check, showing them what they were really up against. But though Hiro posed his biggest business threat, compared with the monsters Raiden had vanquished in his time, Hiro was harmless. No, his senses couldn't be going haywire to herald his approach.

Turning to Megumi, he saw her eyes fixed, vaguely noted the glazed look in them, the tremor in her lower lip. His focus left her behind as the disruption grew in intensity.

Then he was facing Hiro…and the woman he had on his arm. And the realization was instantaneous.

She was the source of the disturbance.

She was the only female around who wasn't Japanese. Even the non-Japanese businessmen in attendance were married to Japanese women. It was the only way to truly enter society, the path to the most solid form of business alliances in Japan.

Every eye in the ballroom seemed to be following her.

The Japanese had strict parameters for their women's beauty. But most were enamored with Caucasian beauty and coloring. Most men obsessed about Western women, even if few approached them, because many of the qualities they so admired in the safety of fantasy proved intimidating in reality. All of those qualities were present in this woman.

She towered above everyone, flaunted her height even more with high heels. Hiro was tall for a Japanese man at almost six feet, and she stood taller. Only a couple of inches short of looking six-foot-four Raiden in the eyes.

She stood out in every other way, too. Among all the dark-haired people around, she looked like a flame-haired Amazon, tanned, curvaceous, bodacious, oozing sexuality and confidence. And among all the women in soft or bright colors, she was the only one in fathomless black. She looked every voluptuous inch the femme fatale, the opposite of everything considered desirable in a Japanese woman, the antithesis of the petite, porcelain-skinned, delicate and demure Megumi. Though one look at prevalent Japanese porn said she was the epitome of the nation's not-so-secret fantasies.

But he didn't share those fantasies, had none really. That came from the total discipline he'd trained in from early childhood, to hone his skills to inhuman precision. During his years with The Organization, he hadn't made use of the choice female companionship they'd provided to keep their agents placated. Since his escape, he'd remained as fastidious. The one time his shields had come crashing down had been with *her*.

But *this* woman was evoking the same…compulsion. When she wasn't even looking at him.

His awareness clung to her even as he forced his gaze to pan to Hiro as he bowed to Megumi. Raiden barely registered that her hand dug deeper into his forearm. Everything in him was focused on the other woman.

Hiro bowed stiltedly in answer to his own compulsory bow, before resuming looking at Megumi. "May I introduce Ms. Scarlett Delacroix, Megumi-san?"

As the ladies exchanged bows, his eyes were dragged back to the woman's profile. He barely tore them away as Hiro turned to him, his gaze colliding with his, the arm around Scarlett Delacroix's nipped waist visibly tightening.

Was Hiro announcing his claim? Telling Raiden not to think of making a move? Hiro assumed he would, with his brand-new fiancée standing at his side?

That would make Hiro more astute than Raiden had thought. He did want to make a move. Which stunned him, because he never did.

But maybe Hiro wasn't reading his aberrant reaction specifically, just believed Scarlett Delacroix was irresistible to any male. He would be right about that, too. If he with his ironclad control felt those unstoppable urges toward that vivid creature, other men must be champing at the bit.

But his reaction was indeed abnormal. He waded in gorgeous women and gave none a second glance. But this woman's effect had nothing to do with her physical attributes. It was identical to *her* effect. His every sense was clamoring so loud, as if in recognition...

This was beyond pathetic. Projecting his reactions to a long-gone and deceitful lover onto other women.

But then he'd never had anything approaching this reaction to any other woman. It was only this woman, this Scarlett....

"Scarlett, please meet Raiden Kuroshiro."

Hiro's grudging introduction yanked him out of his

insane musings to find her extending her hand. His rose involuntarily to meet it…and static sparked at their touch.

Her hand lurched away, a gasp escaping her full lips, before they spread in an exquisite bow. "Serves me right for going for an all-synthetic, antiwrinkle gown," she said, explaining away the spark. "Now I need grounding."

Her accent was American, her voice too low to fathom clearly in the background din, but its warmth speared through his loins, made him grit his teeth.

Hiro pulled her more securely to his side. "It must be a mere manifestation of your electrifying personality."

Raiden aborted a snort at Hiro's hackneyed comment. But what he couldn't rein in was his rising hackles at Hiro's possessive attitude. He couldn't believe his reaction. He'd *never* felt confrontational with another man over a woman.

Then she turned fully to him, the smile on her lips not reaching her eyes as they met his for the first time. The bolt that hit him this time almost rocked him on his feet.

Those eyes. Those intense, luminescent sapphire blues. They were the same color of *her* eyes.

It was really getting ridiculous how he was trying to find similarities between the two completely different women.

"I hear congratulations are in order," Scarlett murmured, her gaze flitting from his eyes to Megumi's before he could hold it.

It couldn't be she was shy. This was a woman who knew her power over men, a power that must have been perfected through years of practice and exercised at will. He was certain there wasn't a diffident cell in that voluptuous body. So why didn't she want to look him in the eye?

"Scarlett had a prior engagement." Hiro turned to

Scarlett, his gaze taking on a besotted edge. "But she still honored me with consenting to grace the ball."

"How could I not, when you organize the best balls in the northern hemisphere, Hiro?" Scarlett turned to Megumi with a warm smile. "Between you and me, I was hoping that by meeting the guests of honor of this ball, I might get my first invitation to a high-society Japanese wedding."

"If I'm invited—" Hiro shot Megumi a brief glance before resuming his adoration of Scarlett "—you certainly will be."

"We'd be honored to have you both grace the wedding." Megumi felt nowhere her usual serene self, her words brittle, her expression forced.

She didn't like Scarlett? Probably not many women did. Scarlett must be an ego crusher, especially to those females who considered themselves beautiful. For she was magnificent.

"I trust this is also Kuroshiro-san's sentiment?" Hiro asked, turning his challenging gaze to him.

In their previous meetings, Hiro had been reserved, but he'd made it clear their enmity would be kept to the financial battlefield. This time, though, he was struggling to hold back his aggression. Because he felt territorial over Scarlett?

Not that she'd given Hiro any reason to fear him. She'd barely looked in his direction so far.

Hiro, on the other hand, was still glaring at him, waiting for his corroboration. Raiden gave it to him with an inclination of his head.

Megumi's hand tightened. Was she urging him to vocalize his response? He knew he had to comply, or it would be taken as an offense. His silence so far had been bad enough.

He didn't feel like making a response. Right now the only thing he felt like doing was snatching Hiro's arm off Scarlett's waist and dragging her away from him.

Still, he said, "Matsuyama-san, Ms. Delacroix, your presence at our wedding isn't only our privilege, it's a necessity."

His deferential words didn't seem to appease Hiro. The man's response was perplexing, since Hiro had not only insisted on holding this ball, but had brought to his attention the very woman he was visually wrestling him over.

Thankfully, the stilted meeting came to an end shortly afterward, and Hiro and Scarlett moved on. Raiden forced himself not to watch them walk away. Not to watch *her*. But he could no longer bear having Megumi by his side.

Looking down at her, he tried to smile, failing this time. "If it's okay with you, Megumi, I'll now take advantage of your kind offer to go make the rounds."

"Of course." Megumi stepped back, looking as relieved as he felt to finally separate.

Walking away, he forced himself to stop by a few congratulators. As soon as he saw an opening to get out of the ballroom, he took it. On his way out, he again saw Scarlett. She was heading out, too. Even from the back, and from a distance, the sense of familiarity swamped him all over again. The same intensity he'd experienced when he'd first seen *her*.

Her. That was how he'd always thought of the woman he'd known by the name of Hannah McPherson.

He'd met her in New York one bright summer afternoon five years ago, when she'd swerved her car to avoid hitting a reckless biker and crashed into his car instead.

From the moment she'd stepped out of her car, everything else had ceased to matter to him. The inexorable attraction he'd felt toward her had been something he'd never thought he could experience. He'd always told her she'd literally crashed into his life, and pulverized all his preconceptions and rules.

Ignoring his usual precautions, he hadn't even performed the most basic investigation on her. It had been through her that he'd known her to be a kindergarten teacher by morning, and a florist who ran an inherited shop by afternoon.

When he'd taken her out that first night, she'd made it clear it wouldn't go any further because he inhabited a world alien to hers. She hadn't budged when he'd insisted that attraction like theirs bridged all differences. It had taken their first kiss for her to capitulate, concede that what had sprung between them had been unstoppable. And from that first night, he'd plunged with her into an incendiary affair.

Then after five delirious months, a single inexplicable discrepancy had led him to unravel an ingeniously spun web of fraud. And to an appalling verdict. That her identity had been manufactured just prior to meeting him.

It had all been a setup. Starting with the accident that had brought them together. She must have been sent by some rival to spy on him. And in their intimacy, he'd left himself wide-open. Whatever she'd been after, she could have found it.

But since no one had used privileged information against him yet, either she hadn't found what she'd been looking for or she was waiting for the right time to leverage her intel from her recruiters. Or him. Or both.

Pretending to be oblivious until he'd decided how to deal with her, he'd called her. She'd been her usual bright, eager self at first, then as if hearing through his act, her voice had changed, becoming a stranger's. Then she'd asked if he preferred she called him Lightning, or if he'd left that name behind when he'd escaped The Organization. And he'd realized it had been far worse than his worst fears.

It hadn't been corporate espionage material she'd managed to get her hands on, but his most lethal secret. His previous identity. And she'd known its value, its danger. That its exposure would bring The Organization to his and his brothers' doors. The Organization that needed them all dead.

His blood had frozen and boiled at once as she'd said it was just as well he'd brought the charade to an end so she could make her demands. Some money in exchange for her silence.

"Some money" had turned out to be fifty million dollars.

Enraged, he'd assured her he didn't negotiate with blackmailers. He took them out. So it was in *her* best interest to keep what she knew to herself.

Unfazed by his threat, she'd said he'd never find her to carry it out, but that she'd had no wish to expose him, just needed the money. It was pocket change to him, so he should just pay without involving payback or pride. He also shouldn't fear she'd ever ask for more or hold her knowledge over him in any other way. Once the transaction was complete, he could consider that she'd never existed. As she'd never truly had.

Though bitterness and fury had consumed him, cold logic had said that while he couldn't trust his instincts or her, he could trust her sense of self-preservation. She'd already known how lethal he could be, and she wouldn't risk extorting him again. This would be a one-off thing. It would end this catastrophic breach to his and his brothers' security.

But he'd found himself wondering. If she really needed

the money, he'd gladly help her, if only she'd tell him she'd been forced to spy on him, and that it hadn't been all a lie.

His need to look the other way in return for such a re-assurance had made him even angrier. At himself. Deciding to end the sordid interlude, he'd transferred the money to the offshore account she'd provided, what had been untraceable even to his formidable resources. As per her declaration, he'd never found any trace of her again. It *had* been as if she'd never existed. It had been truly over.

But it hadn't ended. Not for him.

His obsession with her continued to torment him. It sank its talons the deepest when he was at his lowest ebb. It was at such times he yearned to turn to her, the only woman who'd touched his innermost being, to feel her vitality filling his arms, her empathy touching his soul, her passion igniting his cravings. Every time, he'd cursed her even more, for needing her still.

But his anger remained mostly directed at himself—the master of stealth who'd failed to detect the least trace of duplicity in her. And who, even after it had been proved, had remained inextricably under her spell.

Shaking himself out of the bitter musings, he now ex-ited the ballroom in pursuit of that other woman who had wrung the same reactions from him.

Scarlett Delacroix was gracefully gliding across the mansion's expansive terrace, descending the stairs to the traditional tea garden. In the light of a gibbous moon, her red tresses were the only splash of color and heat in the scene's monotone coldness. The layered skirt of her black dress trailed after her like a piece of night that wor-shipped her lush figure.

Noting that Hiro's bodyguards were monitoring her

progress, he waited as she crossed the wooden bridge to the garden house, then set off in the opposite direction.

In minutes, he entered the building soundlessly from its southern entrance. The warmth of the interior advanced as if to greet him, but it was her aura that reached out and enveloped him as she stood looking out the screen window.

It was uncanny. His reaction to her was identical to his reaction to Hannah, when physically she couldn't be more different. Still, he couldn't shake that insane feeling. Or resist the preposterous impulse.

He stepped out of the shadows and strode toward her.

Without turning, she only shot him a sidelong glance. There was no doubt about it. She'd felt him there all along, had been waiting for him to make a move.

His heat rose as she resumed looking out to the exquisite moonlit garden. No one, no woman, certainly not Hannah, had ever treated him with such nonchalance.

He stopped a breath away, bent and placed his lips an inch from her ear. His words rustled the hair tucked behind it. "Why are you out here and not in that ballroom soaking up the collective adulation?"

Without giving any indication if his nearness affected her in any way, she said, "Not that I noticed such generalized fascination, but I came out for some fresh air and solitude. I'm a touch claustrophobic *and* agoraphobic. A full ballroom is my ultimate aversion."

"Is it? Or are you just giving Hiro something he's never experienced—a woman who can leave his side, who isn't trying to court his favor with her every breath? If you walked away to test how deep your hook has sunk into him, are you now disappointed he hasn't come running after you?"

"I plead not guilty to all of your assumptions, Mr.

Kuroshiro. But the question is, why are *you* here? Why aren't you back in that ballroom collecting oaths of allegiance and obedience? Can I assume my so-called hook has inadvertently sunk in you instead, and it has brought *you* running after me?"

"You can indeed assume, Ms. Delacroix." He paused for a second, then decided to act on the unstoppable compulsion, no matter how absurd it was. "Or should I say Ms. McPherson?"

For an interminable stretch, there was absolutely no reaction from her. Nothing but total stillness and silence.

Then she turned her head to him, her heavily fringed, vibrantly blue eyes looking up at him in what looked like amusement. "I heard that right, didn't I? You just implied I'm someone else? Someone you know?" A brief, tinkling chuckle escaped her dimpled lips. "That's one line I was never given."

His hands itched to clamp over the flesh that pulled at his instincts like inexorable gravity. He barely fought the temptation. "Because men approach you with protests that you're like no one they'd ever met? Take heart. You're still unique. So much so, even a totally different face and body didn't stop me from recognizing you."

There. The words were out. And they sounded ludicrous. At least, to his logic. His instincts said different. He'd follow those wherever they willed until it all played out.

Her eyebrows rose in incredulity before a considering expression came into her eyes. "Is this a game? You want me to pretend I'm this...McPherson woman? And will you be someone else, too? Someone free to indulge himself with a total stranger?" She turned fully to him, leaned back against the window frame over arms tucked behind her back. "I did hear role-playing is huge in Japan, but I wouldn't have thought you're the type who'd be into it. But then, maybe you're just that. Someone who became a billionaire so young must lead a very stressful life. Maybe it's your preferred method of defusing the pressures."

Her every calm syllable, her steady gaze, made everything inside him churn.

His lips twisted grimly, mocking his runaway reaction, conceding her effect. "Your on-the-fly performance is impressive. But then, you always *were* the most spontaneous, undetectable imposter I've ever encountered."

Only one delicately curved auburn eyebrow rose this time, and what seemed so much like real interest entered her gaze. "Have you encountered that many?"

"Hundreds. And I've seen through each of them at a hundred paces. It was only you who took me in, all the way. But I'm now immunized for life against falling for your charades again."

She shook her head as if she'd had enough of playing his game. Then suddenly she tilted it at him, her gaze shedding its mockery, becoming smoldering. "You don't need an outrageous approach to hook me, Mr. Kuroshiro. I'm already interested."

That was something he hadn't expected her to say. Not that he'd expected anything. He was flying blind here.

"You are?"

"Every female with only a brain wave would be." She sighed. "Pity you're engaged."

"Does that even matter?"

"I guess it wouldn't to someone like you. Even if I suspect that such a someone doesn't exist, that you're one of a kind. I expect you're bound by no rules and consider no one in your decisions."

"You already know this about me."

"You mean this McPherson woman knows this about you."

"Will you keep pretending you're not her for long?"

She sighed again. "I already told you I'm interested. And since being engaged doesn't deter you, it's something actually in your favor, since you must only want something intense…and transient. The only kind of liaison I'm open to."

"So Hiro hasn't reserved a place in your bed yet?"

"Hiro, like everything else in my life, is of no concern to you and is off-limits to discussion. I do as I please, and no one has any claims on me."

"I bet Hiro doesn't know this part. Or he does, and you're still dangling the bait. And while you wait until he swallows the whole fishing rod, you welcome diversions?"

"Why not? I'm a free agent so far." She uncoiled to her full statuesque height. "But I've had enough of indulging your role-playing fetish. Let's revisit this when you decide to talk to me, not your imaginary character."

Without lingering one more second, she turned away. He watched her receding, a flame-haired goddess of the night dissolving into her domain, his thoughts tangling.

Had he made a gigantic fool of himself? All evidence said so. His instincts, however, still screamed their contradictory verdict.

Exasperation rumbled from his gut as he lunged after her, grabbed her by the waist and slammed her against his length.

A gasp swelled in her chest as he stabbed a hand into the heavy silk at her nape, tethering her head. In the golden illumination of fire-lit lanterns, her eyes held his in utmost composure, belying her ragged moan at his roughness. And he crashed his lips over hers, swallowing the intoxicating sound.

Her lips parted wide under his onslaught, letting him plunge into her depths, her flesh softening to accommodate his impacting hardness. Her surrender blazed through his nerves. But it was certainty that singed his every cell.

This. This was *her* unforgotten feel and taste, *her* inimitable delight. This *was* her.

The beast that had been perpetually clawing inside him finally tore free. It devoured her, everything inside him roaring with remembrance. Of every minute of deprivation of the five years after she'd left him. Craving more. Needing closure.

Then it swelled. Disgust. With himself. Over the only weakness he'd ever suffered, this susceptibility to her. It towered, then crashed, made him tear his lips from hers, push away from the body that had seemed to melt into his every recess.

Stumbling back at the abruptness of his withdrawal, she leaned against the nearest wall, the only discernible reaction to his explosive kiss her faster breathing.

Then, through those lips he'd just ravished, her voice washed over him, calm, collected...but *hers* at last.

"What gave me away?"

Two

"Everything."

The word boomed in the silence of the garden house. Its reverberations hung in the charged air between them, dripping with bitterness, heavy with five years of unresolved anger.

Not even a blip in her gaze or posture demonstrated any agitation. Only a slight tremor of her now-swollen lips betrayed any reaction to his fury. One that stilled at once, making him think he'd imagined it.

Which he probably had. Meeting him hadn't fazed her at all. And why should it have? She'd come to the ball knowing she'd see him. It was he who'd gotten the shock of his life.

Then, as calmly, she said, "We both know that can't be true. Not even I recognize the woman who looks back at me in the mirror as myself."

She was right. Even on such close-up inspection, there wasn't the least trace of his treacherous lover in her. He'd changed his looks to eliminate perfect resemblance to his old self, but she had totally different facial features and bone structure. Even her complexion looked different. Hannah had had alabaster skin, the kind he'd thought would burn, not tan. But this Scarlett's tan looked effortless, her skin even, velvet honey. And the deep shade of burgundy of her hair looked natural, too, when Hannah had been an equally convincing platinum blonde. All those changes were certainly artificial, even if their result looked 100 percent real. The only changes that could be natural were her body's. Maturity and heels could account for the appreciation in her curves and height.

But all in all, this woman bore no resemblance to the one who'd been in his bed every day of those five months, whose every inch he'd memorized and worshipped.

He cocked his head at her, drenching her from head to toe in disdain. "I assume this is my money's worth? This total and undetectable transformation?"

Her expression remained tranquil, assessing him back. "I wouldn't call it undetectable. At least, not anymore. You detected me." She let out a conceding sigh. "I did have some incredibly costly surgeries to reconfigure my face from the bone structure up. And though your money did foot the bills, along with the other cosmetic and stylistic measures needed to complete the transformation, not even all that cost anywhere near fifty million dollars. The whole thing cost around two million. A couple more financed the creation of my new identity with a whole history and paper trail for it."

"So you still have millions to spare. Or did you invest those into billions? Was that how you got into Hiro's inner circle, through the doors only that kind of money opens?"

Her lashes lowered before rising to strike him with a flash of azure. "I sort of…crashed my way into that."

His simmering blood tumbled in a boil. "So you're still using your old tried-and-true methods."

"Why change what works?" Suddenly her expression became distant, as if reversing into the past to the crash she'd manufactured to enter *his* life. "It was a different sort of crash." Her eyes refocused on him, resumed being supremely placid. "Even if just as effective. But though I put your money to the best use possible, alas, the Midas touch that turns millions into ever-increasing billions remains firmly yours."

Teeth gritting, he bunched hands stinging with the need to grab her again at his sides. "You seem very much at ease with divulging your machinations and secrets now."

A graceful shoulder rose in an easy shrug. "You already found me out. And I'm still waiting to hear how you did."

"It was your eyes."

Those eyes filled with mock reprimand. "They were what I worked on most, so I'm pretty sure they're unrecognizable."

"I recognized the color."

"You can't possibly have recognized me from just that."

"It's a unique color, and changes hue in as unique a way. I used to be fascinated by its fluctuations, thought they corresponded to shifts in your emotions. Then I found out you have none, and those were just a response to variations in lighting."

A still moment, then a tinge of sarcasm entered those eyes that *were* totally different, yet, to him, somehow exactly the same. "Are you telling me I owe being exposed to a fixation you had with my eye color and some trick of light I wasn't even aware of? And you're sticking with that story?"

"I *felt* you."

His hiss wiped the provocation off her face. She'd cornered him into admitting her relentless hold over him, and that even without evidence, he'd always know her.

Now that the admission was out, he might as well go all the way. "I felt you before I turned to see you on Hiro's arm. Not even millions of dollars' worth of permanent disguise was able to wipe off the inimitable imprint you left on my senses." He cocked his head, his gaze spearing hers. "How about that story? You find it more plausible? More satisfactory?"

Her gaze had emptied, and now her voice followed suit. "I had no idea I'd left such an indelible mark. It's why I thought it okay to come here tonight. I thought there was no danger you'd sense the least familiarity, let alone recognize me outright. I met many people who knew me well in my previous...incarnations, and none even felt any vague resemblance."

"I'm not 'people.'"

Her nod conceded that. "I know in *your* previous incarnation you were said to have senses so acute, it made you a ninja in a class of your own. I couldn't tell if those reports were exaggerations. Now I know they weren't."

"You had reason to believe they were outright lies, with the way said senses were disabled around you. I had no inkling of your deceit for five straight months of ultimate intimacy."

Her fixed glance remained unchanged as her head tilted to one side, sending the curtain of her loose silk curls swishing over her polished shoulder. "Speaking of that, I always wondered what finally gave me away *that* time."

He was damned if he'd give her the satisfaction, and the security, of knowing it had been total chance that had finally alerted him, and not his allegedly infallible abilities.

"You want to find out so you'll never repeat the lapse,

hone your deception powers to perfection? Sorry, you'll have to keep on wondering. And worrying."

"Oh, I never worry. Even in the rare times I slip up, I always manage to compensate. As I did when I pre-empted you."

How she'd realized he'd found her out back then had remained a major question mark. Needing an answer to it had even outstripped his need to find his lineage in the past years.

Wrestling with the urge to pounce on her and force her to tell him now, he tried to match her nonchalance. "And now? How will you preempt me this time?"

A sigh accompanied a regretful shake of that elegant head. "It really would have been better for everyone if you didn't recognize me."

"Everyone meaning you."

"Everyone meaning everyone. Starting by you."

A vicious huff crackled from his depths. "You're im-plying knowing your real identity poses danger to me, too?"

"It poses danger to you…only." Before he processed that outrageous statement, she added, "And you don't know my real identity."

Giving in, he obliterated the distance he'd put between them. He needed a physical reinforcement of his domi-nance, feeling he was on the losing side of this confron-tation.

He regretted it the moment he drew his next breath. Though she'd been so thorough in her disguise to the point of changing the soap and perfume she'd used be-fore, her own scent deluged him, even through the mask-ing of new adornments. Hot, vital, intoxicating. The exact bouquet that had been the only one to activate his libido.

Glaring down at her, as if it would shift the balance of

power in his favor, he said, "I know this one is fabricated. As was the one before it. Which should be enough. So explain to me how this knowledge, when it's clearly a secret you've kept from everyone here, wouldn't impact you."

"It *would* cause me intense inconvenience. But it's you who stands to suffer major damage if you expose me." Before he scoffed at that preposterous declaration, she asked, "But really, why would you want to expose me at all?"

"To stop you from setting Hiro up."

After a moment, when it looked as if she didn't get his meaning, incredulity coated her face. "What makes you think I'm doing any such thing? Because you consider I set *you* up?"

"And you don't? What do you call what you did to me?" He waved, stopping any argument in its tracks. Haggling over facts turned them into points of view that could be contested and rewritten. And he was damned if he'd let her do that. "Whatever you're doing, it's criminal."

"Because I'm withholding my real identity? Pot calling the kettle black much?" Her full lips twisted. "And if you're citing my past actions in your unsubstantiated accusations, I did nothing criminal with you. I actually... helped you."

It was his turn to cough in disbelief. "Sure, by systematically deceiving me for five months, then leaving a fifty-million-dollar gaping hole in my liquid assets. I bet that's every man's idea of 'help.'"

"It isn't a crime to con a con man. I was sent to expose an assassin who was posing as a squeaky-clean businessman. The only crimes were in *your* past, not mine."

He gaped at her, astounded all over again. Even after he'd found out she'd conned him, after she'd blackmailed him, he'd thought she'd held her own with him only because he'd been in a precarious position, and more important, because they'd had their confrontation over the phone. If they'd been face-to-face, he'd always thought she wouldn't have been able to maintain her poise.

But this woman with the steely self-possession could stare down the scariest monsters he'd ever dealt with and not turn a hair. If she could hold him at a disadvantage with such effortlessness when he'd thought she would be vulnerable and off balance, no one else would stand a chance against her.

He shook his head. "I didn't choose my old persona. It wasn't the real me. This new one I created is. I bet you can't say the same about yourself. So whatever you call what you do for a living, I call you a professional fraud, out of choice. And whatever elaborate deception you're perpetrating now, I will stop you. I let you get away with deceiving me once. I'm not letting you get away with anything again."

He'd let his lethal side surface as he talked. Expecting exposure to it to shake her at last, he was again amazed when she met his menace head-on.

"You can only 'stop' me if you expose me. And you can't, because it would mean exposing yourself."

He coughed in incredulity. "Are you threatening me?"

"*You're* the one who's threatening to strike me down like your old code name. I'm just pointing out that your righteousness is blinding you to the fact that it's in your best interests to keep my secrets. Why do you think I was so free with them?"

"Because you think I can't do anything with what I know?"

"Not if you want what *I* know to remain buried."

"You *are* threatening me, then."

Something like exasperation tinged her gaze. "I once promised I'd never hold my knowledge over you, and I remain at my word." When he glowered at her, failing to find any words to express what collided inside his head and chest, she exhaled. "Listen, Raiden, you're the one who can create this impasse, and you mustn't. Not when you're mere steps from attaining the family and the status you've craved all your life."

His heart convulsed. She knew this?

Though it shocked him, it stood to reason. Through his obliviousness, his misplaced trust, this woman had somehow once found out his every secret. It must have been easy for someone of her shrewdness to extrapolate his life goals and future plans. Now that she knew the arrangement he had with Megumi and her father, as it had been announced in society already, the details must have been as obvious to her.

It made sense, but it still galled him that she knew so much about him when he knew nothing about her, except what she made him feel, how she still had such power over him.

As if reading his mind, something like gentle persuasion entered her gaze. "Whatever you feel about me, no matter your burning desire to punish me for my transgressions against you, I'm not worth tarnishing the perfect image you've worked so hard and long to create. And that would certainly happen if you expose me. For what would you say I blackmailed you for? You can't say that you succumbed to my blackmail, since it would make you look weak, or that you needed to hide something that badly. If you expose me anonymously, once the mess is out in the open, details have a way of surfacing, of becoming land mines you never know which step will set off."

Fury, and something else he hadn't felt since he was a child—futility—mushroomed inside him.

Everything she'd said was true. Any action against her now, in this delicate time, would have consequences, and the fallout would inescapably harm him. If not now, then later. Whatever impacted him, it would surely drag his brothers in by association. So he couldn't act on the burning desire to punish her, as she'd so accurately put it.

When he made no response, she prodded, that same chafing gentleness in her tone. "Why don't you let me be and go about your business? Your wedding and adopting your family name are just over two months from now, and you can't afford to let anything sabotage that."

She was right again. Damn her.

But there was one thing he wasn't backing down from. "I will let you be, on one condition. That you keep away from Hiro. I'm not letting you exploit him as you did me."

It seemed he had finally managed to surprise her. Her eyes, those eyes that in spite of everything he wanted to drown in, widened. "You're really worried about him? I thought, as his number one rival, you'd welcome whatever misfortune befell him."

"I certainly wouldn't. I fight my adversaries with merit. I wouldn't want to win dishonorably."

"It wouldn't be dishonorable if someone else felled him for you."

"It would be if I knew of his jeopardy and looked the other way. And I won't."

"This *is* about honor, isn't it? You're really taking integrating into your new society to the limit, huh?"

"You may never understand what honor is, but it's the most important thing to me, and I would do anything to satisfy mine. Even if it means risking my plans."

He held her incandescent gaze as it fluctuated through

the range of blue-and-violet spectrum in the softly shifting lights. He imbued his own with his contempt, and his conviction.

She finally shook her head. "You don't have to do that. And you don't have to worry about Hiro. I'd never hurt him."

A skewer twisted in his gut. The way she'd said that... That look in her eyes... It was as if she truly cared for Hiro.

Then the icicles of memory sank into his core, numbing the ache. She'd once looked at him with the same profound emotions. Her ability to project genuineness was unheard of. She could be doing the same now. She must be.

"I can almost see you rejecting what I just said as more fraud." Her eyes were opaque, her voice hushed. "I can't do anything about that, but I can about something else. Before anyone realizes you're here with me, leaving your fiancée back there, and you cause yourself unneeded scandal, I'll do you a favor and do what you seem unable to do. I'll walk away. Let me do that and you can forget all about me again."

With that, she strode to the door she'd entered from. At the threshold, she paused, turned, and the crisp night wind blew her hair toward him like tongues of flame.

Before he could storm after her as every cell in his body was screaming for him to, her voice carried to him across the still warmth, lilting, husky, exactly what had poured into his brain on their transfiguring nights of passion.

"You won't believe this either, Raiden, but it was... nice seeing you again. This time, I at least get to say goodbye."

* * *

Scarlett walked away steadily. Her five-inch heels clicked on the wooden bridge leading away from the garden house over the pond in a rhythmic, deliberate staccato.

Inside her, absolute chaos raged.

This confrontation with Raiden had been a total shock. It hadn't even been a possibility in her mind coming here.

When Hiro had called her a few hours ago, insisting that she attended this ball, she'd been loath to agree. Even with a new face and identity, she dreaded social functions and suffocated under scrutiny. Looking the way she did now, and being a gaijin, as foreigners were called in Japan, and Hiro's personal companion to boot, she'd been certain she'd be put under the microscope of public interest. But she'd agreed without letting Hiro know of her aversion. She'd do anything for him.

Then he'd told her he was sending her the dress he wanted her to wear, and her dormant curiosity had been roused. But it had been when she'd noticed he'd sounded nothing like his warmly indulgent and coolly humorous self, but nervous, urgent and sour, that she'd gently probed.

And he'd told her what he'd withheld from her for months—why he'd been holding this ball, and for whom. The woman he wanted. She'd become engaged to another, obeying her family's demands. He'd wanted to show her he wouldn't be mourning her loss, had an exotic beauty on whom to bestow the affections she'd rejected. Then he'd told her the name of the man he'd lost his woman to. Raiden.

After that, she'd been as anxious as he about this ball. During the past three years, after she'd resurfaced with her new identity, she'd seen Raiden many times, all from afar. He'd even been the indirect reason she'd come to Japan. Seeing him up close again was a whole different ball game, the anticipation eating her up with agitation and eagerness.

So she'd dressed up as Hiro had wanted, played the role he'd wanted her to play when he'd taken her to Raiden and his fiancée. Empathy at Hiro's suffering at Megumi's sight had been intensified by her upheaval at Raiden's nearness. Seeing him face-to-face had felt like a direct blow to the heart.

But she'd played her part for Hiro's sake, and had almost sagged in his stiff hold when he, too, hadn't been able to bear Megumi's nearness any longer and cut their confrontation short. She'd thought that had been it.

Not for a second had she considered Raiden might see any similarity between the new her and the casually dressing, flat shoe–wearing, slim blonde he'd once known. So even when she'd felt him following her, she'd thought he'd been pursuing Hiro's new romantic interest. The Raiden she'd known wouldn't have struck at an adversary that way, but then he could have changed since she'd betrayed him.

Then he'd confronted her, and every meticulously erected pillar maintaining her cohesion had crumbled in shock.

But she'd been trained too well, through too many brutal tests. She'd acted her way to perfection through her life's worst situations. And she'd had plenty of nightmarish ones. None, however, had ever affected her as her time with Raiden had.

In the garden house, she'd still fallen back on her failsafe maneuvers, trapping her agitation in her deepest recesses, plastering one of her automated reaction modes on the surface. But then he'd taken her in his arms, drowned her in a kiss that had dissolved the last vestiges of her facade. And she'd given up the pretense.

What had followed had been agonizing. But she hoped she'd maintained a semblance of indifference all through.

One thing held her together now as she walked away from Raiden. Knowing that he'd heed her warning and leave her alone. She'd never see or hear from him again. Or if she did, he'd pretend she was the total stranger he'd just met tonight.

Not that he didn't hate it. She'd felt him seething to obey the urge to do her major damage, equivalent to what he considered she'd caused him. She could feel his gaze on her all the way to the mansion's entrance, bombarding her with his pent-up rage and contempt.

By the time she reached one of Hiro's limos, she'd expended the last of her balance. After forcing her rented apartment's address in Shibuya out of unsteady lips to the unknown driver, she flopped back in her seat, her nerves in pieces, her muscles like trembling jelly.

Exhaling forcibly to expel her agitation, she tried to luxuriate in the sights of Tokyo at night. The city was one of the most exotic and exciting places she'd ever been, and her life had taken her almost everywhere.

She soon gave up, resigned she'd see nothing during the hour's drive but Raiden's magnificent, wrathful face. Would feel nothing but regurgitated turmoil and searing memories.

Had it really been five years? The insane whirlpool of events as she'd reinvented herself since made her feel as if it had been fifty years. But his memory was so intense, it could have been five days since she'd last seen him. She hadn't forgotten a thing about him. His beauty was as indescribable as she remembered, and his effect on her was as overpowering.

When she'd been sent to spy on him, all she'd known was that he was an American billionaire venture capitalist of Japanese origins. His business past was impeccable and his personal one unremarkable, having been born to a single mother who'd died when he'd been ten, placing him in the foster system until he'd been eighteen. Then he'd traveled the world before coming back to the States at twenty-six, and he'd been soaring through the venture capitalism field since. He'd been twenty-nine when she'd met him and already a billionaire. Now at thirty-four, he was at the undisputable top, with a handful of others, one of whom was Hiro.

But her recruiter was convinced Raiden was a former assassin, and had sent her to get intimate with Raiden and get solid proof. And she had. Through the full access Raiden had given her to his domain, she'd used her special training to breach his secret records and gotten that proof.

But it had been years of research later that had put together his real life story. What he himself hadn't known when he'd been with her. It had been just months ago that she'd worked out just how he'd become that ninja assassin called Lightning.

He'd been two when he'd lost his family in an earthquake and tsunami that hit the rural Akita Prefecture in Japan. Taken to a shelter in the aftermath, he'd remained there for two years until his extraordinary agility had brought him to the attention of a "recruiter" for The Organization, a shadow operation that took children and turned them into unstoppable mercenaries who executed top-risk operations for the highest bidders. Pretending she was a relative, the recruiter had taken him only to sell him to The Organization.

He'd been among hundreds of boys taken from all over the world, kept segregated in a remote area in the Balkans, viciously trained and molded until they graduated to fieldwork. They performed missions under strict surveillance from their personal handlers. Death was the only punishment for any attempts at subordination or escape. But he'd been one of a few who'd ever escaped. She suspected some or even all of his partners in Black Castle Enterprises were also escapees.

She'd often wondered if he'd called himself Raiden, the god of thunder and lightning in Japan, to reflect his code name when he'd been the ultimate ninja warrior, so certain no one would ever tie him to his former identity. His cover *was* ingenious, after all, and it *was* a common enough name. As for Kuroshiro, that literally meant Black Castle. She'd also wondered if he'd picked it after the name of his joint enterprise with his partners, or if they'd taken his....

Suddenly she almost spilled out of the limo. Her driver had opened her door. She hadn't even noticed they'd stopped.

Pulling herself together and out of the past, she thanked him, stepped out and walked into her building.

Looking around the chic foyer on her way to the elevator and her thirtieth-floor unit, she felt thankful all over again to Hiro for making it possible for her to be here.

When she'd first come to Japan just over a year ago and tried to rent a place, she'd learned what the Japanese phrase *hikoshi bimbo* meant. It literally meant "moving poor." The humongous sum of cash that renters had to dish out up front invariably left them impoverished.

Since she'd had no cash in any sums, it hadn't been an

option. After she'd met Hiro, and he'd discovered she'd been sleeping on the floor of the UNICEF regional office where she worked, he'd been appalled and insisted on accommodating her.

She'd refused to stay in his mansion, since being in someone's debt and in their domain was anathema to her. Autonomy and seclusion were a vital necessity to her. She'd also declined the exorbitant apartment he'd gotten her near his home. He'd protested that he had billions, was still around to spend them only thanks to her. She'd argued that even if the place came for free, it was too far from her work downtown.

In the end, he'd still gotten her a "mansion," as recently built large apartments were called in Tokyo. The place was expensive, but now that she did some part-time consulting work for him, she could accept the home in lieu of a salary.

She now entered the apartment, sighed in pleasure at feeling cocooned in its sound-insulated exquisite mixture of modern and traditional Japanese ambiance. Kicking off her towering sandals, she moaned in relief as her feet flattened against the *tatami,* the traditional Japanese flooring made of rice straw with a covering of soft, woven *igusa* straw. Walking on it was physiotherapy all unto itself.

Tossing her wrap onto the coat rack, she wanted only to fall facedown on her equally therapeutic traditional Japanese bed and descend into a deep coma. It was a small blessing she had no work tomorrow.

Hopefully, after a day in her pajamas, she'd regain a semblance of the normalcy she'd worked so hard to achieve. A normalcy that seeing Raiden had pulverized all over again.

Crossing the living room on her way to her bedroom,

she suddenly stopped when an electrifying sensation skittered up her spine. All her senses went haywire, telling her she wasn't alone. Before they could tell her more, a voice came from behind her, sending her every cell screaming.

"Welcome home, darling."

Three

Her heart lodged into her throat, fright mingling dizzyingly with incredulity, dismay…and exhilaration.

Raiden.

He was here.

Feet away… Inches away… A breath away now.

Every nerve in her body fired in remembrance, in jubilation at the approach of the essence that had once been as familiar to her as her own. For five blazing months of pure passion and pleasure, before she'd had to sever the bond. She'd been bleeding inwardly ever since.

She had no idea how he was here. But from what she'd learned about him, in her constant search for his news, in her obsessive research of his past, she knew one thing. Raiden could do anything.

As to why he was here, did it matter? It was one more chance to be close to him. A chance that she'd thought she'd never be given again. An unexpected, priceless gift.

That, she knew, was the last thing he wanted to give her. Judging from his tone, dripping in bitter sarcasm and suppressed aggression, he probably wanted to give her five to ten, minimum.

In fact, logically speaking, he should be here to… eliminate her danger. She was the only one who possessed detailed knowledge of the secrets he'd gone to unimaginable lengths to bury. Her existence posed a threat not only to the persona he'd built and the plans he'd worked for since he'd escaped The Organization, but to his very life.

But though he'd assassinated countless people, and she probably deserved to be, in his opinion, she didn't fear for a second that was why he was here. This lethal man with the staggering body count in his past didn't scare her at all.

Not that anything did. With the kind of existence she'd had, she'd never valued her life enough to be afraid for it. The only true fear she'd ever felt had been on his behalf.

"Feet aching, my love?"

Nostalgia skewered through her, made her squeeze her eyes, bite down on the moan that almost escaped her lips.

Welcoming her home, calling her "my darling" and "my love"… They were the same phrases he'd greeted her with that last time in his penthouse in New York five years ago. It had been the first time he'd said things like that…out of bed.

It had been then she'd realized he'd decided to take their relationship to the next level. And that she'd soon be forced to put an end to it.

Unable to face putting a time frame on "soon," that night she'd thrown herself into being with him with all the passion he'd ignited inside her, gulping down every second as if each had been her last ever. But even in her worst nightmares she hadn't expected they would be that for real, that the very next day it would come to such a jarring and dreadful end.

After it had, she'd had no doubt it would remain over.

Then came tonight. Then now. And the bridge into the past she'd thought had burned to ashes had somehow been rebuilt. Because she seemed to have branded him as he'd done her.

He'd already told her that it had been how he'd recognized her in someone else's body. Which flabbergasted her. Even if he'd formed an emotional attachment to her in the past, it had been to the persona she'd played. She'd thought that if he remembered her at all since, it would be with rage and repugnance. She'd never thought he'd obsess over her in any other way.

But by reciting the exact words he'd said that last time they'd met as lovers, he was letting her know he had. From the way he'd drawled the memorized words, he was also letting her know such a hold over him made it more imperative to him to exact revenge for every wrong she'd dealt him, with five years' worth of compound interest.

She would have let him, if it were only she who'd pay the price. But he was in a far more sensitive position than she was. Any impulsive actions would harm him far more than her. And she couldn't let him do this to himself. Not after what she'd done to protect him. She would protect him again, at any cost, even from himself.

It was time to do so, to end this, and this time, make sure it was over for good.

Feeling the heat of his body radiating at her back, tasting the intoxication of his breath as it filled her lungs, she turned slowly, carefully. Her balance was already compromised, and she didn't want to end facedown at his feet instead of on the bed as she'd previously planned.

She almost did so anyway when she laid eyes on him.

Earlier tonight, she'd realized he'd done the impossible, had become even more magnificent than he'd been, his assets having appreciated with maturity, and would no doubt continue to do so. He'd become a god for real, not just in name.

But now… It shouldn't be possible, but he looked even more awe striking than he had an hour ago.

He'd taken off his tuxedo jacket, undid his bow tie and a few shirt buttons, exposing a tantalizing expanse of the burnished flesh beneath. His muscled shoulders and chest seemed wider with just a sheer layer of silk covering them, and in contrast with the now-apparent sparse hardness of his abdomen. And if he looked like this with clothes still on, she didn't want to dwell on the details of his upgrades with them off.

But it was his face that as usual arrested her. His hair was no longer meticulously groomed, the raven-wing, rain-straight locks slightly mussed. It gave him a wild, raw look that made his heart-stopping cheekbones even more prominent, his slanting caramel eyes even more fiery, his sculpted lips more erotic and his chiseled jaw more rugged.

His whole package was enough to compromise her sanity. Not that she'd ever had much to speak of where he was concerned. And that was on the mental and emotional level. On the physical one, just being around him, just thinking of him, made her melt, throb…ache. Her body had been hammering at her, demanding his since she'd laid eyes on him across the ballroom tonight.

His answering appraisal made her core simmer. Then the velvet depths of his baritone drawl almost made it combust.

"Your surgeon didn't only make you a totally different woman, but the most beautiful model possible, too."

She met the eyes that flayed her with contempt with a look of long-perfected equanimity. Even as her insides raged, she injected her voice with the same inexpression.

"Surgeons, in the plural. This result is a collaborative

effort, performed over many stages. But it was I who provided them with this 'model.' I needed to be beautiful."

"You were always beautiful."

Her heart forgot a few beats before it resumed sputtering. Outwardly, she knew he'd see no evidence of the effect his words had on her. "Nowhere like this."

"So you thought you needed to intensify your beauty, to boost your effectiveness as a siren? I thought you'd know from intensive experience that outward beauty only lures men, but what traps them are the brains and wiles behind the looks."

"Since I have those, too, I more than ever have the perfect package." His gorgeous eyes narrowed, his edible lips filled, as if her brazenness aroused him even as it angered him. She pretended to sigh, but really expelled the air that clogged her lungs. "But beauty alone does open doors."

"Doors that might open into untold trouble."

She gave him her best self-assured glance. "True. To inexperienced innocents whose beauty is a bane that makes them a target for exploitation. I, on the other hand, am a seasoned professional who uses my assets as precisely as the situation necessitates. I downplay my looks or even negate them when I want to, and play them to maximum advantage when I need to."

The heat in his eyes rose, even as his expression became arctic. "It must be so freeing, being able to brag about your strategies with someone you've already played. Someone who can't share his insider knowledge with your future victims."

"No bragging involved. Just facts." Before he volleyed a response, she preempted him, turning the focus on him before her heart burst. "Now it's my turn to ask questions."

His lips twisted. "Since you must know everything about me, the only question left in your mind must be how I'm here."

"I do know everything about you," she conceded. "*But* that. So how did you manage to beat me here? And how are you inside my apartment without any sign of breaking and entry? Did you ninja scale your way up here to the thirtieth floor?"

"Contrary to movies, we ninjas don't perform death-defying feats just because we can. We do go for the path of least resistance whenever possible."

"I don't remember ever seeing a ninja bribe a concierge."

"I didn't do that, either." Before she made another comment, he raised his hand, his eyes reflecting his mirthless smile. "I won't tell you how I arrived before you, or how I came in, so save your breath. I'm through sharing secrets with you. And you're finding out no more on your own, either."

She held his gaze. Before she melted into a puddle at his feet, she said, "I bet you didn't sample any of Hiro's first-class sushi or sip his fine *shochu*. I didn't."

His eyes widened at her sharp detour. Before he could adjust, she turned and crossed to her kitchen.

Once there, she looked back over her shoulder. "Seems this is going to be a long night. Want to eat something?"

Raiden watched the one woman he'd been truly intimate with sashay away in that stranger's body.

And his own body roared in unremitting rage…and hunger.

She'd walked away earlier saying, "Forget all about me again." As if he'd ever forgotten about her at all.

But it had been the sane thing to do, to heed her advice. To go back to the ball and his fiancée, to his plans and life, and forget that she existed. Because she in fact never did. Her current identity was just another fictitious figment that would disappear without a trace soon enough, once she'd gotten whatever she was after here. She'd done it once before when he'd been of no further use to her.

But there was nothing sane about what she made him feel. Never had been, and, it was clear by now, never would be. Renewed exposure to her had caused the fever in his blood to relapse as if it had never subsided at all. As it never had.

The need to have it all out with her ate through his restraint. He'd only ever had speculations about her, didn't have a single fact to quench the maddening thirst to know the truth.

But if he and his brothers had wiped their pasts and created new, perfectly verifiable identities, she'd far surpassed their combined undercover prowess. What they'd done only once, she'd done so many times she seemed to have never had an original identity.

As for their time together, which had scarred him in a way not even his nightmarish existence before it had managed to, he had only theories, no real answers to satisfy the gnawing uncertainty that never stopped asking how. Why?

Now he needed to know the truth.

Though he was certain she'd kept her end of the bargain, since there'd been no hint of suspicion in his identity, he needed to know everything to guard against any breach like hers ever happening again.

Or that was what he'd told himself as he'd torn his way over here. That it was a necessity, a prophylactic measure.

Slow steps finally took him to the semi–open plan

kitchen. He found her flitting around, her hair up in a wonderfully messy mass.

As soon as he entered, she looked over her shoulder again, nodding toward the island. "Pull up a chair. I won't be long."

He walked up to her instead, struggled not to pull her back against his aching body.

She continued to work with fast, precise movements, pausing only when he tucked a lock of hair that had fallen over her shoulder back into her impromptu hairdo.

He bent, murmured in her ear, "Don't you think it weird, with our history, for you to be inviting me to a meal?"

She straightened, continued to work with renewed zeal. "Why? I invited you to meals before."

And he'd thought everything she'd served him had been ambrosia. "You were someone else then. Actually you weren't someone at all, just a role. One that necessitated satisfying my every hunger to mollify me enough so you could dupe me. Which you did. No more reason for you to feed me."

She flashed him another look over her shoulder that struck his heart like a bolt, before resuming work. "It's the least I can do after I made a fifty-million-dollar-shaped hole in your pocket."

"A fifty-million-dollar meal, eh?" He stepped away before he lost the battle and devoured her instead of the painfully tasty-smelling concoctions she was preparing. He walked back to the island, pulled out a stool and leaned his itching hands on the marble counter. "It had better be *really* good."

"Of course it will be."

There she went again with that supreme assurance. She'd never displayed anything near it in the past.

But then it hadn't been the real her he'd known. She'd been playing the part of the part-time florist and kindergarten teacher who'd been out of her league in his world. In reality, with everything he was, everything he'd seen and done, the reverse might turn out to be true.

She now placed a plate heaped with triple the amount of hers before him, before taking a seat across from him.

He continued watching her, wondering if this was the real her this time, or if it was just another role.

She raised one elegant eyebrow. "You're starving. Eat."

A huff escaped him. She just kept surprising him with every word and action. "And you know that how?"

She pushed the cutlery pointedly at his hands. "Because I calculated that you haven't eaten in at least six hours. I first saw you tonight five hours ago, and you hadn't eaten at least an hour before that. I remember you needed to eat every three hours, with the level of exercise you maintained, and that nuclear metabolism of yours. You seemed to eat almost half my body weight every day. With your increased body mass, you must be in the red by now."

He was. In every way. And he hadn't eaten since breakfast. He'd thought his appetite, which nothing had ever affected except her, had been stalled anticipating the ball. Seemed it had been an advance alarm. He had been anticipating *her*.

She started eating, and he gave in, followed suit.

The moment the thing he was eating hit his taste buds, an involuntary growl of hunger and appreciation rolled from his gut. "What *is* that?"

"Nasu dengaku."

"What?"

Her lips twitched. "You don't know your Japanese cuisine, do you?"

His gaze clung to her lips as her expression filled with what looked like unguarded humor. But it couldn't be. This enigma probably was incapable of spontaneity.

Compressing his lips, he suppressed the moronic impulse to smile back. "I only look Japanese, remember? I spent my first twenty-four years as an identity-less weapon, then when I got out, I became American. I learned everything I could about Japan before I came, but nothing can replace acquiring knowledge firsthand."

She nodded as she chewed, her brilliant eyes doing this hypnotic color dance. "It is a very complex country and culture. Such an extensive mix of modern and traditional, so many regional variations. You'll need at least six months before you're used to the most common daily practices, and a year to comfortably navigate the land and society."

If he didn't know better, he would have thought she was giving him sincere advice to ease his integration into his new homeland. But he did know better.

So what was she doing? No doubt more acting.

The acute senses that had never failed him clamored to detect her duplicity. But she was truly undetectable.

He exhaled. "Are you talking from firsthand experience?"

"I have been here just over a year now." Her gorgeous head inclined, and her deep red silky hair sparked fire in the overhead halogen spotlights. "Bear in mind, it might be years before you can fully integrate. Good news is, speaking fluent Japanese *will* shorten and ease the process. It did for me."

She'd never let on she understood a word of Japanese.

"I have more factors to shorten and ease the process. I will have a Japanese wife. Something you didn't have."

"I certainly didn't have a Japanese wife."

He held those teasing eyes, and the urge to ask became irresistible. Not one of the dozens of relevant questions, but the one that blocked his throat like a burning coal.

"Is any of this—" he made an encompassing gesture at her "—real? I know your past self was all an act. Is this new persona all a part of your new act?"

Instead of answering with the same directness she had till now, her eyes lowered to her plate as she resumed eating.

He ate, too, because the food was just too delicious and he was famished, and because her silence made him feel as he imagined people did when waiting for a heart-stopping twist in a movie, increasing their popcorn munching in anticipation.

Then she raised her eyes. "I never really acted with you. Apart from the pretense that I was someone... normal, with what that entailed of prefabricated and rehearsed details, everything else—my actions, my characteristics, what I said to you, what I did with you—that was all the real me."

His heart went off like a clap of thunder in his chest. "Yeah, sure."

She nodded, as if accepting his ridicule. "You asked, and I answered. You're free to take my answer or leave it."

"I'll leave it, if it's all the same to you."

"It is."

He just bet it was.

After wolfing down the last piece of mystery food on his plate, he looked up at her again. "So what was that I just polished off? This *nasu dengaku?*"

"It's grilled aubergine slices marinated in a mix of *hacho-miso* and *shiro-miso* pastes, and covered with ginger and toasted sesame seeds. It's one of my favorite dishes."

"And it just became one of mine." He sat back in his chair. "Anything else to eat? Though it was great, it has nowhere enough calories for my so-called nuclear metabolism."

"Of course. That was just the appetizer."

With that she rose, and went about preparing and serving him two more courses and dessert.

All through, he struggled not to become submerged in the surreal feeling that this was the same woman he'd once wanted with everything in him, that he was sharing with her a warm, intensely enjoyable meal at home. The one thing that kept yanking him out of this false scenario was that he was getting hungrier. For her.

Before that hunger overpowered him, he rose to help her clear the kitchen. After everything had been washed, dried and put away, he turned to her.

"That was unexpected, and unnecessary, and certainly not what I came for. But thanks anyway."

"*That* was appalling." She wrinkled her nose. "You owe me no thanks, and you wouldn't thank me even if I save your life now. But I believe you *were* trying to be gracious, and it only came out the opposite."

"I wasn't aiming at graciousness. As you pointed out, I owe you none."

"But you owed it to your fiancée and Hiro, and you were even worse with them. And that won't work if you want to integrate into Japanese high-class society then take it over. Politeness is paramount here, and the higher you go in society, the more vital it becomes. If you can't *act* gracious with your fiancée and the man holding the ball celebrating your engagement, you're in deep trouble."

"Spoken as the ultimate actress that you are. Maybe I should get lessons from you."

"Maybe you should."

Their gazes collided and wrestled for a long minute.

Before he did what he knew he'd regret, he finally asked the question he'd told himself he'd come here to ask.

"Earlier you said you were sent to expose me as an assassin. Explain."

She gave a dismissing shrug. "What is there to explain?"

"Everything."

"Again? I don't have time for your sweeping generalizations right now. So just narrow down what you want to know, please."

Fighting the urge to roar, he hissed, "Who sent you?"

"Boris Medvedev."

That her response was so immediate, so succinct, would have shocked him all on its own. But that name struck him like a hammer to the temple. It made him stumble back a step.

Medvedev. His personal handler, who'd been assigned to him when he'd been ten. Raiden had spent fourteen horrific years under that man's sadistic eye and lash.

Medvedev had been punished, brutally, when he'd "lost" Raiden. All the handlers had been, when each of his Black Castle brothers had escaped. His brother Rafael had been agonized to know that, as he'd considered his handler, Richard, his mentor. Raiden, however, had been viciously glad that Medvedev had been the most punished and demoted. He owed that man a debt of pain and humiliation nothing could ever satisfy.

But Medvedev wasn't only a sadist, he was an obsessive. It had been what had made Raiden's escape the hardest. And while all their handlers had been sent in search of them, he bet it was Medvedev who'd kept looking after everyone had given up, needing to take his revenge. And most important, to reinstate himself. Though Medvedev had been another abductee of The Organization, he'd suffered from Stockholm syndrome and had integrated totally with his captors. The Organization, and his position within it, was everything to him.

But Raiden had thought even Medvedev had given up the search eventually. He'd underestimated his obsession. And his knowledge of him. His former handler knew him so well he'd suspected his new persona.

But suspicion wouldn't have sufficed. Only solid proof would have been good enough to take to The Organization, that Raiden Kuroshiro, the heavily documented pillar of a global conglomerate like Black Castle Enterprises, was the operative who'd escaped them. Escaped *him*.

So five years ago Medvedev had hired *her,* no doubt the absolute best he could find, to bring him that proof. And she'd found it.

But since Medvedev hadn't made a move since, it was proof she'd upheld her end of the bargain. But now that he knew Medvedev had been her recruiter, he couldn't understand how she had.

He looked at her in renewed confusion. "Medvedev was obsessed with me. He must have watched your every step during those five months, must have demanded regular reports of your progress, and evidence that you were on the right track."

Her eyes turned indigo. "I didn't give him any."

"And he kept financing the fictional life you led? For five months with no signs he might get his money's worth? And it would have been longer if I hadn't discovered you and you were forced to end the charade. Then when you struck your bargain with me, you told him I wasn't the one he thought, and he didn't suspect you'd decided it was more lucrative to work for yourself? Doesn't sound like him."

"I can be very convincing. As you very well know."

With that, it seemed she considered the conversation closed, and she walked past him on her way out of the kitchen. He caught her back to him, slammed her for the second time tonight against his length.

As her breath left her in a gasp that flayed his chest and neck, his hands tightened on her flesh. "I'm not done here."

Though she was much smaller now without those precarious heels and felt vulnerable in his grip, the entity that held his gaze was the most powerful presence he'd ever encountered.

Then she huskily said, "I am."

"Maybe you are, Scarlett, or Hannah, or whatever your real name is. But *we're* not done."

In one explosive movement fueled by five years of betrayal and frustration, he lifted her up onto the island, yanked up the flowing skirt of her black dress, exposing honey tanned legs and thighs, wrenched them wide apart and slammed between them.

He held her eyes for one last tempestuous moment. They all but screamed at him, *Do it!*

And he did. He lunged, crushed her beneath him, crashed his lips on hers.

Her cry went down his throat as he poured his growls down hers, his lips branding hers, his teeth sinking in their plumpness, his tongue filling her mouth, over and over, invading her, draining her. Her heat and taste and surrender were a sledgehammer to his remaining shell of reason.

His hands glided all over her silkiness, mad with re-membrance, sinking in her craved delights, seeking her every memorized trigger, until she writhed beneath him.

At her moan, he slid between her splayed legs down to her core. He nipped her intimate lips through her panties, making her cry out and convulse before he pulled them off with his teeth, his eyes never leaving hers. They'd always told him exactly how she'd felt, what she'd wanted. They'd been far more potent than any mind-altering drug. They still were, sending him clear out of his mind with lust.

She'd always been vocal, too, corroborating her eyes' confessions and demands. Now she said nothing. Yet her body spoke for her, her back arching deeply, legs trem-bling out of control, core weeping with arousal. She was so ready for him. As she'd always been. He'd always wondered if it had been part of her uncanny ability in subterfuge, if she had a trick to achieve such powerful arousals and orgasms every single time.

But it had felt real then. And it still did. Now she felt as desperate as he was, her body shuddering, her breath fracturing, her skin radiating heat, her core pouring its plea for his possession, its maddening scent perfuming the room, filling his lungs.

He rose between her legs, freeing his rock-hard erec-tion before pushing her knees back against her body, opening her fully for him.

Holding the eyes that had turned into cobalt infernos, without any preliminaries he rammed into her, all his power and pent-up hunger and anger behind the thrust.

Her cry at his abrupt invasion was a red-hot spear in his brain. Like a glove, her slick tightness yielded to his power, sheathed him, searing him with her fever, until he thought she'd burn him to ashes.

For delirious moments, he stilled inside her. This was the ultimate embrace he'd been going insane for. Everything he'd ever craved.

Then the urge to conquer her, to lose himself inside her crested again, and he withdrew, then plunged again and again, harder each time, faster. Her cries punctuated his thrusts. Every time he sank deeper, the need to breach her, to bury himself into her recesses, blinded him.

He lodged inside her to the root, and she arched in a deep bow, her inner muscles clamping his hardness in unbearable tautness, her face clenching in agonized urgency, her every muscle beneath and around him buzzing on the edge of a paroxysm. Another thrust would make her explode in release.

He gave it to her, with everything in him.

Her shriek pierced him as her core splintered around his girth and his body all but detonated in the most powerful orgasm he'd ever experienced, even with her. His roars echoed her desperation as his body caught the current of her convulsions. Excruciating pleasure shot through his length in jet after jet of white-hot release until he felt he'd drained his essence into her depths.

The world seemed to vanish as he slumped on top of her, nothing left but feeling her beneath him, still trembling, her core still milking him for every last drop of sensation.

In what could have been an hour, the arms and legs that lay nerveless with satiation around him started to tighten, as did the velvet gripping his erection.

She wanted more. She always had. Once had never been enough for her. Or for him. With her, he'd always wanted more, longer, harder, over and over.

Feeling disgusted with himself, he pulled out of her depths, yanked himself from her clinging limbs.

As soon as he stood up, she slipped off the counter, and the dress he'd only pushed out of the way to take her now tumbled down to cover her seminakedness. In seconds she looked as if nothing had happened.

Tearing his gaze away, he tugged his zipper closed and stuffed his shirt back into his pants in suppressed violence before he strode out to the living room to pick up his jacket.

At the door, he turned, found her standing in the distance, the face that had been gripped in feverish passion just minutes earlier a mask of inanimate beauty.

Flicking her one last contemptuous glance, he said, "Now we're done."

Four

Scarlett felt done in, done for. Just done.

As Raiden had said they were.

Last night, his explosive lovemaking—what she'd been yearning for for five interminable years—had inundated her with the physical satisfaction only he had ever given her. But she'd wanted more, far more. A whole night in his arms. A night of worshipping him and giving herself to him in the intimacy she'd only ever had with him, could never have with another. She'd wanted a new intense memory of him to help keep the frozen wasteland inside her from claiming the last flickering flame of life. What had sprung into existence in the first place because of him.

Keeping obsessive track of his news in the past years had been the one thing that had kept that flame from being extinguished. As long as he'd been safe and soaring from one success to a higher one, it had been enough to keep her going.

Then he'd taken her, what she'd never even dared dream would ever happen again. And as he'd filled her arms and body, his eyes burning her with his ferocious hunger, an insane hope had ignited among the hopelessness she'd been resigned to all her life. That she might have him again, without the need to hide anything from him, for a whole night. More, if he would allow it.

But that wasn't what it had been about for him.

He'd needed to get this, and her, out of his system. He'd needed the closure. Now that he had it, he'd finally move on. As she wanted him to. She'd never wanted anything but his peace.

But the way he'd ended the delirious interlude—with disgust, clearly at himself more than her...

Her phone rang. She grabbed for it, thankful for the distraction. It was Hiro. After he'd once kept insisting she was his hero, she'd laughingly told him she'd make his ringtone "I Need a Hero." She had.

Affection welled inside her, played on lips still stiff with Raiden's rejection as she hit Answer.

"I kissed Megumi."

After a moment's surprise at Hiro's blurted confession, she chuckled. "And I thought I'd be apologizing for leaving last night without telling you. Seems I did you a favor. The moment I left your side, you pursued your fantasy woman, got her alone and did what you should have done long ago."

"It's no laughing matter, Scarlett." Hiro sounded as if he'd suffer a heart attack any second now.

It never ceased to amaze her how the ruthless financial mogul could be so different on a personal level. With her, he had a center made of marshmallow. But when it came to Megumi, his insides were clearly more the consistency of Jell-O.

Not that anyone would believe it. The Japanese weren't given to expressing their emotions, even with their closest people. It was probably because she was a gaijin and a friend who had no contact with his close circle that Hiro felt safe to show her a side of him he'd never show his compatriots and kin. Of course, there was also that life-changing experience he'd shared with her, making her closer to him than almost everyone. Certainly closer than the woman of his dreams, whom he'd finally taken a step toward. If a very belated one.

Scarlett didn't understand why he'd never taken it before. He'd tell her why if and when he saw fit. Or not. She'd be there for him, as he was for her, no questions asked.

"I broke my code of honor. I compromised hers, showed her disrespect and exploited Kuroshiro's trust in accepting my tribute and bringing her to my home. It was a total disaster."

Hiro's deep voice was strangled, choking off the measure of joy his call had given her. He was really taking this badly, was calling to share his self-recriminations because they'd become too much for him to bear alone.

She wished she could tell him he should at least feel no remorse on Raiden's behalf. He had not only kissed *her* but had sex with her. But though Raiden was a major concern to him, what so agonized him was what he thought he'd done to Megumi.

Deciding to go for the heart of the matter, she asked, "Did she respond?"

That seemed to surprise him so much, it aborted his agitation, made him sound scandalized as he said, "Is that all you have to say? What's the difference if she did?"

"It makes all the difference. So did she?" Only his deep, disturbed breathing answered her. "Let me put it another way. Did she resist you?"

A heavy exhalation. "No. She melted in my embrace, as I always dreamed she would, gave me her lips to worship." An exasperated exhalation. "But that was no response."

She groaned. "Hiro, Hiro, don't you know anything about women at all? That *was* her response. Surrendering to you, letting you claim her as you will."

She'd done the same with Raiden. Heat surged through her with the memories of what Raiden had done to her, the unimaginable pleasure he'd given her when he'd taken her like that, devoured her without preliminaries, as if he couldn't wait, couldn't breathe if he didn't have her. It had always been intoxicating when she'd met him kiss for kiss, touch for touch, taken what she'd wanted, which had always been all of him. But her utmost pleasure had always been to submit to his dominance, as she had last night.

"But afterward, she looked…shocked."

She barely held back from moaning with the pangs of renewed hunger as she focused on her distressed friend. "Of course she did. You've never shown her signs you have emotions for her, then suddenly at her engagement party, you drag her aside and devour her."

"I did show her my emotions," Hiro protested. "Every time I saw her for the past six months. But my father was Yakuza, and I thought that might be why she'd never consider me."

That was the first time Hiro admitted his late father had been a member of the Japanese mafia, and she wouldn't probe further. "Did you make any actual advances before last night?"

"I invented ways to see her as frequently as I can."

"Did she realize that? Or did you hide your intentions so well, like you did last night, she didn't realize you set those events up with the sole purpose of seeing her?"

"She moves in completely different circles to mine, so I joined every society and charity she works with, when they're completely unrelated to my interests. She must have realized I only did that to see her. And I paid only her compliments. I also mentioned many times how I thought it was the perfect time to marry. It seemed she enjoyed my interest, encouraged it, and I was working up the nerve to go to her father with my proposal. Then a week ago, her engagement to Kuroshiro was announced, a man she met only days before. A man her father approves of."

So this was how recent this whole arrangement was.

She exhaled. "Listen, Hiro, the young woman I saw last night felt uncertain of herself in spite of her incredible beauty. She probably couldn't believe a man like you was interested in her. Maybe she needed a direct approach, not all those elaborate hints. I can tell you for sure that she was seriously agitated when you took me to her and…Mr. Kuroshiro."

"She didn't look agitated." His frown was clear in his tone.

"That goes to show you that you can't read her, and probably missed all the signs of her reciprocating interest. For she was certainly agitated, and it was because of you." She exhaled. "Seems this was a case of tragic miscommunication."

"And now it's too late," Hiro groaned. "I should have sought your counsel before and all this might have not happened. Now I've made it so much worse by kissing her. I'd hoped to continue to see her in a social setting, but now I won't be able to see her again at all. I've truly lost her."

Before she protested that he hadn't, she remembered. This was the woman Raiden would marry in ten weeks. Raiden *needed* to marry her, for a reason no one but she knew. And he wouldn't let anyone stand in his way. It was better for Hiro to forget about Megumi. For she *was* already lost to him.

She wished she could reach out through the phone and hug him. They had even more in common than she'd thought, wanting the one person they could never have. The irony was the two people they wanted would marry each other. But he was in an even worse situation, because he'd always pine for Megumi, think he might have had her if only he'd acted differently. She, on the other hand, had never entertained the possibility that she could have Raiden. The certainty of despair was better than agonizing what-ifs.

"I'm so sorry, Hiro." She groaned her pain on his behalf. "But if this is any consolation, I do believe Megumi reciprocated your feelings. From what I saw last night, I believe she would have chosen you if she could. I also don't think you compromised her honor or disrespected her when you kissed her. You simply let her know you wanted her for her, not for her family connections. That's a knowledge she'll treasure for the rest of her life."

After that, Hiro abruptly changed the subject, as if he couldn't bear talking about Megumi anymore but was too polite to just end the call. She did it for him, excusing herself to finish up her work. From the way he sounded as he said goodbye, it seemed she'd said all the right things to defuse his distress—only to substitute it with despondence.

But he would have gotten there on his own. Losing the only one you want was the most crushing experience one could suffer. She knew. For she'd had too many horrific experiences, and nothing had hit her harder than losing Raiden.

And there was nothing she could do about it. Not then, not now.

But she could do something about the report she was working on. She had to wrap up this last stage in her project, then she could leave Japan. After what had happened with Raiden, she couldn't stay any longer. It had been one thing to be in the same country as him, to know he was getting married, even see him from afar, when she'd thought he'd never recognize her. But now that he had, now that he'd reignited her, she couldn't bear to see him again if even by chance. She'd miss seeing Hiro regularly like crazy, but losing his constant presence in her life was a price she had to pay.

Right now, she had to finish setting up the shelters in Kyoto. She'd no longer stay to oversee them as she'd planned, so she had to have a system in place to make up for her absence.

To think of all the effort she'd done after she'd joined UNICEF, to come to Japan especially to set up branches of the aid organization in Tokyo. She'd long finished setting up the executive headquarters in downtown Tokyo, orchestrating relief, relocation and disaster-counseling services. She'd since been working on a few locations across Japan for shelters and rehabilitation centers for the children who'd lost family and survived trauma related to man-made crises and natural disasters, especially the most recent earthquake and tsunami. Now she'd have to drop everything and leave when she'd thought she'd stay for years to come. Her time here would be weeks at most now. Days if she could manage it.

Then she'd never be in danger of seeing Raiden again.

This time, it would be truly over.

Raiden stood gazing unseeingly from the window of his new headquarters overlooking downtown Tokyo, again trying to bring his rioting senses under control. And again he failed.

His fury was completely directed at himself. This time, she had nothing to do with any of it. It had been his fault alone that he'd succumbed to this sick need for her. Even knowing exactly what she was, or worse, not knowing anything about her, only that everything about her was a lie. And now he couldn't stop reliving every blazing moment of his possession of her.

One thing he had to admit: they were not done.

Having her once wasn't enough. He needed more. Had to have it. It was imperative he got her out of his system. And this wouldn't happen by walking away and trying to clobber that need into submission. It had been consuming him for five years, but after that maddening taste of her, the fire would only rage higher, burn his sanity to ashes faster.

There was one way this could end. If he gave in to his lust to the very end, bingeing on her until he was glutted.

And he had to do it now. He needed everything resolved before his wedding. He wasn't letting anything jeopardize his plans, starting with his own weakness. Everything he'd worked for the past ten years was at stake.

That was how long he'd been looking for his bloodline. Since his escape from The Organization. Not that he'd been doing nothing but. Since then he'd joined his brothers who'd escaped before him, and they'd set up Black Castle Enterprises together. It had taken some doing adjusting his literally deadly ninja methods to a figurative level in business. But searching for his family had remained a major concern. The one time he'd totally forgotten about his quest had been when he'd been with her in the past.

Finally, a couple of months back, with the benefit of

years of research and his brothers' help, especially the last bit of analysis Rafael Salazar had provided, he'd finally reconstructed who he was and how he'd been taken by The Organization.

But though The Organization itself had had no idea who his family was, he still couldn't let his family know that he was their long-lost relative. He was certain The Organization had never shelved his case and might put two and two together if his origins were made public. A child lost in a tsunami returning to such a well-known family as the Hashimotos as such a high-profile adult would no doubt trigger correct deductions.

He'd already had a brush with exposure five years ago. With Hannah…or Scarlett. Now that he knew it had been Medvedev on his trail, and she'd thrown him off once, it was more imperative than ever he maintained his secrecy, or risk arousing that monster's suspicions again.

And he also couldn't risk his newfound family finding his origins. The Hashimotos were among a handful of families in Japan that were second only to the imperial family in lineage, their bloodline reaching back over a thousand years into Japan's history. If they found out anything of his past, they'd reject him irrevocably. They wouldn't care that it hadn't been of his choosing. They had only samurai in their lineage. Ninjas were anathema to them.

But all his life he'd dreamed of reclaiming his family name, of taking his rightful place at its head and in Japanese society, upholding the traditions he'd been meant to, if not for the disaster that had robbed him of his family and left him prey to those who'd exploited him for twenty years. Nothing would prevent him from reaching his goal now.

But since it was out of the question letting his family

know he was his father's heir and the rightful head of the family, he'd concocted another plan that would secure his goals without divulging his real identity.

That plan had come to him while researching Japanese society. He'd found out that adult adoptions were the most prevalent form of adoption in Japan, especially with the son-in-law taking his wife's family name and becoming their heir. Since his father's second cousin, Takeo Hashimoto—now the head of the family—had one unmarried daughter, he'd decided to marry her, and through *yōshi-engumi,* literally "marriage and adoption," become a *mukoyōshi,* an adopted husband.

He'd put his plan in motion a month ago, coming to Japan to dangle himself in front of Takeo, a tycoon any family would do anything to have as *mukoyōshi,* providing the strongest heir possible and taking the family's position and power to new levels. He'd been certain his uncle would make an offer. And he had. He'd offered Megumi, the family name and leadership and the helm of its current businesses.

After pretending to refuse, then to need persuasion, Raiden had accepted. And he was finally weeks away from reclaiming all he'd lost, everything that was rightfully his.

The one thing in the way now was his obsession with Scarlett. There was no other option but to get rid of it.

In an hour, he was sitting in the back of his limo, his American driver-cum-head bodyguard standing outside for a smoke. He allowed it only since he couldn't smell him through the airtight partition. And because Steve was the best.

Nothing on his level, of course. But the best in the private security world.

Suddenly he sat up, his senses on alert. The next second, he saw her step out of the building they were parked in front of.

He'd again felt her before he'd seen her.

Scarlett saw him the moment he saw her, stopped.

Holding her gaze across the distance, he threw the door open. "Get in."

After a moment of stillness, she walked to the limo, her steps graceful, tranquil. The crowds going and coming on the pavement parted for her, everyone turning to look in fascination at the gaijin woman who looked like a living splash of color among the mostly two-tone population.

When she reached the limo, he slid across the back-seat, making space for her, and watched greedily as she lowered her lush, elegant body beside him. Her heat and scent enveloped him, made hunger writhe inside him.

She looked different today, yet another woman. Nothing like last night's femme fatale. A working woman with practical clothes, a scrubbed-clean face and a prim ponytail. She could have been wearing the most outrageous lingerie or even been naked and on erotic display from the way his hormones hurtled in scalding torrents in his arteries.

He sat back and looked away before he dragged her over him or lunged and crushed her beneath him. Steve came in at once and, raising the opaque, soundproof partition between them, put the car in motion as per Raiden's earlier orders.

After a minute when she sat staring ahead and silent beside him, he said, "I have an offer for you."

"I'm listening." The way she said the words, calm yet immediate, told him she couldn't wait to hear his offer.

He couldn't wait to make it, either. "I want you in my

bed, every night, starting tonight. Until I get married. You can ask for whatever *you* want and its yours."

Silence stretched between them after his succinct proposition.

Then she finally turned to him, drawing him to face her as if by sheer magnetism.

Her eyes emitted blue, hot fire in the limo's semidarkness, the one-way-mirror windows dimming the bright lights of the city. What he could see of her expression was enigmatic. "Don't you think a flare of passion is one thing, but an affair is another?"

He shrugged. "It's not an affair. It's an arrangement. A purely sexual one."

Her lashes lowered for moments, before rising. "What about your engagement? Your fiancée?"

"Megumi only wants to honor her family by marrying the most influential man, producing heirs carrying his genes and accessing his power and wealth. She, like me, expects our lives to remain separate, with intimacies practiced only to acquire said heirs."

"So have you started…practicing yet?"

He frowned. After the intimacies with her, the very idea filled him with outright revulsion.

He gritted down on the unwilling reaction. "Of course not. You don't need to worry I'd come to you from her or another woman's bed. As in the past, while I'm with you, I will be with you alone." A vicious doubt twisted in his gut. "I don't know what you did back then, but I expect the same finite monogamy from you now."

"I was with no one else."

And somehow, even though he now knew she seduced men for a living, he believed her.

Silence stretched again until he wanted to grab her and demand she tell him what she was thinking. Now that he

knew she'd tell him, the urge to know her every thought
almost overpowered him. He held back, reminding himself everything he felt was a by-product of intense lust.
Once that was satisfied, curiosity, possessiveness and
everything else would subside with it.

He inhaled. "Now give me your pledge that you will
be at my disposal for the next ten weeks."

At his terse command, her gaze clashed with his in
mock surprise. "You mean you'd believe my 'pledge'?"
At his curt nod, she exhaled. "And I can ask for anything
I want you say?"

"Anything."

"Even if I ask for another fifty million dollars?"

"Yes."

If she had any doubt how much he wanted her, she
should have no doubt now. He didn't mind letting her
know. For the duration of the arrangement, he was giving in to his every urge, saying and doing everything that
came to him the moment it did, no control, no premedi-
tation. He'd plunge whole into this with her. It was the
only way he'd purge her from his system, the only way
he'd ever emerge whole.

For good measure, he added, "I will pay the whole
amount up-front."

Her gaze was more unreadable as she tilted her head
at him. "How can you, the ruthless financier that you
are, pay that exorbitant amount up-front? How do you
know I won't just take the money and disappear like I
did in the past?"

"I know for two reasons. The first is that you did uphold your pledge to me once. You do seem to possess a
code of some sort. The second and more important reason is because you won't want to. I was there last night,
remember? You were as starving for me as I was for you.

I might despise you, might believe everything between us had been a lie, but I know the physical side was real."

"You do?"

Her soft provocation hit him like an ax, snapping the last tethers of control. He gave in, dragged her over his lap, pressed her down on his steel erection.

Grinding up into her, drawing an involuntary moan from her and an answering grind, he touched his open lips to her pulse point. "Yes, I know. I know that I was the best you ever had. That you haven't found anything near what we shared. That after last night, you're burning for more."

Holding him in her hypnotic gaze, she nodded, silently conceding everything he'd said.

Then in a low, raw whisper, she said, "Then give me more, Raiden. Now."

"Yes." The word escaped him on a scalding hiss as he freed himself. Then he bunched her skirt up before lifting her up to hover over his thick crown. His hands fisted at her hips as he tore her panties away, making her gasp.

His erection thudded against her molten lips, making her fingers dig in his shoulders. "Now, Raiden. *Now.*"

Everything in him surged at her tremulous urgency, tensed when she wrapped her fingers around him and positioned him at her soaking entrance, tried to bear down on him.

She was as tight as ever, what had always made him think he wouldn't fit inside her. But their almost impossible fit had always made them incoherent with pleasure, driven them to pinnacles of wild satisfaction. It had again last night. It would always do so. The scent of their lust rose heavy and humid in the limo as he began invading her.

"So ready." He groaned at the delicious agony as she

opened to him, singed him with her heat and honey. "So right."

Her eyes squeezed shut and she moaned as he forged into her clenching depths, stretching her beyond her capacity.

Pressing her lower belly, he slid his thumb between her drenched folds, rubbed her nub in slow circles, and she cried out, clenched tighter around his girth, taking him deeper. She opened her lust-heavy eyes and watched him feverishly.

She was so beautiful draped over him like that, her lithe body straining against and around his, needing his occupation, his pleasuring. He already felt she'd always look like that. To him, she'd always be *her,* the one woman he craved, no matter what she looked like, or what she was.

"Perfect," he bit out, his teeth grinding with the avalanche of sensations as he began to thrust up into her. "Always perfect."

Her heat rose with his praise, and she became even wetter, letting him slide smoothly farther inside her.

"So hot and hard, so deep… You're so deep inside me. Take me, Raiden, do it to me, all the way inside me… *Raiden*…" she keened, over and over, fidgeting around him to ease the edge of pain she'd confessed always accompanied his complete occupation. But he also knew it made her pleasure sharper, her release more explosive. Her body was corroborating his knowledge, rippling around him, squeezing, trembling on the verge of orgasm. And he hadn't fully sheathed himself inside her yet. He was hovering on the edge, too.

Cursing, he knew they were too inflamed, would combust too quickly. But he was damned if he'd let them come without being inside her all the way, as she demanded, as he needed.

Gripping her hips, he leaned her backward, altering the angle of her descent, making her open fully for his plundering. A breathless cry escaped her as she took him to the root.

After waiting out the blinding sensation of being buried inside her to the hilt, he withdrew, dragging a soft shriek from her depths, along with his erection. He thrust back. And she screamed, came all over him, her body lurching in convulsions, inside and out. He rode her harder as she came, his grasp on her hips ferocious. Pleasure spread from where they connected to every inch of his body as he felt her finish, then without pause start to climb again up the spiral of carnal desperation.

"Please…" She lurched forward to press her gasping mouth to his, her fingers gripping his sweat-dampened hair as she rode him, begging him with body and trembling pleas to end her renewed torment. "I'm coming again. Raiden, please, come with me…."

He lost his mind, the need to finish her and empty himself into her taking over completely. Tilting her, he angled his thrusts, pummeling against that trigger inside her. She at once tightened and shook, then exploded into another shrieking orgasm. Grabbing her by the nape, he fed her convulsions, his hips becoming a blur as he pounded into her, making her writhe and moan and come harder, her body heaving with every discharge of pleasure.

"Hannah!" His bellow of ecstasy sounded feral in his own ears as at last his orgasm tore into him, his seed scorching through his length and shooting into her milking depths in jet after agonizingly pleasurable jet.

Their mutual release raged on until he was fully

drained and she collapsed on top of him, a boneless mass of tremors and satiation. She pressed her face to his equally hot, moist neck, her breath gusting to the same labored rhythm as his.

The limo undulated smoothly through the streets of Tokyo as they lay there, like last night, both fully clothed, only merged at their most intimate parts, which made it all more excruciatingly erotic. He finally brushed his lips across hers, as if comforting her in the aftermath of this mind-blowing interlude, what he again hadn't expected or planned.

"Call me Scarlett." Her whisper hit his cheek with her still-gasping breaths.

"Is that your real name?"

"No. But it…has meaning to me."

What was that? And what was her real name? Where did she come from? Would she ever tell him? Should he demand to know?

No. Their relationship would remain at this sexual level, would never go any further. He'd once thought it could, would, but he'd been wrong. Now there was no place in his life for anything but his plans. And even without his plans, he had no place in his life for someone like her. He was sure she had none for him, either.

He carefully disengaged their bodies, even though he was already clamoring for round two, and tidied them both up.

In minutes, she was once again sitting beside him, looking so deceptively prim in her utilitarian clothes and ponytail, as if she hadn't just combusted in his arms and wrung a new level of ecstasy from his every cell. He brushed damp tendrils of hair off her temples, cupped her cheek.

When she shuddered and pressed her flesh harder into

his palm, his lips crooked in a smile. "I trust that was to your satisfaction?"

Her eyes went black. "To my ecstasy. Now I want more."

Pride revved inside his chest. For he was certain she meant it. She couldn't wait to have him again. Even if he didn't already know that, she had no reason to exaggerate. He'd already offered her everything she might want up front.

"You only have to give me your word and you'll have ten weeks' worth of more. With a huge cash incentive. To put things in perspective."

Her eyes grew opaque, making him regret those last words. Before he found a way to take them back, she finally nodded.

But before relief surged, she added, "But since it's for a good cause, how about doubling that cash incentive to a hundred million dollars?"

Five

"Are you mourning parting with your nine-figure sum?"

Scarlett bent over the couch and slid her arms over Raiden's seminaked body as she whispered the teasing question into his ear.

He remained unmoving, staring ahead through the floor-to-ceiling window at the spectacular Tokyo Bay at sunset.

Which was weird. For the past three weeks since they'd started their…arrangement, he'd always met her halfway as soon as she'd entered, always impatient, urgent, voracious.

It had become her nightly ritual, and whenever possible a midday one, too, coming to his penthouse, to which he'd given her full access. He'd gotten this apartment in the first place for her, acquiring it the very next day after she'd agreed to his proposition, to be a few blocks away from her apartment. This, and everything else he did continued to be in the service of her convenience, and to make the most time for each other, wasting as little as possible commuting.

Before she came here every evening, she passed by her place and prepared an overnight bag. When she departed before his housekeepers came, she left no evidence behind to betray that Raiden shared this place with a woman.

She also went home first to shower. *He* showered as soon as he returned home and was always starving for her at the end of his workday, and she couldn't let him take her to bed fresh, or not so fresh, from hers. She'd been flying back and forth daily to the areas still affected by the last earthquake and tsunami in the northeast of Honshu island, and the fieldwork she'd been doing had been grueling. Over three hundred thousand people were still in temporary housing, and over ten thousand of those were orphaned children, the focus of her work. She'd been going all out setting up their special shelters. She needed to get things up and running before she left.

Her departure had become even more imperative now. The day, the *hour* her time with Raiden was up, she'd leave Japan and never come back.

Till then she'd spend every possible second with him. And Raiden was beyond generous with his time. Her days, as per his decree, were hers—*if* he couldn't get away and meet her back here. Her nights were all his. She was so very okay with that.

Then in the mornings they left separately, and they never met anywhere else. There were no lunches or dinners or evenings out. They'd been taking every precaution to make sure their arrangement remained a secret. She was even more careful than he was. When she left this time, she wanted to leave him nothing but good memories, and no lasting damage of any sort.

That was, nothing more than the hundred-million-dollar-shaped new hole in his pocket.

It still flabbergasted her that he could so easily part with that much money. But he had, without batting an eyelash. Right there in his limo, he'd just produced his checkbook from his hand-tailored jacket, and had written the check. Payable the very next day.

At her incredulity that he'd done that when she didn't have the blade of exposure held to his neck this time, he'd shrugged, saying he considered having her those ten weeks as vital to him as keeping his secrets had been. She'd insisted he hadn't needed to give her anything, that what she wanted was only him. And he'd only said he knew that.

But he'd still been ready to part with such a staggering sum. To put things into perspective. So she wouldn't mistake this for anything permanent.

She could have told him there'd never been any danger of that.

But she didn't tell him. Nor did she talk about anything else of note, either. Their time together was about indulging in each other. Ten weeks of pure pleasure.

Not that she thought it would be really that long. There was no way he'd be with her right up to his wedding day.

Swallowing the lump she had no right to have perpetually in her throat, she ran her palms over his chest and abdomen, luxuriating in his velvet-encased steel flesh, tracing every bulge and ridge and groove of his chiseled perfection.

Then she went lower, afraid she'd find more evidence of disinterest to go with his unprecedented preoccupation, and her breath left her in a ragged sigh as her hand closed over his mind-blowing potency, fully, dauntingly aroused.

Her lips shaking in relief, she bit his earlobe as she squeezed him. "I need you to be doing far better things than staring out into the horizon like that. Like taking me right here, right now."

"Scarlett."

That was all he said as he flung his head against the back of the couch, exposing his face and neck to her worship.

But he hadn't moaned her name in pleasure, or in sensual threat. But as if he was…trying to understand it.

Suddenly the whole world turned upside down. He'd grabbed her and flipped her in the air, bringing her down across his body.

Breathless with shock and with awe at his sheer strength and prowess, she gaped up at him. It had been effortless for him to catapult her like this. His hands hadn't dug hard in her flesh to secure her, then he'd applied what felt like antigravity to her descent in midflip so that she landed with the softest of impacts on his lap.

Sealing her open mouth with a kiss that breached her essence, he finally withdrew to look down at her as she lay cradled in his arms, nerveless still with surprise and sheer delight. She would have stayed like this forever if she could.

He lifted a thick lock of her long hair to his lips before winding it around his hand, giving a tug that sent a million delicious arrows shooting everywhere through her body.

One of her various addictions to him was to how he gave her pleasure with every touch, every action. But when he plundered her, he had her screaming with it, tethering her by her hair, harnessing her to make her submit to his every demand. It bordered on savagery, and was pure perfection.

She wished she could ask him to grow his magnificent hair longer, so she could grab it as she held on to him, as he pounded into her, drove her beyond her limits and herself and the world.

But she had no right to ask anything of him, even if his

indulgence of her knew no bounds. And even if she did ask, and he didn't have to keep it cropped for his image and grew it out, she wouldn't be around long enough to enjoy the results.

Megumi would. She knew he believed his fiancée would endure intimacy with him only for the purpose of making their required heirs, but Scarlett believed any woman he touched would crave him forever afterward. As she did.

"It's too obvious," he suddenly said. "To pick Scarlett because you chose to be a redhead in this incarnation."

It was as if he was continuing a conversation he'd been having with himself. Was that why he'd been lost in thought? Searching for explanations as to why she'd chosen that name?

He'd had questions sometimes, what would have led to discussing her past and dissecting it. She'd diverted him every time. But he kept going back to her name, the one she'd chosen for her latest, and she hoped, last identity. It was as if he was trying to grab the end of a thread that would help him unravel her mystery. A person's given name might not say much about them, but a chosen one said a lot, could be a clue that would lead to their truth. What she never wanted him, of all people, to find out.

But instead of evading the question again, she decided to give him a measure of truth. "I did choose the name because it would make people think my parents picked the obvious name for a redhead. But it's just a coincidence, since it has personal significance to me, what no one else would ever figure out."

His focus became absolute. "What is that?"

She gave him another piece. "It reminds me of my mother."

His eyes smoldered. "Did you lose her long ago?"

"Over twenty years ago."

He frowned. "You must have been too young to remember her."

"I was old enough to remember everything."

His gaze grew more probing. "I wouldn't give you more than twenty-five or -six."

"I'm older than I look."

She was actually almost twenty-nine, had been seven when she'd lost her mother. Or rather, when *she* had been lost to her mother.

But she wouldn't pinpoint her age. She drew the line at giving him specifics. But she'd appease his curiosity with one more truth.

"The first fairy tale my mother ever told me at night was *Little Red Riding Hood*. It remained my favorite bedtime story. But since I couldn't have named myself Red, I went for Scarlett."

As soon as her lips stilled, he bent and took them in a long, drugging kiss. As if rewarding her for satisfying one of his curiosities about her.

Pulling back, she noticed a touch of something she hadn't seen since they'd met again, but had seen a lot five years ago when he'd thought she'd been the fictitious Hannah McPherson, the normal woman who'd lost her parents as he had. Empathy. Even tenderness.

Could she be imagining it? She shouldn't.

"I was two when I lost my parents. But you know that already."

She nodded, her throat tightening as she imagined the lost boy he'd been. She realized it was the first time he'd talked about it. She'd never thought he would share any of his scars with her.

He started sweeping her from head to hip in caresses as he talked, his gaze fixed on her eyes but seemingly looking into his own memories. "In the two years I spent in the shelter, no one ever told me that my parents were dead. They probably thought I was too young to understand what that meant, or they weren't really sure they were. There were thousands still missing and unaccounted for."

Like after the last and most powerful earthquake and tsunami to hit Japan. Years later, over twenty-one thousand people were still missing.

"After The Organization took me when I was four, it took a long while to understand I was imprisoned and that I'd never see my family again, the family I barely remembered anymore. It was twenty years later that I managed to escape."

Unable to hold back, she pulled him down to her and sealed his lips with her own, as if she could absorb his remembered pain and abuse.

Letting her drink deep of his essence, he swept her around to bring her beneath him on the gigantic couch. He stretched over her, his daunting hardness pressing where she needed it through their clothes. He was clad only in black pants. The rest of his body was a poem of defined, elegant muscles, packing unimaginable power, flexing and straining their hunger over her. How she'd soon have to live without this unbridled joy of feeling him like this, she couldn't begin to think. She'd done it once before, falling into the suspended animation that had been the only way she could survive. She had no idea if she'd be able to seek its refuge again.

Her heart thudded painfully as Raiden pulled back from their kiss and started to rise. Unable to let him go, she clung to his arms. He let her, surrendering to her caresses like a great feline inviting and luxuriating in a worshipper's petting.

Then his eyes took on that reminiscing cast again. "I was always angry that I didn't even remember my family. I wished I had been older when I lost them so I'd at least have the memories. It made it so much harder finding their trail." His gaze focused back on her, that gentleness entering it again. "But just now as you said you remembered everything about your mother, I realized that I got the better deal. Memories are far more painful than their absence."

Feeling her throat closing over what felt like barbs, she struggled to keep her eyes from filling with tears.

Before she lost the fight, he speared his hand in her hair at her nape, pinning her head down to the couch, tilting her face up to him. "So you're not a real redhead, either."

"No."

His other hand threaded through her hair, combing it over and over. "You made a very convincing blonde, too. Any shade suits you so much it looks as if you were born with it. Until you try the next shade and it's just as incredible on you."

She stored away the praise he lavished on her, saving it for the barren years ahead. Even if it was mostly about her looks, which weren't hers anyway anymore, she would hold on to it.

She shrugged. "Blond colors were the best to turn into others at short notice. Now that I have no need for changing colors, I can maintain a darker one."

"But now that you don't need to change colors, why not just go back to your original one? Wouldn't that be more convenient? Or do you like how this shade makes you stand out here?"

She couldn't tell him she continued dying her hair obsessively because she couldn't bear seeing the thick white lock that had grown in her crown after she'd left him. A glaring souvenir of the most mutilating period of her life.

So she told him the reason she'd chosen this shade instead. "This was actually my paternal aunt's hair color. I loved her so much, thought she looked like a fairy queen with that hair. And I made my face look like a childhood friend. At least, what I think she would have looked like as an adult."

"Are your aunt and friend dead, too?" At her difficult nod, the empathy she thought she saw in his gaze grew contemplative. "So you've created this new identity from the memories of the people you loved and lost, becoming a living memorial of them."

Surprise at his analysis made her lose the fight, hot, stinging tears rushing to her eyes.

Averting them, she whispered, "I never looked at it this way. It just comforted me to look in the mirror and see a reflection of the ones I loved, to hear the name that reminds me of my mother's soft voice telling me stories in the dark."

Bringing her eyes back to his with a gentle hand on her cheek, his fingers wiped away the tears that had escaped, his gaze lengthening, deepening, until she felt he'd fathomed her every secret without her needing to tell him any more details.

Suddenly he asked, "How many disguises did you have in your life?"

Blinking to clear her eyes, she attempted a mischievous smile. "Aren't you all questions tonight?"

His answering smile was equal parts hunger and self-deprecation. "You fascinate me. I thought I was undetectable until you. I'd give anything to pick your brains."

"Anything?" She ran a finger down his chest, then the groove separating his defined abs, then lower.

"Name your price."

"Any price?"

He just nodded, his expression avid, his irises looking as if they had the sunset at his back trapped in them.

God, how could anything be so absolutely beautiful?

Sighing, she arched up into his length, ran greedy hands down his muscled back. "You know my price."

"That's not a price, that's a privilege. One I'll take full advantage of, as soon as you quench my curiosity. So how many?"

"How many personas have I played, you mean? Many."

"I'm sure you have an exact number."

"Sixty-seven."

His eyes snapped wider. He must have expected her to prevaricate, and probably couldn't imagine someone could have played that many roles.

At length, he said, "Counting the two personas I know?"

"No."

At her immediate answer, he pursed his lips. "Why not? They are very well-drawn and distinct personas."

"Just in their different names and life stories."

"Still claiming you never acted with me?"

"You be the judge of that." She took one of his hands, guided it beneath her panties. As his fingers slid between her swollen, melting flesh, his erection grew so hard, it hurt poking into her side. "Can this be an act?"

"Not this, for sure."

Moaning, she opened herself to him, and those long, powerful fingers caressed her feminine lips apart, sawed through her molten need, knowing exactly where and how to press, how hard or soft to rub, how fast or slow to go. She keened, lurched with sensations almost too much to bear. And that was before he dipped two fingers inside her. It again made her feel so acutely how empty she felt. How only having him inside her had ever filled the void.

"Take me, Raiden. No foreplay...please."

In answer, with movements that bordered on magic in their efficiency, he rid her of her every garment, had her naked beneath him in under ten seconds. Before she could fumble with his zipper to release him, clutch him to her and bring him inside her, he slid down her body.

Protesting weakly, yet unable to do anything but surrender, she arched helplessly as he triggered her every erogenous inch, which under his hands was every last one she had. Again and again she tried to drag him up to her until his magnificent head settled between her thighs and his lips and tongue scorched the heart of her femininity. The sight and the concept of what he did to her were even more incapacitating than the physical sensations.

Through the delirium, she watched him cosset her, drink her, revel in her essence, in her need and taste and pleasure. Then, as always, he knew exactly when she could take no more.

His lips suckled her nub, his teeth grazing it even as his fingers strummed her inner trigger. But it was his command that snapped the coil of unbearable tension inside her.

"Let me see and hear how much I pleasure you, Scarlett."

Shrieking with the recoil of sensation, her body heaved in a chain reaction. She held his eyes all through, as he always demanded that she did in the throes, letting him see what he was doing to her.

Finally subsiding, unable even to regulate her breathing, she watched through drugged eyes as he began again, varying his method, renewing her desperation, deepening her surrender.

She knew there was no point in begging for him again. He'd do with her as he pleased. And give her pleasure beyond endurance while at it.

It would be wise to save her breath for the screams of soul-racking ecstasy he would inflict on her all night long.

And if a voice in her drugged mind told her this would end with a far worse scar than in the past, she didn't care.

The end was still weeks away. And she was savoring what she could have with him until the very last second....

The first thing Raiden saw as soon as he opened his eyes was Scarlett. He had to blink to make sure he actually saw her. Nowadays he saw her whether she was there or not. She was all that filled his mind's eye, his every thought and fantasy.

But she was really here this time. Barely. She'd already showered, dressed and packed her famous overnight bag. Her bag of tricks, as she'd once teasingly referred to it. She did have it filled with stuff that tricked his senses into catapulting to a higher realm. Lingerie, oils and an array of surprising enhancers of her own concoction.

Not that those things were what affected him. They did only because it was she who wore them, who wielded them. Now the bag was over her shoulder and she was about to walk out of his bedroom.

Since they'd started their arrangement six weeks ago, this was the first time he'd woken up before she'd left. Which was unbelievable. Not that he'd woken up this time, but that he'd actually slept through all the other times. As someone whose senses had been conditioned to be on full alert all the time, he'd never relaxed around anyone so fully, not even his brothers, to let sleep claim him so completely.

But against all the reasons he had to distrust her, Raiden's instincts told him otherwise. They trusted her implicitly, turned off his every built-in alarm system, to the point that they made him sleep—deep, blissful, rejuvenating sleep—only while beside her. And to continue surrendering to slumber even as she puttered around his domain, knowing he was his safest with her around.

But it never failed. She always left first thing in the morning, never once waking him up to say goodbye. He'd hoped today would be different, since he'd told her he wouldn't go to work before noon today. He'd hoped she'd take this as what he'd meant it to be, an invitation to sleep in with him and have a late breakfast together.

But then why should he feel so disappointed that she hadn't heeded his implication? Beyond the relentless demands he made on her sexually, in anything else he maintained a take-it-or-leave-it attitude. She probably didn't even realize there'd been an invitation hidden in his words.

But his attitude was just a front. In reality, every second he spent in her company, the bad memories of the past faded, as if they'd happened to someone else. He could no longer see her through their tainted prism. He believed he now saw through to her core self, the real woman. He believed he felt what she felt. Though she was vocal only in passion, he could swear he sensed that this was no longer purely sexual to her. If it had ever been.

And he wasn't deluding himself about this. He'd been feeling this even before learning the truth about her current work made him radically change his opinion of her character.

When he'd first investigated her activities in Japan,

he'd thought her humanitarian work with UNICEF was just an ingenious way of wheedling herself into major businessmen's pockets, like Hiro, for donations she'd pocket herself. Then she'd asked for the hundred million, stating it would all be used in her work. He hadn't been in a condition at the time to care why she'd asked for it, had vaguely thought she'd had to at least be exaggerating about the money's intended use. But after he'd given her the money, and she continued working harder than ever, he had to revise his suspicions, since he'd given her more than ten years' worth of donation drives could raise.

Further investigations had revealed the incredible results she'd been consistently getting for the past three years, fifteen months of those in Japan. Everything fell into place in the light of his new time with her. And that was before he'd discovered her most ambitious project was being funded by her own money. The money she'd taken from him.

He'd then realized she'd asked him for it only so it would free her from dependence on donations and other sources of official funding. Those had been limiting the scope of what she could achieve, and she was always threatened by being forced to stop her projects altogether if she ran out of money. He'd even traced parts of the previous sum he'd given her to more of her humanitarian efforts. He now had no doubt the rest of it had been put to very good use, as she'd told him that first night. He'd thought she was being provocative, but she'd only been telling him the truth. And expecting him to believe the worst.

But even doing so, with the way he'd been feeling, he would have given her a billion dollars had she asked. The way he was feeling now, if she asked, he'd sign over all his assets.

Now he watched her from slit eyes as she paused at the door of his expansive bedroom and looked back. In her utilitarian clothes and ponytail, she looked so practical, so young. So fragile. She'd lost a lot of weight in the past six weeks, and he could sometimes swear she was reverting to what she'd been before.

She hadn't realized he'd woken up. And the expression that came over her, the emotions that gripped her features when she thought she was safe from his scrutiny, speared through him.

Such wistfulness, such pervasive dejection.

Long after she'd closed the door and he heard her leave his penthouse, he lay there on his back in the bed in which they'd shared indescribable intimacies, staring at the ceiling.

Why was she feeling that way? *Did* she feel that way?

He couldn't tell for sure. Not as long as he didn't know everything there was to know about her.

What he knew now was just feelings, observations and information about her current status. Her past remained as inaccessible as ever.

After that night three weeks ago, when she'd told him why she'd chosen the name Scarlett, her red hair and that specific face, she'd gone back to evading his probing. Beyond being candid about what she thought in the moment, and explicit about what he made her feel physically, she gave him nothing more that could make it possible to reconstruct her past.

A past he could no longer bear not knowing about.

It was no longer to tie up everything about her neatly, so that when their time together came to an end, he'd stow away her memory in a closed file and move on, with no lingering uncertainties keeping her alive in his memory. Not that he'd ever wanted *that*. He now admitted it to himself that when he'd hit the first dead ends in his search into her past, he'd convinced himself she was untraceable. He'd unconsciously wanted to avoid finding out what would disturb him more. Or worse, what would irrevocably eradicate her from his mind.

Now it was different. This woman he'd been sharing every intimacy he'd never wanted to share with another with *was* the woman he'd thought she was in the past. She'd told the truth when she'd said she'd never acted with him. And she'd never made personal use of the money she'd taken from him, except to build a new persona. He had to find out what had driven her to that mercenary life in the past, then to go through such effort and pain to escape it.

Yet he didn't know how to start a new investigation, or if one would actually lead to anything other than more dead ends.

But he *could* investigate someone close to her. Hiro. His past was heavily documented, and maybe some threads from her relationship with him would lead to unraveling her mystery.

Investigating Scarlett's relationship with Hiro turned out to be a simple matter of entering their names in an internet search engine.

At the click of a button, he got dozens of results detailing the incident that had brought them together.

About a year ago, Hiro was on one of his private jets, returning from a charity event on Kyoto. Scarlett was among the dozen people who'd organized the event and had been invited to go back to Tokyo with him. Then the plane was hit by lightning.

Five people died in the crash, and others had assorted injuries but had managed to pull themselves out of the wreckage. But Hiro was trapped. They'd tried to extricate him, but on realizing the plane was about to explode, they'd run out, leaving him to his fate. All but Scarlett.

Risking her own life, she'd refused to leave him even when he'd begged her to save herself. She'd finally managed to drag him free and away from the plane in the nick of time. Then she'd stopped the bleeding from the major artery in his leg, which would have killed him anyway, and continued to care for him until rescue teams arrived. Through it all, she'd ignored her own injuries.

Hiro had been on record so many times in the media lauding Scarlett's fearlessness and heroism, and stating unequivocally that he owed her his life.

In addition to the press coverage Raiden found, his own investigations revealed they'd been best friends ever since, but that there'd been no hint of romantic involvement in their closeness. Apart from their friendship, Hiro had been donating massive amounts of money to her causes. But there was never enough money to establish the ongoing services she was setting up. And it was far better to have personal money she had immediate access to, since Hiro's donations would always be tied in lengthy legal procedures before being made available for her to use.

That further proved Scarlett was the person he'd always felt her to be, and that what she'd told him about her and Hiro was true. That revelation cleared away his last misconception about her.

But it still gave him no insight into her past.

Which meant there was one last option open to him.

Enlisting the combined investigative powers of his brothers.

He'd never before considered doing that. It had been the last thing he'd wanted—for them to find out about her, and about how close he'd come to unwittingly exposing them all.

But discovering the truth about her had become imperative. It now meant more to him than learning the truth about himself ever did.

Six

"So there's a woman out there who knows everything about you. And you deem to tell us now? Five years after the fact?"

Raiden looked steadily across his executive desk at the three juggernauts who sat facing him in a semicircle, looking like a tribunal of demigods.

They were the three of his six brothers who'd been able to come for the face-to-face meeting. He'd just told them the short version of his history with Hannah/Scarlett.

The first one to talk after he'd finished was Numair, the leader of the Black Castle brotherhood. His leader.

Numair Al Aswad, or Phantom, the name he'd known him by for their twenty years in The Organization's prison, had been the oldest among them and the one who'd been there longest. Each had found him already established as The Organization's rising star when they'd come to the prison they'd eventually called Black Castle. Almost twenty-five of Numair's forty years had been spent there, at first being trained, then later training others, starting with them. He had taught them his every stealthy and lethal method in espionage and execution.

He hadn't only been the best operative in The Organization's history, he'd also been the shrewdest, the one who'd chosen Raiden and his brothers out of hundreds of boys, judging them to be not only the best of the best but kindred spirits. Taking them on, making them his team, he'd guided them through the endless years of captivity. He was the one who'd forged their brotherhood and their blood oath to one day escape, amass wealth and power and bring down those who'd sold them as slaves and The Organization itself.

Numair had worked to that end since he'd been only ten. It had been his mind-bogglingly convoluted and long-term plan that had made it possible for them to finally escape, disappear and create their new identities. He and Richard, Rafael's former handler, had also been the ones who'd led them into creating Black Castle Enterprises.

But like Raiden, Numair had remembered no specific details about his family before he'd been sold to The Organization. He'd only remembered a few names. One he'd ended up calling himself. The others he'd long realized were those of desert kingdoms. He'd searched, like Raiden, for his bloodline since their escape, and he'd recently found out that not only did he come from one of those kingdoms, but before his abduction, he'd been the heir to its throne.

But reclaiming his legacy wouldn't be as easy as it was for Raiden. Numair's return to his kingdom would turn his region upside down. It could even ignite a war.

Which was fine by Numair. Nothing would stop him from claiming what was his. And it wouldn't be the first time he'd instigated armed conflicts.

Now he regarded Raiden with eyes as still and fathomless as an abyss. But his absolute calmness didn't fool him. That abyss was filled with flesh-melting acid.

Raiden had compromised everything Numair had strived for—their freedoms, their achievements, their very lives. Numair was coldly angry. And when he was like this, he was deadly. Anyone with any sense of self-preservation would be afraid. Very afraid.

"So what took you so long to let us know?" That was Wildcard. Of Russian origins, he'd come to The Organization old enough to remember his past life. But he'd chosen not to make contact with his family after his escape, adopting the name Ivan Kostantinov instead. Still a Russian name, but he hadn't told any of them the significance of his choice. Many of his rivals in the cyber development world thought Ivan the Terrible suited him far more.

Ivan's mockery grew more caustic when Raiden made no response. "Did you change your name from Lightning to Turtle without telling us?"

"Maybe since he's a ninja, he's always been one."

Ivan glared at Bones, the most blasé of the brothers. If only in comparison to the rest of them. To the rest of the world Antonio Balducci was a whirlwind of energy and achievements, an enigmatic, awe-inspiring figure who was a wizard in medicine and with the women who catapulted themselves at his feet. As their former medical expert and field surgeon, Antonio was now in charge of Black Castle's medical R&D business and a reconstructive-trauma surgical god whose work bordered on magic.

On the personal level, ever since their days in Black Castle, Antonio and Ivan couldn't stop harassing each other, but neither one could live without the other, either.

"You knew that she knew," Ivan said, resuming the corrosive scolding Antonio had interrupted. "And you not only let her go then, you're back with her again now. Don't you—"

"I had no idea what she was up to until it was too late," Raiden interrupted Ivan. "I let her go because she gave me her word she'd never use her knowledge. She kept it and I—"

"You had no way of knowing she would," Numair interrupted him in turn. "That was a blind, insane gamble. You jeopardized yourself and, by association, all of us. You compounded your mistakes when you made the decision to keep us in the dark. It could have meant our very lives."

From the bare facts, it did look like that, Raiden conceded. But it had been his gut feeling that he'd gone with then. Still, he couldn't admit that. It would make him look even more unreliable, and Scarlett more dangerous.

He finally exhaled. "I made the call to believe her. And I was right to."

Antonio snorted. "How do you know that? There's no proof yet that this woman hasn't leaked strategic info about you, or us, in the past five years. For all we know, every single problem or loss we suffered could have been her doing."

Raiden's answering snort was more spectacular. "Don't you think if she'd leaked info about our identities, the least we would have suffered would have been bullets between the eyes, not the tame business setbacks we did? She leaked, and will leak, nothing."

Antonio shrugged. "Then you lucked out. So far."

"It wasn't luck. It was a judgment. I stand by it."

"I can understand you making a mistake once," Ivan said. "Though I can't get my head around it, not from you. But to be doing it again… That's totally incomprehensible to me."

"Whatever mistake I made in the past, none of the same variables apply now. I'm not making a mistake again."

Ivan's lips twisted condescendingly. "Says the man

whose wedding is in three weeks. The wedding that will secure your entry into the family you've searched for for ten years, an ultraconservative clan who would reject you at the slightest whiff of scandal."

Antonio shook his head. "And you didn't even wait until all the legalities were concluded and you had your family name back to indulge your desire for this black widow."

Ivan nodded. "You are risking everything you've dreamed of and planned for all your life by associating with this woman at this critical time. And worst of all, it seems you don't realize you're doing that."

Oh, he did realize. Especially in the past week, since he'd dropped his precautions, had been surprising Scarlett at work, insisting on taking her out, then to and from home, no longer able to bear getting there or leaving separately, or any other secrecy measures.

When she'd at first refused to relinquish their precautions, he'd insisted he knew what he was doing. Which he certainly didn't. The only thing he knew was that he could no longer compartmentalize her presence in his life. He wanted her with him in every possible moment, couldn't bear wasting the time he could have with her on secrecy procedures. How that would ultimately affect his plans, he was at a stage where he no longer cared. He knew his time with her was draining away like accelerated sand in an hourglass, and such a realization was messing with his restraint, rearranging all of his priorities.

From his brothers' point of view, that would all prove that he'd lost his mind. He couldn't contest their diagnosis. For he had no sanity to speak of when it came to Scarlett.

When he didn't make a comment, Antonio exhaled.

"From her own admission, she's a Mata Hari who's played at least five dozen men before you. You think you're so special to her that she won't do the same to you...again? How could you resume your liaison after she blackmailed you for fifty million dollars?"

"I did after she asked for double that this time." The trio of his brothers just stared at him as if he'd sprouted two extra heads. "Apart from the money she used to create her current identity, she only uses the money in her humanitarian work."

"And you realized that when?" Ivan scoffed. "Long after the fact, I'm certain. This woman demands money, and no matter how outrageous the amount, and whether you have reason to succumb to her demands or not, you give it to her. Without consulting any of us."

"And without letting us know of the danger she could have posed to all of us back then, and could still pose now or any time in the future." Antonio shook his head in incredulity. "This is even worse than I at first thought."

Raiden's gaze swept the three men, felt them passing judgment. From the fury on Ivan's face, the dismay on Antonio's and the nothingness on Numair's, he knew the sentence they would like to pass was a painless death. To put him out of their collective misery.

Cocking his head at them, he sighed. "Are you done?"

"Actually, no," Ivan growled. "How did you expect us to take this? Don't you realize the magnitude of what you risked? And are still risking?"

Numair sat forward, moving in pure effortlessness, the first trait that had earned him the name Phantom before the rest of his stealthy methods had. This meant he'd decided this back-and-forth exchange was over. He'd reached his verdict.

"Give me one reason why I shouldn't leave this office and go eliminate this woman's threat."

Silence detonated in the wake of Numair's tranquil words.

Feeling his heart about to do the same, Raiden drew in a sharp breath. Once Numair made up his mind, nothing could stop him. So Raiden had to stop his mind in its tracks before it latched on to a course of action.

"One reason. Me." His voice was a steel blade as he transferred his gaze from Numair to the others, letting them know Scarlett was one line he'd never let anyone cross. Not even them. Then he let the lifetime of history and empathy between them enter his gaze. "We survived hell, then conquered the world by trusting each other absolutely. You depended on me and my instincts countless times. I now ask you to trust the instincts that never led us wrong."

"They led you wrong in her case," Antonio pointed out.

"No, they haven't. I now believe she'd been forced to spy on me. And this is why I called this meeting, why I told you about her. I need you to help me find out exactly who she is, and how Medvedev found her, and what power he had over her."

"She was a professional honey trap with a long history behind her before Medvedev hired her," Antonio dismissed.

"And I want to find out how that happened, how she'd entered this life, the life she'd gone to such lengths to exit." He gave them a moment to absorb his demands and the new considerations, then went on. "Promise me you'll do everything in your power to help me settle this issue once and for all."

"I can certainly settle her issue with no effort at all." Numair's voice was laced with chilling, hair-raising humor.

"Numair."

At Raiden's booming growl, Numair held his enraged gaze for seconds before he shrugged. "It would be better for you and for all of us if she just…disappeared. If this were my call, I wouldn't forgive anyone who betrayed me. Not for any reason. If I were you, I wouldn't care why she did."

"You're not me, Numair. Now give me your word."

Numair inclined his head vaguely, looking like a malevolent genie from an Oriental fable with his shoulder-length black hair, slanting eyebrows and striking features.

"Give me your *oath,* Phantom," Raiden gritted.

He had to have that, or Numair would leave his office and fulfill his not-so-veiled threat. When it came to protecting their brotherhood, Numair would do, and had done, literally anything. But he also had an unswerving code of honor, would give his life to uphold an oath he'd made. But he had to make it first, unequivocally, not just imply it, before it became binding.

Pursing his lips, Numair regarded him with the same steadiness he had since Raiden had first seen him when he'd been five, that of the stern older brother who knew best. He didn't approve, but he now realized that Raiden wasn't defending his mistakes in the past or his whims now. He was defending the woman he wanted with every fiber of his being.

Though he still had no reason to make that oath, none but Raiden's conviction, Numair finally said, "You have it."

"I don't have good news."

Raiden's heart rammed his ribs viciously at Numair's declaration.

Numair hadn't stood up to receive him when Abbas,

his right-hand man, had let Raiden into his presidential suite at the Mandarin Oriental Hotel. He said nothing more than his opening statement. Instead, he continued staring out of the window at the glittering nighttime Tokyo as Raiden approached him.

Raiden barely noticed his luxurious surroundings as he came to stand before him. Numair only leaned forward on the immaculate brown silk sofa and poured himself a straight whiskey from a crystal decanter. Still without looking at Raiden, he tossed the shot back.

It hadn't surprised Raiden when only four days after his meeting with his trio of brothers, it had been Numair who'd called him to tell him he had what Raiden had been looking for.

As Phantom, his investigative capabilities were unmatched. Now as Numair Al Aswad, or Black Panther as he was known in the intelligence field, where he was now one of the world's biggest experts and contractors, his reach had multiplied a hundredfold. The only one who could rival him was Richard, or Cobra, Rafael's past handler. Not that he'd even considered enlisting Richard's help. Not because he still felt any hard feelings toward him as one of their past captors, but because of the way Numair felt about him. There *was* still a possibility those two might end up killing each other. Whatever made the two forces of nature abhor each other so much, even after becoming allies, neither man would ever say.

Dread eating through the rest of his tattered control, he gritted his teeth. "Just give me what you have."

Numair at last looked up at him. His eyes weren't indifferent anymore. They were heavy.

Then he said, "Sit down. And pour yourself a drink."

He complied, because his legs no longer felt able to support him. He descended heavily onto the armchair across from Numair, a fine tremor traversing his grip as he poured himself a shot. "It's that bad?"

"Worse."

The fist squeezing Raiden's heart tightened as Numair reached for a tablet on the coffee table between them, accessed an app, then pushed the tablet toward Raiden. Raiden stopped its slide, and his heart turned over in his chest at what he saw on the screen.

A photo of an exquisite girl with shimmering dark caramel hair, an impassive face and extinguished eyes. A younger version of the Hannah he'd known, with a different hair color. And without the warm, lighthearted, normal expressions. This was her without the act. The real her. A girl without hope.

His upper lip and forehead beading with sweat, he glanced up at Numair, his insides churning.

Numair answered his unspoken question. "That's Katya Petrovna, whom you knew as Hannah McPherson and now know as Scarlett Delacroix."

Katya. Her real name at last. It suited her. As anything did. She made anything hers. Names, hair color, faces. Him.

Numair went on. "She was born in Tbilisi, Georgia, in the former U.S.S.R., and raised on the Black Sea coast of the Russian Riviera. She was a descendant of a Georgian noble house. Then, during the collapse of the Soviet Union, she was seven when she was separated from her mother in a riot. She ended up in a white slavery ring."

The thudding of his heart escalated until it shook his whole body. There could be a hundred possibilities after this point, all ugly and horrific. But he had the terrible feeling he knew exactly where this was going.

Then Numair validated his suspicions. "By the age of ten, she ended up in The Organization's grasp."

Even though he'd already suspected that, all his nerves loosened with the blow of confirmation.

The crystal glass in his hand crashed on the marble floor in a thousand diamond-like splinters.

Scarlett. Or Hannah. Or Katya. *Her.* She'd been The Organization's slave, too. Just like him. Like all of them.

Without batting an eye at the smashed glass, Numair tossed back another shot as if he needed it. Then he continued. "She was one of hundreds of girls who'd been imprisoned in an all-female installation equivalent to our Black Castle. And like us, the girls were categorized according to their abilities and talents, but also according to their looks. All girls were trained as we were, but the beautiful ones had extra training in seduction and manipulation. They were used as sexual bait for the world's movers and shakers, or anyone The Organization wanted breached, entrapped or untraceably terminated. According to my source, she was the best. But her trail ended five years ago, when she clearly faked her death."

Raiden struggled not to howl in agony. The details Numair had just related so clinically painted a gruesome picture of the life of the girl in the photo. A girl who knew she was lost and no one would ever come to her rescue. Who knew she'd be a hostage forever, living a life of danger and degradation, an instrument in the service of whoever paid her masters for her skills, to be used and abused as they willed. A woman who knew that escape was impossible, and the only way out was death.

He'd started this quest for the truth, hoping to find out she'd been forced to betray him. Now he wished she hadn't been. Being right meant she'd suffered unimaginably, must be scarred for life. Now he would have given anything for her to be just a woman who'd entered the wrong path, then decided to change, to make good.

But she wasn't. She'd been enslaved. And he couldn't bear thinking she'd suffered what he had. And far, far worse.

"I now believe you were right," Numair said. "She won't expose you or any of us. Not when it means ultimately exposing herself, too. We're all in the same boat, so to speak."

He wanted to roar to Numair that he was still wrong, that this wasn't why his and their secrets were safe with Scarlett. But his vocal cords felt fused over molten agony.

"Bottom line is, you can go ahead and indulge your desire for her. As long as you don't jeopardize your relevant plans." Numair stopped, as if debating whether to tell him more or not. Then he exhaled. "There something else you need to know."

In minutes, Numair stopped talking, and suddenly Raiden could no longer bear hearing another word.

He heaved up to his feet before the roaring inside him escaped his lips.

At the suite's door, Numair's warning hit him between the shoulder blades.

"Don't tell her anything."

"Why didn't you tell me?"

Scarlett had known something was wrong the moment she'd entered the penthouse to find Raiden facing the door as if he'd been waiting for her for hours. His hands and face were clenched as he asked that question.

In a heartbeat, she knew what this blazing darkness cloaking him was all about.

He knew the truth. Her truth.

She didn't have to ask how, didn't need to. He just did.

She felt exposed, her every sordid secret on display before the one person with whom she'd wanted to retain a measure of mystery and allure. She knew there was no point in prevaricating.

So she shrugged. "What was the point?"

"What…?" He seemed so stunned by her answer he found nothing to say. Then he blurted out, "You don't consider being the victim of the same organization that'd kidnapped and enslaved me relevant?"

"Not really." She sat down before she collapsed. "Not now that we both got out."

Urgent strides brought him standing above her, and then he descended on the couch beside her, taking both her hands in his. "I need you to tell me everything. I know only who you were, how you ended up in The Organization's hands, how they trained and used you, like they did me. Now I need to know the specifics of your mission targeting me."

She'd always wished she could erase those specifics from her memory and psyche as she'd erased her former identity. Or thought she had. She hadn't. Raiden had found everything out.

But to avoid telling him the full truth would only prolong the torture. She should get it over with. What they had would soon be over. His wedding was in sixteen days.

She left her hands in his, not because his touch and urgency didn't burn her, but because she couldn't pull away.

Barely holding herself together, she started to explain.

"Medvedev worked on occasion on our side of the operation. He was my handler's lover. She was the one who recommended me to him when he described the skillset he required to set you up. I realized later this was his personal vengeance on you, and if he was right, he wanted it to be his triumph, and his secret shame if he was wrong. He told my handler no specifics. Though he must have told her something lucrative enough to get her to make The Organization believe I was on a mission for them. She gave me all the time I needed to take care of you. Medvedev told her not to worry about watching me, since he'd do it, and he would deliver me back to her at the completion of my task."

She paused to adjust her breathing, which had started to hitch under his laserlike eyes.

"It was a very difficult task, he told me, since your records were somehow expunged from The Organization's system. There were no photos, no fingerprints, no voice recognition, no retinal scans and no DNA to match. Even your implanted tracking devices were deactivated. I assume that was your doing." Raiden nodded, then gestured his impatience. She continued, almost choking on every word. "His only evidence was that you resembled his escapee, and he had a feeling about you. But he couldn't build a case on mere resemblance and his feelings. He needed evidence. Evidence I had to provide."

Pretending to adjust her position, she pulled away from him. He only compensated, touching her along her whole left side, zapping every inch of her flesh with agitation. She had to spit out a conclusion and hope it would satisfy him.

"When I asked what would happen if I couldn't get close enough to you or if it took too long to do so, he said not to worry. He'd do everything to give me all the resources and time I needed to get him his proof. Then, I guess to make me committed to his cause, he said if I got him the proof he needed, he would ensure my freedom from The Organization."

Everything she'd said so far had been specifics of the facts he had already known or deduced. Nothing seemed to surprise him.

She went on, "He said he'd extort you for a huge sum,

pretending it was his price for not exposing you. He said he'd give me a portion of the money to build a new life for myself, and to fake my death so The Organization wouldn't look for me. Just promising me that behind my handler's back, he told me he would betray anyone to get what he wanted, starting with me. But I had no option but to do as he wanted, and to keep his secret. It was clearly implied my life depended on both actions." She paused, taking a shallow, shaky breath. "The rest you know. I came after you with my fabricated identity, and we became lovers until I slipped and you found me out. We made the deal and I managed to escape Medvedev after misleading him. I used the money to create a new identity and fake the death of the old one."

She fell silent, but Raiden's eyes continued to set her every nerve aflame. He was waiting for her to confess more.

She couldn't. The rest was just too horrible.

When he made sure she wasn't adding more, Raiden faced her fully. "Knowing Medvedev and his obsession with me, and what I cost him when I escaped him, being thwarted once wouldn't have stopped him. He would have never stopped. That was the biggest question I had when you told me he was the one who recruited you—how he let you go, how he didn't come after me again. But now I know how."

Her heart stopped as she prayed he only thought he did.

Then he went on and her prayers were aborted.

"He died five years ago, stabbed in the eye in a hotel room." His eyes turned to infernos as he pulled her closer. "It was you who killed him, wasn't it?"

Seven

Raiden's words weren't a question. Just a statement demanding only the corroboration of details. They ricocheted in Scarlett's head until she felt it would burst.

It was you who killed him, wasn't it?

Needing to silence the reverberations, she tore herself out of his hold, feeling as if her flesh had peeled in his hands.

But he wouldn't let her get far. He caught her back into a fierce embrace. "Just tell me, Scarlett."

The terrible memories welled like poison-tinged ink in her system. "Please, Raiden. Don't make me."

His embrace tightened, the hand pressing her head into his expansive chest, convulsing as if he wanted to push her into his rib cage, hide her inside him. "Let it all out, Scarlett. Let me relieve you of it. Let me take it all on for you."

She writhed in his hold, as if she was drowning and trying to kick to the surface. But he held her tighter, letting her know he wasn't letting it go this time. For he must know she hadn't told him everything. Not only about Medvedev but about her, them, everything. And he wouldn't be satisfied with anything less than the whole truth now.

Unable to make such confessions while in his arms,

she choked, "I'll tell you everything...just...just let me breathe."

Cursing himself ferociously, Raiden let her go at once, thinking he'd been suffocating her. She didn't have enough breath to tell him he wasn't the one starving her of oxygen. It was the thought of letting go.

It was harder than she'd expected to let go of the masks she'd hidden behind since she was seven years old. Tearing off her facade was almost as scary as the thought of tearing a layer of skin off her face.

She sat there beside him, feeling his empathic gaze sear her, gathering every spark of will and courage to do what she must do. Show him the real her for the first time.

Inhaling one last bracing breath, she looked him in the eyes and let her barriers crumble.

Raiden's eyes shot wider, his nostrils flared, his chest deflating as if she'd punched him in the gut. That meant she'd managed to show him inside her. And it flabbergasted him.

She let go of her last reluctance. "About Medvedev..."

A finger on her lips stopped her halting words, his face gripped with emotions she'd never seen. They were so complex, she couldn't fathom them. "Start at the beginning, Scarlett. Tell me everything from before you approached me."

Nothing but every last detail would satisfy him, would it? As it shouldn't. She owed him at least that.

Nodding, she let out a ragged exhalation. "Before I did, I investigated you, as I always did, to tailor my approach to every...case. But you were an enigma, with no information indicating your character. So I watched you, and from my observations, I knew you wouldn't respond favorably to a direct approach, wouldn't respond to overt seduction, like almost all men in my experience."

His teeth gritted, his frown deepening. No doubt he hated hearing how he'd been a mission, how there'd been so many before him.

But she already knew he'd feel that way, and she was only telling him the details of what he already knew. So she continued.

"I set up that car accident, created that steeped-in-normalcy persona, because I'd judged only a woman like the fictional Hannah McPherson would have the best chance to make you feel safe enough to let her come close. And I was right."

His hand grabbed the back of her head, his eyes so fierce, as if trying to compel her to believe him. "You were wrong. It was you, the woman beneath the act that I responded to. I proved that when I responded to you again, when you projected a totally different persona." His hand gentled at her nape, making her melt in his grip. "But you said you never acted with me. Was that because once you met me, you judged I would respond best to the real you?"

And she made the first irrevocable confession. "Until I met you, I didn't know there was a real me."

His eyes flared like supernovas, and his grip twisted in her hair with the same ferocity, making her gasp with pleasure and ratcheting heartache.

Suddenly, confessions felt like poison she had to spit out. "From the moment I met you, all my scenarios evaporated, and I was unable to be anything with you but the person you knew, the person I didn't realize existed. It was with you that I became aware of my true personality." At his groan, she turned her face into his shoulder, escaping the intensity in his eyes. "I realized almost at once that I was actually feeling something for you. And among all the dangers I ever faced, those unknown feelings were the most dangerous thing that ever happened to me. It was as though you were my first intimacy. And you were. Any other man I've been with was a mission, an evil I've been forced to endure with a seductive smile while my soul retched or, at best, was numb."

"Scarlett…"

She burrowed into his chest, unable to let him interrupt. The floodgates had opened and everything came gushing out. "It was with you that my senses were awakened for the first time and I realized what intimacy was, what transfiguring passion felt like. You were my first pleasure…then you become my first and, I'm certain, my last love."

Never. Never in his wildest dreams had Raiden expected this. His best hope had been that she'd tell him the truth, and that it would include an admission to validate his feelings. That he hadn't been just a mission to her, that she'd felt something real for him. Then, and now. Never had he dared wish she'd say anything near the things she'd just said.

But she'd said them. She felt them. Had always felt them.

And it felt as if the last barrier he'd erected inside him to protect himself from the heartache she'd caused came crashing down. Admissions rushed in, swamping him in the truth of his emotions for her.

Just as she'd come to life with him, so had he with her. Just as he was her first and last intimacy, her one and only love, so was she his.

Emotions rose like a tidal wave inside him.

With trembling hands he tried to lift her head from where she'd buried it into his chest, needing communion with her in those transfiguring moments. "Scarlett, darling, please, let me…"

Resisting him, she kept her head plastered over his thundering heart, words rushing out of her again, drowning whatever he would have said. "But it wasn't only when I realized I'd fallen in love with you that it became imperative I ended the danger to you. From the first moment I met you, I knew you weren't one of the sleazebags or criminals I was always sent after, and who deserved everything I did to them and more. You were everything I didn't think existed—a noble man who used your powers for the greater good, and who never advertised your benevolence. It was by following in your steps that I ended up in my line of work now."

She raised her head then, and he felt as if he got a direct blow to the heart. Her eyes. God, her eyes.

The emotions in them were staggering. As if everything she'd ever suppressed, ever hidden from him, from the whole world, was flooding out. He felt submerged.

She threaded shaking hands in his hair, such tenderness in her touch and gaze. "Then I found out that you were like me, but that you had escaped when I knew I never would. If I loved you with all my newly forged heart before that, I loved you even more then, with the broken parts of me before the whole ones I discovered inside me because of you. All I cared about from then on was protecting you at all costs."

Her hands smoothed over his head, chest and shoulders, becoming feverish, as if she wanted to make sure he was here, safe, whole, and that she had protected him.

"To protect you, I had to throw Medvedev off your scent. So I stalled him until I figured out how to prove you weren't his escaped agent, and to be with you for as long as I could."

Every word she said felt like a stab, their collective pain pouring out of him on a butchered groan. "Why didn't you tell me everything? I would have taken care of Medvedev and saved you from The Organization."

Her eyes shot up to his, the tears filling them rippling like a pool in an earthquake. It was clear she'd never thought this even an option.

"Did you fear I'd punish you if I knew the truth?"

Her expression made it clear that wasn't something she'd considered, either. "I was only afraid you'd go after Medvedev, and I couldn't risk you. He was an unpredictable monster."

He grimaced at her misplaced fear. "Didn't you know enough about me to know I could have handled Medvedev in my sleep? Or did you think I would, but still wouldn't help you?"

Her eyes implored his belief, when he'd sooner doubt himself rather than her now. "I only cared about your safety and the new life you'd built. And I wanted to end Medvedev's danger to you without you finding out the truth about me and how I came to be with you. I wanted to remain the one you trusted implicitly, wanted totally. I couldn't bear seeing the trust and passion in your eyes turn to contempt and disgust if you knew. I wanted to hold on to the memories. Those months with you, the way you looked at, the way you treated me, meant more to me than anything."

"More than your life?"

"Yes."

He stared at her, the implications of her cried out affirmation boggling his mind.

She'd truly thought holding on to her memories and to his good opinion of her more important than escaping her enslavement, or even preserving her life.

Being unable to reach into the past to make her realize that he would have forgiven her anything, that there'd been nothing to forgive, corroded his sanity. Her false belief had deprived him of the chance to protect her, save her.

He couldn't even avenge her. Medvedev was already dead.

But, no. He'd been working to bring down The Organization—for himself, his brothers and all the unknown children who had been abused. But now, more than ever, he would destroy it on her behalf. His vengeance would now know no bounds. He would wreak unimaginable pain on everyone who'd had a hand in a single moment of her suffering. And when she hadn't told him the worst parts yet... Though he no longer knew if he could withstand hearing them.

But he would, no matter what it did to him. He had to relieve her of all of her burdens, in every way he could.

A distant look came into her eyes. "But all my precautions were in vain. When you called me that last time, the moment I heard your voice I knew you'd found me out. I knew it was the end and I wasn't ready. I would have never been ready. Everything I feared came to pass. You sounded as I always dreaded—angry and disillusioned and disgusted. I was only grateful I didn't see all that on your face. And there was only one thing I could do. Make it all worse."

She looked into his eyes with everything she was on display for the first time. And it was beyond his imagining.

"I wanted to disappear," she said. "Make it impossible for Medvedev to find me. I also wanted to help others in my same situation, but I knew our collective freedoms would cost a huge amount of money. So I blackmailed you for it. That also served to end everything between us on the worst note possible.

"But before I could leave the country, Medvedev walked into the hotel room where I was under a false name. He was shrewd enough to sense I'd make a run for it. I told him I just wanted to escape The Organization, that I thought he wouldn't come through for me since I only had proof you weren't his agent. But he was convinced I had proof you were, even deducted I'd blackmailed you myself, though he assigned me purely mercenary motives for that. He said once I gave him the info, he wouldn't only extort you himself, but your partners, too, whom he was certain were the other operatives who escaped, making this more lucrative than he'd ever thought."

She paused to draw in a shuddering breath. "I failed to divert him, and he just knew everything. I knew he'd turn your hard-won freedom into a new prison, would end up turning you over to The Organization to redeem himself. The one card I had left was that he needed solid info, and I wouldn't give it to him. At first, he still promised he'd keep his end of the bargain if I did mine. But I refused, told him he couldn't do a thing without proof. And he started torturing me."

Something fundamental charred inside him. Red-hot wrath against a dead man he couldn't kill again almost ate through his arteries.

"I knew I wouldn't walk out of that room alive, but I could still save you if I took him down with me. With the last strength left in me, I stabbed him with a stiletto I used as a hair clip. I know how to kill a man with one strike, but he was no ordinary man. Instead of going into instant shock, he was all over me. He almost killed me… before he succumbed."

His whole body started shaking, on the verge of exploding. Scarlett had fought a monster like Medvedev and sustained near-fatal injuries…for him.

"I managed to stem my bleeding, to leave the hotel without being seen, to barely reach a secret medical center before I collapsed. It took them days to stabilize me."

She stopped, and her silence stretched. His blood burned and congealed in his arteries each single second.

Then she talked again, as if in a fugue. "As soon as I was well enough, I started acquiring this new face and a new identity. I came back here believing I'd have the painful pleasure of seeing you from afar without any danger of you recognizing me. But you did recognize me, and now you've even found out everything I thought would forever remain hidden."

Long minutes after she fell silent again, agonized beyond endurance, he choked out, "Why didn't you tell me all this when you met me again? When there was no more danger to me? Why did you let me think the worst of you?"

Suddenly her eyes looked exactly as they had in the photo Numair had showed him. Lifeless, hopeless. "Because there was no point. I came here thinking you'd long forgotten me. Then you recognized me and offered me this arrangement, and I knew I was just passing through your life. I only wanted to have this time with you before I moved on. I knew you'd go on to have the life you worked so hard to establish and you'd never think of me again. And I didn't want you to. I wanted to give you the closure I deprived you of the first time."

"I didn't want closure, Scarlett." He gripped her face, his hands shaking, needing her to know every single thing he'd felt all these years. "I lived all these years going insane for an explanation, *this* explanation. I was unable to come to terms with the discrepancy between what I felt with you, from you, and what it had seemed to be. I've been unable to have any kind of intimacy again."

"You mean you didn't…?" A tiny flame leaped in her eyes before it was immediately extinguished.

He crushed her in his arms, his heart convulsing at the despondence in her eyes. She'd never even considered it was possible for him to feel the same for her as she felt for him.

Needing to make her believe he'd always been hers, to erase every terrible moment she'd ever lived, he raised her face to his and held her eyes. "I didn't. I couldn't. I was yearning for the only woman I ever wanted, and it was excruciating because I thought you were a lie. But not only have you always been real and everything I ever craved and more, you protected me and my brothers from exposure. You saved our lives. And it almost cost you your own."

It cost me something more precious to me than my life.
Scarlett barely caught back the cry.

She couldn't let him know that. Not that. But she couldn't let him make it sound as if what she'd done had been a sacrifice. Giving him up had been that. Protecting him with her life had been a privilege.

She tried to wave his gratitude away, but he persisted.

"You must accept your dues. And you will have the gratitude and lifelong allegiance of my brothers, too. Yes, my partners in Black Castle Enterprises are all The Organization's escapees. We formed a brotherhood within our prison, swore a blood oath to escape, become unstoppable and bring down The Organization and anyone associated with it. We're going through the list from the outside in, and from bottom to top in such convoluted-ways, they wouldn't know what hit them before they're destroyed." Suddenly he frowned, as if remembering something. "What happened to the people you wanted to help?"

She remembered the friends who'd held her together all these years, before and after Raiden. They were now safe in their new lives, which made her aching lips spread in a smile of relief and thankfulness. "I got them out, built them new identities, too. I told you I put your money to the best use."

His gorgeous eyes poured what looked like pride over her, making her heart flutter like a hummingbird.

Then the frown of murderous wrath was back, even blacker. "Are the faint scars on your abdomen Medvedev's stabs?"

The noose of agonizing memories choked her again as she nodded, averting her gaze so she could tell the half-truth. "They were aesthetically revised during my other surgeries."

"Tell me he died in horrific pain."

At his vicious growl, she attempted a shrug. "Probably. I was too busy with my own pain and peril to notice his."

His fingers sank into her shoulders again. "Why didn't you call me? For God's sake, Scarlett, did you think I wouldn't save you?"

His rage at the long-dead Medvedev was palpable. But it was his frustration with her, for not seeking his protection at first, then his help later that he seemed unable to handle. For a man like him, one who took charge and resolved problems, feeling helpless must be the worst thing that could happen to him. He must feel the same now, being unable to change the past.

"I told you what I thought," she murmured. "Contacting you again under any circumstances wasn't even an option."

"Even if you thought you were dying?"

"Especially then. I left to protect you. I would never have considered dragging you to a crime scene, risking your reputation and putting you under the law's scrutiny."

Her rationalizations seemed about to cause him an apoplectic fit. He seemed to vibrate as he struggled with bringing the tirades storming inside him under control.

Then he attacked on a different front, bombarding her with questions. "What were your injuries exactly? How long did it take you to heal? Do you suffer from any lasting damage or ongoing pain?"

I suffer both, she wanted to whimper.

But this was the one thing she wouldn't tell him. This was her loss and she couldn't let him share it.

But he would ask and push until he left her no place to hide any secrets. And she had to keep this one.

To shut him up, divert him, and because she couldn't bear wasting one more moment with him, she clung to him, her hands digging into his luxurious hair, tugging him closer. "No more questions, Raiden. I want you right this second."

He bared his teeth on a silent growl, his body lurching, tensing as if at the shock of a lash.

Peeling her hands off him with his own trembling ones, he held out a warning finger. "Don't, Scarlett. I'm not in control of myself. I was never in this condition."

Disregarding his warning, she lunged at him, tore his shirt out of his pants, attacked his zipper. "I want you out of control. I want you savage and rough and unable to stop. Take me hard and fast and now, Raiden. I can't wait. I *can't.*"

His harsh intakes of breath confessed his pleasure at

her frenzy, but he ended it, capturing her feverish hands. When she writhed against him, raining bites and kisses anywhere she could reach, the last of his restraint crumbled, and she finally made him do what she wanted him to. He hauled her up in his arms and hurtled with her to his bed.

Once there, he flung her down onto her stomach, then launched himself over her, covering her with his great body. It was as if he was shielding her, hiding her, and poignancy welled out of her depths on a keen. Rumbling incessantly, he sounded like a beast, one protecting his mate, maddened and heartbroken he hadn't been able to prevent her injury before he got to her.

Aching at his protectiveness, intoxicated by his possessiveness, she raised her head and met his wild eyes in the mirrored headboard. The sight of their replicas in the coolness of glass—how he dominated her, how she looked taken whole by him—ignited her down to her last nerve ending. And that was before his words scorched her.

"Five years, Scarlett, five interminable years, struggling with losing you. Now it's even worse, knowing you struggled, too, suffered more." Crying out at the desolation in his voice, she arched back into him, needing to absorb it. "But I have you back now, and you just gave me back every memory I thought I couldn't keep. It was all real. This is real. *This.*"

He pressed against her harder, as if he couldn't bear the physical boundaries separating them, his hardness digging into her yielding body. She went limp under him, showing him she wanted him to assimilate her, wanted to dissolve in him.

His eyes kept hers captive, and his hot breath scorched her face, filled her lungs. "I went insane every night, needing you like this and knowing I'd never have you again. Hunger built inside me without even hope for relief."

The first time he'd confessed this, her mind had swerved around his words, shying away from registering them. It was too huge to contemplate that he hadn't had any intimacies since her. This time there was no escaping his meaning. And it was still almost incomprehensible.

Tentatively, she met his gaze in the mirror. "Do you really mean you didn't...didn't...all this time?"

"Yes, I damn well really mean it." He ground harder into her, liquefying her even more. "Since I was a child I achieved absolute control over my urges, to hone my skills. It made me uninterested in sex, especially since I abhorred the form available to me. The Organization provided us with other captives to vent our libidos with."

Their eyes clung, and she knew he must wonder if she'd been one of those captives, if someone he knew had used her for that purpose.

Unable to bear it, she lowered her head to the bed, burying her face in the silk covers, tears starting to pour down her cheeks.

A trembling hand pulled her up to meet his vehement conviction. "I don't care and neither should you. We both did so many things against our will, and we're not responsible for any of it. It doesn't make us less or worse. It actually makes us more and better. We're survivors, conquerors, winners. But you... You're perfect."

Feeling as if her heart had expanded to fill her whole body, she twisted beneath him so hard, she made him roll off her. Then she was all over him, clinging with arms and legs and lips, tears now flowing with gratitude, with relief.

He let her deluge him for a while before taking over,

groaning into her lips. "My brothers used to call me The Monk. I thought I was, until you. Then I became insatiable. After you, after I experienced true passion and ecstasy, I couldn't settle for the sexual relief I never wanted in the first place. I wanted you. Only you. Even when I thought I'd never have you again. But now I do, and all I can think of is having you, doing everything to you, with you."

"Everything?" She moaned, undulating against him, needing him to combust. "Like what? Show me."

"Like this…" He flipped her onto her back, gloriously rough, dragging her top over her head and spilling her swollen breasts into the large palms they'd been made to fill. He kneaded them with a careful savagery that had her bucking beneath him, had her frantically trying to tear his clothes off his back. She needed the crush of his hunger, the oblivion of his possession.

Grasping both her hands in one, he did what she'd failed to. He shredded his shirt, flinging off its tatters. Her salivary glands stung, needing her lips and tongue all over his flesh, her teeth in it.

"And this." He slid down her body, the velvet of his skin sparking her every inch into a conflagration. "And this." He nipped each nipple in turn, had her crying out, before settling into suckling that escalated into ruthlessness, had her core pouring, until she was pummeling him for the release only his invasion would grant her.

He escaped her clawing hands, went down farther, taking her skirt and panties off with him. "And this."

Holding her feet apart, alternating kisses between them, he suckled her toes, forcing her to withstand the sight and sensations of his ownership, his worship. "And this." He bit into her calves, kneading them with his teeth as he trailed up to her inner thigh, before opening the lips of her core. Tantalizing her, he lapped up the flow of her arousal in long, leisurely licks before growling, "And this." He pinpointed the bud where all her nerves converged, took it in a sharp nip.

The discharge of all the pent-up stimulation was so explosive, she heaved in detonation after detonation until she felt as if her spine might snap.

He had no mercy. He pushed two fingers inside her, sharpening her pleasure until her voice broke. He didn't stop even then. No, he sucked every spasm and after-shock out of her, blasting her sensitized flesh with more growls. "And this." His thumb circled the swollen nub, had her writhing under the renewed surge, the need for release a rising crest of incoherence.

"Come for me again, my darling."

It was that "my darling" that hurled her into another orgasm.

After he'd finished her, he came up to loom over her, watching her tremble with what he'd done to her, his hand tracing soothing patterns on her back and buttocks. Mute, saturated with pleasure, hungrier for him than ever, she watched him, the emotions on his face coming too fast and thick for her to decipher. To withstand.

Spreading her legs wide, she begged him, "Inside me, Raiden. Come inside me."

He looked down at her, sable hair cascading over his leonine forehead. "I want to be inside you all the time, Scarlett. And I couldn't be for five years. Because you didn't trust me to understand, didn't give me the chance to help you, to protect you, to save you."

Her body contorted under the onslaught of his impassioned upbraiding. "I'm sorry... I didn't think..."

He captured her face in urgent hands. "You thought too much, and all wrong. And you should be sorry. When

I think what you almost did to yourself, what you cost us when you kept me in the dark, thinking you were protecting me, my head almost explodes."

"I did protect you," she protested weakly.

"And I want your word you'll never do anything like this again. Never hide anything from me again, Scarlett."

"I won't." She was half lying, for she was still hiding things, but she had to protect him from further pain. Needing to distract him, needing him beyond endurance, she wrapped herself around him. "Don't punish me anymore. Just take me."

His body turned to granite in her arms. "You punished us both when you sacrificed yourself for me. Don't you know I'd rather die than see you hurt? And for you to be hurt on my account... God, I don't know how I'll live with that knowledge."

She stared into his pained eyes, distress expanding in her throat all over again. No, she hadn't known that. She'd never dared dream of anything even far less.

Contrition suffocating her, she needed to take him away from the maddening what-ifs, bring him back to her in this moment. "You're hurting me now, Raiden, making me wait."

It was as if some switch was thrown inside him, the consternation on his face switching to voracity.

In full predator mode, he rose above her, rid himself of his pants and briefs. She felt the usual clench of intimidation at the sight of his girth and length, at his beauty and sleekness. She craved his invasion, not only for the ecstasy it forced from her flesh, but because it was the most intimacy she could have with him.

"Just take me, *please*...."

And he finally did. He rammed inside her, all his power and the accumulation of frustration and hunger behind the thrust. The head of his erection, nearly too wide for her, rubbed against all the right places, abrading nerves into an agony of response, pushing receptors over the limit of stimuli. Even after the releases he gave her, she was so inflamed that it took only a few unbridled thrusts for her to arch up in a deep bow and scream. In her ecstasy, she saw only his beloved face in focus, clenched in pleasure, his eyes vehement with his greed for her.

Every time with him it got better. Excruciatingly better.

"I can't… Please… You…you… Now…"

He understood, gave her what she needed. The sight of his face seizing, his roars echoing her screams, the feel of him succumbing to the ecstasy she gave him, the hard jets of his climax inside her. They hit her at her peak, had her unable to endure the spike in pleasure, then everything dimmed, faded.…

Heavy breathing and slow heartbeats echoed from the end of a long tunnel as the scents of satisfaction flooded her lungs. Awareness trickled into a body so sated it was numb.

She felt only one thing. Raiden. Still inside her, even harder, larger. She opened lids weighing half a ton each, saw him swim in and out of focus. He was still kneeling between her legs, her buttocks propped on his thighs, her legs around his. One of his palms was kneading her breasts, the other gliding over her shoulders, her arms, her belly.

"You are mine. *Mine*. As Scarlett. As Hannah. As Katya."

She lurched at hearing her real name on his lips. She'd known he must know it now, but hearing him say it…

She moaned as he ground deeper inside her, reaching

the point where the familiar expansion turned into almost pain. An edge of dominance that was glorious, addictive, overwhelming, even a little frightening. The idea of all that he was, melding with her, at her mercy as she was at his, filled volumes inside her, body, mind and soul.

"Say it. You're mine. All of you. Every version of you."

"There was only ever one version. The version born to love you."

She truly didn't know what happened after that.

Raiden devoured her, finished her, then did so again and again.

It was as though his passion had always been curbed, but now all his shackles had been broken. He showed her what it could be like with him fully unleashed.

It was beyond description.

After the nightlong conflagration, she lay in his arms in a stupor, every cell in her body overloaded with bliss. At least before the ticking timer inside her resumed the countdown.

Her ten weeks were almost up. No matter what he'd said now, how he felt, his plans were more important, couldn't be changed. And she'd have to exit his life soon.

But she couldn't even contemplate being cut off from him forever.

There was only one way she wouldn't be.

Unsteadily, she struggled to prop herself over his endless chest. Looking down at him, she marveled again that all this beauty and power could be hers, even if temporarily.

Then she made the tentative bid for permanence.

"I want to amend our arrangement, Raiden. I want to remain your lover after you're married."

Eight

Raiden sat up slowly, not only because Scarlett's offer had rocked him to his core, because he felt he'd drained his very life force inside her. Four times.

After that statement, that she'd been born to love him, he didn't know what had happened to him. It was as if every iota of control he'd ever practiced had been building up an opposite wildness, and only a measure of that had been released in the past with her, probably because on some level he'd felt there had been something not quite right. Since they'd been together again, their whole situation had rationed his uninhibitedness. Then she'd made that declaration, and it had been as if the dam inside him had burst.

The way he'd taken her, in a sustained eruption of raging hunger, the way she'd surrendered unconditionally, and the explosive pleasure they'd wrung from each other... It had been transfiguring, transcendent.

After that last time he'd taken her in the shower, he'd taken her back to bed and had been feeling another cataclysm building. Then she'd staggered up and made that out-of-the-blue offer and everything had dissipated with shock.

She was now looking at him avidly, her hair hanging

around her gleaming shoulders in thick, wet locks, her lips and body showing the effects of his fierce possession.

He'd never seen anything more beautiful, known anything more overpowering.

The seductive smile playing on her kiss-swollen lips didn't reach her eyes. Those were faltering as she painted his chest in caresses. "Powerful men in Japan almost always have mistresses, and it's accepted as long as they're discreet and don't disgrace their wives and families. I will abide by any precautions you need to maintain our secret." She pouted in a rickety attempt at reprimand. "You'll certainly have to curb the impulses you've been having of late, popping up wherever I am, taking me out or home for all to see."

He suddenly wanted to get up, get away and stop this.

But before he could move, she hugged him fiercely around the waist, laid her hot face over his thudding heart. Her lips trembled against his skin as she spelled out her offer. "If you can't have enough of me, as I can't have enough of you, this doesn't have to end. I don't want to lose you, and I'll do anything, stay anywhere, as long as I can have you like this. I know once you get married your situation will change, but you don't have to leave me behind to have the family, the heritage and the heirs you've planned to have for so long. You can have me indefinitely if you want, and also have everything else you ever craved and deserve."

Raiden's head filled with cacophony, every response that screamed in his mind jumbling together, paralyzing him, muting him.

She was giving him a carte blanche to her life.

It was again the last thing he'd expected. Not that he'd expected anything, being tossed about in last night's tumult.

But if he'd been able to think, he would have come to one conclusion. That it was no longer a possibility he'd give her up on their agreed-on date, or at all. He couldn't even think of a life without her now. Couldn't think of another reason to live but being with her, being hers. He was finally free to face that he'd loved her from the first moment and had never stopped loving her. But he now loved her with a profundity he hadn't thought himself capable of. And he now knew she reciprocated his emotions in full. If he'd thought at all, he would have thought he'd be the one to plead with her not to leave his side.

But she'd preempted him, offering herself without reservations, relegating herself to a permanent position in the shadows in his life.

What hurt most was that she believed it was her natural place, that it was all she was worth, to be hidden as if she was a shameful secret. She believed she was, saw herself as tainted with a stain that would never be cleansed.

Before he voiced one of a million vehement arguments to the opposite, the color suddenly drained from her face.

"You—you don't want any more time with me, let alone indefinitely, do you?" Her bloodless lips contorted. "It—it's just when you said… I thought you… Oh, God, I'm sorry I—"

Her stumbling apology came to an abrupt end as her eyes rolled back in her head and she sagged back on the bed in a dead faint.

The detonation of terror almost made him follow suit.

He didn't, only because he'd turned to stone with fright.

Then shock splintered and he pounced on her, his heart rupturing. "Scarlett… God, Scarlett, darling…"

She didn't move when he shook her. His hands were shaking so hard, he couldn't detect her pulse….

Stop it. Get yourself under control.

He heard himself barking the self-admonition, tried to force himself to think, but could only think she was lying there, ashen, unmoving. And he couldn't rouse her, couldn't tell if she was breathing.

Yet even panicking, his mechanisms of performing under maximum duress kicked in, making him go through emergency procedures.

Then he did the one thing he'd always done when he or any of his brothers was injured or unwell. He called Antonio.

As soon as the line clicked open, Raiden choked, "Scarlett fainted. I can't wake her up."

Without preamble, Antonio went into doctor mode. "Place her on her back, remove any constricting clothing, raise her legs above heart level about twelve inches, then check her airway for anything blocking it. Watch for vomiting. If she vomits, immediately place her on her side."

"I did all that, and she still won't wake up." His voice barely came out, futile tears starting to run down his cheeks.

"Give me her vitals."

He gritted out her breath and heartbeat count.

"Slow, but not dangerously so. Neurologic status?"

"Reflexes are normal. But she won't wake up!"

"That on its own means nothing. Whatever the reason she's unconscious, she isn't in any immediate danger."

"You can't know that!"

"Given your report, I can. Did you call an ambulance?"

"I called you. You're the best there is. Get your ass over here *now*."

"I assume 'here' is your new residence?" Raiden's

apoplectic expletive made Antonio sigh. "Calm down before you give yourself a stroke. I'd rather have only one patient on my hands when I arrive." Before Raiden yelled the building down, he heard slamming doors on the other end of the phone, then before the line went dead, Antonio said, "I'm already on my way."

Shaking out of control, Raiden threw the phone down and pounced on Scarlett. He checked her pulse and breathing over and over, caressed and crooned to her to please wake up.

She didn't. She remained unconscious until Antonio arrived, what felt like an eternity later. It had actually been only ten minutes, which he'd counted second for second. From his perspiring condition, it was clear Antonio had run the whole way from his hotel a few blocks away.

In those endless minutes, Raiden had dressed Scarlett in her underwear, then wrapped her freezing body in the comforter. He'd been wrapped around her to transfer his body heat to her when Steve had let in Antonio. He could now barely relinquish her still form and stand aside to let Antonio start his exam.

Antonio had come prepared, with his magical medical bag as they called it, with supplies and instruments inside ready to handle anything from simple cuts to major field surgery.

He examined Scarlett with all-knowing hands and all-seeing eyes, took her pressure, drew blood, performed neurologic tests, used a few instruments Raiden didn't recognize. Then he finally put everything back into his bag.

Out of his mind by now, Raiden growled like a cornered beast. "Why didn't you wake her up?"

Antonio looked up at him serenely. "Because I can't."

"What do you mean you can't?"

Antonio looked at him with those imperturbable green eyes. "I might be capable of almost anything medically, but contrary to common belief, I can't perform miracles."

"It would take a miracle to wake her up now?" He nearly choked on the words.

"Stop making the worst assumptions, Raiden, for your own health. What you see in movies with instant injections and slaps and smelling salts are just for drama's sake. In the real world you *should* leave an unconscious person to wake up on her own, as long as we've made sure nothing else is wrong with her."

"But there has to be something wrong with her. She just turned off and won't turn back on!"

"I have a diagnosis for that." Antonio stood up, looked him in the eyes like someone about to impart something that would change his life. Then he did. "She's totally exhausted. And seriously upset. *And* certainly pregnant."

Scarlett surfaced from what felt like an abyss.

It had been dark and oppressive down there. But she'd been unwilling to escape it. It had at least been safe, and better than the alternative. That of coming out only to face a far worse bleakness. That of Raiden's rejection.

She'd offered him herself, no strings attached, forever if he'd take her that long. The dismay on his face had hurt so much, she hadn't been able to handle it. She had wished she'd just stop feeling anything so it wouldn't hurt anymore.

She realized she'd fainted. Which was weird. That was the first time her consciousness had given out, yielded to the refuge of oblivion. Not even in her worst of times, and she'd had some nightmarish ones, had it come to her rescue like that. But then, none of those times had been as brutal as knowing it was over with Raiden. Now she was reluctant to exit its protection, wanted to remain in its cold cloak forever.

But there was no use. She was already awake. Even before she opened her eyes, she knew what she'd see. Raiden.

He was standing beside the bed, looking down at her. She could feel his gaze on her, emitting impatience, no doubt for her to come around. There was something else, too. Agitation.

Was that on account of her fainting, or of the offer she'd made before she had? Or both? Did he think he'd have a hysterical female on his hands once she woke up? One who'd start clinging and causing him problems he couldn't afford?

Might as well open her eyes and reassure him that he had nothing to fear from her. She'd made a desperate bid for more time with him, and she'd lost. As she'd known she would. But she'd had to try. Now it was over, and she'd go in silence as she'd intended. But he didn't know that. It was time to let him know.

She opened her eyes, and his image filled her aching gaze. He'd put on pants, was standing over her like a monolith, every muscle in his majestic body bunched, making him look even more perfect, more intimidating. That body that had owned and pleasured hers in magical ways would soon be only a memory. Just like everything else with him. Even his confession that he'd been with no other woman. No matter how he desired her, his plans were what mattered to him. As they should.

Struggling to prop herself up, she pushed hair out of her eyes. "Sorry for passing out on you like that."

"How can you apologize? It isn't as if you could have done something about it."

He sounded hoarse. She did, too, her voice abused with too many cries of pleasure. It felt so strange, made her feel so cold, after that indescribable interlude of intimacy, for him to be standing there, separate from her. But she'd known all along that this was coming. Maybe this fainting spell had been timely, ending the scene she would have so impulsively caused. Now discussing it would be without the flagrant emotions of the moment, would be distant and detached.

She sat up. "I guess not. But I do apologize for what I said before I fainted. It must have been the euphoric high after the incredible sex. But I'm taking back everything I said and we're returning to our scheduled separation. In fact, I think I just pushed the date forward. We had the revelations and confessions and got everything out in the open and off our chests, and had an unprecedented session worthy of a last hurrah. Anything after that would be redundant, so it's time to say our goodbyes."

She flung the comforter off as if it burned her, even if it acutely dismayed her to be seminaked in front of him now. Now that their intimacies were over, she felt as she had all her life, stripped of her every dignity and hiding place. She felt far worse than she ever had. With any other, she hadn't cared about feeling like a sullied, expendable object.

She talked as she started to dress. "I'm leaving Japan within a week. So it will be before your wedding. This time when I disappear, you won't have to worry you'll ever see me again."

"Was that the original plan? To disappear without telling me?"

She blinked up at him. His face was gripped in some emotion she couldn't fathom. Every angle in his masterpiece bone structure jutted out more against his burnished skin, as if he was straining under an insupportable burden.

"Telling you what?"

"That you're pregnant."

If Raiden had told her he was an alien, then flew around the room to prove it, she wouldn't have been more stunned.

She must have gaped at him for minutes before she closed her open mouth and tried to overcome her shock.

"When were you going to tell me, Scarlett?"

Slowly, carefully, as if testing her voice for the first time, she said, "Never, I guess. Since I'm not."

His eyes suddenly took on a faraway look. "I *have* been feeling it in every inch of you. The changes in your body, in your appetite, the extra sensitivity to some scents, to my touch. But I didn't reach the obvious conclusion, because I thought you'd tell me if it was true. But you didn't." His eyes focused on hers again, something enormous roiling in their depths. "Why, Scarlett? Was it because you thought we'd say goodbye and I didn't have to know?" His face drained of all color suddenly. "Or was it because it was a mistake, one you intended to…fix?"

She shook her head, his every word making her more nauseous. "If you're suspecting I fainted because I'm pregnant, don't. I can't be."

"Why can't you be? I haven't taken any precautions."

She raised her hands, needing to stop this before she fainted again, or vomited, or both. "You didn't because you assumed I did. So if you're thinking you shouldn't have left this in my hands, that if I'm pregnant it would cause you major trouble, don't be. I am *not* pregnant."

It was his turn to gape at her. "You're really not aware that you are pregnant, are you?"

"Listen, Raiden, I'm not only not pregnant, I *can't* be pregnant. So stop it…*please.*"

"What do you mean *can't?* You are."

"No, I'm not." He opened his mouth to persist, and her voice rose to a shriek to drown out his. "I can't *ever* be pregnant. I had a traumatic miscarriage and doctors told me I'd never be able to get pregnant again!"

Raiden staggered a step back. Even the most innocuous words from Scarlett hit him harder than any of the vicious blows he'd had in his life, literal or figurative. But this blow almost felled him, when nothing before had ever even compromised his balance.

She truly had no idea she was pregnant. She thought she couldn't become pregnant. Because she'd…she'd…

It made sense, explained the pervasive loss in her eyes that not even her past or their present situation explained. That was what he'd still felt her holding back from him. And he had to heal that wound that remained open inside her.

"You were pregnant with my child?" He made it a question, in case it hadn't been his. She hadn't given a time frame, and it might have happened long before they'd met. Even though everything inside him screamed she'd lost his—their—baby.

From the wounded look in her eyes, his care seemed to offend her. "You think I would have let myself get pregnant by another man? Protecting myself was the first thing I was taught in the business I was pushed into."

His heart squeezed and expanded at the same time. Her pregnancy had been premeditated. Out loud he still asked, "You let yourself become pregnant with my child?"

She looked away, as if she could no longer bear looking at him. "I knew there was no possible future with you, but I wanted to at least have a part of you with me always. I had this plan that I was going to save you from Medvedev, escape The Organization and go somewhere safe and raise the baby on my own, give it the life we've both been robbed of. But we both know how this plan went."

Was it possible there was always more pain? He felt a new level of agony contemplating the incredible courage and selflessness and love it took to make those plans. It was excruciating imagining how she'd felt—the resignation that she'd never have him, the hope she'd considered the epitome of her ambitions, the determination to have a baby, alone, make it safe and loved, as she'd never been.

He struggled not to sag to his knees before her, not to beg her to forgive him for not being there for her, for being oblivious, for not giving her everything she deserved. He choked out his words. "It went spectacularly for the most part. You did save me from Medvedev, did escape The Organization."

"Not because my plan was masterful or anything. The one reason I pulled it off and I'm not dead is because Medvedev underestimated me and underestimated what I'd do to protect you. It was all touch and go and the price was our—" Her face seized, as if she'd caught herself in a terrible faux pas. "The baby. Now I'm unable to have any other."

Before he insisted she'd always call it "our baby," before he convinced her she was already having another one, there was one more poison he needed her to purge from her system. "It was Medvedev's stab that aborted our baby."

Her throat worked as she nodded, confirming his statement, her face that impassive mask he now realized she'd tailored to obscure enormous emotions and suffering.

"They told me it was the baby that saved my life, taking most of the damage for me. But the damage to my uterus was too extensive. They told me I'd never have children again."

He was unable to find words to express his pain and regret and rage and frustration that he couldn't change the past, couldn't give of his own life and flesh to defend hers, to wipe away her scars, mental and physical. And that he couldn't punish Medvedev a thousand times over. But he promised himself again he'd punish everyone who had a hand in Medvedev's existence, and in her suffering, past and present.

But now he had to dispel at least one of her agonies.

Producing the proof from his pocket, he took her hand and placed it in her palm. "This is a blood-testing chip that our resident medical genius in Black Castle Enterprises has patented. He says it yields one hundred percent results in diagnosing a variety of conditions, one of which is pregnancy. He came to my rescue when you fainted and performed the blood test, and his diagnosis is unequivocal. You *are* pregnant."

Scarlett dazedly looked down at the credit card–size transparent plastic chip. The slot for HCG, the hormone detecting pregnancy, was a bright positive red.

Shaking her head, she raised disbelieving eyes to him. "It must be a mistake. I—I can't be pregnant."

"Antonio doesn't make mistakes, Scarlett. The ones who made a mistake were the doctors who gave you that verdict." When she shook her head again, she swayed and he surged to steady her, taking her by the shoulders. "We'll redo the test just to put your mind to rest. But we always trusted Antonio with our very lives. If he's certain, so am I. He believes you're eight weeks pregnant."

Still shaking her head, looking punch-drunk, Scarlett whispered, "That's how long ago our first night was."

Poignancy tightened his hands, bringing her beloved body closer. "I do have a feeling you got pregnant that night."

Tears suddenly welled in her reddened eyes, then flowed down her cheeks, cutting streaks into his heart. "But I saw the CT scans. The damage was too extensive. Even if I'm pregnant…it can't be possible I'll carry the baby to term. Or it's even worse, and it's an ectopic pregnancy. That would still yield a positive test result."

The thought that she could be right about either possibility gripped his heart in crushing dread. He ran to call Antonio.

At his barked order to come back at once, Antonio only asked if Scarlett was awake. Raiden affirmed that, and Antonio only told him to put him on speaker.

Vibrating with anxiety, Raiden complied, though he didn't know why he'd asked that. Antonio was a prankster, but he wouldn't tease him about something like this, and certainly not now of all times.

Once on speaker, Antonio addressed Scarlett. "I assume you didn't realize you're pregnant? Because you thought it wasn't possible?" Scarlett looked even more dazed that Antonio knew what both of them hadn't known. "And now that you do, you're worried about the viability of your pregnancy? And that's why Raiden is working on a stroke again?"

After Scarlett nodded weakly as if Antonio could see her, Antonio went on as if he had. "I can see why you thought that. I performed a thorough exam with ultrasound, but Raiden must have been too agitated to notice, or he didn't recognize my patented handheld ultrasound for what it is. I did see your old scars, inside and out, and from their site and extensiveness, I can see why your doctors would have given you a prognosis of sterility. And they would have been absolutely right, if not for something exceptional about you.

"You're one of a rare percentage blessed with no scarring tendencies. This means your wounds heal almost as elastic as your intact tissues and skin. It's why your esthetic surgery is virtually undetectable. From the current condition of your uterus, I believe you'll carry your baby without incident and with normal activity to at least thirty-two weeks. After that, I recommend bed rest until term. Your miracle baby's development is above average, and you'll surely do everything so it continues to grow at the same rate, so by thirty-six weeks it should be mature enough to be delivered. I recommend C-section, which I'll of course perform."

After Antonio finished his thorough medical report, he promised he'd allocate her a whole day for a total checkup. He suffered Raiden's overwhelmed, overwhelming thanks and ended the call because he was in the middle of surgery.

She remained staring at Raiden all through, her face a mask of shock. Then suddenly the mask cracked and the whole spectrum of emotions fast-forwarded on her face. What she'd just learned, what she'd long craved and despaired of, coming true so unexpectedly... It must be changing everything inside her, rearranging her life and expectations forever. As it was his.

Not that the pregnancy changed what he felt, or what he intended to do. His love for her had already changed everything. The pregnancy, especially one thought to be impossible, was just an extra jubilation. And it was the least fate owed her after all she'd overcome, all she was doing to spare others what she'd suffered.

And it would be only the beginning. She'd have love and safety and cherishing and everything that he was and had to give for the rest of his life.

"Raiden…" She swayed again, and he caught her, swept her up in a fervent embrace and took her back to bed.

He knew she fell asleep the moment she touched the sheets. It had all been too much for her. But now it wasn't a dead faint that claimed her, but deep, recharging sleep. The heartbreakingly blissful smile on her lips said that.

All he wanted was to strip both of them and fuse their flesh and go to sleep wrapped around her, enfolding her and their coming baby in his love and protection.

But before he did that, his phone rang.

Thinking it must be Antonio calling back to add medical advice, he eagerly and not a little anxiously answered.

"Raiden-san, you must come to my office at once."

His uncle's clipped command shot through him with dismay.

The call was over the moment he said, "Of course." Whatever his uncle had to say, he would say only to his face.

In the next second, a smile played on his lips. He marveled at how everything was conspiring to come together. Numair's discoveries had led to Scarlett's confessions, then to Antonio's revelation. Now, from his usually courteous uncle's coldness, this was leading to the confrontation Raiden had been expecting. But instead of placating his uncle and taking a slap on his wrist for his public indiscretions with Scarlett the past two weeks, he'd inform his uncle he was no longer his future father-in-law.

* * *

In half an hour, he entered his uncle's office, found him standing behind his desk, leaning on it, palms down. From his wiped-clean-of-expression face, and that he didn't meet him at the door and didn't salute him now, Raiden knew the man was furious.

Good. It would make this easier. It was always harder giving people their marching orders when they were nice.

Takeo Hashimoto started without preamble. "We've found out about your illicit relationship with that foreign woman."

Just as he'd figured. He was even wondering why this confrontation hadn't happened earlier.

Raiden regarded his uncle calmly as he took a seat across his desk. It was regretful Hashimoto would not become family. He'd been starting to feel he was truly his flesh and blood. But this was probably the last time he'd see the man. Or if he saw him again, it would be as antagonists, at least on Hashimoto's side. Breaking his honor-bound pact would be an irreparable insult. There was no coming back from that.

"We? You mean you've told Megumi?"

"She's the one who told me."

That surprised Raiden. Not that Megumi knew, for of course she'd have been the first to be made aware of his indiscretions. But he hadn't thought she of all people would care, let alone run to her father with the information.

"It was that mongrel Hiro Matsuyama who set this up. And now he claims this woman carries your child."

This straight-out flabbergasted Raiden. Had *everyone* realized Scarlett was pregnant before they did?

But he asked his uncle the question relevant to him. "What does Hiro have to do with any of this?"

Hashimoto looked at him as if he'd dropped a hundred points of his IQ. "He brought her to that ball, where he pretended to honor your and Megumi's engagement. But he only did so he'd put that professional seductress in your way."

Dread zapped through Raiden. Was it possible Hashimoto had found out about Scarlett's past identity? No. He couldn't have. But why would he say that about her if he didn't?

Sitting forward, he picked his words with care. "She's a humanitarian worker, and she's Hiro's best friend. How did you come up with the theory that Hiro threw her in my path so she'd seduce me? Why would Hiro want that anyway?"

"Because he covets Megumi," Hashimoto barked. "He not only wants to stop your marriage, but he needs to do it with a scandal big enough that the ensuing disgrace would make it impossible for us to aspire to another worthy match. Then I'd be forced to accept someone like him as a husband for her."

This was yet another surprise. Raiden hadn't detected that Hiro was attracted to Megumi. But then, in the only time he'd seen them together, he'd been busy thinking that Hiro was besotted with Scarlett.

But now that he replayed that ball in his mind, he could see the whole thing in a new light. Hiro's aggression toward him had been over Megumi. And Megumi's agitation had been over Hiro.

Those two were in love!

That must be why Megumi had told her father about him and Scarlett. So he'd break off the engagement and she'd be free to be with Hiro.

God, how blind had he been?

But at least no real damage had been done. He'd call

Hiro after he broke things off with his uncle, telling him to rush to make a huge bid while the man was most open to compensatory offers. Even from someone he considered socially abhorrent.

For his uncle's sake, Raiden hoped he'd accept Hiro right away. His snobbery, though socially dictated, was starting to grate. If he exercised it on Hiro now that he realized there was mutual love involved, he'd show him his displeasure. He was sure his uncle wouldn't like to see his displeased side.

"So you just found out?" he asked.

"Megumi first told me three weeks after the ball."

Raiden's eyebrows shot up. That far back? The only way Megumi could have found out when he'd still been discreet was through Hiro. Being close to Scarlett, he must have noticed her sudden change of schedule, and all the other telltale signs of a woman being regularly, ferociously loved. Hiro could have also had a report of their garden house meeting and put one and one together. Maybe he'd even followed them to cement his deductions. As for how he'd realized Scarlett was pregnant, she did have all the signs for someone who was looking.

He sighed. "What kept you silent all this time?"

Hashimoto's dignified face darkened with disapproval. "At first you were discreet, and I thought you'd indulge in this woman for a while before settling down to a life of respectability with my pure daughter. Then you started getting careless, letting our partners and rivals see you flaunting that loose woman everywhere, taking her home with you for all to see. It's two weeks away from your wedding and I'm sure I just pulled you out of that woman's arms."

Raiden sighed again. "Yes, you just did."

"Is it also right you've impregnated her?"

The idea that hadn't sunk in fully yet, of Scarlett carrying his baby, a miracle baby by all accounts, spread his lips with its intense delight. "That is absolutely right."

Hashimoto looked at him in such horror, as if he'd just watched him cut off his own arm. "Don't you realize the magnitude of scandal this will cause?"

Raiden nodded calmly. "It won't be as bad as you think."

If he'd married Megumi, then had an illegitimate child with Scarlett, that would have been the stuff of permanent social stigma for the Hashimotos. But breaking off the engagement, even at this late date, for his pregnant gaijin lover… That would only be the stuff of malicious gossip. The most the Hashimotos would suffer would be a period of social ridicule. As for Raiden, he'd leave Japan, never to return. His exit from the scene would soon douse the scandal.

"Raiden-san, I truly expected better from you, far better. I never suspected you'd be so gullible that a woman like that could trick you into such a catastrophic position."

He pursed his lips. It was time to put him straight and end this. "Ms. Delacroix is a noble, courageous and benevolent woman, Takeo-sama, and I won't allow even a hint of disrespect toward her. She is the woman I love, the mother of my future child and the one I'm going to marry."

Hashimoto now looked as if Raiden had hacked off *his* arm.

Raiden exhaled forcibly. "I truly hoped we'd be family, Takeo-sama. I would have been honored to be your adopted son. But this will ultimately be for the best. I'm sorry I didn't end this earlier, but circumstances dictated the timing. You beat me to this confrontation, but the result would have been the same no matter who instigated it."

Hashimoto sagged down to his chair as if Raiden had shot him between the eyes. "You can't do this, Raiden-san... You can't. I—I called you here to demand you end your liaison right away, send that woman..." At his warning glance, Hashimoto swallowed. "Send Ms. Delacroix out of Japan."

"And now you know why I came to see you."

"But even if you no longer care about entering our family, or about destroying our honor, there are billions at stake. For everyone. And everyone includes Yakuza bosses."

This brought Raiden to the edge of his seat. "What the hell are you talking about?"

"Did you think a merger of this magnitude can happen without them insinuating themselves in it for a sizable piece of the pie? There are a dozen Yakuza branches counting on you becoming the head of our family, once this marriage comes through, *and* remains solid and producing heirs. But thanks to your lack of discretion, they found out about your liaison with Ms. Delacroix and were worried."

Before Raiden said everyone could go to hell for all he cared, Hashimoto drove his point home. "They are waiting like vultures for the mergers to occur so they'd have their commissions. They were already considering intervention to put an end to your liaison when they had no doubt you'd still marry Megumi. If they find out you won't, Ms. Delacroix will become an obstacle in the path of their interests. They wouldn't think twice about removing her from yours...permanently."

Nine

Raiden stared down at the city of Tokyo, sizzling with light and nightlife, his uproar ratcheting with every breath.

Unable to bear looking down anymore on this city where he'd once felt an intense sense of belonging, he closed the automatic blinds and crossed the penthouse in the dark.

Not that he needed lights. He'd operated in darkness more than half his life. He'd needed nothing but his skills, his will and his brothers. To succeed, to excel, to survive.

To live, he needed only Scarlett.

Everyone kept telling him he couldn't have her. His brothers, his uncle, society. All these didn't matter. Their opinions could be either changed or disregarded.

The Yakuza mattered. Their opinion was unchangeable.

And they'd sent him his uncle with a simple message.

Get rid of Scarlett, or they will.

He'd thought he'd once known fear, as a helpless child in the hands of monsters. He hadn't experienced its acrid taste since he'd become part of his brotherhood, had long forgotten the sensation. But he'd never known what fear really felt like. Now he knew. Fearing for her safety was unadulterated, sanity-destroying dread.

His uncle had told him he wouldn't make public Raiden's intention to cancel the wedding and to marry Scarlett instead. Not until Raiden decided how to handle the Yakuza's threat. Though he'd been angry and upset that Raiden had reneged on his promises, he was more worried about him.

When Raiden, murderously angry, had told him he could protect himself and his own, his uncle had made valid arguments to the contrary.

The Yakuza needed an ongoing merger to reap the benefits, the kind that came only from stable marriages and legitimate heirs. They'd already bought stock and placed bets depending on the marriage that wouldn't come to pass. His relationship with Scarlett had already hurt their business, but they probably hadn't removed her nuisance already since they expected Raiden to do as he was told, and they'd rather not alienate him unnecessarily. But if they thought they were losing him anyway, they'd have nothing at risk. Eliminating Scarlett would serve as a punishment to him, and a cautionary tale to anyone else who didn't abide by their rules.

He'd sworn to his uncle he would kill them all first.

His uncle had only looked at him as if he'd lost his mind. Then he'd told him he'd do everything in his power to mollify them, to buy him time, until Raiden got his act together.

Even in his maddened wrath, Raiden had known that his uncle was right. Killing them all wasn't a viable option.

He alone could eliminate a dozen Yakuza heads before the night was out. Enlisting his brothers' help would widen his preemptive strikes by a factor of six. But there was no way they'd get everyone. The Yakuza were a cancer. Remove the main tumors and others sprouted in their place. There would be retaliatory hits sooner or later. Apart from keeping Scarlett hidden indefinitely, or changing her identity all over again, she'd always be in danger. Even if he disappeared with her, that still left his brothers. The Yakuza didn't forget their vendettas, needed to demonstrate their lessons viciously to keep their future quarries in line. When their original target escaped them, they forced the target to surface by hitting at their nearest and dearest. If that didn't work, they'd at least made an example that would ensure no one crossed them again.

No. Neither striking first nor hiding was the answer. Too much was at stake. Everything was at stake.

Scarlett was everything.

Keeping her and their baby safe required a different mode of attack. And for that, he needed his brothers. All of them. This had to be planned with no margin of error. None.

He entered his pitch-dark bedroom, knowing without needing to see that Scarlett was still out on his bed like the lights. Her scent enveloped him; her essence permeated him.

Doing what he'd wanted to do before his fateful meeting with his uncle, he stripped, joined her on the bed, rid her of her own clothes and cocooned her in his body, as if he'd taken her inside him, where she'd be totally safe.

He had to rest now, while she did.

Tomorrow a war began.

Raiden woke up the moment she did.

Keeping his eyes closed and his body relaxed, he hid the fact that he was awake, too. He needed her to go about her daily business as if nothing was different. The Yakuza would be watching both him and her more closely now that they'd sent their message. Yet he couldn't alarm or distress her a moment before he had to. It already killed him that he would soon have to.

He lay there on his side as she separated her precious flesh from his, as she'd been doing every morning, gently, careful not to disturb him. Then as if she couldn't help herself, she pressed back to him for a moment, feathering his chest with kisses. His heart almost imploded.

Pretending to turn in his sleep so she wouldn't feel it thundering against her chest, he separated from her. A tiny sigh escaped her, a blissful little sound, as she placed a final kiss over his shoulder, then left the bed.

In the fifteen minutes it took her to get ready to leave, he almost suffocated with a dozen conflicting urges. To drag her back to bed and drown in her, to grab her and run out of Japan and disappear, to tell her everything now, not later. But the main need remained to go out and take down as many of those who threatened her as possible. A need he knew would go unfulfilled. But he still swore he was adding those goons to his list of undetectable and unendurable punishments.

But her safety came first, and last.

As she exited the bedroom, he thought he heard her humming a song. His heart stopped to make sure he'd heard right, before it rocketed into a whole new level of turmoil. She'd never done anything so spontaneous around him. He'd never heard her sound so…cheerful. For the first time in her life, he believed she was happy.

And he'd soon have to mar that happiness.

The moment the penthouse door clicked closed behind her, he exploded from bed. In minutes, he'd set off the general alarm, set up a meeting with those of his brothers still in Japan, with the others joining them on videoconference.

He needed a solution before this day was over.

And he *would* have it.

"Which Yakuza bosses made this threat?"

That was Numair, as usual the first one who spoke up with the most relevant question or comment after one of them made a report on a problem they were gathered to resolve.

Raiden had made his investigations. He now knew where the threat was coming from. He told his brothers.

All of them had intimate knowledge of every figure of power in the world, from heads of state to criminal masterminds. The names he'd just mentioned were among the most vicious.

After a minute of silence, Richard was the first to talk. "Are you sure you want to antagonize those vipers? You Japanese people have this weird obsession with honor and ritual, your vendettas last centuries and it makes your criminals the most tenacious on the planet."

Raiden turned to hold the Englishman's gaze. "I wouldn't only antagonize the very devil for Scarlett, I'd die for her and take down anyone with me. But that's why I gathered you all, to find another way that doesn't include antagonizing them. I want this done gracefully and faultlessly, to ensure no fallout of any kind, ever."

"I'm missing something, it seems."

This was Jakob Wolff, their resident Norse god, as the media called him and as all women agreed. Having been given the codename Brainiac during their years with The Organization, he'd turned his weaponry and tech virtuosity into an R&D division that produced the next level of technology, probably Black Castle's highest grossing. He and Raiden had always had their…differences.

Jakob now looked out of the screen at him, his steel-hued eyes boring into Raiden's. "I assume when you say you'd take down anyone with you, that includes us? And we should agree to that, why?"

Raiden shot him a glance in lieu of a *kakato-geri* ax kick over his thick head. "Because you *owe* Scarlett your fortunes, your security and your very lives. Medvedev uncovered my identity and by association yours, and was coming after all of us. She almost sacrificed her own life taking him down. That's why."

Jakob met his infuriated gaze in utmost composure. "Now, that's a good reason. I thought you expected us to do that for you. My bad."

"Shut up, Brainiac."

Numair's silky command got a dismissive grunt from Jakob. But he did break off the visual duel with Raiden. Numair would always remain their commander. They'd entrusted their lives to him when they'd been children, and no matter how they changed or how powerful they grew, they'd always take orders from him, and he would always have the last say.

"What do you need us to do, Raiden?"

That was Rafael, probably his closest brother, and the one Raiden had been reluctant to call, since he was a newlywed with a baby on the way, too. Raiden hadn't wanted to take him from Eliana's side. After that memorable encounter with her before their wedding in Brazil, where they'd settled down, he had a permanent soft spot for Rafael's bride. Eliana was also just the kind of friend he wanted for Scarlett.

"I want you to use every resource and connection at your disposal, call in all your favors and practice every pressure tactic to make sure it's in the Yakuza's best interests to forget Scarlett exists."

Rafael was the one who nodded immediately. Raiden

could see the others thinking of the logistics of his demand, wheels turning in their heads as they planned its execution.

Not that he even considered any of them would reject him. He knew they'd do all they could to help him. But he had to leave them in no doubt how grave the situation was.

"If I can't be assured of her total and permanent security, I won't only relinquish my identity and fake my death and hers, like we did before, but when we resurface, to make sure all of us remain safe from retaliations, I won't even tell you as whom. You'll never see me again."

"And how can any of us live without your aggravation, Lightning?" That was Ivan, his tone teasing, but his eyes alarmed, unable to contemplate losing another of their own. Like they'd lost Cypher.

Richard added his vote. "You and Rafael are the only reason I put up with this group of weasels and your moose of a leader. I'd do anything to keep you around, lad."

Richard's comment was met with generalized snorts, before each man followed with his own pledge in his own way.

"Losing one of us, even pains in the neck—" Numair's gaze singled out Jakob "—or extra baggage—" his gaze flicked to Richard "—is never an option." He stopped, no doubt remembering how they'd lost one of their brothers before, and hadn't been able to do anything about it. Cypher had disappeared without a trace. They all carried guilt that would never go away for their roles in his loss. Numair exhaled. "As for your beloved…"

"She's my *everything*." Raiden interjected forcefully. "And now she's giving me even more than that. She's carrying our miracle child."

Looking gratefully again at Antonio, the one who'd

given him the best news of his life, he explained what made their baby such a miracle. His brothers took a minute to digest the new info before they bombarded him with their teasing and congratulations.

He allowed himself those moments to accept yet another form of his brothers' support, his heart stuttering at realizing he was beginning to feel like a proud—and insanely anxious—father.

Then came Numair's summation, the decree they'd all abide by. "We would have scorched the earth for Scarlett, just because she's yours. But now we know she almost sacrificed herself for you, and us by association, and we know what she suffered because of her sacrifice, what it almost cost her, and you, anyone daring to threaten her will pay. Long after they back down." Numair looked around, getting corroborating nods from everyone. Nodding in turn, he drummed his fingers on the arm of his chair as he sat forward, as he used to when a direction was settled and it was time to drum out details. "Now let's see how we'll make the Yakuza offer to guard Scarlett and your baby with their lives, for life."

For the next three hours they discussed every detail and possibility, and came up with a plan. Then Ivan and Antonio left, and the others signed out of the videoconference, each going to initiate his part in the tapestry of manipulation.

Numair stayed behind a few minutes longer to make sure Raiden wouldn't postpone the first thing he had to do.

Pain crushed his heart as he conceded the necessity of that action. It was the hardest thing Raiden would ever do. Giving the Yakuza what they were now waiting for.

And he had to make it look convincing.

* * *

The first thing Scarlett noticed as she walked into the downtown office was the avid looks everyone gave her.

She'd already been drawing extreme interest since Raiden had first come for her here. And that was before they'd learned who the god who regularly swept her away in his chariot was.

But now they were making no attempt to hide that they were talking about her. Gossip was a paramount pastime around here, even more than anywhere else in the world she'd been, and she'd already been the subject of the mandatory form, as a gaijin who looked the way she did. But now she couldn't understand the reason for their sudden in-your-face nosiness.

She didn't wonder long. Finding Hiro waiting for her in her office explained everything.

Hiro was the second billionaire who'd come for her in as many weeks. Not only that, but she'd recently learned he was one who was considered a hero of the people, a man who had left his father's path in crime and made himself into a major power in Japan out of nothing. And while it was common knowledge they were friends, her colleagues had only heard about this, as they always met outside of their respective workplaces. For him to be here must be the stuff of folktales to them.

She was happy to see him as usual, and just truly, deliriously *happy* for the first time in her life. Her lips spread wide as she rushed toward him. Deciding to give her openly watching colleagues more to gossip about, no doubt all over the cyberspace everyone here practically lived in, she hugged him exuberantly. She thought a few took photos.

She pulled away, still holding Hiro by the arms. "To what do I owe this wonderful surprise?"

"You won't think it wonderful when you know why I'm here."

It was then she noticed his pained expression, her delight turning to concern. "Is something wrong with you? With Megumi?"

Hiro gave a difficult nod. "There is something terribly wrong. Something she and I are guilty of."

"For God's sake, Hiro, just tell me what it is."

Looking as if he'd choke on guilt, Hiro stood with shoulders slumped. "That night of the ball, one of my guards told me he saw you and Kuroshiro arriving at the garden house one after the other. Afterward, you were… different, and I just knew it was because of him. So I followed you. The moment I became certain that the two of you had something going on, I told Megumi."

She gaped at him. That was out of left field. She'd never suspected *he* suspected a thing. Went to show how totally blinded by Raiden she was. She was unable to see anything but him.

She sighed, led him to her couch, pulled him down with her. "You wanted Megumi to break the engagement."

"There *is* no engagement. He's seen her exactly five times in the past nine weeks and never alone. He's with *you* all the time. But when she told her father that, he told her it's expected that men like Raiden would have a mistress."

She winced at the word *mistress,* and the fact that now Megumi's father, the man who'd become Raiden's adoptive father, knew about her. But from his nonchalant reaction, it meant Raiden had known what he was doing when he'd started being open about their affair. He'd realized his uncle wouldn't care, that it wouldn't jeopardize his marriage adoption. As she hoped nothing would.

She hadn't given it any thought in the tumult of last night, but now she did. She knew her pregnancy would change nothing, nor did she want it to.

But maybe Hiro had just delivered the best news. If Raiden's uncle didn't care, maybe she could remain in Raiden's life as she'd suggested before her pregnancy had been discovered and the subject had been dropped. She could be with him at least until she started to show. Having a mistress was one thing; having a pregnant one was another. One of the main reasons he was getting married was to have heirs—the legitimate kind. An illegitimate child would be a problem to any man, as illegitimacy was a huge issue here. But for someone in Raiden's sensitive position, being so newly added to such a noble family register, it would be untenable.

But no matter what happened, it was enough for her to be carrying his baby. *His baby.*

The fireworks of disbelief and jubilation went off in her blood again.

She'd been shocked, then incredulous, then so frantically elated, she'd shut down again, unable to handle the surge of hope and happiness. Becoming pregnant had been so impossible in her mind, she'd disregarded all the very definite signs of pregnancy she'd been having. But what had been the height of her hopes in the past, and what she'd long given up on, had really come to pass. Antonio might consider it was a physical fluke about her that made this pregnancy possible, and far better, viable, but she preferred to think her love for Raiden had healed all her scars. She also thought maybe fate had finally seen fit to make it up to her, with a miracle whose joy would erase everything she'd ever suffered.

"Scarlett?"

She blinked, and Hiro's worried face filled her vision.

She'd melted back on the couch as she'd continued her giddy musings. And *giddy* also described her physical state. She must be looking as dizzy and nauseous as she felt. She hoped she didn't vomit in Hiro's presence. Again. She'd done so last week and had thought she was coming down with something, had even made the oblivious comment then.

She struggled to sit up. "Sorry for zonking out on you like that. Seems that bug I caught is tenacious."

"I know you're pregnant, Scarlett."

Her smile froze and her mouth dropped open.

"I've seen all the signs during the past two weeks. You vomited, you couldn't bear the scent of my aftershave though I didn't change it, nothing tasted the same to you and your perception of warmth and cold had nothing to do with the actual weather."

She shook her head, stunned. "Wow, you sure know your pregnancy signs and symptoms."

"I have sisters and ten nephews and nieces. I know everything there is to know about pregnancy."

"I guess there's no point in denying it. But I can trust you to keep my secret, right?" She elbowed him playfully.

"Actually, you can't."

Her mouth hung wide again. "Huh?"

"That's what I'm here to confess." Hiro's agitation ratcheted with every word. "I wanted to expose Raiden, to corner him into doing the right thing by Megumi and by you. I went to Megumi's father with my discovery, and I was…loud. I think everyone in his office heard me. It was long after I left that I realized I'd exposed you, too, and betrayed your trust. I still hoped nothing would come of it. Then I woke up this morning and saw it, rushed here to at least explain before you did."

Her heart seemed to hold its beat. "Saw what?"

"The news of your pregnancy all over the newspapers and the internet."

It had been two hours since Hiro had left. She was still sitting where he'd left her. All she'd done since had been reaching for her tablet to check the tabloids.

And it *was* all there, complete with a thorough photo documentation of all of her appearances with Raiden. The feverishly gossipy articles dissected their torrid affair, and ended with the speculation she'd been having about the possibilities in their future, just in outlandish versions. One article hypothesized that Raiden would convert to a religion that would legally allow him to practice bigamy.

All in all, it was an unqualified disaster.

And its shock waves must have reached Raiden by now.

In fact, it must have reached him long before now. So why hadn't he contacted her? She had to see him at once to figure—

"Scarlett."

Raiden. Here. As if she'd summoned him.

She turned her head so suddenly, the world spun again and she slumped back on the couch. He rushed from the wide-open door and swooped down on her, looking exactly as she imagined herself to look. Harassed, unsteady and nauseous.

Not that he could be physically nauseous as she was, but he must be sick to his stomach with the developments.

Before she could say anything, apologize for the trouble this would cause him, he caught her head in both his large hands, hitting her like his namesake with an enervating bolt of craving. He claimed her lips in a devouring kiss that mimicked his latest overriding possession.

She'd become a puddle of longing by the time he pulled back to sear her in the roiling emotions radiating from his gaze and every pore of his body. Then he spoke, and every supporting impulse in her body gave way.

Catching her in a fierce embrace, he repeated what he'd just said, every word expanding inside her until she felt she'd burst with the enormity of it all.

"I love you, Scarlett. I've always loved you, and I will love you to the day I die."

He'd said it again and again before she could at last vent a measure of her shock. "Oh, God, Raiden…you do?"

"What did you think our magical five months were about? And the five years I didn't even think of having another woman? And the past miraculous eight weeks, with their heaven-sent outcome?"

"I—I didn't think, I just loved you, just wanted to love you…and loved every second with you."

"You didn't know I loved you in the past? You didn't feel me working up to ask you to be with me forever?"

"I—I thought you loved Hannah, who didn't exist."

He ran his fingers through her hair, his eyes a blaze of sincerity. "I only ever saw *you,* whatever name you used or whatever facade you wore. You admitted that you were always yourself with me, and I already told you it was you I felt, you I wanted. But I never confessed completely. Now I am confessing. I will never again hide an iota of what I feel for you. I love you. I worship every breath you take. You're everything to me, my darling, everything. You and our miracle child."

She closed her eyes, wanting to trap that image of him as he looked at her with his whole being, the tremor of truth vibrating through all of him, as he confessed his equal and total involvement.

Then she opened her eyes and she felt as if she'd been born again. Born to a world where she didn't have to be alone, but had the love of the only person she'd ever loved with everything in her, with all of her past and future, her strengths and scars.

"Now I want you to do something for me," he said. "Without questions."

She grabbed his hands, her heart ricocheting in her chest with alarm at the darkness that tinged his face and voice. "You know I'd do anything for you."

"I want you to leave Japan. Today. I want you to pack your essentials and go back to the States. I'll pack everything else for you once you give me an address to send it to."

She gaped at him, her mind shutting down, unable to reconcile the purity of his heartfelt confession with his sudden demand for her to leave.

Had he just confessed his love only to tell her he could no longer afford to have her near? She'd always thought his desire for his family name and heritage was the most important thing to him, that she'd end up losing him sooner rather than later. But after he'd told her she was everything to him, and she believed he meant it, what could his abrupt demand mean?

"Do you trust me?" His clipped question cut through her chaos.

She did, with her life, and now the life of their baby. Whether she'd ever be in his life again… That was what she didn't trust.

He repeated the question, more urgent and agitated, and she nodded weakly.

"Then trust me now. Trust that I love you, and that I'll

do anything for your love. For *our* love and *our* child. Trust that without a single second of doubt…and leave. Now. Please."

The entreaty for an explanation congealed in her throat. She had to trust he had the best reason for jump-starting her heart, which had been smothered in despair, only to rip it out of her chest by tearing her from his side so abruptly.

She hung limp in his arms as he helped her to her feet, then fetched her stuff and fitted it over her shoulder.

"Steve is waiting outside. He'll be with you all through. Take this phone. Call me the moment you board the plane."

Her hand trembled around the phone he'd pushed into it. Then he stood back, deprived her of his warmth and touch. She almost heaped to the ground without his support.

But he nodded for her, imploring her to go. Numb, she acquiesced, stumbled away from him to the open door, found most of her colleagues out of their offices, hanging in the corridor, openly watching. They must have witnessed the whole episode. And no doubt documented it, too. It might already be on the internet and trending on some social media site.

Uncaring what they did, or who saw this, feeling destroyed, even more than the first time she'd walked away from him, she turned to take what felt like her last look at him.

Raiden. Her only love.

He was looking back at her as if she'd taken his heart with her and was dragging it away from his body.

Though he'd made it sound as if she'd definitely see him again, that this was merely some emergency damage-control maneuver he had to execute, she felt this was the end.

Saying goodbye in her heart, because hope was more mutilating than despair, she turned and walked away from him.

Ten

Raiden watched Scarlett walk away unsteadily, passing through her colleagues, feeling as if his life force was draining out of his body with her every receding step.

Now that everyone realized this was for real, that he'd just sent her away, their yammering curiosity turned to vocal concern. Some strode by her side, anxiously asking if they could help, if she needed anything. The way she waved away their interest and offers of help told him she was barely holding herself upright and together. He wanted to roar for everyone to leave her alone, but had to stand there and suffer every heartbreaking second of her disappearance.

The moment he could no longer see her, he turned away, struggling with the tears that surged from his depths. He didn't want one of those people catching a photo of him in this condition. It might undermine all he was trying to do.

Getting his phone out, he called Steve, went over the details of the next few days. The specific bodyguards assigned to Scarlett's constant guard duty, the protocols they'd follow, the hourly reports they'd relay to him and everything else that ensured she'd have security no head of state ever had.

Afterward, he stood there, in the office that was no

longer hers, waiting for Steve to take her away from him, struggling not to run out after her, come what may. Letting her go was the hardest test of his control ever.

But he had to do it. He had to make the Yakuza think he'd given her her marching orders. And he had to do it where people would witness it and run to make it public knowledge.

He didn't know how long it would be before the plan he'd concocted with his brothers worked, and worked perfectly. And the next two weeks, until the date of his supposed wedding, were the most dangerous time for Scarlett to remain here.

After the threat had been made, her continued presence, especially now that her pregnancy was a widespread scandal, would be considered a direct danger to the Yakuza's interests, and a flaunting of their displeasure. The Yakuza might consider both transgressions worthy of a disciplinary strike.

He'd hoped he could have only explained why he couldn't risk her staying even the night here. But all he'd been able to do was tell her how he felt, promise her forever, even as he begged her to leave. He'd hoped she'd believe him, in her heart at least, until he could explain more. And that her stunned confusion as she'd walked away would convince anyone this was an abrupt and permanent separation.

Now he'd wait until she was out of even his bodyguards' earshot to call her on the secure line he'd given her and explain. He was taking no chances she might be monitored now, since he couldn't be. He had to convince the Yakuza he had complied.

But he wouldn't fully explain the kind of danger he was protecting her from, couldn't bear causing her even more agitation. But at least, until he resolved this situation, she was safe.

Yet even he, with his unlimited resources, knew there was no way to keep her perfectly safe for more than a few days without imprisoning her, and alerting her stalkers to the fact that they were on to them. So those days would have to do. He and his brothers had a brief window of time to bring this to a permanent end.

Needing to put the last touch on this scene, he walked out. The office denizens flocked around him as they would a rock star, asking him questions as the paparazzi would.

Once outside, he finally acknowledged he wasn't walking alone, turned to them and gave the statement he knew would travel around Japan in minutes afterward.

Every lie cut him deeply, but he forced them out with what he hoped was a smile of nonchalance and not a grimace of agony.

"Regretfully, Ms. Delacroix won't be back. But she will continue her excellent work remotely until her projects are up and running. As for her pregnancy, it was a false alarm. And yes, my wedding is still in two weeks' time."

A dozen voices rose with a dozen questions, but this time he waved them away and entered the other limo waiting for him.

As they drove away, he put up the privacy barrier and sagged back into his seat, counting the minutes before he could call Scarlett again. After that, he'd begin counting the seconds until he could see her again.

And this time remain with her forever.

"This damned plan is taking *forever!*"
Raiden's vicious growl was followed by a minor crash.

He'd startled the flight attendant placing his meal in front of him out of her wits, making her drop the tray.

Gritting an apology and waving away her attempt to put things straight, he turned a blind gaze out of the window of his private jet, trying to rein back the constant boiling inside him. Not even the martial arts techniques he'd perfected had managed to bring him a measure of relaxation. He was spiraling out of control.

"It's been only two weeks." Numair's calm response through the phone line only poured fuel on his fire.

"That's temporally speaking," Raiden bit off.

"I wasn't aware there was another parameter we can measure time with."

"Phantom, attempting wit on me right now might cause me that stroke you all keep saying I'm trying to give myself." He paused for a second then almost shouted, "I don't care how long it's really been. It's been longer than my endurance."

"Your endurance lasted two seconds after she left."

He opened his mouth to blast him back with something, then closed it. For said endurance had been depleted *before* she'd left.

Numair was also right. Logically speaking, it hadn't been too long. Though the combined might of his brothers was mind-boggling, it couldn't have possibly taken them less than two weeks to untangle and reroute the web of interests, to tie all loose ends and to put all safety measures irrevocably in place.

But his brothers had already done that. It wasn't until the wedding invitees had filled the ballroom hours ago that Numair and Richard had given the signal that all danger was over. Hashimoto had then walked in to announce the cancellation of the wedding. Raiden had followed his speech, apologizing for the last-second change of plans and assuring everyone dinner and entertainment were still on. Then he'd hurtled out of the hotel and onto his jet heading to New York. To Scarlett.

Then damn Numair had called him after takeoff to tell him to come back, or at least not to go to Scarlett, and wait in New York until he told him he could see her. Numair claimed they weren't finished yet, and that he'd jumped the gun.

Numair insisted that they had yet to put on the finishing touch, what would have everyone willing to kill each other to keep Scarlett and their child safe.

Now everything inside him snapped. "Finish this, Numair. Kill whomever you have to kill and finish it. And don't say I have to wait again. I *can't.* And even if I can, I already called Scarlett and told her I'm on my way. And I won't disappoint her again. I won't. *Do you hear me?*"

After his last bellowed words, total silence ensued on the other side.

Then he heard snickering. Snickering?

"I think the gods of Olympus heard you, Lightning."

"I didn't know you had it in you, Phantom."

Raiden frowned. That was Richard's voice, followed by Jakob's. What was going on here?

"We made a bet whether Phantom would have the heart to pull your strings, Lightning." That was Ivan.

"I bet against him, said he couldn't torture you a second more than you've already been tortured." Jakob groaned. "Now I have to submit to *his* torture for a whole day. He'll probably make me endure his company."

Rafael's apologetic voice came on. "I tried to stop them. But you know not even bullets can stop that herd."

"It's a send-off gift from all of us," Ivan teased. "For the way you've abused us all during the past two weeks."

"You tortured me most of all." Antonio yawned loudly

before continuing, "Calling me one minute for updates on my role in the plan, and the very next minute with obsessions about Scarlett's pregnancy. Do you know I slept on my feet during surgery today? And dreamed?"

Raiden shook his head, not really taking it all in. "You mean there's no finishing touch?"

A beat passed, then he heard more groans.

"He didn't even register that this was a prank," Jakob lamented.

"Good for you, Raiden." Rafael laughed. "You turned the tables on them without even meaning to."

"Should have known there was no pranking a love zombie," Ivan sniggered.

"God, that love malady is horrific." He could hear the disgusted shudder in Jakob's voice. "Bones, have you invented a vaccine for it yet? I'm willing to be your test subject."

"There *is* a finishing touch," Numair spoke up, ending his brothers' to and fro. "And it was put in place before we gave you the go-ahead earlier today. The Yakuza would now kill themselves and their families before they came near your wife and child."

After that, he could no longer hear anything. He didn't even know when the conversation came to an end.

All he knew was that he could finally be reunited with Scarlett. And that Numair had said *your wife and child.*

His wife and child.

Scarlett and their miracle.

His, at last. As he'd always be theirs.

Fifteen hours later, he stood on Scarlett's doorstep.

He'd spent hours of that time with her on the phone, telling her everything, now that it had all worked out. When he'd sent her away initially, he'd told her only that he was involved in a very delicate situation that he had to resolve with her out of the way. Finding out the details and magnitude of the averted danger had made her break down again.

She'd had frequent crises during the past two weeks. Though she no longer had any doubt that he was hers, she'd had so much terrible misfortune in her life, she believed something, anything, would happen, and prevent them from being together. No matter how he swore nothing would, the fear, their separation and pregnancy hormones played havoc with her moods and nerves.

Then she opened the door.

It felt as if his very heart, what had been ripped from his chest, stood across that threshold. The desolation of the time without him, the dread that fate would deal her another blow—this time a final one that wouldn't be survivable—lined her face, streaked her cheeks, hunched her body. She looked as terrible as he did. And like the most beautiful thing he'd ever seen. She was the one thing he wanted to see, to savor and wonder at for the rest of his life.

Then they were fused, straining to get closer, kissing, moaning, smiling, shedding tears, tearing clothes, pleading for more, for now, for everything, always everything.

Then she was in his arms, taken, contained; then he found himself on top of her on a bed and they were almost fighting each other for a faster descent into oblivion. Then finally they were merged, cresting then crashing into ecstasy.

Their union was brief, ferocious and earth-shattering, releasing all their pent-up dreads and longings.

A long time afterward, from the deepest well of satiation, he heard her voice, raw with her episodes of weeping, and just now with her abandon.

"I never wanted this."

He rose on his elbow, frowning down at her.

She elaborated. "I never wanted you to leave all your plans and dreams behind for me. With everything in me I hoped that you would reclaim your heritage and have a family, your family, again."

He smiled his adoration and indulgence down at her. "*You* are my family. And you're even giving me two family members at once. As for my heritage, I will have one. The one we'll make together and pass on to our child."

Her turbid eyes filled with the tears that now came so easily to her. "But there must have been a way to have both—your heritage and me. I would have been yours no matter what. I don't need legalities to make me yours."

"But I need to make you mine with legalities and with every other way there is or is still to be invented." When she grimaced and buried her face in his chest, he pulled her back. "I want you as my wife, and I want to be your husband. I always wanted that, from the first moment I saw you. And I continued to want you against all odds, all through the years." He suddenly huffed as a memory hit him. "Do you know that before I met you again and I thought I'd have to have heirs, I was resigned that I'd have to close my eyes and think of you so I could…perform?"

"God, Raiden, don't—"

"If you can't even stomach thinking of me in a hypothetical bed with a hypothetical woman—"

"Megumi wasn't so hypothetical."

He threw his head back on a delighted laugh at her growl. "See? You may think you could have shared me for the sake of my mission to reacquire my family name, but you're almost sick to your stomach just imagining it in retrospect, even when you know it will never happen."

"I would have stomached anything to be with you. At

least, I would have lived with permanent nausea. I was a beggar who didn't dream she could be a chooser."

He crushed her to him, his eyes reproving. "You were never a beggar. You were always my mistress, in all meanings of the word. Mistress of my heart, queen of my life. I was born to love you, too."

He received her surge as she flung herself at him, squeezed her tighter into himself. "I dreamed of reclaiming my heritage and my family because I thought I'd be able to fill the emptiness inside me with duty and tradition, that they'd be anchors to give my life purpose. Then I found you, and I no longer needed anything but you. I only searched for them again when I lost you, to fill the void your loss left behind. But you're back with me, and you're mine, have always been mine like I've always been yours. You fill my every emptiness—you are my anchor. You and the family we'll create together. You are my counterpart, the other half of my soul, the only one who's ever understood me, the darkness and pain and scars I have inside me, and also the power, resilience and indomitable will. We're the same, and we're the only ones to soothe and heal each other, and to give each other the endless love we need."

After dragging him down for a fierce, thankful kiss, she sank back, playing lovingly with his hair, her brilliant eyes glittering with tears and adoration. "When I wanted to do something that mattered, all I could think of was you, when you were a child, helpless and alone, and I wanted to help all the children who found themselves in your same situation."

His heart convulsed at yet another proof of her total love for him. "You suffered worse. Why didn't you direct your efforts toward girls who suffer the same as you did?"

"Because I love you more than I love myself. Way

more." And he believed her. For he loved her way beyond how he loved himself or anything else. "Imagining your pain hurt me more than remembering experiencing my own. But once this shelter project is up and running, I'll do what you suggest, too, in my original region. But there, I won't be up against natural disasters, but organized crime." She sank kneading fingers in his arm. "I'll need your muscle there."

Body going rigid with arousal all over again, he groaned. "My every muscle is at your disposal. And my brothers', too."

She giggled. "Are you sure they'd be open to that? Antonio called me when you were on your way and begged me to get you off his back. The poor man is entering chronic sleep deprivation because you're obsessing about my pregnancy."

"So what? That man can operate in his sleep. He actually did yesterday." She chuckled again, and he melted a caress down the delightful curve of her cheek. "So how do you feel about adoption?"

After a moment's surprise at his abrupt change of subject, she smiled widely. "I feel that now that I'm going to have a billionaire ninja husband, I'd like to adopt four children."

His eyebrows shot up. "Why four?"

"Because I have my eye on two girls and two boys in the shelter. And they have their eye on me. Ages two to six. I was thinking how I would be able to adopt them alone, but now..."

"We'll adopt them together. And our baby will be born to find she or he already has a huge family waiting to love her or him."

"Uh...why don't you think about it some more? Adoption is a huge decision, even bigger than deciding to have a biological child."

"I know that. And I've already thought. Why do you think I asked you what you feel about it?" A consideration suddenly hit him. "Or did you only consider adoption when you thought you wouldn't have a child of your own?"

"Knowing I'll have a child of my own doesn't change a thing. I want to help as many children as I can, give them security, and if possible, a loving home."

"You're saving the child I was in them, aren't you?" When she nodded and buried her face in his chest, he lifted her chin, held her swimming eyes that glittered azure in the soft lights. "And we'll also save the child *you* were. An older girl who's been passed over for adoption from your part of the world."

She dived into his arms again with a smothered cry of poignancy...and the doorbell rang.

Frowning, he sat up. "Expecting someone?"

"I didn't even tell anyone I was back."

On alert in a split second, he sprang from the bed, making her whoop in delight at his elastic rebound.

"Wow," she breathed as she rushed to put on her dressing gown. "One day you must show me all the ninja stuff you can do."

"I showed you many so far." Then he showed her another trick, literally jumping into his pants.

As she jumped and clapped, he placed his fingers on his lips as he rushed soundlessly out of the bedroom.

She rushed after him. "Didn't you resolve everything with the Yakuza? Why are you alarmed now?"

He again gestured for her to lower her voice. "Because no one should be calling on you, now or at all."

"Aren't your bodyguards still around?"

"That's what's worrying me. That they didn't give us a heads-up and let someone come all the way to your door."

"Then they must have thought that someone would certainly be welcome."

"I'm not taking any chances."

She suddenly slapped her forehead. "You made me forget I have a video intercom."

He blinked at her. It seemed his circuits had been irrevocably fried, wiping out all his ingrained training. He'd have to train all over again. He'd have to reinstall simple logic.

Feeling sheepish, he followed her as she checked the video feed. With a gun pointed at the door.

Then he saw who it was and his arms fell to his sides, the gun dangling loosely in one hand.

It was his uncle, Megumi and Hiro.

With a cry of surprise, Scarlett rushed to open the door.

Raiden stood frozen, unable to even come up with a reason that the unlikely trio was here. He'd thought he'd never see them again, let alone together.

He watched Scarlett welcome them inside, hugging Hiro, her face alight with pleasure at seeing her friend, and he could swear she was really pleased to see the other two, too.

The trio looked over at Raiden, their gazes drawn to the gun in his hand.

He waved it in self-deprecation. "I assume I don't need this and that you come in peace?"

Megumi giggled. Giggled! And such a merry sound, too.

Seemed it had been the prospect of marrying him that had been the reason for her stilted attitude.

As he put the gun away, Scarlett invited them all into her living room.

As soon as they sat down, Hiro blurted out, "I wouldn't have blamed you if you shot me on sight, Kuroshiro-san."

"When I thought you were interested in Scarlett, you were definitely in danger. Now, as her best friend, you've been drafted to the role of mine, too."

"It would be my honor to have you as a friend and ally, Kuroshiro-san." Hiro extended a hand to him, his eyes warm for the first time.

Raiden shook his hand. "If we're going to be friends, you'd better get used to calling me Raiden. And I'll call you like my lady calls you…Hiro." He slapped Hiro on the back and winked at his absolute surprise. "Next time you want to force me to do the right thing, just pick up the phone and threaten me. I'd rather be given the chance to avoid being smeared all over the tabloids and the World Wide Web." Hiro looked so mortified he took pity on him. "And if we're going to be friends and allies, we need to start working on your sense of humor. I was only teasing."

"You shouldn't be," Hiro objected. "I thoughtlessly caused you and Scarlett, and at the time Hashimoto-sama and Megumi-san, a terrible scandal."

He grinned as he gathered Scarlett to his side. "From where I'm sitting, what you did was part of a sequence of events that led to me being here, the happiest man in existence."

Scarlett raised her hand. "Happiest woman in *history* here."

Though they'd just said the truth, she was clearly unable to bear seeing her friend beating himself up over this and she needed to make him exonerate himself. He felt the same way. Even if Hiro's actions could have caused untold damage, they hadn't. And what he and Scarlett had now was so unbelievable, he could forgive anyone anything.

"And then you were only defending your beloved," Raiden added. "Saving her from a fate worse than death—marrying a man who loves another while she loves you." He grinned widely at Megumi, then at the still-chagrined man. "So that makes you a hero in my eyes."

"You might both forgive me in your magnanimity, because somehow my actions caused you only temporary distress. But that things were resolved so spectacularly was no thanks to me. So I reserve the right not to forgive myself, and to be forever at your disposal, should you require satisfaction."

"Just take that get-out-of-jail-free card, Hiro. I will no doubt need one from you at a future date." At Hiro's reluctant nod, with one last smile, Raiden turned his gaze to his uncle. "Not that I'm not thrilled for this unexpected opportunity to see you again, but I really thought I never would. So what brings you here? Whatever you needed, you know I'm forever at your disposal and I would come to you wherever you are."

"I had to be the one to come to you to make the offer," Hashimoto said.

"What offer?"

"When you terminated the marriage adoption, I felt disgraced and wanted to forever cut any ties with you. But then I remembered how I worried about you when you were under threat, and realized I already consider you family. The real disgrace would be to cling to pride and put gossip and public censorship ahead of true relationships."

Hashimoto suddenly leaned forward, took Raiden's hand and Scarlett's, gathered them together and held them in both of his. "After all the dust settled, I remembered when you said how you'd wished we would have been family. I still feel the same way. I am here offering you the name of our family, and the place at its head—the same things you would have gotten through the marriage adoption. But now I'm offering them through adoption alone."

Though that was yet another development in a string of unexpected ones, the strange part was what Raiden had been so passionate about ten weeks ago didn't turn a hair in him now. He truly had everything he wanted or needed as long as he had Scarlett.

He shook his head. "This is no longer something I want or need. My family is right here." He tightened his arm around Scarlett's shoulder. She only looked up at him with eyes that were at once stricken and admonishing.

"But this time we don't only want you, we want to adopt you as a married couple," Hashimoto rushed to add. "And this is what our family hopes you would both consider—both of you taking our family name, making our family yours."

A long moment of silence followed his offer.

Then Raiden exhaled. "That's a very generous offer, Takeo-sama, but I still have to decline."

"But why, Raiden-san?" That was Megumi, at last breaking her usual silence. "We would have been cata-strophic as spouses, but I just know it's because you were meant to be my brother. And I would love nothing more than to have Scarlett-san as my sister."

"And now Hashimoto-sama has agreed to give me

Megumi-chan's hand in marriage," Hiro said eagerly. "I would no longer be only your friend, but your brother, too."

Delighted for both him and Megumi, Raiden clapped him on the back again. "You move fast, don't you, Hiro? Good for you." He turned to Megumi, who was blushing delicately. "You two feel to me as if you were once one whole that was split into two. It's so good seeing you becoming one again."

"So won't you reconsider?" Megumi asked, her eyes entreating. "Why are you refusing at all?"

He turned somber eyes to Hashimoto. "Because I haven't forgotten what you said about Scarlett, how you viewed her. Scarlett is and has always been the most upstanding and heroic person I know. I don't only worship her, but I respect and admire her more than anyone in the world. I would have nothing but the absolute best for her, and I would certainly never expose her to being considered an evil to be tolerated but secretly reviled, because your family still needs me."

Scarlett threaded her arm through his and looked up at him, her eyes silently scolding. "Mr. Hashimoto was under too much pressure at the time, not to mention misconceptions."

Hashimoto jumped on Scarlett's life raft. "That is true, and I now regret my words, and my thoughts. I had no proof to support them but hearsay, just because your presence went against my family's best interests. Can you possibly accept my apology and my assurances that my opinion was one of ignorance and self-service, but one that I have irrevocably changed?"

"Of *course* I accept, Mr. Hashimoto," Scarlett said

fervently. "I almost caused you all huge losses, just being there, just loving Raiden. And like Hiro said, it's no thanks to me that everything has been averted and we've reached this happy moment." As Raiden began to protest, she turned to him and hugged him around the waist, all her love in her eyes. "Let's not dwell on anything that happened before today. The past is dead and gone. Let's only remember the good parts of it, and look forward to a magnificent future."

He knew what she meant. They might never be able to forget the past, but it had led them to this point, where they were unimaginably blessed by having each other.

She brought him down to her for a fierce, brief kiss. "But we both do need a family, to make up for the ones we lost. And it will be the best thing for our coming baby, and any other children we will have, to have a big family to dote on them."

Suddenly unable to wait a second longer, he swept her in his arms, heaved up to his feet and strode back to her bedroom.

At her squeaking protest, he stopped, looked back at the trio, found them on their feet, looking crestfallen.

He raised a mocking eyebrow at them. "Uh, sorry, were you waiting for a response from me?" He groaned in pleasure as Scarlett gave his jaw a punishing nip. His eyes laughed down at her, then back at the guests. "Let me give you a tip for future reference. Once Scarlett has spoken, I am but the executor of her will. She wants us to be family, we *will* be family."

After a moment's uncertainty, the trio's faces split with smiles, then they each advanced on them, all delighted relief.

At Scarlett's loving nudge, he put her back on her feet so she could receive with him the hugs of the three people who would be their family.

After an interlude of mutual thanks and excitement, especially on the side of the ladies, who seemed to be delighted to have a girlfriend in their testosterone-dominated lives, Raiden swept Scarlett back up into his arms.

This time their guests took the hint and rushed to the door. Scarlett spluttered that he put her down, that they should stay longer, that she hadn't even offered them something to drink. But this time he didn't heed her, and the trio insisted on leaving. It was time, Hashimoto said, to leave the two of them to continue their reunion after such a harrowing separation.

Raiden called after them when they were at the door, "I *am* grateful we will be family. But remember, we will only be because Scarlett decreed it. Now you all owe her."

Their voices rose in corroboration as they closed the door behind them. Then he raced with her to her bedroom.

Putting her down on the still-rumpled sheets, as if he was laying down his heart, he pulled off his clothes, then hers, and came down into her arms.

"I wasn't just making him squirm, you know," he said against her lips. "I was going to insist on refusing."

She flushed with passion and embarrassment, unable as usual to take her dues. "But you didn't, and now you'll have everything you ever dreamed of and deserve. I won't have to feel perpetually sad and guilty that my presence in your life deprived you of such a huge thing."

"It will be huge only because I will share it with you.

But if not for you, for your forgiveness and your desire to be part of a family, I wouldn't have accepted. So they do owe you. Just as I owe you my happiness, my very life."

Crying out, she pulled him down to her. "And I owe you mine."

And she took him inside her, taking him home, his one and only home, forever.

* * * * *

MILLS & BOON®

Why not subscribe?
Never miss a title and save money too!

Here's what's available to you if you join the
exclusive **Mills & Boon Book Club** today:

✦ *Titles up to a month ahead of the shops*
✦ *Amazing discounts*
✦ *Free P&P*
✦ *Earn Bonus Book points that can be redeemed*
  against other titles and gifts
✦ *Choose from monthly or pre-paid plans*

Still want more?
Well, if you join today we'll even give you
50% OFF your first parcel!

So visit **www.millsandboon.co.uk/subs**
or call Customer Relations on 020 8288 2888
to be a part of this exclusive Book Club!

214_ST_5